WHEN BLACKNESS WAS A VIRTUE

T0151601

WHEN BLACKNESS WAS A VIRTUE

a novel

MICHAEL GRANT JAFFE

DZANC
BOOKS

DZANC BOOKS

5220 Dexter Ann Arbor Rd.
Ann Arbor, MI 48103
www.dzancbooks.org

WHEN BLACKNESS WAS A VIRTUE

Copyright © 2014, text by Michael Grant Jaffe.

Published 2014 by Dzanc Books
ISBN: 978-1-938604508
First edition: January 2014

This project is supported in part by the National Endowment for the Arts and the MCACA.

Printed in the United States of America

10 9 8 7 6 5 4 3 2 1

For Scout & Esmé,

For Georges & Anne

Anger be now your song...

—Homer, *The Iliad*

WHEN BLACKNESS WAS A VIRTUE

The light in the first-floor window is operated by a timing device. Each evening before dusk it suddenly illuminates, casting a tangerine glow behind a pair of loosely drawn curtains. There are four copper-plated numbers tacked to the doorframe, slanted from high to low. The narrow walkway leading to the house is bordered by flowerbeds teeming with snapdragons, tulips, and wild geraniums. A coil of candystriped rope, perhaps a child's toy, dangles from the second-story gutters. Another splash of color, a yellow and blue circular from a local pizza delivery, among a thorny web of hydrangea branches. Today there was rain; the concrete steps are still dark with water.

In the distance comes the steady hum of a lawnmower. Then the faint smell of burning charcoal. I watch two squirrels skitter across the lawn, chasing each other in drunken parabolas around the trunk of a broad sugar maple.

More time passes before a green Buick pulls into the driveway. The woman is talking to someone as she climbs from her car. After a moment the rear doors flare open, nearly in unison, revealing two young boys with matching backpacks.

"It's not the kind of macaroni I like," says the boy on the passenger side, the one with longer hair.

"Well, I can fix you a sandwich," says the woman. "Or we might have some leftover brisket."

She searches for the house key, balancing a grocery bag on her hip. It's not until they reach the side door that she notices me—crossing the street at an easy pace, careful not to draw attention to myself. The bag starts to slip before she catches it against her thigh. I jog the final few yards, taking the groceries from her and setting them on the pavement.

"I'll be right there," she says, ushering the boys into the kitchen.

"I'm hungry, Nana," says the boy with longer hair.

"Okay, okay." She wipes her hands on the tail of her blouse. "Go watch TV—you can watch TV. I'll fix you something to eat in a minute."

"Hey, Marky," shouts the boy from inside the house. "Nana says we can watch TV."

I smile because, really, there is nothing else. I remove a small notepad from the breast pocket of my jacket. *Lillian Doughty.* She's older than I expected.

"My daughter got stuck at work." She leans against one of the door's hinges, her hands now pinched in the small of her back. "Those are my grandsons." She's breathing quickly, the air leaving her lungs with a short whistle. "I never would've…I mean…"

"Take it easy," I say.

Reaching into her groceries, I remove three tomatoes from a small paper sack. I motion for her to place the bag over her mouth and nose. She follows my instructions but continues talking. The words are strained, lost to crinkling paper and wheezy breaths.

Then a noise from the door—one of her grandsons standing between the parted screen.

"What're you doing, Nana?" "I just got a little lightheaded." She fans herself with the bag, trying to put the boy at ease. "I'm fine, honey. Just go back into the living room and I'll be right there."

After the boy disappears she returns the tomatoes to the bag, one at a time. She smoothes out the front of her blouse and slacks.

"Please tell Mr. Eugene that I need a few more days."

"Friday?"

"Yes." The relief comes slowly—and when it's nearly upon her, I can almost see her mouth rise into the hint of a smile. "Oh, Friday would be good." She bends down and embraces the bag of groceries. "Please tell Mr. Eugene I'm sorry—it won't happen again."

She takes a hesitant step toward the house. And another. Then she's half-inside her kitchen.

"Friday," she repeats.

My foot is pressed against the base of the door. When she reaches for the knob, I lean forward with all my weight. The edge of the door catches her above the right eye. There is blood, slow then fast. She staggers back. A red crease rises from the meaty ledge of her brow. She slaps at the counter, trying to steady herself as she moves into darkness.

I hear her reedy moans from behind the sealed door.

"Friday," I say, walking down the driveway.

Sitting behind the wheel of my car, I leaf through the pages of my notepad. I use an obscure brand of Japanese marking pens I've only been able to find at a local art shop. They have tiny tips, like the head of a needle, that work well with my precise style of handwriting. I remove one from my sun visor, where it's held in place by rubber bands. To the left of Lillian Doughty's name is a small box that remains unshaded. Beneath a pair of horizontal lines I've written her address, phone number, car model and color. Last, parenthetically, is a dollar figure—*twelve hundred*—which I encircle. I also put today's date and, following an asterisk, a notation that she has two young grandsons. I didn't know about the boys.

Suspended by chain from the ceiling of my garage is a battered heavy bag. Many nights in darkness, my mind churning, I'll get clipped by the bag—on the elbow, the knee—as I make my way into the house. I once spilled a takeout dinner, a chicken burrito that hit the ground with such force it blasted beans and rice and

guacamole across the grill of my car. The next morning I caught a
pair of skunks perched on the bumper, scratching at dried whorls
of Mexican food. It took nearly a week for the stink to fade.

I walk into the laundry room, toss my jacket on the hood of
the washing machine, and take a beer from the fridge. Arranged
neatly across the dining room table are a dozen or so greeting
cards—a new line, all "heartfelt," from Silver Springs, the company for which I work. I'm supposed to familiarize myself with
the stock. "You've gotta know what you're pushing," says my
boss, Dennis Gaines, who often pounds his desk for emphasis
as he speaks.

I sit on the couch, feet propped against a coffee table. There's
a ballgame on TV. The beer is cold and I touch the bottle to both
cheeks, roll it gently across my forehead. Outside someone has
the same ballgame on a radio. I try to follow the sound while mut-
ing the television, but there's a slight delay, the picture coming a
few seconds ahead of the radio broadcast. I'm ready for another
beer, maybe something to eat. But I can't seem to propel myself into the other room. My mind starts to inflate with a list
of things I'd wanted to accomplish during the day. From the
supermarket there was deodorant and dishwashing soap, sandwich meat, bread, vanilla-crème cookies, juice boxes. I forgot to
reschedule an appointment for a magnetic resonance imaging
on my back. And, responsively, my doctor won't prescribe more
painkillers until he reads the film…

A trip to the mall near Clayton for new bed sheets and bath
towels. I also have to return a pair of loafers that's been sitting in
my trunk for a month. Beside the shoe store is a boutique that
sells greeting cards, wrapping paper, and inexpensive curios—
scented candles, glass figurines, picture frames. I have to talk with
the manager about the amount of floor space she's allocated our
lines. Though the store technically falls in my territory, one of
my company's other sales associates, a half-wit named Josh Dyer,
visited the mall a week ago on a family outing. Dyer has long had
designs on a senior managerial position.

Speaking in the urgent cadence normally associated with weightier matters—emergency room exchanges, roadside automobile breakdowns—he called a meeting to discuss the boutique's dearth of Silver Springs cards. Afterward, Gaines pulled me aside to explain, "in no uncertain terms," that this was *my* responsibility and—finger-slapping a nearby copy machine to stress certain words—I needed to make regular visits to the shop until the oversight was corrected. Then, in a final gasp of indignation, he promised if I couldn't fix the problem to his satisfaction, he was going to send Dyer. Later that afternoon, dizzy with rage, I beat a man with a steel lamp I tore off his kitchen wall.

Across the room, I notice the red light blinking on my answering machine. Twice I lob wooden coasters at the button, on a lark, to see if I can get the messages to play. Instead I capsize a coffee cup filled with pens, pencils, and a pair of scissors. The ballgame erases into a sitcom, the evening news, and finally a succession of movies with similar endings.

I'm awakened by a series of sharp pinches running down my left leg. I have a herniated disc and, on occasion, if I sit in the wrong position for too long, a numbing pain will spread concentrically from a place deep within my hip. Amid the TV's cathode blur comes an impossibly flat-stomached woman selling a fitness device that resembles an oversize gyroscope. Her voice is loud, filled with a disturbingly high level of cheer. She follows me as I stagger into the bathroom. I take a long, swaying piss with my arm braced against the towel rack for balance.

It's nearly five thirty. I can't decide whether to try falling back asleep.

I make my way to the bedroom. On the nightstand is an empty bowl of mint chip ice cream from two nights earlier. I woozily undress, dumping my shoes into the hamper before realizing my mistake and placing them on the closet floor. A sliver of soft light guides me through the blackness. Though it's been a couple days since my daughters were here last, I've forgotten to turn off their nightlight—a dancing pink elephant that allows them to navigate the bathroom (left, then right) after dark.

Standing at the end of a wood and brass bar, I watch the guy enter with two of his buddies. They're business types: suits, ties, newly shined shoes. Usually, when I'm running a job for Mr. Eugene—collecting gambling debts—I like to get the person alone. That way, if it turns bad, I don't have to worry about anyone else.

But these jokers come in loud, calling out their drink orders before the door behind them has a chance to close. The one on the right is nearly as big as me. He's got broad shoulders and big hands. He carries himself like an athlete—maybe he played rugby or small-college hockey—walking with a slight bounce that starts along his quadriceps.

I make my way toward them. I've discovered it's better to deal with these things quickly. I don't want the guy to get comfortable with his surroundings; I don't want the liquor to give him a false sense of bravado.

The three of them are watching a large TV suspended in the corner. I've left him a half-dozen phone messages, folded a note in the mailbox at his apartment building.

"Ben Coakley?" I say, tapping him on the elbow.

His friends are still focused on sports highlights.

Slowly he turns from the bar. The color drains from his face with such swiftness it's as though a valve has been released under his chin. He lifts his beer, reflexively, then lowers it again without taking a sip.

"I've been meaning to call you." His eyes dart to the door, window, and back to the door. "I've had a *crazy* week." He emphasizes the word crazy, staying on it a beat too long—perhaps buying himself more time to think. "Shit, I was gonna call you this morning but I got dragged into a meeting."

I nod.

In most cases, I find it's better for me to say as little as possible. People have a way of talking a lot when they're stressed. They will often narrate the previous few days of their lives, at abnormally high speed, until, eventually, they lead themselves back to the moment of our encounter. Then, usually, they'll take a deep breath, and the situation will resolve itself.

While Ben Coakley's nervously blathering on, gesturing wildly with his arms—even splashing himself with beer—the larger of his two friends takes a sudden interest in our conversation.

"Everything okay?"

I carefully spread my feet apart, shoulder width. I want to be in proper position to throw a punch—or catch one.

"I guess…" says Ben Coakley, sputtering.

Now his other friend has also turned his attention toward me. Coakley begins telling his story: A couple months ago he won big on the Yankees; he let it ride on a Cardinals-Dodgers game; and he lost, then lost again when the Red Sox blew a six-run lead in the eighth inning against the Devil Rays—"the *Devil Rays!*"—and, well, suddenly he's in the hole seventeen-fifty, plus the vig.

"Listen, pal," says the big guy, standing. "He's good for it. Maybe he wins next week. And then *we're* coming to *you* for money."

Because I've been here before, I know what comes next.

On the bar is a half-empty beer stein made of thick, dimpled glass. I raise it, cautiously, so the handle remains firm between the crease at the base of my palm. In a single motion, I cock my elbow and thrust the mug forward until it collides with the big guy's nose. There's a detonation of glass and pale beer. Toothy mug shards erupt into a dozen geometrical shapes, glimmering in the green light from a neon bar sign.

A rope of blood hangs across his face like an inverted horseshoe, connecting one eye to the other. I punch him two more times, in rapid succession, until he drops to the ground. The big guy's holding his face and groaning. His legs are splayed against the slick tile floor, his loafers scraping for traction—

I pause for a moment, wanting Ben Coakley and his other friend to see the damage. Then I suggest we move outside.

By the time I reach the sidewalk, Ben Coakley is pawing through the bills in his money clip.

"What do you have, Ryan?" he says to his friend.

Ben Coakley races back through the doors. From where I'm standing, half-shielded by his friend pressed against the window, it appears Ben Coakley's convincing the big guy, still knotted between the legs of a barstool, to surrender the contents of his wallet.

"I've got three hundred and eighty-three dollars," says Coakley, short of breath. "But there's a money machine across the street. I can get you another four hundred."

I feel a sharp pain in my right hand and start massaging my middle knuckle—a gesture Ben Coakley misinterprets as a sign of aggression.

"I *promise* I can get you the rest tomorrow."

His arm is raised and trembling. The bills are poking in a half-dozen strange directions between the slats of his closed fingers. Across his shoulder I can see the big guy struggling to stand, using a pair of barstools as crutches, all wobbly and awkward like a baby doe. His face is still leaking blood: smeared down his lapels, collecting in a puddle near his shiny brown shoes. I watch the bartender offer him a small towel.

This would be a good time to leave, says a voice in my head, clear as each of Ben Coakley's heavy breaths. I take the crumpled money and stuff it into my coat pocket.

"By noon," I say.

Coakley thanks me, nodding again and again.

I start my car, letting the engine run for a moment. Coakley and his friend are still standing on the sidewalk, peering out toward separate spots in the darkness. I make a wide U-turn and my tires grind against the curb. I roll down the passenger window.

"You know the place?"

He nods, retreating a step. I wrote the name of a cigar shop on the note I slid into his mailbox. He'll leave the balance of his debt with a cashier, who'll place it in my cedar-lined locker in back.

Slowly, I drive away. I steal a glance in the rearview mirror. Coakley and his friend have come together; their arms pressed flat at their sides, they cast two long shadows in the bleached light. My window is still cracked and I can hear the tires hiss against the cool asphalt.

The afternoon sun has set their hair aglow. They are seated together on a narrow brick wall, feet bumping in loopy figure eights. Tig is wearing a red-and-white gingham dress and black Mary Janes. Her frilly socks are folded down so they half overlap. Nearby is her older sister, Callie, whose tanned knees are visible through twin holes in her jeans. A large red crest covers the left side of her soccer jersey. In a pile on the ground, a pair of backpacks with matching lunch boxes. Tig holds a sheet of rolled construction paper to her right eye like a telescope. I race behind a thin tree on the school's lawn, pretending to hide from the sweep of her makeshift spyglass.

"Oh!" she shouts, dropping down from the wall. "I see you, Dad."

I take an emphatic step out onto the walkway; I throw my arms skyward, shaking my fists in mock frustration.

"I was gonna sneak up on you."

"*Dad*," says Callie, her voice filled with impatience. "You knew she was watching you."

"No, I really—"

"Just tell her the truth."

Tig greets me with a tight squeeze around the waist. I hug back, crouching to kiss her on the head. I hold her for an extra beat, two, slipping my fingers below her armpits. Our embrace is so wonderfully pure, so perfect, I can feel my heart thumping against the side of her cheek.

"Mmmmm," I say, kissing her again. "Can I keep you this way until dinner?"

"Da—" She shakes free. "I coul'nt breathe."

I reach for Callie. But she is reluctant, pulling away. We're entering a new territory, a different phase in our relationship, and I don't know how to interpret her actions. Maybe she doesn't want her friends to see us hugging. Or maybe it's something else—a passive-aggressive response to my behavior toward her mother. *Let it be*, my sister has advised me. Try to avoid giving these little exchanges too much weight.

Callie pats me quickly on my back, as though burping a baby. "Okay, ladies. Do you want a snack?"

"Ice cream," says Callie.

"We *always* have ice cream," says Tig.

"You want something else?"

"I want something else." Tig crosses her arms against her chest, as though deep in thought. "I want a canna-lope."

"Cantaloupe?"

In explaining her sister's curious choice, Callie describes a school assembly that morning where an author read from a book about a butterfly who befriends a talking cantaloupe.

"And you want to *eat* the cantaloupe?"

"Yes," says Tig, her eyes meeting mine. "I'll have canna-lope."

I carry their backpacks and lunch boxes to my car. As I make my way around to the driver's side, Callie leans between the front seats—she's rummaging for gum or candy or breath mints. She once poured an entire container of Tic Tacs into her mouth and we had to stop at a convenience store to buy something for Tig —peanut butter cups, I think—to make it fair.

"The good news," I say, handing them both a stick of gum from my pocket, "I know a place that has ice cream *and* cantaloupe."

"Where?" asks Callie, suspiciously.

"We've gotta go to the grocery store. We need something for dinner—and for your lunches tomorrow."

They both let out throaty groans. Callie kicks the back of the passenger seat, snapping her head from side to side as though she's suffering a seizure. Tig shreds an old greeting card. She tosses the tiny pieces across the armrest below my elbow.

"Guys!"

"I *hate* the grocery store," says Callie, pressing her face against the window. "We just went with Mom."

"It's boring," says Tig.

"We'll make it quick, I promise."

"You *always* say that. 'Oh, we only need a few things,'" says Callie, offering an unflattering imitation of my voice. "And then we get, like, everything."

For a moment there's silence. But then comes a reprieve from Tig, sweet and innocent, as though nothing had preceded it.

"We can get canna-lope?"

"Yes, honey," I say, smiling into the windshield. "We can get all the cantaloupes you want."

"Good."

"Geez," says Callie, realizing she's now outnumbered. Then, mostly to herself: "I hate the grocery store."

The noise comes from two aisles away. I walk past the dairy section, a case of bottled water tucked beneath my arm. Tig's screaming madly from the front of a shopping cart, like Lucifer's hood ornament. Callie gives another push, powerful and deliberate. As the cart races toward me, it nearly collides with an unsteady pyramid of laundry detergent. Before I can caution them, before I can speak the same words they've heard during a hundred previous visits to the grocery store—this is *not* a playground and most people don't enjoy heart-stopping encounters with runaway shopping carts—Tig reaches for a box of Fruit Roll-ups and asks, "Can we get this?"

I nod, as I always do, and gather them back under control. It's been a long day; I can see the girls are tired. Callie walks beside me—a lean, a bump, another lean with her heavy head against my hip. Tig has climbed inside the cart, retreating to a corner with our growing pile of purchases to keep her company. I follow her pink fingers moving gingerly across the wax-paper coating on a sack of cookies. She begins to separate the adhesive flap.

"What're you doing, Tig?"

She lets the package slide casually down her leg.

"Nuthin'."

"Okay," I say, and give her a wink. "Just making sure."

The girls help me load the groceries onto the black conveyor belt at the register. But their attention span is short. Callie starts leafing through a teen magazine crowded with glossy photographs of young celebrities. Tig's still chewing on a plastic spoon she got from the bakery aisle, a woman handing out samples of bread pudding. Tig adjusts herself in the cart, peering over Callie's shoulder.

"Stop!" says Callie, shielding the magazine with her back.

"I can't see."

"I'm looking at this one." Callie takes several steps toward the cashier. "Get your own."

"Come on, Cal," I say, gently nudging her back in the direction of her sister. "She just wants to look at the pictures with you."

Then comes a long sigh. She stomps past us, returning the magazine to its rack with an exaggerated swing, as though pulling down a window shade.

"Oh, that's silly." I slide my credit card into a gray box suspended above the conveyor belt, then let Tig press the appropriate sensors on its keypad. "You'd rather stop looking than share?"

"Yes!" says Callie, crossing her arms defiantly. "I never get to do *anything* by myself. I hate having a sister."

"I don't want to hear that, Cal." I take hold of her shoulder, turning her so our eyes meet. "What am I always telling you guys?"

Behind us stands a sixtyish woman in a brightly colored house dress. She's already segregated her groceries from ours with a plastic dividing rod. Though she's thumbing through a small bundle of torn coupons, held together by paperclip, I can tell she's listening to our conversation.

"You've only got one sister in this world," I say, gesturing toward Tig. "And you need to be good to each other. Here's something I absolutely promise: One day you're going to be best, *best* friends."

"Anna's my best friend."

"Ruby's my best friend, Dad," says Tig.

"I know, I know." The woman in the bright dress smiles, then pretends to search for another item in her now-empty cart. "Anna and Ruby are great friends. But someday—I don't know when—you two are gonna be closer than peas in a pod."

"*Eeew*! Peas in a pie."

"I never heard of a pea pie," says Tig.

The woman starts to chuckle and turns her head.

"Not a *pie*," I say, mussing up their hair. "It's *pod*: peas in a *pod*."

Later, after surrendering a dollar to a teenage boy who loads our groceries into the trunk, I can hear Tig muttering to herself in the back seat. "Peas in a pie," she whispers. "Peas in a *pod*."

The girls are squeezed onto a small stepladder beside the bathroom sink. As they brush their teeth, Tig leans forward and spits a foamy stream of saliva. "Oh, Jesus," says Callie, surprising me; I can't recall her using Christ's name as an exclamation. Because I know what's coming next, I grab her toothbrush and rinse it with fresh water.

"She spit on me!" says Callie, wiping dry her arm against a towel. "It got on my hand and toothbrush and—"

"It was an accident," I say.

"I didn't mean to..." says Tig.

Callie storms out of the bathroom, giving Tig a little shove on the way.

"Hey," I say.

I follow Callie into the hall, pinning her gently to the wall with my elbow. She's now talking at hyperspeed—about sisters and spittle and privacy. I place my finger over her lips.

"What's my number-one rule?" I lean close, rubbing my nose against hers. "We do *not* hit."

"I didn't hit her, Dad."

"We don't bump or bite or kick..."

She pushes my finger away. Then, curiously, she asks: "Can we move?"

"Why?"

"I want my own room. None of my friends have to share a room with *their* little sisters."

"I want my own room, too" comes Tig's disembodied voice.

"Well…" I hoist Callie onto my back, walking her to the upper bunk bed. "It's something we can consider."

"You're just saying that because you don't wanna talk about it anymore."

I pull Callie's moon-and-stars quilt up to her chin.

"No, I'm serious. We can look at the rentals in Sunday's newspaper."

"Promise?"

I nod.

"Sack of grain!" shouts Tig from the bathroom.

Since the girls were toddlers, I've had a few different ways of carrying them. Tucked beneath one arm we call "loaf of bread." Or there's "like a baby," which is when they're cradled against my outstretched forearms. But Tig's favorite, "sack of grain," is where I haul her belly-down across my right shoulder. Sometimes, like tonight, she grabs the door's molding and I stop dead in my tracks, pretending to be alarmed.

"Whoa," I say, spinning a revolution, two, before dumping Tig onto her bed.

"Tell us a story," says Callie.

"Tell us about when you were a kid," says Tig.

For some reason, they've grown to love fairly pedestrian tales from my youth. They're especially fond of the ones where I get into trouble, or where I'm the target of a joke. I sit on the edge of Tig's lower bunk, chin on fist. Finally, because I'm tired and nothing is coming to mind, I settle for an old standby—one of their favorites.

During my senior year of high school, my mother asked me to return a basting pan to my aunt. It was a brutally cold day, with temperatures never rising above zero. Because my pickup wouldn't start—the next morning it would require a jump—I borrowed my mother's Volkswagen convertible. My best friend,

Doug Sullivan, came along for the ride. We were silly teenagers and we decided to lower the soft-top, driving hunched forward, shivering against the frosted dashboard. I remember people staring at us from the warmth of their cars. Mostly they shook their heads, wondering what would possess two otherwise normal-looking boys to travel with the top down on the coldest day in a decade.

After pulling back into my driveway, Sully helped me return the roof to its original position. But the frigid air had turned the metal support beams stiff and brittle. We leaned forward with the heft of our bodies. To this day, I can still hear the pop in my ears—it sounded like a pencil being snapped across a knee. Sully's jaw dropped and his mouth formed a near-perfect O. We both understood the gravity of our actions.

"What happened to your friend?" asks Tig, though she already knows the answer.

He ran home, leaving me to face my mother alone.

In the darkness, I can see the whites of my daughters' eyes. Here comes the part they like best: When I describe their nana's reaction, I make funny noises—mimicking the sound of exploding dynamite on the old Road Runner cartoons. I use my fingers to trace spiraling stars and detonated fireworks above their grandmother's head.

"Nana was mad," says Tig.

"Very."

"Was that the maddest you ever saw her?" asks Callie.

"Probably," I say, rising from the bed. "And you know what?"

"I know!" shouts Callie.

"Me too, me too," says Tig.

"She never let you drive that car again."

"Nope," I add, kissing them both on their foreheads. "Never again."

His eyes turn stern and narrow. As Dennis Gaines's face grows flush, he strikes the conference room table with the side of his fist. It's a common mistake—one I've made a hundred times. The words escaped from my mouth before I'd paused to think; but the moment I spoke them, conjoined familiarly together, I knew there would be unpleasant consequences.

"They're not *greeting cards*," he says, with emphasis to illuminate my error. "Harpon makes greeting cards. Not us. We offer *social expressions*."

I nod absently.

My eyes lock with Bill Sweeney's. He's fighting back a smile. Slyly, he removes a credit card from his wallet and pretends to saw open his wrist.

"I understand," I say, suddenly, after Gaines has turned his attention again to me. "It was a slip of the tongue."

"Listen, I don't mean to overreact." A few of the other salesmen in the room instinctively shake their heads. "But this is the very crux of what we're doing here."

Afterward, I retreat to the kitchenette near my office for a fresh cup of coffee. Sweeney's knocking on the Plexiglas window of a vending machine, trying to get a steel spring to release its hold—just another quarter rotation—on a Kit Kat bar.

"Are you out of your mind?" he asks.

I nod.

"Oh, Christ. You were killing me in there."

From above the refrigerator he removes a narrow rod of metal, roughly the length and width of a yardstick.

"Did he actually use the word *crux*?" I ask.

"Yeah," says Sweeney, sliding the rod between the hard rubber seal of the vending machine's door. "I think he did."

"Crux," I repeat aloud, if only to hear its sound again.

There's a splashy thud as Sweeney is finally able to free the candy from its perch. As we walk toward our desks, he breaks the chocolate into fourths, stuffing the scored wafers into his mouth one after another.

On my chair is a bundle of make-readies—rough-draft versions of greeting cards—squeezed together by fat rubber bands. It's a courtesy passed along by the creative department (after years of heated discussions). In theory, sales representatives have an earliest-possible opportunity to review the company's product line—in this case, Mother's Day. But I can't remember the last time I looked at a season's offerings until they were in final form. Some days, impulsively, I'll spread the cards across my desk to create an illusion of diligence. At the very least, it will save me from another excruciating conversation with Gaines should he pass my cubicle and notice the still-bound packet.

Behind my left shoulder I hear the sound of fingers trawling through a glass candy dish filled with sour balls. I pretend to work, focusing on a spreadsheet glowing from my computer screen. I'm now relying on my peripheral vision; I watch Josh Dyer examining one of the sweets. Orange. Or maybe he's holding a pair of them, yellow and red, blurred together against my occipital lobe. He sighs, as if the whole thing is too much for him. Then he blows off a speck of lint, a smudge from his own hand, before dropping the candy into his mouth.

"Good day?" asks Dyer, sucking a scrap of sour ball from between his teeth.

"First rate."

I begin typing random numbers and letters into my spreadsheet, hoping the appearance of labor will scare him away.

"Listen..." He reaches across my desk and removes a yellow Post-it note. He folds the tiny square of paper against itself, two, three times. Then he uses the spiky cone to pry candy from behind his eye tooth. "Gaines asked me..." He stops and crosses his arms. "Are you planning to visit that shop in the North Ridge Mall?"

I nod.

"Carol's? Caroline's?"

"Carmella's Paper & Things," I say, without looking up.

"Right—that's it." He tosses the now-twisted Post-it into a wire trash can beside my desk. "Carmella's."

Near my right hand is a large paperweight—a painted rock Tig made for my birthday one year. I lay my forehead against its grainy surface and hold my position, as though in prayer, waiting for the sound of Dyer's parting footsteps.

The hot dog is baked inside a flaky, buttery cinnamon roll. A teenage boy holds the samples aloft on a plastic tray, bite-sized servings of the magical pairing speared by colored toothpicks. I've eaten three and would've gone for more had the boy not retreated behind a group of small children. Instead, I walk to a neighboring counter for free chunks of bourbon chicken. Though I'm trying to improve my diet, I've somehow convinced myself that if I don't actually purchase the food, it doesn't count against my list of restrictions.

I make my way toward the Java Hut, where a young girl offers thimble-size paper cups filled with peach smoothies. The first drink hits the back of my throat like a shot of flavored schnapps. As I reach for another—maybe two at once—a familiar face enters the ceiling of my vision. This has been happening with greater frequency: I recognize someone, I *think* I recognize someone, from whom I've collected money. I try vanishing into a line for giant pretzels, but at six five I'm hardly inconspicuous. I crouch forward, pretending to rub a soreness from my knee. From the corner of my eye, I watch him sprinkle parmesan cheese or garlic salt onto a slice of pizza. He's middle-aged with a stubby nose and a wide forehead, emphasized by his slicked-back hair. If it's the same guy, I once pinned him to the door of his car—my forearm against his throat—while I removed some money from his wallet. And because he was still a few hundred dollars short, I cracked him on his left ankle with an aluminum softball bat I took from his back seat.

Stoop-shouldered, I shuffle through a knot of shoppers. Once I reach the airy hub of the mall, concealed by barking fountains and potted trees, I glance back for a more direct view. It's been about a year since our encounter, but I half-expect him to be limping, his foot still smarting from the bat's damage. He studies the space around him, presumably looking for a place to sit. He's holding his pizza in one hand and a tall soda in the other. A shopping bag hangs from his left forearm, awkwardly bumping against his thigh as he walks. He takes a bite of pizza—couldn't wait any longer—and after a couple powerful chews he stops. Now his fingertips scratch at his tongue—he's balancing his pizza while attempting to remove a corner of wax paper from his mouth. His movement causes the soda to splash the side of his shopping bag and, when he adjusts the drink, his slice somersaults toppings-down onto the floor. Then he's on his knees, scooping up hot cheese and pepperoni with a pair of flimsy paper napkins.

He looks sad and ordinary. I feel remorse welling inside me. It starts small—a germ of guilt. But a momentum deep within my imagination is building: he's just a man trying to get by in this life. Maybe he's divorced, like me, with a couple kids he doesn't see enough. He's struggling to make it through this day, and the next. Then he received a tip from a friend—Penn State will cover. A gift from the football gods; a way to make his paycheck last a little longer. But the Nittany Lions pulled their starters late in the game. And then a meaningless touchdown by Wisconsin. Except it wasn't so meaningless to this guy. A week later comes another game to make the first one right. Then one more. And suddenly he's on his knees in a wet parking lot, protecting his head with his arms while some big guy he doesn't know stands over him with a shiny silver-and-blue bat...

Maybe it's not him, I tell myself, now desperate to break the connection. I look down at him from the escalator, my eyes narrowing against the light, and for the first time I notice a squid of tomato sauce on his shirt.

A delicate chime signals my arrival at Carmella's Paper & Things. I'm greeted by a head-spinning cocktail of lavender and vanilla. A small display table holds several examples of wedding invitations—creamy cardstock with loopy, gold-leaf embossments. Nearby is a shelf crowded with boxed stationery in powder blue and ecru and white. There's also a glass jeweler's case filled with three rows of expensive-looking pens resting on a burgundy sash of crushed velvet.

"Can I help you?" asks a woman's voice.

I poke my head down one aisle then another.

"Here!" says the woman, slapping at the carpet behind me.

She's sitting on the floor, unpacking a large box of one of my competitor's cards. When I see a three-quarter view of her face, my stomach seems to float into my esophagus. I take a couple brief steps and steady myself against a wooden cabinet. She has coppery hair in a blunt cut, ending near the crest of her jawline. Fat black eyeliner makes her green eyes look translucent. She's dressed in a tight gray t-shirt and fashionably distressed jeans. Her toenails—she's not wearing shoes—are painted silver. Without looking, she lifts a bundle of envelopes and stuffs it into a slot above her head.

"Can I help you find something?"

She is beautiful and intriguing and, entwined on the nubby showroom floor, seems like someone I'd like to know.

"I'm here to see Leann," I say, offering a business card.

"Leann!" she shouts.

As I wait, I continue watching her remove rectangular packets of greeting cards and matching envelopes. She tears the cellophane wrapping with her incisors. Then she blindly plugs each sheaf into the rack against her back. She finishes every cycle by crossing off a corresponding line on a clipboard pitched across her lap. I imagine my fingertips grazing the raspberry blush of her cheek, tucking a rogue strand of hair behind her ear. I can nearly feel the soft skin of her neck pressed against mine, the two of us joined together like a pair of feathered hinges. It seems strange to be ferried along this path of infatuation with a woman I've never met. The last time I had this type of instantaneous and all-encompassing feelings for a woman was ages ago—perhaps on the evening I met my ex-wife. It's almost as though an electrical current has alerted my senses, causing the prickly hair on my limbs to rise to attention.

My trance is broken by the squeaking of firm leather shoes coming from a nearby aisle. They belong to a middle-aged woman in a tan pantsuit. She's wearing narrow, gold-rimmed eyeglasses and a jade necklace that nearly reaches her navel.

"Mr. Fanning," she says, extending her hand.

"How are you, Leann?"

I position myself in such a way that I can maintain eye contact with the woman on the floor.

"Is this a social visit?" asks Leann.

"I wish …"

As the words leave my mouth, it occurs to me that I'm still staring at the woman behind her. I take several steps to my left and extract a pair of Harpon greeting cards from a display cabinet.

"This entire side is supposed to be ours," I say, rubbing the cards together. "*And* the endcaps."

Leann adjusts a crooked envelope, then crosses her arms.

"I told you last time—we just don't have the space."

"It disrupts the continuity," I say. "It ruins the whole theme we're trying to achieve with our line."

For a moment we're both silent, only the gentle *thunk* as more of my competitor's cards are lowered into their respective bins. I gaze dimly ahead and wonder if Leann has any idea how much I don't care where she puts this crap. "In fact," I want to tell her, "if my boss wasn't such a red-ass I wouldn't care if you took every Silver Springs greeting card—nay, *social expression*—and ignited them in a giant bonfire in the center of your goddamn store!"

"Maybe we could tighten things a titch," she says. "I could get you another panel or so, but that's the best I can do." She takes a deep breath, letting her eyes drift. "Our standalone stores are a different story."

"You're killing me, Leann."

"Another panel," she says, with hard-edged finality.

"Oh, you hate me." I thread my fingers together, as though in prayer. "It's difficult to capture a mood when you're putting our 'heartfelt' next to a photocard of some fat kid picking his nose."

She calls to the woman kneeling behind us. Her name is Nina and, when she appears, I can feel the last bit of fight I have for this whole fruitless exercise escape my body like a cloud of winter's breath. Leann explains her decision to Nina, then nods politely in my direction before waddling to the back of the store in her too-tight shoes. I'm still clinging to my business card, and I return it to my wallet. In a tiny show of disgust, Nina slaps her thighs and plucks several stacks of recently shelved greeting cards from their display. They hit the floor with a skin-against-skin smacking sound.

"I'm sorry," I say.

"Not a problem," says Nina. "It's part of the job."

"Yeah, but—" I crouch down beside her. "I created more work for you."

As she leans forward to separate a pile of fanned cards, the V-neck collar of her shirt pulls from her skin. I follow the lacy trim of her brassiere—a perimeter of intricately stitched flowers in white and gray. Even as I try to look away, my eyes catch on a constellation of light freckles that spill into the narrow valley between her breasts. Next I'm staring at her lower lip, knotted and pink, as she bites down, straining to reach a stray envelope.

And for the first time in a long, long while, I'm wondering what it would feel like to kiss someone. Not to sleep with her, not even to put my hands on her body—fumbling with the plastic latch on her lacy gray-and-white brassiere. Not to sink my fingers down the small of her back, inside the waistband of her jeans, let her cotton underpants stretch across my knuckles. Only: How would she taste, lips against lips?

My face turns warm. I take a step back, then another. In what seems like slow motion, I feel my elbow puncture the side of a wood-and-paper lantern.

"Oh, God," I say, trying awkwardly to reassemble the fangy pieces.

"Don't worry about it." Nina rises—she's taller than I expected—and removes the damaged lantern from the table. "Happens all the time."

"I'm just making a mess of your day."

"*Please.*" She wraps the lantern's black cord into a tight lasso, stuffing it through the collapsed side. "My day was a mess long before you got here."

I can't think of anything else to say, but I'm not ready to leave her yet.

"What kind of lamp *was* that?"

She leads me to a shelf supporting a collection of similar lanterns in red and violet and green. She flips a switch, and a sheet of cylindrical paper with tiny die-cut figures begins turning carousel-like inside the cube. The figures cast galloping blue ponies against the wall, a box of stationery, and, finally, against Nina's cheek.

"Mostly people buy them for kids' rooms."

"Let me pay for the one I broke."

"I'm not gonna take your money," she says, smiling.

Her teeth are fine and straight and smooth as marble. Anything I say now would feel forced—a clumsy transition from courteous professional banter to something more desperate. I have to come back here again, at least once every six weeks. I lack the skill and dexterity of language to propel us forward in incremental (and non-threatening) stages.

"Listen—" I say, rubbing my palms against the thighs of my pants.

"Go, go!" She grabs me by the arm and leads me toward the entrance to the mall. "It'll be fine. I promise."

I watch her walk away from me, cradling the lantern like a leaky melon. I'm hoping she'll turn around, take a quick peek across her shoulder. But she keeps moving until she disappears against the light and clutter of the store.

The pitch and volume of the siren rattles the window above the sink. Tig's running from dining room to kitchen, waving her arms and screaming, "Fire! Fire!"

"There's no fire," I say.

Stretched to full extension, I try unscrewing the smoke detector from the ceiling of our hallway.

"Too loud," says Callie, her hands pressed across her ears.

I can't get the faceplate to release. The siren continues its shrill whine.

"Turn it off, Dad," says Callie. "It's making me crazy."

"Fire, fire!"

"Tig!" I say, racing to my bedroom. "Stop saying that."

I remove a hockey stick from beneath my bed.

"Okay—now watch out!"

I take a mighty swing, from my hips, and carve a crescent of plaster from behind the still-screeching smoke detector. "Shit," I say, moving closer. My second swing connects, flush against the stick's sweet spot, and the smoke detector explodes into a dozen pieces of jagged plastic and ruptured wire. A small, rectangular nine-volt battery ricochets off the bathroom door, leaving a dent, before fracturing a hotel ashtray filled with loose change.

"Ooooh," says Callie, hands dropping from ears to cheeks.

"That did it," announces Tig.

I sweep up the mess with the blade of the hockey stick.

"Put it on the pad," I say.

Beside the phone in the kitchen we keep a narrow pad of paper listing our errands for the week. Groceries, school supplies.

"Is *detector* spelled with an e-r?" asks Callie.

"O-r."

"New smoke detector," she repeats, aloud.

"Can we get a different color this time?" says Tig. "Pink or purple?"

"They don't make *pink* or *purple*," says Callie, her voice hard with contempt.

"Well, if—"

"They only make white."

"Our old one's not white."

"It's *beige*. That's almost like white."

"Okay, okay," I say, ushering the girls back into the kitchen. "We'll see what they have at the hardware store. In the meantime, let's have dinner."

The television plays in the background as the girls set three places at the table. I heat a dish of leftover macaroni and cheese in the microwave. Then I peel half a medium-sized cucumber— Tig doesn't like the skin—and chop it into ten slices. Once the steaks are finished I cut them into pieces, oozy with blood, small enough for the mouths of young girls. There's also fresh cider and wedges of cornbread left by Miss Simone, our cleaning lady.

As soon as the plates hit the table, Callie begins spearing the cubes of meat and stuffing them into her mouth.

"Slow down, sister," I say. "There's no more steak in the kitchen."

She nods.

"I wish I didn't like meat so much." She takes a breath. "I also love animals. I always think about that cute widdle pig in Charlotte's Web when I'm eating bacon. But I still love bacon."

"Yeah, bacon is *so* good," says Tig.

"We don't eat a lot of meat," I say.

"The other night we had chicken," says Callie. "*That's* meat."

"Chicken's meat."

"Actually, it's considered poultry."

"What's poultry?" asks Tig.

"It's still a dead animal," says Callie.

"Hey—let's talk about something else." I flick a cucumber seed across the table, bringing smiles to the girls' faces. "How was school?"

"Callie has a crush on Adam Unger," says Tig, slurring the boy's name into a single word—*Adamunger*—so it sounds like an obscure African dialect.

"Really?"

"No!" Callie gestures at her sister with a fork. "She doesn't even know who he is."

"I heard you talkin' about him."

"Shut up."

"That's enough," I say, tapping my knife against a glass.

We eat the rest of our dinners in silence, a TV news program playing from the living room. Both girls have ice cream sandwiches for dessert and I wash the dishes. The phone rings—Callie rushes to answer it. She's talking to her mother, who's called to wish the girls goodnight. Once they've finished recounting the highlights of the day, Tig waves to me. "Mom wants to talk to you," she whispers, covering the wrong end of the phone with her little hand.

The earpiece is sticky with ice cream and smudged chocolate fingerprints. I hold it away from my head. Liz has never been good with transitions. There's no small talk, no brief exchange of pleasantries. She begins as soon as she hears the sound of my voice. Something about a bill from a recent dentist appointment for the girls. "This is *your* responsibility, Hayes," she says, spiraling into a caustic loop. When she pauses, if only to determine whether I've terminated the connection, I try explaining the details of our shared parenting agreement. (This is familiar territory.) A monthly stipend is extracted from my paycheck to cover the girls' medical and dental insurance. But all wellness visits to pediatricians and, in this case, their dentist, are to be covered by her—unless it exceeds two hundred dollars, in which case we split the cost equally.

"That's bullshit, Hayes," she shouts. "I don't—"

I unplug the phone from the wall. Because all of my phones operate from the same base station, this ensures any return call will be dumped into voicemail. Next I reach for my cell phone, on the counter, and switch off its ringer. Too often our "discussions" devolve into long, gainless arguments, wars of attrition that don't end until I've conceded the point. "We paid nearly fifty thousand dollars for a divorce," I've pleaded with her. "Look at the document. We are bound—*by law*—to follow its orders."

Over the years, I've done my best to keep the girls out of harm's way. I have tried desperately to convince Liz to restrain her emotion. I remember a day, during our first year of separation, when she began screaming in her driveway because I planned to take the girls to a friend's farm in northern Kentucky. With Callie and Tig belted into the back seat of my car, tiny valises at their sides, I listened to the recurring voice of a psychologist friend thrumming through my head: *Extricate yourself from the situation.* Calmly, I assured Liz that everything would be fine; I promised to have the girls call her each evening. As I backed us slowly into the street, Liz dove onto the hood of my car. She slapped at the windshield with her open hands. "Stop! Stop!" she shouted. "He's taking my kids!"

The girls were terrified—this was their *mother* clinging to the hull of a moving vehicle. Soon they too were crying, confused. I could see Mr. Harter's reflection in the side mirror, pushing a lawnmower and pretending not to notice as our circus life played itself out on his normally tranquil, tree-lined street. I shifted the car again into park, hoping this act of hesitation would be enough to disarm Liz, proof that my motives were sincere. But her fists came through the open window, striking me in the ear, against the side of my face. "*Please,*" I said, my hands forming a protective barrier against her glancing blows.

Again the psychologist's voice, clear and stern: *You cannot raise your arm in anger. Not one time. Or you will lose your children.*

She pulled the girls, still crying, from the car and led them back into her house. I could feel a warmness swelling along my left cheekbone. In the background the trippy buzz of Mr. Harter's lawnmower, working its way across his yard in a diagonal pattern.

I sat alone in my idling car with the same thought turning over again and again: How do you explain this awful thing to your daughters? They're young—hopefully too young to remember this in a few years. As I'd done before, I prayed for the failure of their sweet little minds. Let this memory stay behind, like a puddle of dark oil beneath an old car.

For me, the best part of a romantic relationship is its first few weeks, or, if you're lucky, months. Fueled by equal doses of promise and lust, prospective partners are cautious about what they reveal to one another. Potentially toxic secrets remain stored away in some dark closet, awaiting a slow and often damaging release. It was no different for Liz and me.

During our third date, we sat parked behind a restaurant called the Wagon Wheel. Though we'd already said our goodbyes, I didn't want to leave her. I climbed into the back seat of her car. She peered back across her shoulder through the gullwing gap between the bucket seats, and I could see the primary features of her face—lean eyebrows, tall and angular cheekbones, rose-petal lips—illuminated by a flickering streetlight. I took her fingers in my hands and rubbed them with my thumb, smoothing past a pair of antique gold rings. I could feel a twinge in my buttocks as I leaned forward and kissed her, first on the mouth and then on the downy side of her neck. In those days, Liz was swimming for exercise, and I tasted chlorine on her skin. How will it be possible, I wondered, for this relationship to progress—for us to discover if the pieces fit together—when all we want to do is put our hands on one another?

In the weeks that followed, we couldn't imagine ending the day without a phone call. I'd lie in bed, my room hidden by darkness, with the phone turning warm against my ear. We'd talk about otherwise meaningless exchanges at work and irritating lines at the post office and shortcuts home to bypass rush-hour traffic until one of us finally heard a scratchy tiredness in the other's voice.

It didn't take long before we both realized this thing between us could be something wonderful. Sometimes it's difficult to parse genuine memories, events that actually occurred, from the florid make-believe that clouded my mind during those early days. One winter afternoon, Liz and I went for a walk along the banks of the Chagrin River. Near an icy bend, I lost my footing and slid knee-deep into the cold, running water. I remember grabbing a handful of snow from the shore and tossing it at her. For years, I had this memory of the two of us engaged in a snowball fight—I plodding through the clear water, my arms sprung from my body for balance, and Liz lofting damp snowballs that quickly dissolved after splashing between my legs. I know we ended up sitting beside a fire at a local Rotary Club, sipping hot cider through cinnamon sticks. But soon after Callie was born, I retold the story in bed, with Callie sleeping between Liz and me, and Liz said the snowball fight never happened.

I'm not convinced she's right. She's just chosen to forget that part for some reason neither of us understands.

The day's newspaper is spread across my floor like broken tile. I remove an empty glass of grapefruit juice from my nightstand, fill it with sudsy water in the kitchen sink. The house is dark and quiet. For a moment, I stand in the girls' doorway and listen to the gentle sounds of their sleeping. Tig rolls onto her side, pushing a fuzzy polar bear across her pillow. I can hear an oyster of phlegm in the back of Callie's throat with each sticky breath.

Because I'm alone, because it's the middle of the night and I love my daughters with a force that sometimes makes me tremble—especially on days when they're with their mother and I'm left only with thoughts of a failed family—I squeeze into the bottom bunk beside Tig. Her small body is warm and soft. Almost immediately she presses against me, as though magnetized, her little rump and thigh squished against my leg. Tig's hair is still damp from her bath, smelling soapy and clean. There's also a light scent of coconut from her sister's moisturizing cream.

I curl my arm across her waist, pulling her tight along the well of my belly. As she bends her legs, I take her right foot in my hand and begin kneading it with my thumb. When she was a toddler, during winter months, I'd lift her onto my lap and rub her feet together in one palm, sometimes blowing warm breath so loudly it would cause her eyes to grow wide as daisies. "Footsy warmer, Daddy," she'd say, her toes wiggling with excitement.

From above comes the squeaking of wooden bed joints as Callie finds a position of comfort. Divinely, her thin white hand drops down from the side of the mattress. I reach into the night, resting my elbow against the ladder, and thread my fingers through hers, our paired hands casting swollen shadows against the wall behind the small pink elephant light. And surely this is as perfect a moment as I'm entitled—lying in stillness, a human conductor between my young daughters. The only noise now is our syncopated breathing, low and gentle, just us three.

Four black leather couches form a lopsided square in the center of the room. Pressed to the walls is a collection of large cedar-and-glass cases, each holding a half-dozen shelves of yawning cigar boxes. A brushed-steel coffee table rests on a Persian rug, its surface crowded with ashtrays, wooden matches, magazines, and a tray of picked-apart sweet rolls. Below the cash register is a waist-high, glass-and-metal display case filled with expensive lighters and leather goods and polished mahogany humidors. A man with a red thunderbolt tattoo across his right forearm is sealing three cigars in a Ziploc pouch.

"Fanning," he says, nodding.

I remove a thick, stubby Maduro from a colorful box. The wrapper is black and oily and webbed with veins. I use a guillotine to sever its cap, quick and precise, then touch a jet-flame to the blunt end until the cigar ignites. A tail of peppery smoke leaks from the corner of my mouth.

Several neon signs shaped like cigar bands illuminate a back hallway. Stenciled in white letters across a dark green door is the word *Private*. Big Dave, the guy with the tattoo, depresses a small button beneath the counter, releasing a lock on the green door. I enter a dimly lit office that smells, queerly, of turpentine and wet bark.

Seated near the entrance is an enormous man, a mountain with legs, his cannonball biceps straining the sleeves of his black t-shirt. Across the room is another beast, his head shaved clean save for a dark Fu Manchu-style mustache. He glances briefly in my direction before leaning over a pool table to measure his shot.

Behind a desk congested with papers and books and a sleek laptop computer is Mr. Eugene. He's wearing a gray chalk-stripe suit and pale blue shirt. Tucked into his breast pocket is a silk handkerchief in violet that glows under the muted desk lamp. Mr. Eugene's salt-and-pepper hair is slicked back, revealing a sharp widow's peak in the middle of his forehead. In his right hand is a silver and crimson lighter made of smooth Chinese lacquer that pings whenever he snaps open its lid. Lying on the corner of his desk, atop a stack of manila folders, neither hidden nor exposed, is a holstered nine-millimeter pistol.

"Come over here, Hayes," he says, punctuating the address with a ring of his lighter. "Let me get a look at you."

I stand in a halo of smoky light. I wipe my palms dry on my trousers, twice moving my cigar before reaching into the pocket of my sport coat. I carefully place a white envelope, with the Silver Springs logo embossed in its upper left-hand corner, beside a ceramic mug filled with pens and markers. Written on the envelope, in faint pencil, is the encircled figure $7,850.

"How are your girls?"

"Good, good." I have trouble meeting his eyes. "They're wonderful."

"Must be getting big?"

I nod.

He turns toward the pool table. "Hey, Linus," he says, gesturing with a gold letter opener. "Get Hayes a couple of those things Ricky brought us." He pauses. "They're in that box by the file cabinets."

The guy with the Fu Manchu mustache sets down his pool cue. I can hear the scrape and slap as he rummages through tight cardboard packaging. He makes his way around to Mr. Eugene.

"Take these for the girls," says Mr. Eugene. "Kids love this shit."

He hands me two individually wrapped personal DVD players and I thank him, two or three times, bowing uncontrollably like a nervous Japanese waiter.

"Well…" He sighs, smoothing down the lapels of his suit jacket. "You had a little trouble with the Coakley kid."

His remark is surprising, though not unexpected. I've said nothing to Mr. Eugene or during my occasional phone conversations with his assistant, Dove. Still, whenever I've had a problem with one of my collections, no matter how small, Mr. Eugene seems to know before I can tell him myself.

"It worked out okay," I say.

"Everybody's a tough guy," he says, shaking his head. "See what happens? His idiot friend's got a busted nose."

"I hit him too hard." I'm now staring at the floor, my foot pawing the fringe on a dark rug. "Maybe I—"

"Nonsense! The motherfucker owed me money. That's how it goes." He takes a breath. "Listen, if the kid didn't want to see his friend get popped, he should've just given you the cash. Right away—no monkey business."

I nod.

For a moment, Mr. Eugene turns his back to me. Then he licks his thumb, counting out seven crisp hundred-dollar bills. I stuff them into my pocket.

"Don't give it a second thought, Hayes," he says. "Some of these people are sick." He taps the side of his head with his index finger, a stack of fresh bills still pressed against his palm. "Not two hours ago the kid called to put a nickel on Southern Cal."

I must look surprised, because Mr. Eugene continues: "My hand to God."

In the back of my freezer is a glass jar filled with coffee beans. I release the lid, pouring the cold black beans onto the kitchen counter. Near the bottom is a steel, soup-can-sized cylinder I once purchased from a military supply store. Slowly, I unscrew the two sides, springing to life a tight coil of paper money, mostly hundreds. I press the fresh bills from Mr. Eugene against the others and wind them up again. After returning the jar to the freezer, I block its view with a casual placement of brightly designed boxes—toaster waffles, sausage sandwiches, ice cream bars. The refrigerator door is crowded with signs that for half the week I'm not alone: photographs of Callie and Tig; calendars of their soccer games, dance recitals; quiz papers with red stars or smiley faces; and colorful drawings—my favorite, a painting of "Dad" with a triangular head, yellow necktie, and four-fingered hands.

Cresting from the top of the icebox, like an oversized visor, is my portfolio—a black leather case I haven't touched in more than a year. Not long after college, I was hired by Silver Springs as a designer. I created greeting cards for dozens of different lines. There were rustic Western scenes, still lifes, romantic couples wandering white sandy beaches. I worked in a "bullpen" with other artists: a collegial setting where we'd often break the tension by playing a hybridized version of Wiffle ball along the enormous corridor beside our desks. In six years, it rarely felt like a job.

Shortly before Tig turned three, I was working on a collection of pastels for Valentine's Day when another artist, Alice Jernigan, walked into my cubicle, anxiously twisting a piece of oilcloth.

"Did you hear?" she asked, her face lean and white. "Tomorrow they're announcing layoffs. Lots of them."

The next morning I sat in my boss's office as she described the details of my "very decent" severance package. We were joined by a representative from human resources (in case I had questions) and a doughy, middle-aged security officer (in case I didn't handle the news with dignity). Because I was among the first in my division to be released, I remember staring at the list of other names on my boss's desk and trying to read them upside down. I'm not sure what I expected. Would I sprint from the room, shouting hysterically, "Save yourself, Alice Jernigan! Save yourself"?

In hindsight, the layoffs should have come as no surprise. We had watched the company's stock plummet from nearly thirty dollars a share to under five. The corporate types blamed Silver Springs' financial problems on a mild recession: the public had less to spend on discretionary purchases—greeting cards, pricy stationery, collectibles. But a few of us—a group of recently fired employees who met for drinks three days after losing our jobs—had our own little theory. Poor management. The company is run by a pair of brothers, David and Lyle Silver, third-generation CEOs left to guide a business started by their grandfather. Unfortunately, they've paid far greater attention to their own pursuits: David spends most of his time racing sailboats near Palm Beach, and Lyle's still working to extricate himself from a bad—and breathtakingly expensive—marriage. I'd often gossip with other designers over coffee in the main cafeteria, and we'd playfully suggest that the best way to succeed at Silver Springs was to associate yourself with a catastrophic failure—the bigger the screw-up, the higher the promotion. Someone would invariably cite the company's creative director, Connor Brisco, as a sterling example.

Though in his forties, Brisco dressed (and behaved) like a teenager desperate for attention. His closely cropped hair was bleached nearly white. He had a curious fashion sense that we deridingly described as part staff sergeant, part Sex Pistol. Regardless of season, he wore military fatigues, chain-link belts, motorcycle boots, and a "trademark" lavender scarf. He was almost singlehandedly responsible for a series of blunders so magnificent, so completely without redemption, that they would've cost an entire division of mortals their collective careers. My favorite was sparked at a corporate retreat, when one evening during dinner he began scribbling on the back of a cocktail napkin. "Oh, goodness," said a woman in middle management, her hand pressed to her chest. "He never knows when inspiration will strike." The resulting concept was a brand of characters for children—toys, clothing, Saturday morning animated series—called the Burger Bunch.

A short time later, I remember sitting in a company all-hands meeting as Brisco—flanked by the Brothers Silver—announced the launch of this latest venture. We were told that the Burger Bunch was a team of crimefighting superheroes comprised of anthropomorphic fast-food products—Chico the Chicken, Hot Dog Helen, Chip Chips and, of course, Blaze Burger. I was awestruck, having temporarily lost my powers of speech and motion. An editor named Artie Walton had the nerve to ask whether we—not wanting to offend, he chose his pronoun carefully—truly believed young children would be drawn to animated fast-food products and, more to the point, their retail tie-ins. (Hours later, Walton would be reprimanded for what was perceived as a lack of solidarity.)

In the ensuing months, the Burger Bunch lost many millions of dollars for Silver Springs. The weekend cartoon never attracted an audience and was canceled after its eleventh episode. All associated toys were remaindered by the end of the fiscal year. On a Friday in March, a letter was sent to all company employees via inter-office mail, signed by both Silver brothers, congratulating Connor Brisco on being named vice president of creative development.

I thought of Brisco the day I packed my belongings into a box. From my bulletin board, I removed a colorful Burger Bunch lapel pin I'd helped design.

All told, I was out of work for about five months. It was a marvelous time because I spent a magical ribbon of uninterrupted days with Callie and Tig. But it also signaled the end of my marriage: By the time I returned to Silver Springs, part of an employee retraining program in retail sales, I'd come to understand that Liz and I were awful together.

My second week back on the job, I lay in bed, pretending to sleep. Liz tossed and turned; she slapped the sheets, exhaled a loud, throaty sigh. She wanted to talk. There would be tears and shouting and insults. The vortex was swift. "You're *right*," I could say, repeating the paired words a hundred times. It wasn't enough. She would come stronger and stronger until the sun appeared like dripped wax against the horizon, or one of the children was awakened, the soft sound of crying bleeding through the walls.

Sometimes it's the easiest thing in the world, like grabbing a sack of cheeseburgers from a drive-thru concession. Globetrotter's Travel sits near the corner of Banks and Livery. An image of Earth is painted across its window, thrice encircled by the white vapor trail from a lean aircraft. The walls are covered in glossy posters of exotic locations—Bali, New Zealand, Greece. Making my way to the back, I pass four display stands stuffed with travel brochures.

The side of his metal desk has been defiled by a patchwork of vacation-themed decals. As Donald Katz speaks into a headset, he types frantically on a keyboard resting against his lap. He can see me approaching from the corner of his eye. Raising an index finger, he mouths the words, "One minute."

There's an empty seat beside Katz. I lean forward, pretending to stare at a framed photograph of, presumably, his wife and two children. In truth, I'm looking for anything he may use to protect himself—pocket knife, letter opener, scissors. A woman calls to me from the front of the room, wondering if she might be of service. I shake my head.

"We have coffee," she says.

I wait for a long moment. Then, once Katz has ended his phone conversation, I ask the woman for a cup. Black. In the hopes it will distract her from my business with her colleague.

"So, what can I do for you?" he says, half-standing before the cord tethered to his head causes his knees to buckle.

"I'm here for Mr. Eugene."

His face turns flush.

"Oh, God—oh, Jesus," he says, rolling back in his chair.

Mostly, I'm prepared for whatever comes next. I prefer doing business in public places, in crowded parking lots or bustling office buildings. People are less likely to make a scene—screaming and cursing and, occasionally, defending themselves—when others are watching. Still, I've become a keen observer: I follow sly hands dipping into coat pockets; I notice feet shuffling into position for possible egress.

"I'm sorry," he says, bracing his chin between his palms. "I'm so, so sorry."

He begins talking, but stops when the woman delivers my coffee. As she proceeds back toward her desk, Katz describes his busy week. He's been preoccupied with a chartered Caribbean cruise package for a group of senior citizens from Dunkirk. In detail, he explains the varied accommodations and connecting flights and assorted meal restrictions he was required to arrange.

"I absolutely meant to drop it off on Tuesday." Beneath his desk is a weathered brown briefcase—the kind with a shoulder strap. He digs through papers and saved magazine stories and bound travel pamphlets. "Here—here we go."

He surrenders a light gray envelope with the Globetrotter's Travel insignia printed in the space for a return address.

"It's all there," he says, slapping his thighs. "Count it."

I pull back the flap, peeking briefly inside. I've become pretty good at measuring money by sight and weight, within a reasonable margin of error.

"We're good," I tell him.

As I leave, I glance back at the woman. She breaks into an uneasy smile. Then her lips start moving. I'm about to ask her what she said when I realize she's talking into a headset—the same model as Katz's except for a pair of flowers pasted across its bridge.

One of the things that ignited the flame of attraction between Liz and me was her comical absentmindedness—a strain of needy behavior that caused her to lock her keys in her car or misplace her purse or forget important dates. She needed someone—she needed *me*—to gather the reins on her life. How could she survive—how had she lasted *this* long—without a well-intentioned soul to remind her the stove was still on?

There's a wonderful photograph of six-year-old Liz standing beside her school playground that for a long time I carried in the pocket of my wallet. Liz resembles one of those old-timey children from *The Grapes of Wrath*, plucked from a swirling dustbowl. She's wearing a dirty blouse whose buttons and holes don't align; the left-side tail hangs lower than the right. Liz was always tall for her age, and the bottoms of her trousers end a couple inches above her ankles. She has sandy smudges across her cheeks and knees. She's missing one sneaker and her hair, short and choppy, appears to have been styled by electricity. Just by glancing at the photo, I could tell Liz was the whirling dervish of the sandlot—first in line for relay races and kickball games and monkey-bar scaling. Still, there's a gentle sadness in her squinty brown eyes—a suggestion that this level of activity comes with a heavy toll: homework assignments forgotten in her bedroom, lunch money left on the kitchen counter, missed school buses.

About a month after we started dating, Liz invited me to a chamber music concert—she had a friend who played the cello. She and I dressed for the occasion—I wore a navy suit; she wore a red brocade dress and her aunt's pearls. We had dinner at a fancy French restaurant and split a bottle of wine. As we approached the concert hall, Liz's face turned a chalky white. I thought maybe the rich food hadn't agreed with her stomach.

"Oh, Jesus," she said, slapping her silver-and-black clutch against her hip. "I forgot the tickets. They're tacked to my refrigerator."

At first, I thought she was joking—I gave her a playful sock in the shoulder. But then I watched her eyes turn red and watery. She stammered and shook her head. "I'm *so* sorry," she said, hiding her face in her hands.

It wasn't a big deal, I assured her. There would be other concerts. Instead, we ate soft-serve ice cream with sprinkles, sharing a park bench and making up stories about the passersby.

"That guy," I said, motioning toward a burly, construction-worker type. "He's wearing Daffy Duck boxers."

"His wife's," said Liz.

"His *wife's* Daffy Duck boxers?"

"No," she said, kicking my foot. "He's wearing his wife's panties—the thong kind that rides up his ass."

In the warm night air, we talked and giggled; we were loud enough that several people took a second glance, as though they'd missed something. I found Liz's forgetfulness endearing—there was a fissure, a natural place in her life where I could belong. Moving forward, I'd be responsible for reminding her to lock the car and close her blouse and take the concert tickets from the refrigerator door. This was a sudden obligation—a service she would surely find sweet and reassuring. I pictured her staring blankly out the windshield of her car, pausing for a moment, until I surrendered a set of keys that had been resting beside a vase of crépe-paper flowers on her kitchen table. She would softly tap my thigh, as if to suggest, "What would I do without you?"

They don't make pink smoke detectors. Nor purple, nor blue. The salesman at the hardware store suggests, if I'm in a bind, purchasing white—the only color they stock—and spray-painting the device a shade of my choosing. But his brow creases when he tells me the company won't guarantee the reliability of its product once another element—in this case, paint applied by aerosol—has been introduced. I thank him and buy a white one and a corresponding nine-volt battery.

Afterward, I take a short detour into the mall for a hot cinnamon pretzel and diet cola. I make my way through the food court, hardware bag tucked beneath my arm. I'm moving in syncopated harmony, taking a bite of pretzel after each step. Near the exit doors I stop, pretzel suspended above my gaping mouth. I raise my elbow to wave—has she seen me?—and the smoke detector drops from my armpit. She rushes forward to retrieve my bag, her hair rusty and straight. But she's holding a tray of her own. "I've got it," I say, spraying embarrassing flecks of pretzel.

For a moment we stand opposite each other, like gunfighters waiting to draw. Then Nina reaches forward with two fingers, wiping something from the edge of my mouth.

"Just some food."

I bury my face in my shoulder, rubbing clean the remnants from my snack—cinnamon dust, crystallized sugar, scraps of dough.

"Better?" I ask.

"Much."

I follow her to a small wire table tucked behind a potted tree. She sits down and motions for me to join her. Nervously, I begin peeling the waxy dermis from my cup.

"I don't want to talk about work," she says, removing the tomatoes from her tuna sandwich. "I get thirty minutes for lunch, and the absolute *last* thing I wanna do is yack about frickin' cards and wrapping paper."

"Sounds reasonable."

"Oh, I'm sorry." She offers me one of her potato chips. "It's just—I'm in a mood today."

Her skin is smooth and shiny, like a ripe fruit. She's wearing a lime-colored polo shirt and a matching barrette fastened just below her part. I watch her thin fingers as she tears the sandwich into bite-sized pieces. On the side of her lean neck is a tiny, moon-shaped birthmark.

"So, you're back to see Leann?"

At first, I have no idea what she's saying. Leann? It takes a moment.

"No, no."

I wave the bag from the hardware store.

Then comes an awkward silence—but it doesn't last. She sips from her drink and says, "Okay: If you could have any meal from this food court, what would you choose?" Before I can respond, she offers a disclaimer. "And your health's not an issue—I mean, you don't have to worry about calories or cholesterol or any of that crap."

"Anything, huh?" I say, trying to think of some way to impress her with my answer. "I'm kinda partial to Chinese—even *bad* Chinese. So, I might say General Tsao's chicken, pork fried rice, spare ribs and—what the hell—a wonton soup with extra wontons."

She nods.

"Oh—and a Diet Coke."

For emphasis, I shake the ice in my cup.

"Amateur."

"*Amateur?*" I pause, crossing my arms. "Okay, your turn."

"Boom—" she's pointing at a Mexican restaurant, "cheese empanadas from Tico Taco." She continues gesturing with her arm. "Boom! Side of *shrimp* fried rice. Boom! Pancakes and sausage from Benny's Breakfast Anytime. Boom! Half a cheesesteak from Philly's Finest. Boom! Fries from McDonald's—I can't believe you didn't say fries from McDonald's. And *boom*, strawberry shake from the Creamery to wash it all down."

"Oh—"

"Hey, I didn't say you couldn't mix and match."

"You're right." I touch her lightly on the back of her hand. "But I thought we were talking about a *meal*. Not a long list of foods you couldn't possibly finish at a single sitting."

"Oh, please."

"Nope."

"I may be thin, but I'm scrappy."

It's been a long time since I've flirted with a woman. I'm grasping at a sea of unfamiliar levers, looking for a way to make this last.

"We're making a date," I say, letting the sentence escape too swiftly. "Right now. The two of us. And if you can eat all that food, I'll pay for it."

There's a terrifying pause before she responds. I instantly regret invoking the word *date*. My confidence is foundering, overtaken by a great wave of insecurities. Why would she agree to such a plan—even with these feeble terms?

But then: "Get your money ready, pal."

She has an espresso smile that makes my heart race like caffeine. Incredibly, fantastically, she scribbles her phone number on the back of my business card. I repeat the seven digits, again and again, all the way out to my car.

The pounding makes the kitchen fixtures rattle. I open the door to the girls' room. The music is loud and brassy, blaring from a cheap Burger Bunch CD player perched on a windowsill. The girls are dressed in leotards, bright blue and yellow.

"Watch this, Dad," says Tig, leaping from the ladder of her bunkbed.

Across the room, Callie executes a cautious pirouette. The floor is littered with pink feathers from a pair of shedding boas the girls wear looped around their necks.

"Did you finish your homework, Cal?"

"Yes!"

"All of it?"

"I just have some reading."

"I have some reading, too," says Tig.

"Okay—so let's clean up in here. Get your jammies on, brush your teeth. Then you can read in bed."

"Just a few more minutes," says Callie, pumping her fists like a sprinter.

"We're *dancing*," announces Tig.

As though on cue, Callie rolls her head in short, quick arcs, causing her hair to slap across her shoulders.

"I'm gonna finish washing the dishes," I say. "You have exactly *three* more minutes."

"Thanks, Dad," says Tig—always first.

Then, from Callie, as if the word causes her physical pain: "Thanks."

Back in the kitchen, I chop the remaining carrots and wrap them—five sticks for each girl—in tin foil. I store them in the fridge for tomorrow's lunch. As I return a pot to the cupboard, I recall an evening when Liz and I prepared a large spaghetti dinner for some friends. We were working together, as a team, boiling noodles and frying sausage and seasoning the sauce. ("Think it needs more *zip?*" she asked.) In the heat of the stove, I remember thinking that couples require a shared appreciation that this marriage business is hard work. We need the other person to goddamn root for our success to have a chance at making it.

As I finish rinsing down the sink, I hear the girls leave their bedroom. I'm waiting for the usual sounds as they jockey for position on the footstool in the bathroom, fight over who gets to brush her teeth first. Instead, there's an abrupt noise at the rear of the house.

"Dad, come here!" shouts Callie. "Quick!"

Both girls are crowded against the back door, their mouths forming small clouds of moisture on the glass.

"Omigod!" says Callie, tucking her hair behind her ears. "It's *so* cute."

Shielding my eyes against the glare of the light, I look outside. It takes a few moments before I see what the girls are cooing over. On the corner of our deck, beneath a vinyl and aluminum chair, is a kitten—wiry and orange, with matted fur pushed back from its face, giving it a windblown appearance. As I reach to unfasten the lock, the kitten scurries toward the middle of our yard. It watches the three of us crammed into the doorframe.

"Here, sweet kitty," says Tig. "We won't hurt you, kitty, kitty."

I rub my fingers together, pretending to offer a nugget of food. Tig copies me.

"What do you think it's doing here?" asks Callie.

"It probably doesn't have a home," says Tig.

"How do you know?"

Tentatively, the kitten begins creeping forward. It turns sideways, licking its right front paw. I back slowly into the house.

"Stay here," I tell the girls.

I run into the kitchen and pour a shallow bowl of milk. I also grab a small can of tuna fish.

"We'll see if he likes this stuff," I say.

Popping the lid on the tuna, I use my hockey stick and gently guide the tin across the wooden boards of our deck. I try the same thing with the bowl of milk, but twice it nearly capsizes. Instead, I carry it to the edge of the stairs.

"We should have some kitty food," says Tig.

"That's stupid," says Callie. "Why would we have cat food? We don't even have a *cat*."

I press my index finger against my lips. The kitten is illuminated by a splash of light from our neighbor's garage. It continues cleaning itself—paws, head, ears. Suddenly, as though signaled by a bell, the kitten scampers onto our deck and begins sniffing the fish.

"Is he eating it?" whispers Tig.

I nod.

"Can we bring it inside?" asks Callie.

"Oh—it can sleep in bed with me," says Tig, loud enough to startle the kitten.

"No, no," I say, easing the screen door closed. "I'm sure it has a family somewhere."

"I bet it doesn't," says Callie. "It looks a mess."

"We would take *much* better care of it."

I lift Tig against my chest, carry her into the bathroom. Sweetly, reassuringly, Callie has her finger hooked through a belt loop on my jeans. When I reach down to rub her head, I notice that her eyes have turned glassy and moist.

"Honey?" I kiss her lightly on her hair. "What's wrong?"

"I'm worried about the kitten."

"I'm worried, too," says Tig—though as she speaks, I catch her watching herself in the mirror.

"Guys, it'll be fine. I promise."

"Remember that big raccoon?" One day several months ago, we returned from dinner to find an enormous raccoon foraging through our trash. For days afterward the girls were frightened to walk outside—they'd leap at the first sound of a blowing leaf or skittish squirrel. "Maybe it'll eat the kitten?"

"Raccoons don't eat kittens," I say. Then I dig my fingers into both girls' bellies and twist until I hear laughter. "*Only little girls!*"

In the darkness of their room, I tuck them into bed. We have some familiar rituals: Callie says she's not tired before drifting immediately to sleep. Then Tig whispers, "Come here, Dad."

I lean down, my ear pressed to her lips. She wants me to lie down beside her—"Please, *please*. Just for a minute."

Tig's on her stomach. As lightly as possible, I trace tiny circles onto her naked back with my fingertips. "That's the ticket," she says, once I have the right combination of rhythm and pressure. Soon, she too has her eyes closed, breathing in a drowsy cadence I recognize from my room in the deep hours of the night.

After we separated, Liz and I spent nearly two years in mediation, followed by nine months working with psychologists. Eventually, on the advice of a wealthy friend, she hired a sadistic attorney whose practice was run like a building contractor's: keep as many jobs going as possible. During the course of my divorce trial, he requested—and was excruciatingly granted—seventeen continuances. I'd wait five months for resolution only to learn a day before our court date that we were again being pushed back on the judge's docket.

On a Friday in July, I rushed home from a vacation with my girls in hopes of inching closer to freedom. I sat beside my attorney in the courtroom, quietly paging through a binder of outdated subpoenas. After about an hour we realized that neither my soon-to-be-ex-wife nor her lawyer had any intention of honoring the day's commitment. I'd seen enough TV legal dramas to know what came next. "I'm holding them both in contempt of court," I imagined the magistrate barking into his phone. "I want them *arrested.*" Instead, he seemed delighted to suddenly have a free afternoon. He could only manage a shrug when I asked if they'd be punished.

On my drive home, I remember my hands gripping the steering wheel so tightly they began to cramp. And then my rage erased into sadness, and I was riding in aimless circles, tears leaking down my face. Only a few days earlier, I'd scavenged coins from my apartment—an ashtray in the hall, a Silver Springs coffee mug on my desk, even the girls' piggy banks—to pay for necessities, gasoline and food. I'd made light of the fact that we'd eaten buttered noodles and carrots twice for dinner. ("I'm sorry," I told the girls. "I haven't had a chance to go grocery shopping.") I'd parked illegally outside the courthouse, risking a ticket, because I didn't have enough cash for the garage. It shouldn't be this hard, I repeated to myself, as I drove on and on.

Because calamity rarely follows a natural order, I began thinking about the previous Saturday, when the girls and I were leaving a soccer game. They were in the back seat arguing about a portable video game, and three times I asked them to stop. Suddenly, Callie turned her back to the door and kicked Tig with a cleated foot; Tig responded by biting her sister. There was crying and screaming. After pleading with them for quiet—"I'm driving," I shouted. "Do you want me to get into an accident?"—I swung, blind and wild, making contact with both girls.

I have no excuse for striking my daughters—the confluence of stress and failure was simply too much. *I'm trying,* I wanted to tell them, tears welling in my eyes, I am *trying* to do better. They both gazed at me as though I was an unfamiliar animal who'd suddenly poked its head from a dark hole.

At seven the evening after being stood up in court, I found myself at Gilberto's Cigar Shop, where they let me run a tab. I'd been a frequent visitor over the previous few years. Mostly, I gained some relief in the mindless conversations with other patrons, talking about politics, sports, even bad marriages. Today I stared numbly at a ballgame, my ears full of lead. I felt the hand squeezing my shoulder before I realized someone was speaking to me. Surely I seemed confused and, perhaps, even derelict— tie pulled loose, shirt half-untucked, powdery trail of salt across my cheeks.

The guy's name was Victor. He was stocky and muscular, with a thin, serpentine scar curled against the back of his wrist. I quickly surrendered the details of my day, and of the countless awful months preceding it. Victor nodded and took a long pull on his cigar. He was a former member of the Israeli Special Forces who now ran his own import/export business. He was detached, objective. I needed a way to alleviate the hard-wound tension knotted in my chest, he said. A *release*. And there it was: distilled to its brutish form. "You cannot *heet* your wife's lawyer," he said. "I don't think you can *heet* your wife. But you have to *heet* sometheen, no?" After digging through his wallet, he gave me the card of a friend. "Go see him."

A few weeks later, I was making a sales call to a store on the border of Petty Township and I noticed a sign in a neighboring window—*Krav Maga*, outlined in the same blue cursive as on the business card Victor had given me. The inside looked like an old-time boxing gym. Despite a pair of creaky, oscillating table fans, the air was thick and damp, rank with perspiration and sour breath. There were suspended heavy bags, padded mats on the walls and floors, broomsticks wrapped in foam and silver electrical tape. The only modern concession was a set of six stereo speakers bolted to the ceiling. Rave music blasted so loud the woman behind the desk wore protective earmuffs. (Later, I would learn the music was a necessary evil: It taught students to ignore peripheral distractions and focus on their approaching assailant.)

The owner was a guy named Eli, who'd learned his craft in the same Special Forces unit as Victor. "In Hebrew," he said, placing a meaty paw on my shoulder, "Krav Maga means contact combat, or close combat."

Though I initially registered for a brief trial course, I was soon visiting the studio four or five times a week. Some days I would spar during my lunch break and return for another workout in the evening. It had been a long time since I'd had such a pure adrenaline rush—I could feel the fury and stress escaping my body with each right hook, thrust elbow, and side kick. Many years earlier I had attended a small college in upstate New York, where I'd played tight end on the football team. In my four seasons I rarely caught a pass, even during practices. But I was a fierce blocker: I relished the collisions, the impact of hurtling into another man—all knotty forearms and slappy pads and hard-churning thighs—as I tried to bust him on his ass. Sometimes even that wasn't enough; I would sprint over his prone body, looking for another player to capsize. On two occasions, my temper roiling like a deck of misfiring pistons, I had to be separated from defenders—arms braided together, facemasks kissing, fangs of spittle and sweat shaking from our chins as we wrestled for leverage.

This was the hole that needed filling. A relief. I now had a place to drive out all that worry and contempt. Some nights I stayed at Eli's gym until my clothes were dark and sealed to my skin with perspiration. I'd sit in my car, still breathing heavy, unspooling the gauze and tape that bound my bright red knuckles. I'd have to wait for my spent quadriceps to stop twitching before I could drive home.

One summer evening I was invited into Eli's office for a glass of cold vodka. Because I hadn't eaten since lunch, the liquor made me feel warm and lightheaded. For a few minutes, I wondered whether this was another of Eli's lessons—he was going to see if I could handle myself while loopy on booze. Instead, he told me about his childhood in Rehovot, his time in the Israeli army, and his journey to the United States. As I prepared a response—still tipsy, I first spoke the words in my head—he complimented me on how much I'd learned.

"But I'm *vedy* worried," he said, tapping the metal top on the vodka bottle.

The things that made me successful in his classes—size, reach, aggressiveness, and a cavalier attitude about personal safety—also made me a dangerous man.

"I never thought of myself as a 'dangerous man,'" I said, smiling. "I like the sound of that," squinting like a movie villain, "*dangerous man.*"

"No, no," he said. "Hazardous—a *hazardous* man. With letter 'H'."

Later, I took a long, dizzy shower and thought more about what Eli had said. He believed I had other, less honorable intentions for my training. "Only for protection," he'd said, raising his arms like a cornered fighter. "Only as last resort"—though his accent gave his words a skewed meaning: *last result.*

I lay on my bed, naked and dripping. The vodka turned the stucco swirls on my ceiling into familiar shapes—an angry dog, a dorsal fin, a pair of stacked chairs. I wondered if Eli frequently had this conversation with his students. Or was I unique? "Hazardous," I said, aloud. "Haz-er-*duhs.*"

Her voice is loud and full of good cheer. The song has a relentless bass line, making the speakers in my car doors puff and pound. Both girls know all the words—they're strapped into the back seat, singing and mimicking the arm movements from a music video. Callie turns toward her sister and shakes her head: "*Trickle* not *rickle.*" She sounds exasperated. "There's no such word as *rickle.*" To young girls, this is the height of comedy, and they both erupt with laughter.

A few blocks from school, Tig opens her lunchbox and removes a foil pouch of gummy candies. She lowers her hands behind the front seat, in hopes of shielding my view in the mirror.

"Put it away, honey," I say. "That's for lunch."

"Ohhh." She kicks the seat. "I was only gonna have one of 'em."

"Hey, I may have been born at night—but I wasn't born *last* night."

The girls are in a fine mood. They break into more laughter, though I'm not certain they understand the joke.

The parking oval in front of their school is cleaved into neat halves by an enormous flagpole. A steady wind slaps a steel cable against the pole's base—pa-*ting*, pa-*ting*.

"How 'bout some sugar?" I say, as Callie prepares to step from the car.

She leans forward, permitting me to plant a kiss on the top of her head. Tig is more affectionate—or perhaps less fearful of her friends' appraising eyes—and she grabs my face in her little hands, kissing me full on the lips.

"Thank you, honey," I say. "Have a *great* day."

"Mom's picking us up?"

"Yes—Mom today, me tomorrow."

As she backs away, I can see her mouth moving as she repeats the schedule. I watch her slowly navigate the path to the building. She passes a group of concrete benches and her backpack slips from her shoulder. Instead of restoring its position, she lets it drag behind like a cumbersome pink tail. I reach for my window— "Pick it up," I want to shout. But I'm silent. Then she's lost behind two boys, the glass door glimmering in the sun.

The houses are in various states of disrepair—peeling paint, missing shutters, sagging doors on ruptured hinges. Some of the windows are covered by thin planks of wood, their surfaces a chaotic snare of graffiti. The mouth of a rusted grill blooms with soggy newspapers and broken bottles and a loose coil of razor wire. Pages from a magazine, torn and crumpled, drift like tumbleweeds. One porch is trussed in yellow police tape, a railroad tie sprouting strangely from between its stairs.

Near the end of the block is a vacant lot surrounded by chain-link fencing. Inside, cars are parked bumper to bumper— protected from trouble by a man sitting in a guard shack, illuminated by a portable TV with a coat-hanger antenna. A .410 pump-action shotgun rests across his lap.

He gets a gratuity, I learned on my only other visit. I press ten dollars into his palm and take a wobbly stone path to the side of a neighboring house. Beneath the awning is a narrow shelf holding a pad of white paper and several pens. I print my name on one of the slips, then stuff it through a horizontal mail slot. After a moment the door sighs open and I'm swallowed by a pod of hot air.

To my left stands an elderly black man in a shallow laundry room. He's framed by a pair of industrial dryers, each tumbling with what appear to be full loads. I'm greeted with a short, quick nod. He hands me a set of warm linens—two white towels, two white bed sheets—and a key tethered to a wooden block, painted with the number nineteen. As I make my way down the hall, I notice the walls are sloppy with moisture. I retreat into a dark locker room with rugged, cast iron benches and cement floors. I rapidly undress, stuffing my clothes into a slim locker, and wrap myself in the twin sheets. The stink of fabric softener, sweet and florid, makes me sneeze.

A narrow passageway leads to the second floor: dingy rooms configured into a giant sauna—or *shvitz*, as it's called in Yiddish —with crates of scalding stones positioned concentrically near the stairwell. Packs of soft, angry men sit wrapped in toga-like bed sheets, the heat turning their faces bloated and pink as coral. Someone pours a tin cup of water over the stones, producing a cloud of shimmery blue steam.

I'm wearing a pair of paper slippers. I shuffle across the warped floorboards, leaving a slick, pigeon-toed trail. From within the cottony tendrils of fog comes a familiar voice.

"Right here," says Mr. Eugene, slapping the bench to his left.

I sit awkwardly beside him, squeezing a teat of cloth in my fist. I have never felt particularly comfortable in rooms filled with naked men. In college, after football practice, I would often dress alone—obscured by a strategically stacked tower of padding, a gaping locker door—or race home to shower in privacy. My doubts about my relationship with Mr. Eugene manifest themselves in an assortment of nervous tics: restless (and bouncing) leg, wandering eyes, fidgety fingers.

"You like this," he says, more statement than question.

I nod.

I press my sticky thighs together. I watch a single droplet of water quivering on the tip of Mr. Eugene's tanned chin.

"It's good for the sinuses." He demonstrates by inhaling a nose-full of hot air. "Good for the pores, the lungs—even the ticker," he says, clapping his sternum.

Already my breathing has become slow and labored. It feels as though my chest is holding a pile of cinderblocks.

A small, lean black man enters the room. He's wearing tight white shorts and a white t-shirt. "*Platza?*" he asks, glancing from face to face. A guy with curly red hair nods. As he rolls onto his sizable belly, his bed sheets spill to the ground. The black man ladles soapy water across the redhead's back; he drags leafy oak branches down his arms and legs, across his square, wrinkled buttocks.

"A few more minutes," says Mr. Eugene, abruptly. "We'll talk during lunch."

I can't recall if this is a "dry heat" or the other kind. I don't know the difference. Neither of them I find very enjoyable. When the black man finishes with the redhead, he starts moving in our direction. I'm filled with similar dread as when a roaming musician sidles up to my table during an intimate meal, suddenly making me the center of attention. ("Go away, go away," I say to myself.) Soon he disappears into another wing of the house.

In this room, I have no concept of time. Did Mr. Eugene just speak? Was it ten minutes ago? He rises, bed sheets pasted to the creases of his skin—elbows, armpits, behind his knees. I follow him into a cramped blue room that reeks of chlorine. Three carpeted stairs lead to a cold pool. Standing on a deck of perforated aluminum, Mr. Eugene disrobes and lowers himself into the water.

"Whew!" he shouts, raising his head.

I climb down across from him. Instantly, the air leaves my lungs and I can feel my muscles contract. My limbs lock into place, the joints now rigid and tight. I'm overcome by the freezing temperature, my teeth clattering against themselves. As I race back to the deck, I slip and gouge my kneecap on a jagged screw head. I walk behind Mr. Eugene, wrapping myself in damp sheets and massaging my wounded knee.

We enter a dining hall crowded with seasonal patio tables. There are dozens of men swathed in twisted bed sheets, like some ancient Roman senators' meeting—assuming the learned counsel drank Johnnie Walker Black and Budweiser tallboys. We take a table against the far wall. A waiter hands us a fresh-baked loaf of rye bread and a silver chalice filled with pickled tomatoes. There's no menu because everyone gets the same thing: rib steak and hash browns.

"Medium rare," announces Mr. Eugene to our waiter. "But make the hash browns real crispy."

"Same," I say.

Resting between us is a bottle of scotch with Mr. Eugene's name written across a piece of masking tape. There are also two empty glasses and a porcelain bowl filled with ice. From beneath the table, Mr. Eugene removes a thin black case he'd stored in his locker. He clips the ends from a pair of double coronas and offers one to me. For a moment his face is lost behind a wheel of gray smoke. He waves his hand, then slides a gold lighter in my direction.

"You know Norm Keesey?" he asks.

I shake my head.

"You wouldn't—I mean, there's no reason you *should* know him."

Mr. Eugene sits quietly smoking his cigar, eyes surveying the room. The waiter arrives with our food. Before he can leave, Mr. Eugene raises a finger. He carves into his massive slab of beef, nodding as he examines its bloody-red core.

"Norm Keesey," he repeats, mouth full with ribsteak, "is a guy I've known forever. Christ, we used to play stickball together on Union Avenue."

I gently balance my cigar against the edge of the table.

"Motherfucker's been placing bets with me for—" He pulls a piece of gristle from between his teeth and tucks it under his plate. "Well, he's been placing bets with me for a *long* time."

I'd forgotten the steaks come smothered in fresh garlic. The seasoning and sauna have made me desperate for something cold to drink.

"Six months ago—fucking outta the blue—he decides, 'I'm not payin' the vig.'" Mr. Eugene has now stopped eating. He stabs his knife into his steak and rests his jaw on its wooden handle. "Not paying the vig? Holy Christ. *Everyone* pays the vig. I'd make my sainted mother—rest her soul—pay the fucking vig."

Vig is short for *vigorish*—a slang terminology for a bookmaker's commission on every wager. If a guy loses a hundred-dollar bet with Mr. Eugene, he's got to pay him $110—a hundred bucks for losing the bet, another ten to cover the vig.

"It's not an insignificant number."

I place my hand over the bowl of half-melted ice and pour a stream of water into my glass.

"You thirsty?" Mr. Eugene grabs a passing busboy by the arm. "Bring him a—whaddya want?"

"Diet Coke," I say, directing my answer at Mr. Eugene.

"Diet Coke—get him a Diet Coke." As the busboy starts walking to the kitchen, Mr. Eugene shouts: "And a *clean* glass."

We sit eating silently for a few moments. Mr. Eugene taps his hash browns with his fork, trying to conjure the pulled thread of our conversation.

"Keesey, Keesey," he says, nodding in agreement of nothing. "Um—it's not a little number. Guy owes me fourteen hundred bucks."

My drink arrives, and I take a long swallow. The carbonation burns my throat.

"This has to be handled real carefully."

Mr. Eugene reminds me that he's known the family since childhood. Because he's fond of Keesey's sister, a nurse who lives in Hudson, he doesn't want me to speak his name during my visit.

"He'll know who you're talking about," says Mr. Eugene, taking a sip of scotch. He pauses, crossing his arms. "She's a sweetheart."

In the relatively short time since I started working for Mr. Eugene, I've never seen him so preoccupied with the details of a collection.

We finish our meals and, without provocation, our waiter delivers two magnificent wedges of coconut cream pie—dense and creamy and topped with cuticles of toasted coconut.

"Oh, Christ," says Mr. Eugene. At first, I think he's referring to the imposing plates of pie. But then he continues: "There's probably something else I should tell you." He leans forward and grips the table. "He's a cop."

I can feel my head snap back with surprise.

"Keesey?"

I speak the name superfluously—a bridge to carry us across this sudden chasm of tension. Now I understand Mr. Eugene's unexpected showiness, his motivation behind the sauna and steaks. My mind's racing with images of a collection gone wrong: I picture myself sitting in a squad car, hands fastened behind my back; I'm guided into a courtroom, sleepy and unshaved, wearing one of those bright orange jumpsuits; and then an interrogation chamber, like the kind I've seen a million times on a million cop shows, where I sit across the table from Callie and Tig, searching desperately for words that might make sense to them.

"Just lean on him a little," says Mr. Eugene, sensing my apprehension. "I don't care so much about the money. It's the *precedent*. I mean, I'm trying to run a business."

I feel disoriented, reaching for my cigar instead of my fork.

"Listen, you can keep half the money." His face glows with approval. "It's yours. I just don't—" He straightens the links on his chunky gold bracelet. "You understand why this is important to me?"

I nod.

I watch Mr. Eugene chase a bite of pie with some scotch. A queasiness rises from low in my stomach. There must be a way to refuse him, I think, staring at a speckle of dishwasher soap on my spoon. But I can't think of an answer—at least not one that's coming to me in the muggy clamor of this house. In the end, it's the oldest story in the world: a simple act of commerce. I need the money—for child support and alimony, mortgage and rent.

My boots stretch before me like a pair of slender washtubs. I have enormous feet, size fourteen. Years ago, when I grew tired of people stepping on my toes in crowded places, I started wearing Red Wing work boots with toe caps of reinforced steel. I now own three pairs—two brown, one black. They're great for kicking things. (I once put my foot through the side of a motor home and barely felt a thing.) They're also good for transporting my daughters around the house. Today, Tig's standing across my laces in stocking feet while I dance her from living room to kitchen.

"Go faster," she says.

I list from side to side, joints locked, like a tin robot.

"It's *my* turn," says Callie.

She squeezes behind her sister. Now it's the three of us shuffling together down the hallway, and I pretend to lose my balance, bumping my shoulder clumsily into the wall. The contact shakes a film of dust from a bookcase.

"Keep going, Dad," says Tig.

My calves start to burn. I ferry my weight back on a thick rubber heel, spinning in tight circles until both girls tumble dizzily backward. They break into laughter.

"Again," says Callie, reaching up.

"No, no," I say. "Get your shoes on. We're going to dinner."

They whine in unison. Neither wants to leave the house. Because I allow them to watch TV during dinner—something their mother's against—they nearly always prefer eating at home.

"I don't wanna go out," says Tig.

"We're going."

"You could make macaroni and cheese," says Callie. "I *know* we have that. I saw some in the cupboard."

She races into the kitchen, and when she returns, she's shaking a blue and orange box.

"See—right here!"

"I'm not discussing it." I retrieve their shoes from near the side door. "Let's go, ladies."

Tig runs down the hallway, jumping onto her bed. Callie stomps her foot.

"I hate this place—I *hate* it!"

She throws the box of macaroni in a shallow arc. It collides with the sharp corner of an end table, bursting before it hits the ground. Elbow noodles, hard and trim, skitter across the wooden floorboards. Some splash against the couch, finding creases between the squared cushions. In the stillness as Callie awaits my reaction, she stares with squinty-eyed anger, the smooth skin of her forehead now compressed with rows of spiky lines. From the bedroom, I can hear Tig shouting in a singsongy voice, "I'm not going either! I'm not going either!"

Years ago, a friend of mine who's an elementary school teacher told me about the Seven Mississippi Rule: Count to seven Mississippi before responding to a defiant child. Slowly, I begin counting (*one Mississippi, two Mississippi*). Callie watches me with a blank look on her face, lulled into a false sense of security. As she marches toward an adjoining room (*three Mississippi, four Mississippi*), I reach out and grab her by the arm. I can feel the rage rising inside me (*five Mississippi, six…*).

"I'm staying home," she says, in a last gasp of insolence.

I reach back and swat her forcefully on the ass. Her eyes grow wide and watery. She screams, digging her fingernails into my forearm.

"Omigod!" she shouts, now crying. "You hit me!"

Tig appears in her doorway.

"You wanna get spanked, too?" I ask, turning toward her. "Get fucking ready!"

In a frantic whirl of preadolescent bodies, Tig rushes past me in search of her shoes; Callie sprints in the opposite direction, to my bedroom, and dives for the phone.

"I'm calling Mom," she screams.

"Oh, *no* you're not!" I wrestle the phone from her hand and swing it against the bedpost—two, three times—before cracking it in half. "Get your *shoes!*"

As I pick up slivers of chipped plastic and a perforated metal disk from the phone's mouthpiece, I hear the girls whimpering in the living room. My temper instantly subsides—I'm overcome by the sound of Tig's staccato sobbing as she gulps for another breath. This is not the kind of childhood I want for my daughters.

So I run to them, collapsing at their feet. I rub their knees, their shins. I start to speak but my voice is reedy and fragile, cracking on the second word. I lay my head in Callie's lap. Tig reaches across and gently strokes my sideburn.

"It's okay," she says.

Then I apologize in a short speech that's fraught with hypocrisy. I lean on words like stress and frustration and disappointment. I tell them it's never "okay" to put your hands on another person in anger. More than anything, I want to set a good example—I need them to know that some things can't be made right simply by acknowledging the mistake.

"But I *am* sorry," I say, kissing them each on the cheek.

There is nothing else until we hear the ugly scrape of a car's bumper against a hydrant outside.

The paper placemats are congested with ink-line caricatures of the Chinese zodiac. A blue pen clutched in her fist, Tig draws large feathery wings along the spine of a rat. Callie spears a dumpling with her chopstick, dipping it into a bowl of tangy sauce. She holds the dumpling erect, like a lollipop, and nibbles its sides.

"One time," starts Tig, suddenly, "we went to dinner with Nana and the waitress gave us about ten cherries in our drinks." She's still looking down at her artwork. "We got Shirley-templers."

"Shirley *Temples*," says Callie.

"Shirley *Temples*," repeats Tig.

My hands are cold. I lay them lightly around the teapot.

"Do you think a genie's gonna come out of there?" asks Callie.

"Maybe."

"You get three wishes," says Tig.

I smile and slowly massage the sides of the teapot, making eerie whistling noises with my mouth.

"What would *you* wish for?" I ask.

"Oh—I want a pair of red fashion boots I saw in this catalog at Mom's," says Tig.

"*Sheesh*," says Callie, shaking her head. "Why don't you ask for a million dollars? Or *ten* million dollars? Then you could get whatever you want."

"Yeah, yeah!" Tig drums the table with her pen. "I'd wish for ten million dollars! Then I'd get those red boots *and* a bunch of new outfits."

"You're so stupid."

"Stop," I say, shaking my head at Callie.

"With that much money you could buy the whole store."

"Okay, I'd buy the store," says Tig. "And I'd call it Ella's Fashion Place."

"Ella's?" I ask.

"There's a girl in her class named Ella and—"

"No!" says Tig, straightening in her seat. "That's not why. I just like the name."

"Nothing wrong with that." I reach across the table and tighten one of her pigtails. "It's a nice name."

"I'd buy a houseboat," says Callie.

"A houseboat? What would you do with that?"

"I saw one in a movie," she says, submerging another dumpling in her bowl of sauce. "It looked really cool. This girl—the actress, who's about my age—she lived on the boat with her family. I mean, they could go swimming whenever they wanted."

"Why not just buy a pool?"

"'Cause a houseboat's better."

I nod.

"I like it," I say, taking a sip of hot tea. "Just one question: Where would we put it?"

"We'd probably have to move."

"I wanna move!" says Tig. "I wanna move to Kansas."

"Kansas?"

"She thinks it's like *The Wizard of Oz.*"

"Dorothy lives there."

"I already told you," says Callie. "Dorothy's a *character* in a *movie.*"

Tig returns to her drawing. She's focused, tongue curling out from between her lips.

"Maybe we could find a big lake in Kansas?" I say, winking at Callie. "There's no place like *houseboat.* There's no place like *houseboat.*"

"Dad!" Callie rolls her eyes. "That's so idiotic."

I hold up my index finger and use Tig's pen to write something on the back of my placemat. Then I turn it so both girls can see: "Dads are cute."

"No."

I shrug, holding my shoulders for an extended beat.

The leaves were bright and vibrant, as though someone had taken each tree and dipped it into an enormous kettle of freshly stirred paint. Burnt orange and goldenrod and radish red. Liz and I wandered the hilly fields of Paterson's orchard, eating apples— Granny Smiths, Honeycrisps, Pink Ladies—and tossing the cores into the neighboring woods. For a while we were quiet, listening to crackling branches and dried brush underfoot, and the melodious chirping of birds. Finally, Liz began telling me about a homecoming dance her senior year of high school with a harvesty theme. Each table had centerpieces crafted from Bartlett pears and apples and seasonal flowers. Her date was a kid named Alan Greene, whom she'd known since third grade. But she wanted to attend with a boy on the soccer team, Ben Fallon, who, she was quite certain, didn't know she existed.

Later, during the obligatory senior breakfast, she stood in the hallway at one of her classmates' houses and watched Ben Fallon making out with his date. "I could literally feel my heart dropping into my stomach," she said. As a bleachy sun rose above the horizon, she sat on her bed and stared into an oval-shaped vanity mirror at the fangs of mascara drooling down her cheeks. Liz's parents had been dead for several years by then, and though her aunt and uncle were kind and generous people, they simply weren't equipped to parry questions from a lovesick teenager. Soon Liz was crying so hard she could barely catch her breath. It was the first time, she told me, she remembered feeling truly alone.

We stood beside a creek clogged with matted leaves and loosely gathered sticks. She's *still* alone, I recall thinking. This poor, lost child—the same one from the photograph of the playground, dressed in a hastily buttoned shirt and dirty trousers. I could feel a wave of emotional truth wash through me. Was this love? Or maybe the next best thing: A desire to be so close with someone that you share her pain—help her carry the water—and, at the same time, let her siphon off a part of the goodness in your life. I wrapped my arms around Liz's waist and drew her close, resting my chin against the knot of her spine.

"What's wrong?" she asked, her lips brushing my earlobe.

"Nothing," I said.

And nothing was wrong, because I could suddenly read the mossy symbols that until now had appeared only as labyrinthine code. This was what I wanted from a partner—someone who made me feel useful and loving; someone I cared for at least as much as myself.

A gentle breeze rustled through the orchard. Liz and I turned toward the car, our bodies pressed together, hip to hip, causing us to walk with a rhythmic limp. As our shoes touched the stony surface of the parking lot, we paused, and I kissed her on the corner of her mouth. There was a lightness to my movement that I could sense in my arms and shoulders and every time I lifted my thighs, as though banded weights had been torn free. On our drive back through the color-splashed countryside, I caught myself looking at Liz—three, five times—her face turned mostly to the passenger window.

His hands are trembling as he tries to strike a match. With each fractured breath, a crinkled cigarette waggles in the corner of his mouth like a conductor's spastic baton. He's wearing a tweed sport coat, faded blue Oxford-cloth shirt, and chinos. He lowers himself behind a massive antique desk that's covered with intricate carvings and angled, swooping scroll-work. The room is cluttered with books—stacked in towers on the floor, lining the walls, some resting horizontally across the spines of others. Piled before him are reams of academic-looking papers with frayed edges, bent corners and ring-shaped stains from muddy beverages. He's framed by lead-paned windows that have turned orange in the kerosene sunlight.

"I'm usually pretty good about this," he says, exhaling a swift spike of lungsmoke.

In my black notepad, I write the word *anxious* beside his name.

"I had a little setback." He lifts a manila folder from his desk, as though half-expecting to find some misplaced money beneath it. "I don't have—I know I was supposed to square up last Tuesday."

I give him a grim and hopeless stare—straight mouth, arched eyebrows, arms crossed against my chest. He starts to cough and struggles to catch his breath. Sinking his head near his knees, he grabs a rolled chair.

"Whaddaya got?"

"Pardon?" he says, letting his chin fall slack.

"A payment schedule." I push aside some papers and take a seat on the corner of his desk. "What can you give me right now? Today?"

Purposefully, he reaches into the breast pocket of his jacket and removes his wallet.

"Not much," he says, counting out thirty-seven dollars. "I'm a college professor." He pinches down the thighs of his trousers. "I was doing fine. It's just—I *never* bet the over/under."

We sit together in silence. Finally, he rises—seemingly inspired—and motions me into his living room. There's a large, crushed-velvet couch in emerald, surrounded by several wooden chairs with floral seat cushions, a glass coffee table, two worn Persian rugs, and a mahogany hutch with dull brass handles. He walks toward the fireplace.

"You can take *this*," he says, reaching for an ivory-colored statue of a nude woman reclining on a tangle of cloth. "As collateral—until I make good on my payment."

I glare skeptically at the statue. It's heavy and smooth, with a sheen of black dust clotting the tight crevices.

"It's worth a great deal," he says. "Far more than I owe."

I stand with my legs planted firmly, moving the statue between my hands.

"And *this*."

He fumbles with his wristwatch—gold with a white face, brown crocodile strap—and thrusts it toward me.

"I'd get them back, of course," he says. "I just need a couple more weeks."

Below the mantle is a rack of cast iron tools designed for tending fires. I grab a pointed rod by its pewter handle, and begin a progression of theatrical flourishes—waving the rod near my waist, stabbing the air with a back-forth pumping action. He watches me, shifting his weight uneasily from one foot to the other. A sloppy floe of mortar curls upward from between the fireplace's stones. I measure its distance and take a tomahawk

swing with the rod, discharging sandy, sparkly debris across the
rug. He raises his elbow near his face, as though for protection,
and shuffles back.

"You can't bet," I say.

I knock the rod against the bottom of my boot.

"Huh?"

"Until you're paid off," I say, resting the rod on my shoulder,
"you can't place any more bets."

"Of course," he says, nodding frantically.

I start walking toward the front of the house. I let the iron rod
drop casually to the floor, creating a hollow clanging sound. He
looks startled, jerking sideways like a whiplash victim, his arms
pulled rigid against his body. Patting his pockets, breast and rear,
he removes a pack of cigarettes and fishes through the cellophane with his fingers.

I let my eyes roam the hallway. This is nothing more than a
cagey game of chicken. I'm an intimidating presence, large and
menacing, with a reasonable excuse for being here in the late
afternoon. I can take anything I want from this guy, assuming
he believes I will do him harm. Conversely, if he doesn't think
I'm a threat, shows no fear, he can tell me to take his thirty-seven
dollars and go screw myself.

As I drift through the adjoining rooms, I make a point of examining his possessions, all showy and disdainful, lifting a crystal
decanter and a silver cocktail tray. I fiddle with the knobs on his
hi-fi equipment. There's a large, jewel-pocked frame bordering a
photograph of the professor and a ruddy-faced woman.

"My wife," he says, softly. "She's not living here right now."

Most people haven't been in a fistfight since grade school.
Though some talk tough, hoping to impress, they have no desire
to greet the ugly side of violence. The threat of spilled blood,
especially when it's their own, often carries the same weight as
the act itself.

I run my finger against a hinged lacquer box, and it reminds
me of a similar item from my attorney's desk. Ironically—or fit-
tingly, depending on your view of the legal profession—I began

my career as a bully-for-hire while sitting in my lawyer's office. After several years, I signed my final divorce papers and I owed my attorney a sizable sum of money. He understood that I was on the verge of bankruptcy and, unlike the professor, didn't have any pricy art for collateral.

"Bear with me," I said, refusing eye contact. "I'll figure it out."

Later, ridiculously, I asked if there was anything I could do for him—perhaps a new design for his business cards? Or even manual labor? He chuckled and shook his head. Half-jokingly, he said, "Not unless you can get this asshole off my back." Apparently, he wasn't earning enough revenue for his firm and, according to rumors, one of the senior partners wanted him gone.

I was desperate and broke—the primary ingredients for every great vehicle of change. Three nights later, after a little research, I sat parked in darkness on Bloomfield Drive, waiting for the senior partner to return home. I knew what kind of car he drove, a large Mercedes sedan, and every time a pair of headlights crested over a neighboring hill my heart felt like it was going to punch past my lungs. After he finally pulled into the mouth of his long, serpentine driveway, I watched him make his way around the front of his car to retrieve a stack of mail, thorny with catalogs and different-sized envelopes. Go now, I recall thinking. *Wait any longer and you're gonna lose your nerve...*

My limbs were possessed, moving under a power of their own: gently opening the car door; carrying me quietly across the street; allowing me to approach him with a furtive caution. Twice I touched a note in my pocket, making sure it was still in the same place—an act of thuggish compulsivity. He didn't notice me until my foot collided with a patch of gravel, the flung stones ringing against the rims of his wheels.

"Can I help you?" he asked.

He didn't seem particularly concerned, still flipping through his mail.

"Let him be," I said, maybe too quickly. I'd rehearsed my dialogue in the mirror a dozen times.

I knew better than to mention my lawyer by name. But I provided the senior partner with plenty of what he would call circumstantial evidence, enough specifics so that he'd understand exactly whom I meant.

"Are you serious?" he asked.

I closed the distance between us. I wanted to look down on him—he was maybe six inches shorter than me—and emphasize the difference in our heights.

"*Very* serious," I said, though the words lacked the impact I'd imagined earlier in my bathroom.

I delivered a slight forearm shiver to his chest, knocking him into the mailbox. Then I walked to the side of his car and removed the note from my pocket, laying it neatly beneath his passenger-side wiper blade. As I moved past him again, he stepped back, instinctively, squeezing the pile of mail against his abdomen.

"I have a gun," I said, suddenly, surprising myself. "Close your eyes and face the house."

"Listen—"

"Just turn around."

He followed my instructions.

"Now, count to a hundred before opening your eyes."

He nodded.

I didn't want him to see my license plate. As I climbed into my car, I called back to him: "I can't *hear* you!"

"Fourteen, fifteen, sixteen…"

My foot stamped the gas pedal with controlled force, leaving a smudge of tire rubber against the black-tarred roadway. I reached the hill and glanced in my rearview mirror. He was still standing in the same spot, his trousered legs pressed close enough together to form a single billowy pylon. By the time I crossed Fleming Street, several blocks away, my hands were trembling on the steering wheel. Then came a dark curtain of guilt and remorse. *What did you do? Oh, Christ—people have gone to prison for less. A gun? Why'd you tell him you had a gun?*

But then…

A wonderful dizziness drifted through me—a near-toxic spurt of adrenaline that clouded my vision, forcing me to the side of the road. Next came a shower of black dots, like when you squeeze your eyes closed for a few minutes and then open them too quickly. A rush of primal emotion, base and masculine and sodden with testosterone, that reminded me of a perfect block in football—*decleating* is what we called it when you knocked a guy off his spikes. I was embraced by a muzzy warmth, the glow of this new authority. It felt familiar and rewarding—a place I wanted to visit again.

By week's end, my lawyer was called into the senior partner's office and told his standing at the firm was no longer in question. This was followed by a cautious silence. The only thing I'd written on the note I left behind was the college mailing address of the senior partner's middle son.

Now, standing in the foyer of the professor's house, I remove a leather satchel—*his* leather satchel—from a hook by the door. I fill it with the nude sculpture, wristwatch, thirty-seven dollars, and a gleaming silver table clock.

"Thank you," he says, because that's what they always say when they don't get hit.

The noise comes in a dream. A brassy ringing from a bell on a ferry boat. I reach into the abyss and try to stop it, but I'm too far away. As I start running, the deck expands, creating a nautical spire against the distant horizon. My feet are slipping on the varnished boards. I grab a guardrail to keep myself upright. A frothy wave, like the back of a broom, slaps me sideways. And the bell continues: *brrrr-iiing, brrrr-iiing…*

Then I'm standing near my refrigerator, in darkness. The familiar voice comes from my hand—the last voice I want to hear at four seventeen in the morning. She sounds muffled and frantic.

"There's someone in the house," says my ex-wife.

"What do you mean?"

"I hear someone—*something*—moving around downstairs."
She takes a short swallow. "The girls are in my bedroom closet."
We only live a few blocks from each other, a decision I made
to ease my daughters' transition during our initial period of separation. It can't take me more than a couple minutes to reach Liz's
driveway. Beneath my seat is a small steel case, roughly the size
of a dictionary, filled with die-cut foam padding in the shape of
a handgun. I remove a nine-millimeter pistol—a matte-finish
Heckler & Koch—and release its safety. Near the garage is a
bulbous gas grill, and I open the lid, retrieving a green rubber
key fob.

I make my way into the back hall, walking on exaggerated
tiptoes, like some mustachioed villain in a campy movie. I can
hear the rustling of papers from the kitchen, followed by something hard and heavy—ceramic coffee mug, fruit bowl—striking the floor.

"Please go!" shouts Liz from the top of the staircase. "I don't
care what you take—just *go!*"

For a few moments, I crouch against the common wall and
listen. There are no weighty footsteps, no drawers sliding open in
search of wedding silver. Then comes a hollow scratching sound,
like a box-cutter pulling through cardboard. I raise the barrel of
my gun, resting my index finger beside the trigger. I turn the
corner, slowly, turning and turning...

Staring back at me from the counter are two black, filmy eyes,
shallow and shiny as fish scales. A spear of light from beneath the
basement door illumines a choppy trail of Cheerios. There are
broken cookies, crusts of bread, shredded barbecue-chip packaging of reddish-silver. I align the three florescent dots on the sight
of my gun.

"Hayes?" calls Liz.

I slap the wall with my free hand, loud and fleshy. The large
raccoon scurries across the counter, nails scraping the steel sink,
before leaping through the open window. A small potted cactus
tumbles to the floor.

"It's okay," I say, hiding the pistol in the rear waistband of my jeans.

Liz races down the stairs, followed by the girls.

"What—what happened?"

"Was it a bear?" asks Tig.

The girls are sleepy-eyed, in matching blue cloud-formation pajamas.

"Oh, God," says Liz, fanning herself with her fingers.

"It was a raccoon."

"A *raccoon*," repeats Tig, nodding in approval.

"Did you kill it?" asks Callie.

"Nope." A low throbbing begins near my left temple. "It ran out the window."

"Well—" Liz sighs, gently ushering the girls back toward the staircase. She doesn't say anything else.

A thousand times during our marriage, I returned from work to a house that was empty and unlocked. Some mornings I'd come downstairs to make coffee and discover the back door had been left ajar, only a poor screen keeping intruders at bay. I would tack up a blizzard of sticky notes—on appliances, dashboards, purse handles—to remind her. It took me years to understand that she's simply wired differently. Kind of flighty, dangerously absentminded.

On nights when I'm not with my daughters, I worry about getting phone calls at four seventeen in the morning because Liz left open a first-floor window. I'm terrified of other intruders, the kind that don't walk on four legs.

"Liz," I say, after kissing the girls goodnight. "You've gotta check the windows before heading to bed. And make sure the doors are locked."

"I know, I know."

Having served my purpose, she's anxious to chase me from the house. This is very different than the way it used to be, as she battled the slippery fingers of abandonment. After all, she'd lost her parents at an early age. During our time together, I did my best to fill the gaping emptiness. But it was too great, and

I wasn't strong enough to make something sweet from her life, and live my own.

"*Liz.*"

"I—"

"You *don't* know. Otherwise I wouldn't be here in the middle of the night."

"I shouldn't have called you."

"That's not what I'm saying." I twirl the key fob around my finger. "*Of course* you should call me. But you should also make sure the house is closed up for the night."

"I will." She's moved to within a few inches, trying to bulldoze me through the back door. "I *promise* I will."

There's more to say. But I don't feel like having a shouting match on the rear deck—the same corrosive exchange we had dozens of times when I was living in this house. Sometimes they were loud enough to draw the attention of our neighbors—peeking out windows, gaining sightlines between the posts of our fence.

As I'm leaving, I miss a step and nearly fall into a row of trash cans. Callie's bike is propped against a lawn chair. The girls have drawn colorful pictures on the driveway with chalk—a rainbow, a yellow dinosaur, a three-story houseboat. For a moment I get emotional thinking about the girls, my girls, creating artwork in the yard without me around to watch them. I make a mental note to buy more art supplies the next time I'm at the mall.

Along the side of the house is an unspooled garden hose, mashed flat in parts by automobile tires. I lay my head against the dashboard and close my eyes. I can hear the steady patter of folded newspapers being flung from a car as it makes its way down the street.

We're sitting in a circular booth at Jem's Bar & Grill. There's a mammoth ring of televisions suspended from the ceiling, a Technicolor halo, each aglow with a different sporting event. Tucker is wearing a white dress shirt, the knot on his brown-and-gold necktie pulled low across his collarbone. He's chewing a plastic straw, working his molars so vigorously that a pearl of spittle squeezes from its red-and-yellow-striped end. He cocks his middle finger against his thumb and flicks a sugar packet across the table.

"This is the honest-to-God truth," he says. "I've had sex once—*one time*—in the past six weeks."

"Hummers?" asks Sully.

"Are you kidding?" Tucker pounds the table with the side of his fist. "I stopped getting those after our honeymoon."

"False advertising," says Cale.

"You know how when your kids want something—a video game or a new pet—they pretend to be all nice?" says Sully. "Maybe they'll straighten out their rooms? Or clear off the dishes without being told? Well, that's how Deb works me now with blowjobs. I don't even enjoy them anymore, 'cause I know she's gonna ask for something when she finishes rinsing her mouth in the bathroom sink."

"Sometimes," starts Cale, crossing his arms and leaning back. "Kristen will be *talking* and *talking*. And for a million bucks I couldn't tell you a single word she said."

We all nod.

"It's like her voice hits a special frequency that I'm incapable of hearing."

I take a drink of beer, slowly peeling the label from my bottle.

"Remind us what it's like to be single," says Tucker, turning toward me. "Only the good stuff."

But there's nothing—at least nothing that's going to bring calls of delight and vicarious fist-bumps.

Cale exhales a deep, watery sigh, and reaches for another slice of pizza.

I start with a description of Nina, full of embellishment, in which she crouches behind a cash register. I provide half-invented details about her low-cut jeans: when she reached for a crate of envelopes, I could see the steep Y of her thong pressed against the rosy skin of her hips.

"C'mon, man," says Cale. "I get *underpants* whenever I drop my daughter at school. She has a twenty-two-year-old student teacher who wears short skirts."

Their eyes are sad and hopeful.

"I'm sorry," I say. Briefly, I consider fashioning a tale of conquest and erotica from other people's conversations—plundered at the smoke shop, in line at a liquor store—but I haven't the strength nor will. "I guess I've failed you."

"It's not the first time," says Tucker.

Our waitress finally returns. Pinned to the pocket of her blue shirt is a citrus-shaped button that reads, *Orange you glad we met?* Tucker reviews our check, holding the trim leather binder like a hymnal.

"Twenty-five apiece," says Sully. "That includes tip."

Arching my middle fingers, I trace small teardrops against my temples. I grow tired thinking about my long drive home, where I'll be greeted by a sinkful of dirty dishes and two loads of laundry.

The high-pitched mewing is nearly lost behind a rush of water. It has its own unique timbre, sharp and trill. The first time I hear it, I'm washing my face in the bathroom. I stop the faucet and hold perfectly still, wondering if it was only the strained sound of water racing through copper pipe. But then it comes again.

I make my way to the back door and notice that the yard's been illuminated by a trio of motion-sensor lights. Perched on the edge of my deck is the same scrawny kitten the girls and I saw earlier in the week. He's peering back at me from behind the glass door. I pour him another saucer of milk, cautiously leaving it under a sun chair. He waits until I'm back inside before starting to drink.

"This isn't your home," I say, though nobody's listening.

He's hunched over the dish, his tail flopping carelessly from one side to another. His tongue moves with such controlled precision there's scarcely a ripple across the plain of pale milk.

When he's finished drinking, he licks his paws and combs them through the fur on his face. He glances casually across the deck. Then he trots toward the door and curls himself into a ball on a bristly shoe mat.

I retreat to my bed. Propped up by a couple pillows, I read the newspaper while listening to a classic rock station on my clock radio. I'm prepared for a restless night; I always sleep better when the girls are with me. I toss the last section of newspaper to the floor and lie in the flinty darkness. One of my neighbors returns home and I watch his red taillights slither across the wall above my feet. I sing a few verses of a Lynyrd Skynyrd song. After years of practice, I've discovered the ideal volume for my radio rests between five and six—loud enough to keep my mind occupied, but soft enough to welcome sleep.

Later this week, I have to submit my sales figures from the previous quarter. I know they're down—I only hope they're not drastically lower than those of the other sales associates. I keep picturing my boss, Dennis Gaines, reviewing the reports in his office. I can see his body contract, slow and slinky, like a sausage casing pierced by a knife. He'll shake his head, smack his desk. "This is lousy!" he'll shout, fierce enough for his voice to carry across the neighboring cubicles.

Silver Springs is a company that rewards mediocrity, and Gaines has managed to fail ingloriously upward. He's simple-minded, with limited vision and less imagination. After every professional setback—ill-conceived holiday lines, poor-selling brands, repeatedly unmet quotas—he climbs another rung on the corporate ladder. A few years ago, when I was still designing cards, I remember hearing about a new initiative—that's what they always call it: an *initiative*—in which do-it-yourself greeting card kiosks were installed at shopping malls. Gaines was leading the charge. The company invested millions of dollars in technology to create video-game-sized consoles. But consumers couldn't figure out how they operated—the greeting cards ended up with dreadful color combinations, incorrect tag lines, outsized envelopes. In addition, the machines were so fickle that teams of repairmen were regularly dispatched on endless service calls. (One of the clunky devices still rests outside the company cafeteria, dim and dusty, like a kitschy conversation piece.)

"*Incredible*," said Crissy Cordaro, an artist who used to work in the cubicle beside mine. "We should spend a week trying to come up with really *awful* ideas. Fart cards that emit a noxious odor. Not-my-mother's day cards for kids given up for adoption. A *spoooky* Halloween collection with photographs of real corpses. Christ, that's the only way to get ahead in this stupid place."

It still makes me chuckle, lying in bed with my radio playing softly. But memories don't always follow a reasonable order, and soon I grow anxious. It only takes a moment to remember that Crissy Cordaro's father was a police officer. And next I'm flooded with thoughts of Mr. Eugene and his childhood friend, Keesey, who refuses to pay the vig.

There are rules, I tell myself. *He knows that. Better than most.*

It takes me a week to call. For a few days, I kept the number on a sticky note pressed to the passenger seat of my car. Eventually, the tiny slip of paper found its way into the house—first beside the kitchen phone and, later, on my nightstand. I don't expect her to answer and I am silent for a long time, half-waiting for a mechanical beep. She remembers me; she also remembers our wager. After our short conversation I am jittery with adrenaline, my nerve endings all sparky and raw. I spend forty minutes hitting the heavy bag in the garage. Then I drink a beer, glancing two or three times at her name on the yellow note.

The booth is in the back of the restaurant. Every couple minutes I rise for a peek at the hostess stand, repeatedly bumping my knee against a support rod beneath the table. I nervously polish my silverware with a napkin. I nibble a heel of bread, then check my teeth in the knife's reflection for stray sesame seeds. She's wearing a short black dress and knee-high boots. Her hair is pulled casually from her face with a narrow elastic headband—the same type my daughters use when I tell them to "look neat." She smiles and waves me back into my seat.

"The ol' bait and switch," she says.

"Pardon?"

"Our bet was for all the mall food I could eat." Around her neck is a leather choker with a brassy coin-sized pendant. "But this place looks a lot nicer than the food court."

"I don't get out much," I say. "I have to make the most of my opportunities."

"So that's what this is?" she asks, drumming her fingers on the menu. "An *opportunity?*"

"No, I didn't—"

"Take it easy. I'm just busting your chops."

Between us is a shallow plate filled with olive oil and grated parmesan cheese. Nina tears loose a piece of bread, dragging it through the greenish liquid.

"This is yummy," she says. "Even better than Mrs. Doyle's Pretzels."

She begins talking at a frenetic pace, as though the words had been tamped down, just waiting to be released. She tells me about her car, a Saab, that she's owned for seven years. She thinks it needs a new fuel pump. Every few days it has trouble turning over. But she's discovered that if she shakes the car she can often get it started.

"Last week it died at a traffic light on Chardon Road," she says, shrugging. "I climbed onto the front bumper and began jumping. People were staring at me like I was crazy. This one guy asked if I needed help—so, that was nice. Anyway, I'm rocking the car up and down. And just to make sure, I stood on the, um, doorframe, I guess, and shook the car from side to side."

She pauses to take a sip of wine.

"But it worked. That's why this mechanic friend of mine thinks it's the fuel pump. He says maybe the jostling motion sort of kick-starts the pump. Or loosens a clog in the fuel line."

"What a nightmare."

"Oh, it's terrible. Every morning I get a knot in my stomach just wondering if the damn thing's gonna start." She takes another bite of bread. "I've been late to work twice already."

In the dim light her skin resembles the vanilla hard candies my grandmother stored in her purse. She has a small rogue freckle, dark as a felt-tip marker, above the corner of her mouth. Four days a week she's taking graduate-level classes at a local university. ("I thought I wanted to teach high school," she says. "But now I'd settle for first or second grade.") Coiled around her right wrist is a collection of bracelets, silver and copper and braids of colorful string. Her fingernails are short and well-manicured, glossy with plum-tinted polish.

The wine reminds her of a story from when she was a teenager. In the basement of her parents' house, near Nashville, Tennessee, she and her best friend found a few bottles of expensive Cabernet. The two girls got drunk beneath Nina's billiard table and tried making crank phone calls. ("We were *sixteen*," she admits, playfully hiding her face.) They didn't have much success because they'd burst into laughter whenever someone answered on the other end. Eventually, the girls staggered into Nina's front yard.

"I was tanked," says Nina, smiling at the memory. "I started making snow angels on our lawn. The only problem: It was the middle of summer. I remember our neighbor, Mr. Markey, was walking his dog—a Border Collie named Dixie. And my friend, Sue Garson, was laughing so hard she had to brace herself against a big oak tree near our driveway." She pauses, and I wonder if that's the end of her story. But then: "Sue said, 'Jesus, Nina. Your neighbor's right *here*. He's watching you roll around all trampy and shitfaced.'"

She takes a drink of wine, then sighs.

"I always thought that was a crummy thing for her to say." Nina's now staring down at the breadbasket. "I was really embarrassed. For maybe the next three months I totally avoided Mr. Markey."

"Your friend—Sue?—she was probably also drunk."

"Sure." On the seat beside Nina is a beige tackle box she uses as a purse. Her finger absently taps against its plastic handle. "It was still rotten."

For some troubling reason, I decide to share a story from my own boozy past—maybe the worst one. A few years after college, I was drinking whiskey with a buddy named Deke. We were watching basketball in a fancy new condominium his parents bought him. During a commercial, I grabbed a free alternative newspaper that was lying on his coffee table and started leafing through it. The back page was a crooked mess of overlapping circles from a chunky red pen. At first, I thought Deke was looking for a new job in the classifieds. But after reading a few of the advertisements, I realized he'd been searching through escort services.

"Guys really *do* that?" says Nina.

"I asked the same question."

After I dared him into making a call, he told the "escort" his address. I remember getting sober real quickly. Soon, I was pacing his shiny blond floors in my stocking feet. "She's coming here, man," I kept repeating. "A hooker's on her way right now." He just laughed, calmly smoking a cigarette on the end of his couch.

About forty minutes later the downstairs buzzer sounded. "I'm not staying," I said, twice. "I just want to see how she looks."

She was prettier than I'd expected: light brown skin; dark, shoulder-length hair; blue dress with a conservative neckline. If we'd passed her on the street, we might've guessed she was a teacher or a clerk.

I introduced myself, idiotically, offering a made-up name—we'd agreed not to use our real names—and shook her hand a couple times. On my drive home, I couldn't stop thinking about Deke alone in his fancy new apartment with a hooker from the back pages of some giveaway newspaper.

"For Chrissakes," I say, slapping the table. "The guy's father is a judge."

"You know, I see those ads all the time. I just never imagined that people actually *called* them."

"Me neither."

There's a brief, awkward silence. And I should leave it alone —allow my poorly selected tale to wither and die. But...

Three weeks later, Deke was helping the woman move into his place.

"That's crazy," says Nina.

"*Crazy.*"

It didn't take long before he realized his mistake. Once a neighbor called the cops because the noise was so loud—she'd been throwing food at him, breaking bottles. The morning he finally gathered the courage to ask her to leave, she invited him into the bathroom. She was holding a thin piece of plastic that looked like a tongue depressor. Slowly, she curled back her finger to reveal a small red cross.

"A home pregnancy test," says Nina.

I nod.

There was a series of long discussions. Deke wasn't sleeping, he'd lost fifteen pounds. Finally, he called his father. After a pair of meetings with the woman's lawyer—she now had a *lawyer*—they agreed to pay her twenty thousand dollars if she would have an abortion and disappear from Deke's life.

"Jesus," says Nina, shaking her head. "That's some expensive hooker."

I smile, because that's what everybody says.

As Nina finishes her salmon, I grow anxious wondering what made me share this story, especially on a first date. It's mildly amusing—the type of seedy encounter that makes you glad it happened to somebody else—but I know it will only persuade Nina to turn the foggy lens back at me. It's the kind of story that practically compels its listener to pass judgment on everyone involved. Maybe she has strong opinions on abortion. Or she'll speculate on the morality of my friends.

"We're not close," I say, suddenly, between mouthfuls of pasta.

"Excuse me?"

"Deke and I—we're not that close anymore." I wipe my mouth with a napkin. "I don't want you to think I hang out with a bunch of derelicts."

"Don't worry about it."

"I'm not worried," I say, taking a short breath. "I just—well, I wish I hadn't told you all that."

"Why? There's nothing wrong with it." She smiles, reaching across the table to pat my hand. "It was…*entertaining.*"

For the rest of our meal, I'm blinded by regret. She talks about her childhood and past boyfriends and work at Carmella's Paper & Things. But I keep replaying a scene from this old movie where one of the actors, after bumbling a date, strikes himself repeatedly on the side of his head while chanting, "Stupid, stupid, stupid."

Outside the restaurant is a small courtyard surrounded by a belt-high iron fence. As we're leaving, a latch on the gate is slow to release. Because I haven't slowed my pace to account for the sticky gate, I bump into her from behind.

"Whoa," she says, raising her hand against my chest.

Stoked by desperation, I lean forward and kiss Nina full on the mouth. I can see her eyes grow wide like blooming flowers. But she doesn't pull away. I thread my fingers through the mane of hair at the back of her neck, making a fist and tugging her chin higher. A soft, dreamy moan comes from the well of her throat.

"That was a surprise," she whispers.

There's a certain fearlessness that accompanies the loss of hope—the way I felt after sharing my ridiculous hooker tale. Or maybe I was pressed into action by residual guilt: I didn't have a single good sex story to tell my friends at dinner the other night. But this is the first time in my life I've kissed a woman without a hint of premeditation. We kiss some more, her lips warm and citrusy. I nuzzle my face along the spill of her neck. Beneath her flowery bath soap and skin cream, I can smell the sweet muskiness of her scalp. My fingers gather against the arch of her armpit. We hear the footsteps of another couple as they walk past us toward the sloppy gate...

The tip of her tongue traces the outline of my mouth, two, three revolutions, before darting between my teeth. Her hand comes to rest on my belt buckle, slow and dangerous. Then I feel the instep of her right boot grinding up and down and up against my left calf.

"Maybe we should—"

"Walk me to my car," she says, taking my elbow.

"Um, that's not what I was gonna suggest."

"Oh, come on," she says, gripping my finger. "Let's save a little something for next time."

This is her first mention of another date. In my mind's eye the prospect takes the form of detailed flashcards, our relationship now progressing at some fantastical speed: I imagine us lying beside each other in my bed; then sharing breakfast at my neighborhood diner; and later, months in the future, I picture Nina playing a board game at the kitchen table with my daughters...

I'm being pulled forward by some sonic momentum. I haven't felt this way about a woman for a long time—since Liz and I met. After a brief glimpse of transparency, a true view, maybe it'll be okay to throw my arms around this thing and squeeze tight in a Christmas-morning embrace...

She lowers herself into her car. I take her arm and kiss her softly on the inside of her left wrist. As I back away, she looks troubled. She's staring into the scores and dials on her dashboard, head nodding swiftly. My hand's suspended in mid-wave when she turns toward me. She shrugs and opens her door again.

"It won't start," she says.

She climbs onto her bumper, palm pressed to the hood for balance, and begins rocking in short, pistony bursts. The car lurches forward then back. I watch the tires stretch and condense against the pebbled asphalt. She guides me to a plastic running strip inside the passenger door; she stands across from me, on the driver's side, her boots hooked to the lower doorframe.

"Go!" she says.

Now we're both leaping, taking turns, first Nina then me. The car pitches from side to side, as though slaloming through a tight line of pylons. I can hear the squeak and rattle of rusty metal parts. Then comes a long hissy sigh from one of the tires or a taxed shock absorber. She raises two crossed fingers. This time the engine starts.

"That's some workout," I say, breathing heavy.

She rolls down her window, kissing me awkwardly across my knuckles.

"You're a good sport."

I bow from my waist, pretending to remove an invisible hat. And then I'm standing alone in a serpent's tail of blue exhaust. I watch her angle-eye taillights glaring back through the briny darkness.

There are too many of them. Keesey's sitting behind a plate of eggs and coffee. Four other cops share his table. I nibble a piece of dry wheat toast, watching from my booth in the corner. After a few minutes their voices turn soft, five heads pressed crookedly together above a black-and-silver napkin dispenser, until the group suddenly disbands in laughter. A bald, chunky cop punches Keesey in the arm. The youngest one rises, wiping his lap. He has shaggy blond hair and a long, slender nose. As he walks to the restroom, he pauses to position his nightstick against the curve of his thigh.

From across the restaurant a middle-aged waitress calls to one of the cops. She's wearing a white polyester dress that clings to her body, collecting above her pelvis in slappy pleats that resemble coiled rope. She rests her elbow across Keesey's shoulder, stabbing the air with a ballpoint pen. A second waitress, red hair nested in a loose bun, refills their mugs with coffee.

As a boy, I would occasionally eat breakfast in a diner like this one with my uncle. He sold insurance—auto, life, homeowners. I would sit across from him coloring paper placemats with crayons I plucked from a dented colander. My uncle read the newspaper, folded in half the long way. Everyone in the diner knew him by name. On days when I'd join him at work, maybe during summer or holiday break, we'd have Chinese food for lunch. "Let's go see the Chinamen," he'd announce.

My uncle was a repository of offbeat information. He had a queer habit of regurgitating strange factoids that had found safe harbor in his brain—a crocodile's tongue is attached to the roof of its mouth; a group of larks is called an exaltation; Canada has more lakes than the rest of the world combined. For a long time, my mother tried to persuade him to try out for a TV quiz show.

Years later, when I was in college, there was a sandwich shop near campus that posted a daily trivia question on a chalkboard behind the register. Correct answers earned you a complimentary lunch. One week during my sophomore year, I nailed four in a row.

I remember sharing this story with my uncle a few days before he died of cancer. He broke into a warm, morphine-induced smile and asked what I ordered. Corned beef, turkey, turkey, and, for a change of pace, eggplant parmesan. "Hayes," he said, short of breath. He waved me closer. "Two-thirds of the world's eggplant is grown in New Jersey." Though I didn't give it much thought at the time, those were the last words he ever spoke to me.

The young cop makes his way back to the table. In unison, the others stand to meet him. They remove tidy folds of cash from their front pockets, peeling off bills and tucking them beneath water glasses. Wallet-less, they contain their money with the same hefty, lime-colored rubber bands favored by Mr. Eugene. I once watched him pluck a half-dozen from bales of asparagus at a local farmer's market.

I'm trying to keep my distance. I fiddle with my check, pause over a story in a scattered newspaper. I shuffle toward the entrance, where the cops have now congregated in a spiny knot.

Keesey wears black gum-soled shoes and an enamel flag pinned to the collar of his shirt. The skin between his eyebrows is pink and freezer-burn flaky. When he reaches the sidewalk, he lights a cigarette and exhales smoke through his nostrils. I'm watching from behind the window, obscured by a cardboard placard announcing a charity spaghetti dinner at the VFW. There are five of them, an odd number; I'm hoping Keesey will leave alone. But he climbs into the passenger side of a cruiser driven by the young guy. I walk to the curb, my arm propped against a parking meter. Keesey blows smoke through his parted door, then tosses his cigarette into the street. I'm trying to think of something to say—a quick batch of words that will convince him to abandon his partner and come talk to me. *Officer Keesey?* or *Can I have a moment of your time?* or *This is really important.*

I raise my hand in a truncated wave, interrupted, a sawed-off gesture. He doesn't notice me in the sealed darkness of his squad car, surrounded by electronics and chrome and kitchen-beige leather. This is my last chance—a mad scramble with the radio dial to find a passed song before it ends. My arm leaves my side, startlingly self-possessed, colliding in three short knocks above the wheel well of Keesey's cruiser.

"You need something?" asks the young cop.

I can feel my nodding head grow wobbly and weak, converting its gathered momentum into a horizontal sway. I'm distracted by sounds of the street—slamming doors, rifled engines, names being called against the distance. My mind's filled with a churning polyrhythm. He asks me if I'm okay.

"I'm fine," I say, taking a pair of toe-to-heel steps backward.

And then they're gone, leaving only the echoing *shush* of tire rubber against roadway and Keesey's smoldering cigarette.

Eighteen was a meaningful number for Liz and me—the date we met; her birthday; the hour of the day, in military parlance, of the first time we made love. On the morning of our eighteen-month anniversary, I sat at a small glass table in my breakfast nook and ate a plate of scrambled eggs. Liz was drinking coffee, a curious smile slowly breaking across her face. She was hiding something in her lap, half-covered by the floppy fabric of her sweatpants. When she finally revealed the package, a medium-sized box wrapped in red tissue paper, I could see a swoopy gold heart pasted against the lower right-hand corner. She had used indelible marker to write our initials, separated by a plus sign, within the heart's borders. I cut through several pieces of carefully applied tape with a butter knife, softly shaking the lid of the box from its bottom. I peered down at a brown leather photo album with the number eighteen embossed in gold on its cover.

For much of our courtship, Liz had taken to carrying around a large, clunky Polaroid camera. Gently, I turned the pages on a random collection of pictures and tokens from our first eighteen months together. There was a receipt from the strawberry tarts we had at a small coffee shop on Gosling Street. A postcard purchased at a Native American museum we stepped into during the summer to escape the heat. She'd even saved the unused tickets from her friend's cello concert, the ones she'd forgotten on her refrigerator, accompanied by a pair of Polaroids—first her then me—in our dress clothes. The transparent plastic shield wouldn't stay down on the page featuring a round cork coaster from a bar called the Barking Spider, where we met. Symmetrically arranged like a child's interpretation of sunbeams were the dried petals from the flower I gave her as an apology after our first argument—I'd been testy that we missed a movie because she misread the time.

There were white-bordered pictures, sometimes as many as six to a page. Liz standing on the bow of a ferry and swinging a tennis racquet and modeling a denim jacket I bought her for Sweetie's Day. A blurred shot of me attempting to juggle apples at Paterson's orchard; another as I hung upside down, heels to buttocks, from a chin-up bar.

A photograph of me lying in the bed of my old pickup, covered by a plaid wool blanket, with a small black box dangling over the side of my truck—a sound speaker from a drive-in theater designed to clip through a lowered window. We had gone to see *True Grit*, starring John Wayne, and had parked my truck backward so we could stretch out as we watched the film. I remember that my arm fell asleep snaked beneath Liz's shoulders, but I was afraid to move it; I didn't want her to think I was uncomfortable. It was a peaceful, star-filled night and I wished the movie could last longer. We stayed in the truck for a while after the others had gone, watching a pair of high school kids collecting debris from the darkened lot. Liz spoke with a sleepy drawl, her cheek pressed against my chest. I listened to the stiff bristles of a push broom scraping the pavement as one of the boys slalomed around the white speaker posts. If only we could stay this way forever, I thought, Liz's knee curled lightly across my thigh.

In my kitchen, I craned lower for a thorough inspection.

"What do you see?" asked Liz.

There was a large paper cup that had been filled with cherry-flavored granules of ice. After we finished the drink we kissed, cold mouth meeting cold mouth. It was a strange and oddly comforting sensation, her chilled tongue and teeth and lips exploring mine—as though she were someone different and this was the first time we'd been intimate.

Even back then, in the early stages of our relationship, I understood that there would be rough times ahead—there always were—but I had a faith in Liz unlike anything I'd felt for another person. A poster for the local Boys and Girls Club tacked near the drive-in's concession stand encouraged readers to "belong to something larger than yourself." I recall focusing on a single word—*belong*—and allowing its red letters to scald themselves against my eyelids. I belonged to Liz and she belonged to me. More importantly, we belonged together.

I reached across the table and took her hand in mine, dryly kissing each of her fingers. If I had been looking for clues, a sign that this thing between us was good, I could've stumbled upon them everywhere. We spent hours sitting beside each other on the couch, silently reading or watching TV, occasionally massaging each other's stocking feet, never needing to speak to know we were content. She relied on me to remember things—locking doors, paying bills, listing groceries—and I needed her to remind me that some things simply don't matter. ("Take it easy, sport—it's only milk. We can get it tomorrow.") When we made love—long, breathless encounters—we connected seamlessly, a single beast that knew how to quell all its desires. And, significantly: Until I met Liz I was a fitfully light sleeper, unable to drift off while lying beside a partner—I rarely brought women home, instead choosing their places so I could leave at will. But now I found it difficult to fall asleep without Liz in my bed, her warm fingers threaded between mine.

Later that day, after Liz had gone to the gym, I flipped through the album again. I examined the pages, appreciating the work that went into completing each one—ordering the events, digging through her drawers for the proper mementos, pasting down four lacy photo corners for each picture. I smiled when it occurred to me that the two of us, together, must have meant something special to Liz also—from the beginning—or she never would've saved all this stuff.

The chair creaked as I adjusted myself, lifting a velum cover on the final page and lowering a pen to the white space below a photograph of Liz and me standing on a sun-washed beach. (We'd asked a lifeguard to shoot us with a hot-air balloon rising above the skyline.) *Mr. & Mrs. Hayes Fanning*, I wrote, like a teenage girl, if only to see how the title looked beneath us.

A gleaming white mortar and pestle, infinitely conjoined, rest on the counter. Below are shelves of vitamins, stool softeners, cold medicines, throat lozenges, acetaminophen (tablets and gel-caps), hydrocortisone (1% cream and ointment), allergy capsules, laxatives, antacid liquids (twelve or sixteen-ounce) in cartoonish pink and teal jugs. Nearby are wire swivel-stands crammed with self-help books from skin care to chronic depression. There's even a dark green paperback titled *Cooking with Broccoli*. Twin aisles of chin-high display racks filled with children's toys, snack foods, and miscellaneous home supplies—paper towels and extension cords, light bulbs and batteries. An elderly woman sits in one of three soft-backed chairs, a glossy magazine winged open across her lap. She reaches forward and pinches a nylon stocking above her spidery calf.

Half-hidden by a linoleum counter, Sid Goldberg affixes self-adhesive labels to a variety of medications—pills and tonics and silvery tubes of salve. He's flanked by dozens of yellowed sills, bristly with pharmaceuticals. Wearing a white lab coat, plaid shirt, and necktie, he says something to one of his assistants and sidesteps his way to the register.

"Mrs. Lipsyte? Your prescriptions are ready."

It takes a moment before he sees me standing near the magazines. He smiles, slapping his hand against his hip.

"Florida's killing me, Hayes," he says, waving me into the restricted area. He's eating leftover pasta from a Tupperware container. "They can't cover."

Goldberg is eager and talkative. Though he's never missed a payment, he prefers that I come to collect his money instead of dropping it at the smoke shop. He says it makes him feel like he's doing something illicit—which, in truth, he is. Several months ago, as I watched him count out a short stack of twenties, he asked me what would happen if he couldn't pay. "Would you get all rough with me?" he said excitedly, raising his fist. At the time, I had a terrible chest cold; I was coughing and hoarse. He poured me a pint-sized bottle of aubergine syrup, a magical elixir called Hycodan which he furtively slipped into the pocket of my coat. The medicine's a semisynthetic opioid, causing the same euphoric sensation as codeine tablets or, I'm told, heroin. I spent the next three days in bed, drifting from one neon unicorn dream to another. By the final few swallows, I was crouched at the gates of chaos—I even questioned the dissolution of my marriage. I tried re-examining my role in its collapse, incredibly, ridiculously, wondering whether my expectations had been reasonable. But it occurred to me in the days that followed, as I battled withdrawal headaches and nausea, that the only legitimate survival technique for living with my ex-wife was an ever-present opiate drip—a rubber bladder of morphine hitched to my back, straw-thin tube helixed around one arm.

Goldberg spears a log of rigatoni with a plastic fork. From where I'm standing, I can see stippled marinara sauce across the collar of his lab coat. He's always asking for my opinion on upcoming games, as though by working for Mr. Eugene I have access to certain covert information.

"What do you think about Iowa?" he asks.

I shrug.

"Come on, Hayes." He drinks from a can of ginger ale. "Eleven points is a lot—even against Purdue."

"Sid," I say, taking two squirts from a sample bottle of moisturizer and massaging the cream into my hands. "I just pick up the money. You *absolutely* know more about these games than I do."

"Oh, please." Reaching into a drawer on his desk, he removes a white envelope and slides it toward me. "Can you tell me which team has the most action?"

I shake my head.

He runs his fingers through his thinning gray hair. A pair of tortoiseshell spectacles hangs suspended around his neck by a bright red cord. He sighs deeply, then polishes the lenses with his necktie.

"Okay."

Together we walk to the front door. He pauses to straighten some magazines on a particle-board ledge. When he glances down, he notices one of the marinara spots on his lab coat. He touches a handkerchief to his tongue and blots the stain with saliva, creating a larger, more diluted blemish.

"Next time," he says, smiling, "*you* pay *me.*"

"Fair enough."

In the parking lot it starts to drizzle. I sit for a moment behind the wheel of my car, staring through the misty windshield. A young mother sprints for cover beneath a green awning; she shakes her hair before noticing that her son is still standing on the sidewalk. He stomps his foot in one of the fresh puddles. She calls for him, twice. Finally she shuffles back into the wetness and hoists him against her ribcage. "Loaf of bread," I say, quietly. It's one of Tig's favorites.

The tables are arranged in a crude, horseshoe formation. A transparent lectern stands in the throat of the open end. Torn pieces of blue masking tape hold a collection of colorful sketches against the rear wall. Nearby is a slick whiteboard with three felt-tip markers, red, yellow, and green, appended by a holster snapped to its frame. My boss, Dennis Gaines, has insisted I participate in Silver Springs' latest Request for Ideation (RFI)—a series of brainstorms featuring employees from various company divisions. In theory, we will meet several times over the next couple months to create a half-dozen prototypes of unique merchandise, with the best of the group—as elected by other "teams" in the RFI—approved for mass production to the marketplace.

Today there are bagels, cream cheese (plain and honey walnut), coffee in a corrugated box with a side-mounted spigot, and a tray filled with gummy-edged pastries. "If nothing else," said Gaines, during our initial conversation, "it will give you some insight into how to work as a member of a team." I could tell from the singsong nature of his voice, exaggerated and condescending, that his remarks were meant to sting.

A few weeks ago, he ordered me to have a stack of invoices on his desk by the following morning. Because I was staring into my computer screen, back facing the entrance of my cubicle, I thought he'd departed. "Fucking douchebag," I said, soft but audible. I could feel my face warm with color when I heard the shuffling of papers, and I realized he was still standing behind me. He didn't say anything for several excruciatingly long moments. Finally, he settled for expedience by simply repeating his earlier command and marching away.

This is the second RFI meeting of the session. I was added only after another participant was forced to drop out for medical reasons. I'm the sixth member of the orange team. (Go, Orange!) Quietly, I sit drinking coffee and nibbling a dry bagel. Our team leader, Layney Marks, is a stout middle-aged designer/manager who's wearing a pair of pricy, intentionally ripped jeans and a sequined blouse. Her swollen feet are wedged into patent-leather pumps with three-inch heels. Once, while standing in line at the cafeteria, I heard two women talking about Marks' clothing. "Oh, *God*," said one. "She thinks by dressing like a teenager it'll make her look younger. Tragic."

Marks explains the manner in which we're supposed to present our favorite concepts, using copy and samples and fleshed-out designs tacked to black polyform boards that lean against the lectern. She reviews some of the group's ideas from the previous meeting: wine-bottle gift boxes, "arty" greeting cards that can be displayed on collapsible easels, talking holiday cards with smart-aleck retorts programmed into nickel-thin digital chips, tiny religious-themed pendants. She's talking and talking, but the words only compress into a drone of endless sound, like the teacher's voice in the old Charlie Brown cartoons: *Waaa-wh-whaaa-whaa.* I glance down and notice a dainty gold chain wrapped around her right ankle. It looks strange, a queer juxtaposition, her thick leg beneath a thread of delicate jewelry.

Across the room sits a guy with bookish black spectacles and a severe haircut—sandpaper short on the sides, gelled rooster spikes on top. He's scribbling into a wire-bound notepad. After every few sentences from Marks, he nods in agreement. Near his elbow rests a pile of books with colorful Post-it notes—pink, yellow, blue—peeking from their spines. Beside him a young woman gnaws on a cheese Danish, a flurry of crumbs collecting on her chest and lap.

Every Saturday morning, my father used to eat a cheese Danish at a delicatessen called Lenny's. He would retire to a corner table with his newspaper, coffee, and a Danish he cut into pizza-style wedges. One day when I was about seven, I sat across from him with a plate of French toast dusted in confectionary sugar. I was reading the comics—or the "funny pages," as my father called them. Suddenly, without provocation, my father said, "You know, I should've been with more redheads."

At the time, I'm not sure I had any idea what he meant. But a few years later, when I returned home from elementary school to find my mother crying at our kitchen table—my father had left us, and I wouldn't see him again for eleven years—I remember thinking maybe he'd gone someplace to get the redheads out of his system.

There was no shortage of reasons to hate my father. After his departure we struggled financially, my mother working a succession of jobs to keep us from sinking. For me there was an emptiness that seemed fiercest in autumn: During my football games I would gaze into the grandstands and count the fathers of my teammates. Or every October when our local Girl Scout troop would host a father-daughter dance, which my sister was forced to attend with my sloppy Uncle Dan. But I harbored the most resentment over something that wasn't in his control.

A few days before homecoming during my senior year of college, I stood in the locker room after practice. I was gazing down at my tattered shower shoes, staring at a tea-colored stain that resembled the outline of Idaho—it's funny the details that remain with us in moments of trauma. My trance was broken when I got called into the coach's office. "Your father's dying," he said, busily shuffling papers on his desk. "We're gonna miss you on Saturday." There was nothing further to discuss—he didn't care that I hadn't seen my father in over a decade, or that I would've preferred playing in the game to traveling to Pennsylvania, where my father lay in a hospital bed.

When I arrived I was greeted by my sister Cameron, whose eyes were already red and puffy. She was the only member of my family who hadn't held a grudge against him. "Some people just need more space," she'd once said, in defense of his prolonged absence. We sat on slippery plastic benches and drank vending-machine coffee until the nurses permitted us inside his room.

He was lean and fragile—his skin the same watery gray as raw turnip. Transparent tubing spiraled down from his nose and arm. Behind him was a complicated panel with knobs and gauges and assorted blinking lights. A dribble of wetness created a dark trail near the collar of his hospital gown.

"You're big," he said, when I crept slowly toward the side of his bed.

For some reason I was preoccupied with his fingernails, which seemed neglectfully long. I also noticed a sharp crescent on the webbing of his left thumb, and I was trying to decide whether it was lead shavings or a dirty scar or, perhaps, a small arrowhead tattoo. His lips were thin and bloodless. When he spoke they turned white as porcelain. He motioned for a plastic cup. As I lifted it toward his mouth, straw bent like a dead tulip, he tapped the mattress near his leg.

"Careful," he whispered. "Don't get piss on yourself."

Dangling from his skeletal bed frame was a catheter bag half-filled with urine—brothy yellow with furry tumbleweeds.

He'd missed so much of my life. Mostly, he wasn't interested in hearing about all the things that had happened while he was away. Instead, there were questions about school now and girlfriends and football. He told me he'd been to see one of my games the previous fall, in Hamilton, New York.

"You made a nice catch," he said. "Really got clobbered by the safety—but you held onto the ball."

It wouldn't have been difficult for him to find me afterward, on the field or outside the locker room. I wanted to know why he'd kept his distance, even when he was only a dozen rows away. But he kept talking. During the game he attended, against Colgate, he'd noticed I had two of my fingers taped. ("Were they busted?" he asked.) There was also a heated exchange with the quarterback after an incomplete pass. He was curious about what we said.

Eventually, a nurse made my sister and me leave the room so my father could get some rest.

"Wait for me," he mumbled, patting Cameron on the hand. "I won't sleep long."

But he was wrong, the way he'd been wrong about everything else. Cameron and I wandered to the cafeteria, where we shared a block of lime Jell-O and a Pepsi. We sat beside a large mural of dancing children, watching a procession of diners—physicians and hospital employees with ID badges hitched to their breast pockets and relatives of sick people—carrying hexagonal-shaped trays past a nearby register.

"He's pretty good," said Cameron, carving a bloom of whipped cream from the Jell-O with a swipe of her spoon. "Although I'm not sure what I expected."

To me, he seemed like somebody else—somebody who wasn't my father. Maybe a distant uncle or the father of a friend. He was just a frail-looking man lying in some anonymous hospital bed. Many years earlier, before he'd left us, we spent a Memorial Day at a local carnival. I was five or six. I remember a long corridor of scarred amusement park rides—carousel, Ferris wheel, bumper cars. Near the end of the afternoon, I'd convinced my parents to let me ride the Whirligig—a spinning, saucer-shaped cart that traveled on a narrow crown of ball bearings. The ride was swift and jerky. By its second rotation, I was terrified—my arms swimming wildly against the rapidly moving air. I could hear my parents' voices squeezed together into a single eager groan. Suddenly—mercifully!—the ride came to a premature end. My father leaped the short fence and sprinted to where I was seated. He pulled back the safety bar, lifting me into his arms.

Carefully, he navigated us through a spoke of steel girders and stilled pistons. I was pressed horizontally across his shoulder —sack of grain!—as he walked toward the gate. He carried me through a jangle of arms and legs and adjustable mesh ball caps. In that solitary moment, as we approached my mother and sister standing on the hot asphalt, I remember thinking my father was the most powerful man in the world.

Years later, when I try to conjure his best-possible image, that's how I picture him. It's a memory that rises through the fog of my (mostly) fatherless childhood, helping me to forget the gaping hole in those football grandstands and, finally, the evening my sister and I returned to his hospital room after cafeteria Jell-O only to watch him being wheeled out for a surgical procedure he wouldn't survive.

As Marks goes on, I watch the guy with black spectacles turn the page in his notepad. The woman beside him taps a final bite of Danish into her mouth. It's an imperfect place, this world in which we live. A piece of blue masking tape on the wall behind Marks suddenly loses its stickiness and one of the colorful sketches flips forward, tumbling to the ground.

They each get orange-flavored juice boxes, carrot sticks, pouches of fruit gummy snacks, and two handfuls of potato chips in zippered baggies. Tig wants a peanut butter and jelly sandwich with the crusts cut off; Callie prefers cream cheese on cinnamon swirl toast. Using a Sharpie marker, I write their names on the brown paper sacks, follow each with a thunderbolt-shaped exclamation mark.

The scream comes as I'm tucking their lunches into their backpacks. At first, it sounds like it's from the morning news program playing absently on the TV. But then Tig races into the living room, crying hysterically, her left forearm cradled against her little belly.

"She bited me," says Tig, straining to catch her breath.

I can see the impressions made by Callie's incisors on Tig's wrist, red and damp with saliva. Together we walk to the bathroom. Callie's staring at her reflection in the mirror, using a large wooden brush to style and restyle her hair. The sink is littered with an assortment of headbands, barrettes, and ribbons.

"What happened?" I ask.

"It was *my* turn," says Callie, refusing to break contact with her image in the mirror. Perhaps realizing the weakness of her argument, she offers more: "And she hit me."

"No, I didn't," says Tig, stomping her foot. "She's *lying*. I didn't touch her."

"Callie—"

"She was totally hogging the mirror." Callie remains facing forward. "I told her it was my turn—and she was about to smack me with the brush."

"What's my number-one rule in this house?"

"No hitting," says Tig.

"I didn't *hit* her."

"Callie," I say, grabbing her by the elbow and spinning her toward me. "That *includes* biting and kicking and hair-pulling—and anything else where you violate a person's space."

"Well," she says, stealing another glance at the mirror, "she was being a…*bitch*."

From the edge of my vision, I can see Tig's jaw fall slack. I squeeze Callie's arm and pull her down from the footstool. As I drag her into the hallway, she starts yelling—she raises the brush into a throwing position, above her right shoulder.

"You say that's your number-one rule," she shouts. "But now *you're* hurting *me*."

"What have I told you about using that kind of language?"

"She *was* acting like a bitch."

"Callie!" I press down tighter near the crease of her elbow. "I don't want to hear any more cursing."

She yanks herself loose, racing toward her bedroom.

"Child abuse, child abuse!"

I lean my forehead against the wall and sigh. I can hear the brush finally leave Callie's hand, breaking something glassy—a figurine, a child's teacup—before it lands on the floor. After a few moments of silence, I kneel beside Tig.

"Were you teasing her?"

"No, I promise I wasn't," she says, her eyes fixed to a spot behind me. "I mean, I wasn't *trying* to tease her."

I tell Tig to get ready for school. Then, still standing in the hallway, I announce a new set of rules: Each girl will get exactly five minutes of "personal time" in the bathroom every morning.

"Does that seem fair?"

"Yes," says Tig, quickly, because she knows I'm in a mood.

"I should get longer," says Callie. "I'm older."

I stagger into the bathroom and turn off the lights. In the darkness, I place my index finger against my temple and pretend to shoot myself, snapping my head sideways with imaginary recoil. Three blocks from the girls' school is a small bakery called Tannenbaum's. Some mornings, if I can get the girls out of the house in time, we stop there for "breakfast." Today Callie's face is besmirched by white frosting from a custard-filled éclair. Her sister has an asymmetrical chocolate mustache painted grimly across her upper lip. In Tig's hands, the giant donut resembles a steering wheel. I'm drinking coffee and skimming the headlines in the morning newspaper. A faint scuffing sound competes with the classical music playing from the bakery's stereo. When I follow the noise, looking down, I see Tig's foot sliding across the linoleum floor. She's bumping it into the side of Callie's sneaker, pushing her sister away.

"Tig," I say. "What're you doing?"

"Trying to annoy me," says Callie.

"Tig?"

"I don't have any room."

"You have plenty of room," I say, clutching the backrest of her chair and skirting it away from Callie. "Leave your sister alone."

Callie squints her eyes, shooting a nasty look at Tig. In response, Tig reaches across the tiny table and pinches a corner of Callie's éclair.

"Dad!"

"Tig."

"That's so gross," says Callie, tearing off the offending section of pastry. "She doesn't wash her hands after she goes to the bathroom—and she touched my food."

"I do *so* wash my hands."

"No, you don't."

"Guys, guys," I say, spanking my knee with the newspaper. "This is the last time we're gonna come here if you can't get along."

After we finish and load into the car, I watch them jostling for position on the back seat. I slap my arm down against the leather upholstery—an unspoken reminder of the dividing line between them. During the short ride to school, I worry about their recent catty treatment of each other. I begin to wonder about my role in their continuing development. Is this simply a stage, the same give-and-take that endures between nearly every adolescent pair of sisters? Or, more terrifying, are they exhibiting a learned pattern of behavior? Is it possible they're mimicking the countless fights between their mother and me?

As we reach the school's entrance, I'm thinking about the times Liz and I have goaded each other into battle, and how easily I could've held my tongue, letting Liz burn herself out, her vitriol stored on a message chip to be erased with two quick jabs of my thumb. Rather than engaging her in petty arguments, our daughters within earshot, I could've just driven away, or hung up the phone. Now I'm left to consider the collateral damage.

"Hey," I say, twisting my body toward the back of the car. "Can you guys do me a favor?"

"We know, we know," says Callie, exasperated. "Be good to each other."

"Right, yes." I squeeze her sleeve so she can't escape. "One other thing?"

"We're gonna be late," says Tig.

"Okay—one second," I say, gathering them in my outstretched arms. "Face sandwich."

"Dad!" says Callie. "Not *here*."

"C'mon. Just a quick one."

Reluctantly, the two girls press their faces on either side of my jaw—cheek to cheek to cheek. I give them both a kiss and watch them race up the path to the building. Then comes a glimmer of hope—Tig stumbles, dropping her backpack, and Callie waits for her, breaking stride, before they continue together past the glass doors. Her momentary pause is a tiny gesture. But it's enough to lift my spirits, making me feel better about the whole long morning.

If the lifespans of failed relationships were plotted on a sheet of graph paper, they would likely resemble a bell curve. But it's difficult to know exactly when the downturn begins to occur—there's rarely a singular catastrophic moment when the earth gives way. Liz and I had everything a young family could want: a cute house on a pleasant, tree-lined street; two cars; a cherubic toddler with another expected in a few short months. But we weren't happy; there was a coldness between us seemingly born from thin air, like a sudden dust storm, that had started forming in the weeks before we became parents. Some of the qualities I once found so endearing in Liz—her vulnerability, her flightiness—now proved to be irritants, a whiny hinge on a door. And I know she held a similar contempt for me. Small misunderstandings instantly turned into referendums on the state of our marriage. A dozen months earlier she might have forgotten her car keys on the table and, after a suitable delay, I would've playfully suspended them from my index finger, and we'd share an easy laugh. But the levity had vanished like a school of frightened minnows. Now, I would give a derisive sigh, maybe strike the dashboard, and Liz would stomp back into the house.

For a while we tried desperately to regain the thing we had lost. There were unexpected gifts and handholding and soft kisses in the morning hours. But it all felt forced, contrived, as though we were following a script of what we thought the other person needed. Our lives became a giant sweater that had begun to unravel, only we couldn't find a place to sever the accumulating thread.

The December before Tig was born, we drove east to Liz's aunt and uncle's house. In the preceding weeks, we'd done our best to refrain from fighting in front of Callie. But the six-hour ride proved too long; shortly after we reached the Pennsylvania turnpike, I started complaining about crumbs from Liz's cranberry muffin falling to the floor. There were angry looks and swatted hands and exchanged laundry lists of shortcomings. Eventually, we had to pull into a rest stop because our strained voices had woken Callie. We spent the last ninety minutes of the trip in a stoic silence broken only by the squeaking rubber bunny being gnawed between Callie's teeth.

Liz's uncle Tony was a hulking man with hands the size of griddlecakes. He greeted us in the driveway, his meaty forearms bracing a small pyramid of knotty firewood. Before Tony had retired to the wilderness, he'd run his own commercial construction company, and his days still began at four thirty with a pot of black coffee.

We were welcomed into the house by Aunt Eileen, who wore a gingham apron and puffy oven mitts.

"I'm baking," she said, wiping a thumbprint of flour from her nose.

Though Christmas was three weeks away, the living room was already decorated for the holiday. There was a sturdy Scotch pine with ornaments and colored lights and a white illuminated angel at its summit. The windows were trimmed with shiny bunting in red and silver and green. A row of stockings hung from the mantel of the fireplace—Eileen had used a glue gun to write our names across the stockings in sparkly gold cursive. A collection of bright poinsettias lined the stairway, their pots shrouded in green and red foil.

After a few minutes of small talk, Liz and I retired to the guest room to unpack. I carefully placed our clothes into the drawers of an antique bureau that reeked of cedar and mothballs. Callie tugged on the cushion of a wicker rocking chair, her tiny pink fingers gripping a corduroy seam. Every time I thought about speaking, even if it was only some innocuous remark— "Your aunt looks great" or "Should I put Callie's food in the fridge?"—I stopped myself, not wanting to reignite the powder keg between us.

Finally, before we shuffled downstairs for dinner, Liz turned to me. "*Keep it together,*" she said, toting Callie in her arms. Keep it together, I whispered, alone, not certain what she'd meant.

That evening I slept on the couch—it was the first time in more than a year that Liz and I hadn't spent the night together. We had an excuse, though—Tony and I were rising before dawn to go hunting and Liz didn't want to be awakened. The Christmas lights unplugged, I lay in the darkness, breathing in the scent of ginger and baked ham. I could hear the floorboards above me wheezing under Liz's uncle's heavy footsteps. For a long time, I couldn't slow my carousel of thoughts. I was filled with self-doubt; I wondered if I possessed the tools to make my marriage work. I asked myself if it was this hard for other couples, or whether there was some secret that we simply couldn't grasp.

In the glow of headlights, Tony and I packed our hunting gear into the back of his SUV. I'd never shot at a living thing and, in truth, I wasn't sure I wanted to know how it felt. But weeks ago, on the phone, Tony had called me a "Nancy boy" when I'd voiced my opposition. "You won't hit anything," he'd said. "It's mostly to get outside—and away from the girls."

We drove for about an hour, to a parcel of land owned by the friend of a friend. It was cold even though we'd dressed in layers—long johns, thermal shirts, sweaters, windproof jackets with Day-Glo bibs, gloves, rubber-soled boots with fuzzy white liners. Tony held a pair of Remington 11-87 shotguns, his pockets concealing their shells. We hiked for a while through a snowy pasture. Beside a narrow, icy creek, he gestured toward a line of trees beyond the next plot of land.

"Up there," he said. "I look for escape routes between where the deer eat and sleep."

We each set up a tree stand about twenty feet off the ground, near a clearing that led to twin alfalfa fields. It was quiet and I could hear the wind whistling across the barren branches. Tony's breath showed in fat white clouds until he got settled, and then it was difficult to see. We sat for a long time, silently, looking for movement in the gray knitting of tree trunks. My fingers were numb and I curled them into the palms of my gloves. Tony was eating half a turkey and lettuce sandwich.

When Liz and I first visited her aunt and uncle, soon after we started dating, we were so afraid our lovemaking would disturb them that we crept into their basement in the middle of the night and had sex against their washing machine. And the most recent time we'd made love, early into her pregnancy, we were clumsy and awkward. Our knees collided; my hand lingered too long in one spot, not long enough in another. Liz said it felt different—"Not bad, just different." Of course, once she'd spoken the words I couldn't shake them.

With my chin resting across the barrel of my shotgun, dropped against a crossbar on the tree stand, I tried to imagine a time when Liz and I would be happy again. Maybe in a few months, after the birth of our second child, all this spite would wash away, like the film on a dirty window. I was working hard to picture us in bed together, lustily entwined, when two loud pops shook me from my thoughts.

Tony had lowered himself to the ground, and I could see a wispy coil of smoke rising from the mouth of his gun. The air smelled of cordite and roasted turkey. I quickly climbed down from my tree stand and followed in his tracks, my boots crunching against the ice. He had shot a doe behind her front shoulder. The animal was collapsed in the snow, head tilted up in an almost regal manner as she struggled to breathe. She had onyx-black eyes and lashes that curled delicately at the ends. Her ears were twitching as though she was batting away insects. A misty spume of blood erupted from her shiny nostrils.

Tony removed a long knife from a sheath on his belt and approached her from behind. He crouched between her front and rear legs, waiting for her to die. Together we sat in silence, watching the movement of the deer's ribcage growing slower and slower. Finally, Tony plunged the knife into the white fur near her forward legs and drew down toward her rectum, splitting the belly as he went. With a large stick employed like a crowbar, Tony pulled apart the two flaps of skin.

"Shit," he said, turning his face from an odor like burnt cabbage—it came from an accidental gash he'd made in the animal's stomach.

He reached into the belly and pulled out a slithery wig of intestines. The liver and kidney and lungs were still warm, and tendrils of steam lifted from them as they lay in the snow. I watched Tony's arm disappear into the hollow cavity again.

"Hold this," he said, moving his shoulder sideways.

I placed my gloved hands together, palms up, and stepped forward. He dropped the deer's heart—scarlet and marbled with papery blue veins—into the cradle of my fingers.

It took us about forty minutes to drag the doe's gutted body back to Tony's truck. By the time we reached a stony ridge near the roadway, a spike of sunshine emerged from the scrubbed gray sky, dancing against the deer's sandy fur. It reminded me of the coat on a friend's Labrador retriever, a dog named Layla that Liz and I had watched over a weekend several years earlier. We'd taken the dog to a park and let her run loose, darting around picnic tables. I remember feeling especially close to Liz that afternoon—she'd sat between my outstretched legs with her shoulders leaning against my stomach, and I brushed her hair aside and rested my cheek on the back of her warm neck. We talked about names, boys and girls, for the day when we had children. It all seemed so immediate, so real, that we practiced calling out our favorite ones to imaginary sons and daughters chasing after the dog—Lily and Sawyer, Emma and Lucas.

Kneeling at the side of the road, I caught my breath as Tony searched for rope to bind his deer to the hood of the truck. "Jesus," he said, tapping my arm. "You can get rid of that thing already—I was just breakin' your balls."

My eyes had gone blurry and wet. I turned my head, pretending I'd been on the wrong side of the wind. I gazed down at the doe's naked heart, still resting in my left hand. It wasn't easy to watch something beautiful get torn apart in such a violent and careless way.

At this time of the afternoon, with the sun dangling above the horizon like a high-wattage bulb, it's difficult to see through the window. I can barely make out his figure standing at the counter. (Has he paid yet? Is he talking to the owner?) When the door finally swings open, he's carrying his dry cleaning, wrapped in plastic, draped across his forearm. He's still wearing his uniform.

On his way to the parking lot he slows to light a cigarette. I shuffle along behind him, my heart chugging frantically.

"Um, excuse me?" I say, in a voice that's high and brittle. "Officer Keesey?"

His shoes are so shiny that even at a few paces I can see my own distorted reflection in their gleam. I take a moment, gather myself. Then the words start pouring from my mouth at a savage rate.

In truth, all he needs to hear is one syllable: *vig*. He begins walking again, hitching his dry cleaning to a hook inside the back door of his car.

"Listen up," he says, crossing his arms. The movement changes the angle of his badge, turning it toxic orange with sunlight. "I'm gonna tell you the same thing I told your boss: I pay my debts. But I'm not handing out free money."

I've rehearsed a silly little speech about the nature of this business, and the need for a *vigorish* to keep bookmakers from going bust. But he interrupts me, blowing smoke through both nostrils.

"I'm not negotiating," he says, tapping his belt—a belt that, incidentally, carries an automatic pistol, a taser, a nightstick, and handcuffs. "So, if you have something in mind—if he sent you here to rattle me—then let's get to it."

I nod, slow and empty. Standing in the parking lot, I wait as he lowers himself into his car. Finally, as if to demonstrate how unthreatened he feels by my presence, he makes a call on his cell phone. He's talking and laughing—once he even slaps the dashboard in delight. When he's finished, he drives across the lot and down a low-grade decline toward the merging roadway. He never looks back, refusing to acknowledge my image in his rear-view mirror, my feet still planted in that place where blacktop and gravel meet grass.

There were a great many temptations, villainous nicknames I could've programmed into my cell phone and conjoined perpetually to Liz's number. I considered downloading a cartoon devil that would appear in the phone's tiny window every time she called. But I recognize it's not the type of example I want to set for my daughters. I have a Pavlovian response to Liz's calls: the sharp stitch of a distance runner beneath my left ribcage. She usually wants to make a last-minute change to our shared parenting schedule, or maybe she didn't receive her monthly support payment.

This is in stark contrast to the way I felt when Liz called during our early months dating. We couldn't wait to speak with each other, share the details of our days. Conversations often lasted entire car rides—so long, even, that I'd sit in my driveway, the concrete cool under the heels of my hands, because I didn't want them to end.

But somewhere it all turned fragile—not with a mighty blow but, rather, with a dull and constant pecking. Our love was a beautiful orchid that had been neglected, left outside during a frost. There were times, in the beginning, when the only thing we wanted was what we had. An unexpected caress, a compliment about her outfit or new haircut. Maybe a genuine curiosity about her job as office manager for a construction firm. But casually, as the days passed, our shared kindness was replaced by something different—withdrawn apathy followed, in close succession, by sudden contempt. We'd lost our hold on the one thing that truly mattered. And the more we tried to pull it close again, the more it slithered through our joined fingers like a vital mucus. I wish it could've turned out differently—for Liz, for me and the girls. Still, I don't believe anything would've saved us.

We simply didn't have the proper components to stay together for the long haul.

The afternoon sun is blazing down as I stand in the shadow of an innocuous office complex, surveying the mirrored windows, granite benches, slim sidewalks carved from vibrant green swatches of lawn. An intentionally battered wooden sign reads *River Run Plaza.*

Three times I walk around the largest building, my hot fist bumping against my thigh. I try to calm myself with a Krav Maga breathing technique—I have business to conduct. A cement patio, listing sideways, reminds me of a date early in my courtship with Liz. We'd met for coffee and dessert on the open-air terrace of a French-themed café near her apartment. It was a warm evening and a row of boxed trees was threaded with strings of icicle lights. We sat on wire chairs, peering across a lacy tablecloth. There is something exhilarating and addictive about gazing through the peepholes of a new relationship: a chance to discover—and weigh—the various quirks of a prospective partner. I watched with a mixture of joy and fascination as Liz used a teaspoon to dig out the filling of her lemon pie because, in her words, she only liked "the inside part." I found this revelation endearing, matched later by a photograph she pulled from her purse of a four-year-old version of herself lying limp and shut-eyed across a picnic table. "See what I mean," she said. "When I'm tired, I can fall asleep anywhere." Afterward, we wandered for blocks with our index fingers looped together, tenuously, as though tethered to helium balloons.

I'm still tight with anger during my elevator ride to the fourth floor. I stare at my reflection in the coppery doors, my left heel nervously kicking the wall. It's nearly dinnertime and most people have gone home for the day. I move gradually along the outside of the cubicles, reviewing rows of gray and white nameplates.

Many of the employees at Reece & Goble, an independent accounting firm, have made feeble attempts to personalize their workspaces. There are framed photographs of family members, pennants and posters of professional sports teams, hand-clipped cartoon panels, bumper stickers, decals, wooden plaques with inspirational sayings. Dorothy Karns has painted intricate daisies around her name with Wite-Out. I nearly stumble over a small Astro-Turf mat with an ivory hole die-cut from its center. Several golf clubs lean against a neighboring doorway. I pass a kitchenette that smells of burnt coffee and microwaved leftovers.

It's been nearly two weeks since I first tried contacting Roy Hibbert. I've left him a number of phone messages. Three times I visited his apartment building, twice ringing his buzzer without getting a response, and once sneaking in behind an elderly woman who'd been walking her dog. I knocked on his door long enough to bring a curious neighbor into the hallway.

He's sitting behind a dark, L-shaped desk, illuminated by his computer terminal. He looks about forty, with a receding hairline and rough skin. Near his elbow rests a tottery stack of manila folders, spiny-edged papers sticking out at random. A small replica of London's Big Ben ticks between twin mugs filled with writing utensils and blue-handled scissors. Tacked neatly across his bulletin board are four symmetrical columns of white bond paper—phone extensions, important dates, instructional shortcuts. On the corner of his bookshelf is an old birthday card—not a Silver Springs—showing an office worker posted glumly behind his desk. Against the far wall sits a black, three-drawer file cabinet with a college basketball schedule taped to it. There's also a transparent glass bowl filled with colorful M&Ms.

I knock softly on the plastic molding of his cubicle.

"Two down," he says, peering into a binder fanned across his lap.

"Pardon?"

"Jefferson is two doors down." He pauses, lifting his head for the first time. "Oh—I thought you were the delivery guy."

We stare silently at each other for a few seconds.

"I'm here for Mr. Eugene."

Perhaps it's the comfort of his surroundings, but he doesn't seem alarmed. He leans back in his chair, threading his fingers together behind his neck.

"I got your message."

"*Messages,*" I say, emphasizing the last syllable—*jhez.*

"I was gonna call him today." There's a silver-plated letter opener lying beside his phone. "I really like Auburn on Saturday."

"You're down two dimes."

"That's what I'm saying—I want to put it on Auburn, giving six."

I shake my head, lifting a heavy crystal paperweight and shifting it between my palms. "You've gotta pay off first."

He begins to look uncomfortable, hands dropping to his lap. Distracted, he moves his binder from one thigh to the other.

"That's a lot of money," he says, any edge of bravado now gone from his voice.

"Right."

I've never had a problem reconciling the physical part of this job—especially on days when I'm stoked by the residual madness that comes after most dealings with my ex-wife. In truth, I'm grateful for the release. Nobody put a gun to Roy Hibbert's head and made him wager more money than he could afford to lose.

"Well…what…" he stammers, "what happens if I don't have it?"

"We'll give you some time—a few weeks. Charge you points."

He nods, seemingly relieved to learn that we're not opposed to negotiation. I replace the paperweight on the corner of his file cabinet. Then I take his letter opener, wiping it clean against the forearm of my shirt. He looks stunned when I jab the point into the short webbing between his left pinkie and ring finger. I lean forward and my body's weight drives the letter opener through his flap of skin and into the desk below. He squeals, but not loud enough to draw interest from his fellow accountants.

After removing the blade, he dabs at a cuticle of blood with paper napkins he keeps stored in a drawer. He wants to say something, but one of his colleagues suddenly appears.

"Hey, do you have any 8917s?"

Hibbert nods, gesturing to a tidy row of vertical files.

"Blue folder," he says, hiding his injured hand between his knees.

Together we watch his visitor rummage for forms.

"Sorry for the interruption."

After the visitor returns to his desk several cubicles away, I write my phone number on a sticky note and press it against Hibbert's breast pocket.

"Don't lose this," I say. "I'll need something by Thursday."

He nods, now clutching his hand beneath his left buttocks. I reach forward and he jumps. I scoop a plastic spoonful of M&Ms from their bowl, tossing them one at a time into my mouth. The candies are slightly stale, limp and waxy. After I dump the remaining few into a trash can near the kitchenette, I notice green and orange tiger stripes across my palm. I lick away the stickiness. As I wait for the elevator, Hibbert scurries through the cubicle maze behind me. I think I can hear him asking for a Band-Aid.

The early days are filled with promise and pleasure. Everything's still possible in this new dimension of us. And because I want the feeling to last—concealing my flaws for as long as possible—I've intentionally limited my contact with Nina. Our phone conversations have been brief and infrequent. I've loaded my schedule with make-believe meetings and imaginary engagements. Our next date is still lingering in the distance, enticingly, like a strawberry sundae after a plate of spinach. I've become a furnace of pheromonal heat, rattly with anticipation. Each afternoon I listen eagerly to my phone messages, hoping to hear her voice.

Earlier in the week, I sat through another agonizing RFI meeting. There were more new concepts—personalized storybooks, raised wording on sheets of tin, cardboard foldouts with slots for photographs. The tide of voices became overwhelming; more than once, I nearly drifted to sleep. Then I started thinking about Nina—the way the streetlight caught against her hair; the smell of her neck and wrist; the trill of her laugh as it rose along her throat. She wore silver rings on her forefinger and thumb. During long silences at dinner she tapped them together like castanets. I watched her pull a loose thread from her sweater using her teeth. When she drank, I noticed a fine, C-shaped scar beneath her chin. She told me it happened when she was six. She chuckled, slapping the table, and explained how she'd been playing circus with her brother. He was a lion tamer; she was a lion. As she leaped through a hula hoop, she caught her thigh—her brother was pulling it in the opposite direction—and struck the driveway with her face. "There was so much blood," she said, tracing the puckered skin with her fingertip, "that I needed a whole box of Kleenex on the ride to the emergency room." But the worst part, she recalled, was the drive home from the hospital. Her mother had stopped for a bucket of fried chicken. "I was so hungry," she said. "But I was all bandaged up. I couldn't eat solid food—the doctor said chewing might tear my stitches—for, like, three days."

Seated in my meeting, I tried to summon this image of Nina, nearly the same age as Tig, in the back of her mother's station wagon. Her unbalanced pigtails resembling geysers of rusty water leaking from her head. Hitched below her lemon-drop lips was an upside-down turban of gauze and adhesive tape. I could almost picture her eyebrows arched in anger as the smell of warm chicken filled the car.

I didn't realize we were going around the room, one at a time, offering final suggestions for this stage of the RFI project. Twice my name was called before I shook from my daydream. I had to scramble—give them the only thing I could snatch from my imaginary scrapbook haze. There was the gauzy, white dressing on six-year-old Nina's chin. In that moment of desperation, the gauze appeared to me like fragile and wispy lace. It suddenly seemed reasonable, inspired even, to propose greeting cards with lace borders.

"I like it," said one of the designers, nodding her head. "Perfect for baby announcements and wedding showers."

"My mother used to sew dresses," said another designer. "I think she still has a box of lacy fabric in her attic. Maybe I can dig it up for the prototypes."

"Well done," said Jamie Mason, a lackey in the company's content management division. He was tracking the various ideas on a leather-bound legal pad.

A few minutes later we took a break to replenish our soft drinks and use the restrooms. One of the copywriters, Bill Larone, patted me on the back. "Nice save," he whispered. I basked in the afterglow of my unfamiliar success. For now, my "team" had a different opinion of me. And, if nothing else, it would give me a little positive ammunition during my next job review.

The sound resembles the plucking of a high-pitched stringed instrument. Half-asleep on my couch, I hear the noise above an old movie playing on TV. Then comes wood on wood—a *thuda-thud* of the rear screen door against its frame. In the muted darkness of my back porch, I can see the skinny orange kitten, its fur pressed into sooty gray darts, clutching the screen with its claws. The other day the girls made me buy a small sack of cat food, each nugget formed like a different feline delicacy—salmon, drumstick, rib-steak. I pour the food into a cereal bowl and push open the door. Tentatively, the kitten inches forward. He sniffs the floor, the bowl. Then he retreats back to the porch. Again, he moves forward and starts eating—I can hear the little shapes crunching between his teeth. He pauses and lifts his crooked head, pawing the left side of his mouth.

When he's finished he takes several cautious steps deeper into the house. Suddenly, as though pricked by a needle, he explodes down my hallway, racing from room to room like a bead of water on a hot skillet. His claws pinch and scrape the floorboards.

"Whoa—take it easy," I say.

He flies across my stocking feet and leaps against the door, his nails now clinging to the interior of the screen. Slowly, I nudge the handle and the kitten drops to the porch. He runs across the yard, triggering the motion-sensor lights, and disappears through a thorny hedge beside the garage. For a long moment, I stare into the leafy green bushes, waiting for him to return.

This afternoon there's only two of us. Callie's at a friend's house working on a math project. In the rearview mirror, I can see Tig's head cocked sideways. She vigorously scratches her chin with the eraser of a pencil.

"Dad?"

"Yes, hon?"

My wipers squeak in the steady rain. They're old and brittle, turning my windshield into a slurry mess. I have to crane my neck and squint to see the road.

"How come boys' underpants have lines on them?"

"Lines?"

"You know," she says, touching the pencil to her lips. "The lines in front."

It takes a moment before I realize what she means.

"Oh," I say, chuckling. "They're actually overlapping flaps of fabric—so boys can stand up when they go pee."

"Whaddya mean?"

"Well…" I pause, trying to think of a delicate explanation—one that will make sense to a seven-year-old girl. "Sometimes, when boys only have to go pee—"

"Not poop."

I nod my head.

"Sometimes when boys only have to pee they stand up. And they poke their, um, penises through the slots in their underpants. That way they don't have to unfasten their belts and pants and undies."

"Girls don't pee standing up."

"No, they don't."

"Do boys ever miss the toilet and pee on the ground?"

A large truck pulls in front of me, splashing the car—and my clouded windshield—with a fat slap of water.

"I suppose they do."

"Have *you* ever peed on the ground?"

"Gee, I hope not," I say, smiling back at her. "At least not on purpose."

She giggles.

"Maybe somebody could walk into the bathroom while a boy's peeing. And he could turn around and—" she takes a quick breath "—get pee on them."

"Yuck!"

She's now laughing harder, kicking the back of the front seat. "That'd be gross."

"Oh, you're just being silly," I say, stealing another peek in the mirror.

She jiggles with delight, lifting her legs so I can see the dimpled soles of her sneakers. I wonder what causes her to think of these things. Did someone put the idea in her head? Her little mind racing from one disconnected subject to the next. Juice boxes, ID bracelets, ten extra minutes of recess. Even the overlapping flaps on boys' underpants. New words, awkward and unpronounceable, that sail through her consciousness. Half the time she doesn't know what they mean, just a collection of familiar symbols. Several months ago, I remember the two of us watching a TV commercial that featured a couple in a long embrace. "Why are they *sexing?*" she asked, struggling both with form and definition. In truth, "sexing" could've meant any number of things to her—sprinting down a beach, rubbing someone's back, the soft arch on the inside of a person's foot.

Before we reach the next intersection, she nods her head contentedly. Maybe she's satisfied with her image of some boy accidentally urinating on his father's shoes. Or perhaps she has moved on, thinking about popcorn or amusement parks or a song on her radio earlier in the day.

For many years I didn't have a place for all my anger. Sleepless, I'd lie in bed and think about a recent fight with Liz, the right words only later coming in the right order. Her voice would rise and rise, drowning my reply in a cascade of ratty feedback. Often I'd wonder if this would be the day she'd finally hear me. Instead, it would all slip greasily away. We'd repeat the same mistakes, find ourselves in some endless cycle of tucks and jabs. My emotions were suddenly divided: a part of me was fixated on our incessant bickering, and another part was focused on protecting our daughters, terrified and confused, watching from nearby—a kitchen window, the back seat of my car, the open space of a parking lot.

One spring afternoon, I remember waiting for the girls in Liz's driveway when I noticed that the side door of her house wasn't fully closed. I leaped from my car and pulled the door shut, causing the knob to yank loose in my hand. I could hear the other half drop—*tink!*—inside the house. By the time the girls had climbed into my back seat, Liz was standing beside me. There was no exchanged greeting—a quick nod, instructions for the following day. She was already flush with annoyance. As I clutched the brass knob, she shouted and brayed, slugging the doorframe with her square fist. Like everything else that had gone wrong in her life, this too was my fault. She claimed my constant double-checking of doors—making *sure* they were locked—had caused the knobs to grow weak. It didn't matter that I hadn't lived in the house for years.

I stood silently, my daughters' sweet faces staring back at me through tempered automobile glass. The choice was simple. I could defend myself, engage in a ridiculous argument with Liz about a doorknob that had finally broken free in my hand. Or I could walk away, which, in this case, meant calling a handyman to repair the busted door and—"as long as he's coming," insisted Liz—have him haul off the old water heater from the basement.

It had taken me years of evolution to reach this place—an understanding that no higher purpose would be served by fighting in front of my daughters. But I was left with the taste of resentment on my tongue, a sourness I couldn't spit out. I would often stand in a hot shower and replay a different ending to our most recent encounter, violent and felonious. "You want me to *pay* for a new doorknob?" I'd imagine saying. Then, in my stormy mind's eye, I'd usher the girls inside the house before cracking their mother with a tire iron. Even in this warped fantasy, my forearms tighten with tension.

A friend of mine once suggested meditation. "It'll help you clear your head," he'd said, offering me a book by a Buddhist monk. I tried it a few times, sitting cross-legged on the floor of my quiet living room. But invariably I wasn't able to extinguish the inferno that simmered beneath my calm exterior. Maybe I'd recall one of Liz's insults, or a painful line of questioning from our divorce trial, and suddenly I was picturing myself thrusting a Phillips screwdriver through her attorney's kneecap. I could see him lying on the courtroom floor, convulsing in pain, a worm of blood winding down his shiny trousers. The rage would overtake me like a seizure, pushing my imagination past the limits of sanity. Now there was also physical movement—the heel of my palm striking the sofa as I broke his nose and dragged him necktie-first into an old steam radiator.

For the rest of my life, or at least the next eleven years—until my legal accountability for the girls has ceased—I'll be inextrica-

bly tethered to Liz and, by definition, to this bottomless cauldron
of animus. Sometimes the weight is crippling. I keep looking
for better ways to manage my relationship with Liz and, ines-
capably, my associated rage. There are support groups, websites,
textbooks written by psychology experts. "Try videotaping her
next outburst," said my lawyer after an ugly incident. "We can
hold her in contempt of court for violating your shared parenting order."

About eighteen months into our separation, I was forced to
give a deposition. I sat in a conference room and drew geometric
shapes on a yellow legal pad. There was a nautical theme to the
three paintings hanging from the walls—a fishing boat, a schoon-
er on the high seas, a lighthouse at dusk. Across the table sat
an attorney who represented one of my creditors, First Federal
Bank—I'd fallen woefully behind on my MasterCard payments,
and I owed them nearly seventeen-thousand dollars. There was
also another five thousand on a Visa card, and monthly car vouchers and mortgage payments. Eerily detached, I listened as my lawyer explained how the court had made an error in my temporary
support payments—they were garnishing more than twice the
appropriate amount from my biweekly paychecks. Several times
we'd been scheduled to speak with a magistrate about the mistake. But before every hearing Liz's lawyer would file another
continuance. *This is how poverty feels*, I recall thinking.

After the ninth continuance, I broke the law, if only a tech-
nicality. It was a warm June morning and I was dressed for court.
On my drive downtown I received a call from my lawyer, who
told me the continuance had been granted. Though I was legally
prohibited from speaking to the magistrate without either Liz
or her attorney in attendance, I waited in the hallway outside
his office. A couple hours passed. Finally, a few minutes before
lunch, I intercepted him near the restroom. The words came in
a feral rush—months of grief and frustration hastily uncorked.
I pleaded with him to schedule a make-up conference for later
in the week. "I've reached the end of the line," I said, my voice
trembling. "I'm broke." I told him I didn't have enough money

to pay for the parking garage beneath the courthouse. Palms together, I leaned forward in supplication and begged for compassion. As I started to cry, my words became even less coherent. I told him about my creditors; I told him about taking money from my then-three-year-old daughter's piggy bank to pay for gasoline. There had also been a call to my mother, I said, the kind of call no middle-aged son wants to make. I needed to borrow money to pay for my utilities. (Try explaining to your daughters why the lights don't work.)

The magistrate took me by the elbow and led me into the restroom. He handed me a couple paper towels to dry my eyes. Then, standing before a urinal, he promised to do what he could.

Every day we read newspapers or watch TV and, invariably, a story will come to our attention that causes us to shake our collective heads. *Oh, people are sick.* We each have a moral compass—some nebulous line in the sand that we *know* we're not willing to cross, regardless of circumstances. But then the road gives way beneath our feet. And, suddenly, we're all turned around, desperate to get back to that place we were standing. Would you do *anything* to make your life whole again? What if you had two little girls whom you loved dearly? What would you be willing to do for *them*?

The money had come from the back pocket of an old pair of trousers. A folded ten-dollar bill. And because it was found money, I treated it as such: I bought a Partagas Lonsdale and smoked it, slowly, on one of the black leather couches at Gilberto's. Maybe if I had used the money for groceries or if I'd smoked the cigar a little quicker or if I'd left the first time I thought about leaving, none of this would've happened. But I was talking to a guy named Navigator Bob—he was big and friendly and excited about a new motorcycle he'd purchased earlier in the week. His cell phone started ringing, but he couldn't extract it from his pocket because something was blocking its path. After a couple seconds, he removed a giant fist of cash—dirty green bills double-banded into a tight cylinder. There were questions and more questions. Then, weeks later, an introduction to Mr. Eugene.

"I have a daughter," said Mr. Eugene, finally, fishing for a connection. "And a *challenging* ex-wife."

The job didn't require a significant learning curve. There was a name and a phone number, maybe an address. There was also a specific dollar figure.

My first collection was at a carpet and flooring store in a strip mall on Mayfair Road. I stood in the parking lot for twenty minutes, gathering my nerve. I'd made two calls to Navigator Bob, who assured me there wouldn't be any need to get physical—he knew the guy. Later, I learned that violence was rarely required; the *threat* of violence was usually enough to convince people to part with their money. As I walked to the back of the store, I grew lightheaded from the chemical smell of new carpeting and my racing pulse.

Adam Gravitz sat in a windowed office, behind a desk with a wooden nameplate that read *The Boss*. He was talking on the phone when I reached his doorway. He raised an index finger and rolled it against the air, as if to suggest he was anxious to reach the end of his conversation.

This could go horribly wrong, I remember thinking, gauging my distance from a large black security guard who was wandering the showroom floor. But Gravitz finished his call and I introduced myself, gently closing the glass door with my foot. When he turned away it felt like my heart would explode. Was he calling the cops? Reaching for a weapon? Instead, I watched him open the door to a wooden end table, revealing a small charcoal-colored safe.

"The Magic Kingdom," he said, counting out fifty-three hundred dollars in new bills.

"Excuse me?"

"Oh, I'd promised to take the wife and kids to Disney World —the Magic Kingdom—for spring break," he said, slipping the money into a manila envelope. "This is our vacation."

There was nothing else. Maybe a few words about a power forward on the Phoenix Suns who'd missed his free throws. Afterward, I sat in my car, doors locked, and counted the money three times.

The elevator is enormous, nearly the size of a physician's waiting room. Against the rear wall sits a crescent-shaped desk with a receptionist who wears her hair in a tightly wound bun. I can feel us trembling with movement; the crimson numbers have flickered into triple digits. Suddenly, a large window appears, and I watch as we're carried above an assortment of neighboring rooftops. I begin walking toward the receptionist—I want to know when we're going to reach our destination. But my feet are losing traction against the slick floor and my arms flail wildly, as though swimming through an imaginary current. Then the air tastes sour and toxic. I can feel a hand on my shoulder, moving and squeezing…

The noise rises out of the darkness. It's a familiar voice, in achy tones, now whining close to my ear.

"Dad," says Tig, her fingers buried in the fabric of my undershirt.

She's shaking me and I can see her pale knee folded against the edge of my mattress.

"Dad," she says again. "I can't sleep."

A cluster of jumbled words skip across my dry throat. I wonder if I spoke them aloud—to Tig or my elevator receptionist?

"Can I call Mommy?" asks Tig.

It's nearly four thirty. I reach into the night and hug Tig close to my chest. She's crying now and I feel her damp eyelashes against my neck.

"Did you have a nightmare?" I ask, though I know otherwise. She shakes her head.

Yesterday afternoon, as I waited for the girls beside my car, Tig's teacher, Mrs. Archer, waved me into the school. We sat across from each other on a pair of miniature chairs, my knees rising near my armpits. According to Mrs. Archer, Tig had used a hefty textbook to destroy a diorama of Lincoln's bedroom built by John Martin.

"She was quite animated," said Mrs. Archer. "I was very surprised—she's usually such a sweet, even-tempered girl."

Mrs. Archer wanted to know if, perhaps, Tig was experiencing some difficulty outside of school. I shook my head and shrugged. "Nothing unusual," I said, though it's hard to know when the splintery pieces of the girls' busted life will draw blood.

During my meeting with Mrs. Archer, Tig sat in the hallway and blinked back tears. She had never been in trouble at school and she wasn't sure what came next—how her parents, who could rarely find common ground, would respond to this sudden delinquency. By the time we reached the parking lot, Tig was crying so hard her face had turned red. I was caught between diametrically opposed poles—I wanted to punish my daughter for her curiously destructive behavior; and I wanted to comfort her, let her know that everything would be alright.

"Ooooh," said Callie, standing near my car. "Tig did something bad."

"Keep your nose out of other people's business," I said.

But maybe it was *all* of our business—this rough road Liz and I had erected for our daughters might only get worse. Hidden beneath every mile of pavement was another potential hazard that wouldn't reveal itself for years, slippery and dangerous as mercury.

In the glow of my digital clock, I see Tig looking up at me. She apologizes for "smashing" John Martin's project, claiming she got angry when he pushed her on the playground during recess. I kiss her softly on the back of her head and rock her in my lap.

Before my daughters were born, I had a great many notions about "good" parenting—my intended reactions to certain types of behaviors. But now I often feel as though I've failed them. The only thing I want is for my girls to be happy, and that seems impossible given all they've witnessed between their mother and me. I wonder when Tig's fuse first started to blossom. Would she have these same vengeful desires if she'd been raised in a more conventional family? I wish Liz and I could put our differences aside—maybe have a brief conversation about Tig's little misstep without looking to cast blame. We could discuss the proper ways to discipline her; both of us on the same page.

My baby girl is still weeping, and in the empty night I only want her sadness to go away. I gently squeeze her skinny thigh between my index finger and thumb. I start singing a song from when she was little, barely above a whisper.

> Once there was a way to get back homeward,
> Once there was a way to get back home,
> Sleep pretty darling do not cry,
> And I will sing a lullabye.

She pushes away from me, her hands still spread across my forearms.

"But I *am* home," she says.

"You are."

"Where was the girl going?"

"What girl?"

"In the song."

"I'm not sure," I say, wiping Tig's face with a corner of my bed sheet. "It's only a song—from when you were a baby. Do you remember it?"

She shakes her head. Then she lies down beside me, her tiny feet rubbing against my inner calf. We are quiet for a long time, until I'm almost certain that she's asleep. But then she moves, suddenly, turning her face across my shoulder.

"It was pretty good," she says.

"What?"

"John Martin's project."

She lowers her head again and closes her eyes. In the waning darkness, I see a triangular indentation across her wrist caused by the zipper of her sweat jacket.

On the lower level of a Tudor-style carriage house is a two-car garage that smells of oil paints and turpentine. She's wearing denim overalls and a frayed t-shirt. An inverted wire coat hanger holds a portable radio suspended from one of the ceiling beams. It's an old song, Boston's "More Than a Feeling," and I'm transported to a junior high dance in a brown and blue gymnasium. I remember standing against the wall, below six backboards that had been jackknifed against the rafters to create additional room. I was awkward and oversized; my feet, slightly pigeon-toed, seemed to make a half-dozen calibrations—nearly imperceptible movements against the crackling cartilage of my ankles—before they collided with the ground, like some steel-socketed landing gear on a clumsy aircraft.

It's strange the way some inconsequential memories seem to gather significance over the years. During maybe the first dance I ever attended, I couldn't muster the nerve to speak with any girls. I made my way down a neighboring hallway, "More Than a Feeling" echoing off the tinny lockers. I drank from a husky metal fountain, dribbling water across the front of my shirt. There was plenty of time to kill: Dale Tremont's mother wasn't picking us up for another ninety minutes. I strolled past a row of display cases in the school's front lobby, gazing at recent newspaper clippings, awards presentations, athletic ribbons and trophies. I kicked a forgotten tennis ball against a plastic garbage pail.

From nearby came a foreign sound, the gentle yelps of an animal, though not in distress. The door to the nurse's office was ajar, and slivery streetlight from an outside window spilled across the floor. I moved closer. The air was hot and tangy with the kind of moisture that comes from laboring bodies. In a quick glimpse, I could see Chad Van Der Meer, long and blond, sitting on one of the examination tables with a sandy-haired girl folded crookedly across his lap. His head was tipped sideways, eyes closed, his starfish-sized hand creeping down her back. Their cheeks were lean and hollow, pulled taut by distended chins. I'd never seen two people kissing this way, not people my age.

I quickly retreated to the checkerboard tile lobby. As I made my way again toward the gymnasium, music growing louder, I couldn't shake the image of Van Der Meer tongue-kissing with the sandy-haired girl. It seemed unreal, impossible even, that someone in my grade would already be making out (in the nurse's office!) when I couldn't bring myself to ask a girl to dance. Was the gap between our social development really that great? (It was.) How long would I have to wait for my first real kiss? (It would be another three years, on a grassy hill at Damon Park during a James Taylor concert.)

This is what's threading through my head, in the doorway of Nina's garage, when she screams and stomps her right foot.

"Christ! You scared the crap outta me."

She's surrounded by three enormous canvases, a triptych, featuring lifelike soldiers on a wintry battlefield. Some of the men are wounded and bloody, leaving burgundy boot prints in the crusty gray snow. Curiously, she's created a jumble of eras and weaponry—Revolutionary War-type Minutemen firing M203 grenade launchers, modern-day paratroopers toting sharpened spears and stone-head mallets, Confederate soldiers aiming crossbows into the black-crow darkness. Near the upper right-hand corner, a scrum of Prussians ready a catapult against a low-flying Apache attack helicopter.

"Is that Napoleon?" I ask, pointing toward a diminutive officer on horseback.

"Could be," she says.

"This is really amazing."

She thanks me, washing her hands in a large brushed-steel utility sink. Then she hoists herself onto a wooden table and dangles her feet, leaving her beefy-soled work boots to clomp together. When she reaches toward the ceiling, stretching limbs and back, her tiny t-shirt hikes past her ribcage, and I catch a glimpse of her stomach between the side panels of her overalls. The skin across her abdomen is tight and dimly pleated with muscles. I think she's talking, but I don't hear anything because I'm fantasizing about kissing her along the tender ridge of her pubic bone.

This next part happens so quickly I'm not sure if it's real or imagined. She leans sideways, popping the stiffness from her vertebrae, and I see a slender band of white cotton bisecting her lower hip. Then comes a dreamy flutter of erotic imagery—pebbly razor stubble bordering a triangle of coarse hair between her legs. Or maybe it's sheared to resemble a slim business card, no wider than twin sticks of chewing gum. Or, finally, I consider a hairless vagina, Nina's smooth labia squeezed together like curled fingers.

"You're early," she says.

A small box-shaped refrigerator, similar to the ones used in college dormitories, rests beneath the table. She nudges open the door with the toe of her boot, igniting the tinkling sound of glass bumping against glass. She retrieves two beers, then braces a bottle along the table's edge and slugs it with the heel of her hand. The cap hisses loose, tumbling to the floor like a damaged coin.

When I lean close to take my beer, a strand of her long bangs brushes across my cheek. I breathe deeply, my nostrils filling with a tart gust of perspiration. I'm caught by a vague sensation, pure and carnal. In this fleeting moment, it suddenly feels as though everything in my life can be made right by this one freckle-skinned woman. A single kiss, warm and composed, to help me forget my laundry list of troubles.

Craning forward, my lips touch the hidden slope on the back of her scalp. She wraps her arm around my waist, pulling me close, and we press our bodies together, collarbones connecting in a lopsided X. Then comes the hopsy stink of beer and evaporating paint remover. As I steady myself, I glance down and notice a hand-drawn heart on the side of her boot. I carefully move my fingers through the side of her overalls until they come into contact with her skin. But the beer's still cold, and when the bottle touches her body she jumps.

"You want something to eat?" she asks, shimmying down from the table.

I shake my head.

"Oh, come on." She moves to a wobbly staircase against the wall. "Don't be shy."

We make our way to her apartment—a cozy loft above the garage. The main room features a small kitchen, a dining table and chairs, a couch, a coffee table (with neatly arranged magazines and a book on Asian art), a pair of matching floor lamps, a hand-painted purple-and-white writer's desk, and an old television resting on a doily-covered peach crate. Her bedroom and bathroom are separated by narrow panels of matte-white drywall. Several framed canvases in various sizes, presumably painted by Nina, hang in random locations. In the far corner are a potted tree and a leafy philodendron, but no cats. Below one of the windows hunches a squat bookcase made of dark wood, crowded with colorful spines in assorted heights and widths. A large spiral-bound sketchpad and a tin of charcoal pencils are balanced against the arm of the couch.

"You okay with dairy?" she asks, placing a tray of cheeses on the kitchen counter. There's also fruit, crackers, and a crusty French baguette.

Her inquiry reminds me of someone I dated for a few months after college. I tell Nina how the girl was lactose intolerant and, during our breakup, she dropped a paper sack filled with everything I'd ever given her—old t-shirts, postcards, leaping dolphin earrings—on my doorstep. There was also a note in which she said she'd rather eat a giant bowl of cottage cheese than spend another day with me.

"Ouch," says Nina, pretending to gag.

My friends thought it was hilarious. For months, the letter remained tacked to the side of my refrigerator. "She's not lactose intolerant," said my buddy Doak. "She's *Fanning* intolerant."

Nina loads a sesame-seed cracker with Gouda and sliced strawberry.

I'm distracted by thoughts about what comes next. It's been a long time since I've been intimate with a woman and, sitting on a wicker stool, I begin to worry about my limbs and lips racing to their own reckless engine. My penis is already erect, pressed against the inside of my thigh. I'm fearful that a simple caress—on my wrist or elbow or knee—will push me to a state of near manic arousal. After taking a swallow of cold beer, I feel the wind preparing to rush from my lungs.

"Have you lived here for a while?" I ask, nervously tapping a red grape against my plate.

"Are you listening to me?" She cocks her head and smiles. "I just *told* you: I've been here since Christmas."

The back of my neck erupts with prickly heat. No, I haven't been listening to her—I'm not listening *now*. I bite the inside of my cheek, trying to force myself into paying attention. She's saying something about an icy driveway and a rental truck sliding into a lamppost. Then she raises her arm, revealing a short scar near the arc of her bicep. I nod, stupidly. But I'm thinking about the two of us lying on her floral comforter. It would only take a slight flick of my thumb to release the cleats on her overalls. There'd be gentle kissing below her naval, my eyelashes lightly tickling the skin of her pelvis…

She says something else that I don't hear. I'm staring into her eyes and, after a moment, it becomes clear that she's waiting for a response.

"I don't know," I say.

"You don't know if you want another beer?"

"I mean—" I take her hand and hold it against my chest. "Are *you* having another one?"

She shakes her head and fills two stemless glasses with the remains from a bottle of red wine. I follow her to the couch, walking hunched and hurried to conceal my erection. She gives me a funny look.

"My back is killing me."

She nods and lights three candles on the ledge beside us.

"I'm a little ripe," she says, pinching her t-shirt and lifting it from her body. "The afternoon got away from me—I was planning to take a shower."

She unfastens the straps on her overalls and folds the bib down across her lap. My heart's racing and, absurdly, it occurs to me for the first time that I should've jerked off in anticipation of this moment—built up my resistance after not having sex for many, many months.

We start slow and soft, our lips meeting sideways because of the angle at which we're sitting. Her mouth is warm and boozy. I roll my leg across her thigh, hooking her with my knee. After a few minutes my fingers crawl beneath her shirt, but she taps them casually down again.

"Whew—take a breath, boy," she says, reaching for her wine glass.

I slide to the corner of the couch and squeeze a throw pillow against the buckle of my belt. She lays her head on my shoulder, her hair fanning across my shirt. Maybe it's my story about the cottage-cheese girlfriend or the day's waning sunshine, hot as a dentist's lamp, that stirs her memory. But she starts telling me about an overnight camp in Maine that she attended the summer she turned fourteen. A row of clapboard cabins, painted bright red, stood between a small lake and a dark, endless forest. There were slow-turning ceiling fans, metal bunk beds, tattered rugs, and poorly measured swatches of mosquito netting stapled across the otherwise empty window frames. Near the tobacco-colored water, canoes crowded the shores like enormous melon rinds. According to Nina, it was a "*camp* camp"—a motion-picture version replete with swimming, sailing, bug-juice punch and lanyard kits for rainy days. In a form of old-school segregation, the boys' groups were named for birds of prey—falcons, eagles, hawks—and the girls' groups were named after more docile species—sparrows, thrushes, purple martins.

"I was a robin," says Nina, using her index finger to trace the veins along the inside of my wrist.

On Saturday nights, the camp held mixers around a bonfire that was half-encircled by parenthetically shaped columns of tumbled-smooth stones. There was also a large gazebo decorated with paper lanterns and braided spirals of white lights. The air stank of smoldering Citronella torches that pierced the pressed-dirt landscape. Bordering a sand-and-gravel pathway that slithered into the dense woods were several pairs of split-oak logs, bolted to abandoned railroad ties, which were used as benches. Behind a short hill that supported the camp director's cabin was a courtyard striped with pole-to-pole volleyball nets. In the pitch-black night, campers were told to avoid the area for fear of being clotheslined. Once, recalled Nina, a boating instructor concussed himself after sprinting forehead first into a steel post.

During one of these mixers, Nina sat waiting on the oak-tree benches for a friend. "Her name was Hannah," says Nina. "I think she was from Georgia." It was late—nearly time for an announcement over the loudspeaker that everyone should return to their cabins for the night. She could feel something move in the darkness behind her shoulder. Suddenly, a thin, sun-scorched face appeared from within a webbing of branches. He was a junior counselor, wearing chinos and a white polo shirt. His canvas belt had small blue anchors embroidered in its fabric. He tapped Nina on the back. "Come here," he said, pressing down a tree limb to free her path.

She followed him for about a dozen yards—until they'd reached a short clearing where Nina could see a wool, military-style blanket lying on the ground. There was an empty punch cup and an overturned half-pint of gin screwed into the mud. Nina wanted to run. But he was a couple years older and she feared what he might say about her the next day. They sat on the blanket, his arm now resting across her knee. His hands were dry and cold. She could feel a strange dizziness start along the slope of her right eyebrow. And she was trembling. The trees squeezed together in a swift picket fence—a pointy crown spinning and spinning against itself. In the distance, she could hear the playful sounds of other campers as they trudged back to

their rooms—cracking twigs, hand-slaps, high-pitched giggles.
Never in her life had she wanted to be somewhere else more
than at that moment…

He said something and smiled, revealing a front tooth that
was the color of weak tea. She stared at the tooth for several seconds, wondering how it got that way. Maybe he'd fallen from a
bicycle or been plunked by an errant elbow. It occurred to her,
still peering into his mouth, that he was a good deal bigger and
stronger than she was. For the first time since childhood, she
considered her size in relation to the outside world. She hadn't
the wit nor will to shed his ropy body if he moved any closer.

"Wanna mess around?" he asked, lurching forward with his
ugly dead tooth.

She was too frightened to speak—too frightened, even, to
shake her head.

An unfamiliar noise came from the woods behind them—a
foot stomping against a hollow bleach jug, or a counselor's clipboard striking a tree. He turned away and, in that sweet stillness,
Nina's legs lifted her from the blanket. Though her mind was
focused on the boy's fuzzy chin, thoughts clouded with perilous
images of the night ahead, she ran toward the blossom of light she
knew was a lamp affixed to the mess-hall porch. She moved with
wild abandon, twice failing to shield herself from stray branches
that smacked and scraped her face. Words she didn't hear came
from the boy. ("Hey, wait!" or "Where're you going?") But she
continued running until she saw the red wooden robin nailed
above her cabin's door. She was breathing so hard that with each
new gulp of oxygen the springs of her bed would shiver and
squeak.

"You okay?" asked Hannah, hanging her head down from
the top bunk.

There was a nod. Then she curled herself into a fetal position
with her spine against the headboard. She didn't sleep, instead
watching the evening's events replaying continually in her mind.
Pressed against the gummy crease of her right fist was a Swiss
Army knife her father had given her for camp.

"I'd never done physical harm to anyone," says Nina, still lying in the furrow of my arm. "But all that night I stared across our cabin. And if that boy had walked through the door, I would've stuck him with a knife."

In a lame attempt to lighten the mood, I wiggle my fingers across the back of her neck. But she waves them away, sliding down and resting her cheek on my chest. I can feel her warm breath through the fabric of my shirt.

I sigh loudly.

"What?"

We've reached the end. There may be more kissing, some petting. But, intentionally or not, she's drawn a line for tonight.

"That's an awful story," I say, rubbing tiny circles around her elbow.

"I hate it." She squeezes my hand. "I mean, he didn't really *do* anything. But I've never felt more helpless—and afraid."

"I'm sure."

"We're talking about something that happened *years* ago— when I was a kid. And I still catch myself wondering about that night. Crazy stuff. Like, what if I didn't get up and run?"

She adjusts her body, gaining leverage by pushing her fingers against the couch—an otherwise innocent movement that causes her wrist to bump against the zipper of my jeans. It's been an endless string of months since a woman has touched me below the waist, even accidentally, and my crotch is ablaze, finding hope where there's none. We lie together, silently, watching the shadows grow narrow. I'm nearly asleep when she interrupts me, her voice light and whispery.

"You're a big guy," she says, her speech vibrating across my sternum. "I bet there haven't been too many times that you've been afraid—I mean, *physically* afraid."

I shake my head.

As a tingling numbness shoots down my right leg, I twist my hips and find a fresh corner of seat cushion on which to rest my ass.

"Almost the opposite," I say, making a blocky fist and waving it—*Bang! Zoom! To the moon!*—over her head. "My size can make me seem imposing."

"You get what you want."

I nod.

"And that's such a bad thing?"

"Not usually," I say, smiling.

"So—"

"Well…" I exhale, watching a blue light blinking on her microwave. "Because I'm big and—for lack of a better description—*intimidating*, people sometimes expect a certain reaction."

She sits up, turning to meet my eyes.

"They assume you're going to—" she pauses, searching for the right words, "—get physical with them?"

"Sometimes."

"Really?"

I nod.

"And *do* you?"

From the manner in which she's now positioned herself, left arm forming a barrier between us, I can tell she's not comfortable with this potential revelation.

"I try to avoid it."

There is only silence. For a moment, she's staring into the space across my shoulder.

"But you've hit people?"

"I have."

"To get what you want?"

"I—"

"So, it's not just your size that's imposing?" We're no longer touching, her body now turned to face me. "Maybe you could injure someone?"

"That hasn't happened."

"But it could."

"I suppose it *could*," I say, scratching my chin. "But someone *could* drop a piano on my head."

She chuckles, breaking the sudden tension.

"Hawking greeting cards? I don't think so."

"Me neither."

She leans back, kicking her chunky boots onto the coffee table. The small black heart, sketched with permanent marker, jiggles from side to side. For the first time, it occurs to me that she may have blotted out a name that once filled the heart's interior.

Bordering the southern edge of Carbon Mills is a four-lane road called Ripley. It's hemorrhaging with strip malls and fast-food restaurants and warehouse-sized discount stores. Eventually, about five miles from town, Ripley bottlenecks into two gravel-covered lanes. At the second traffic light, across from a pair of cone-shaped structures where the Department of Transportation stockpiles great pyramids of rock salt, sits a small shed with blue neon burning from its doorways. The word *Dinks* is written in red cursive across a large chilidog fastened above the middle of three service windows. In the dozens of visits the girls and I have made to Dinks, we've never ordered anything that didn't include frozen custard—waffle cones, sundaes, milkshakes.

We're sitting on the last of four picnic tables, surrounded by a field overgrown with fescue and wild oat. Tig's using a plastic spoon to blend fudge sauce into her vanilla custard.

"That's disgusting," says Callie.

"I like it this way."

Callie's nibbling on a "red bonnet"—a chocolate-and-vanilla swirl with hardened cherry topping. I watch her feet shuffling in the dirt. Both girls are making pleasant humming noises from deep in their throats.

"Pretty good?" I say, raising my own dish.

They nod.

"Dad," Tig starts, wiping her mouth with the back of her arm. "What's your favorite thing in the world?"

"You girls."

Callie groans.

"Not like that," says Tig.

"You mean, what's my favorite *food*?"

"No—"

"What's the best thing that's ever happened to you?" asks Callie. "And don't say 'When you girls were born' or something stupid like that."

"Oh."

"Like if you won a contest," says Tig, offering a smile.

"Or a big trophy."

"Geez, that's a toughie…" Rising from the table, I toss my dish and napkins into a trash barrel. "Let's see." I pause, tapping my chin for emphasis. "Okay, this is *one* of my favorite things. You might think it's silly."

The girls exchange suspicious glances.

"When you were babies, Mom and I would wrap you tightly in soft flannel blankets—it's called *swaddling*—and lay you in the middle of our bed. I used to love curling up beside each of you, pressing my nose against the skin of your tiny necks."

"Sheesh," says Callie.

"You guys would rock and twist. My *favorite* part was the way you smelled—this mixture of sweet cream and talcum powder and clean linen." I move back to the table. "Sometimes, if my nose got too close to your mouths, you'd try sucking it. You thought it was Mommy's boobie."

"Eeeew," says Tig, laughing.

"That's so nasty," says Callie.

"But it's true."

"Maybe I was trying to *bite* you."

"Not me, Daddy," says Tig.

I give her a gentle squeeze on the shoulder.

As the girls finish their ice cream, Callie's eyes suddenly grow wide and worried. She scoots to the end of the bench and ducks her head beneath the table.

"What're you doing?" I ask.

"*Shhhhh*," she says, raising her index finger. "That's Adam Unger—from my school."

"You should say hello."

"Dad!" She slaps her knee. "I don't want him to see me."

"Why?"

"She has a crush on him," says Tig.

"I do *not* have a crush on him."

"You like him," insists Tig, nodding slowly.

"Dad!"

"Okay, okay." I walk to Callie's side, shielding her from a cluster of people standing near Dinks' menu board. "Finish up and we can go."

"*Adam*," says Tig, though not loud enough for the boy to hear.

"Tig! Shut up!"

"That's enough," I say, taking a paper napkin and playfully stuffing it into Tig's mouth.

In the car, Callie crouches low in her seat, beneath the line of the window. She's obscured by the door when Tig shouts Adam's name, again, as we pull from the parking lot.

"Dad!" says Callie, busting her sister in the arm.

Tig grabs her wound, then flails out and swats Callie on the side of the head. Both girls begin wildly exchanging blows across the back seat. With my eyes on the road ahead—a large truck's approaching from the opposite direction—I peek into the rearview mirror. Awkwardly, I lean back and windmill my arm, blindly swiping anything within reach. The girls scream and curse at one another.

"Guys!" I say, pinching a leg. "Stop it! Right now! Do you want me to get into an accident?"

"I don't care," says Callie. "She's such a bitch."

"*Callie!*"

"A 'bitch' is a girl dog," says Tig, still rubbing her arm. "And I love dogs. So, I'm glad you called me a bitch."

"Good, 'cause you *are* a bitch."

"Enough! Stop using that word—both of you."

They're quiet for a while. On my dashboard, an orange *check engine* light ignites for a few miles before turning dark again. Then comes something from one of the girls, a request, but I'm not paying attention.

"Dad, Dad, Dad," says Callie.

She calls for me several more times in an annoying staccato, *rat-a-tat-tat.*

"What?"

"Can you play my CD?"

"The fourth song," says Tig.

"No, just start at the beginning."

"Last time we were gonna hear the song I like, number four," says Tig, her voice sounding ragged and whiny. "But then we had to get out of the car."

I turn the radio to a sports talk station.

"Not *this*," says Callie.

"We're gonna listen to what *I* want for a change," I say, smacking the seat beside me. "This is what happens when you fight with each other."

"This sucks," says Callie.

"Callie!"

"What? 'Sucks' isn't a bad word. People *suck* things all the time. They suck lollipops and Lifesavers and cough drops."

Tightening my eyes, I shoot an angry look into the rearview mirror, though I'm not sure she can see me.

"You're being mean, Dad," says Tig.

"Keep behaving this way—you guys will *really* get a taste of mean."

After a few minutes of silence, I start feeling guilty. By tomorrow they'll be with their mother. If my moods were charted on an index card, most of the lows would be on evenings after the girls have been with me. In the beginning, when Liz and I first separated, I would often cry myself to sleep once I dropped the girls at their mother's house. Reluctantly, I press the CD button and allow their syrupy music to play for the rest of the ride.

"Thanks, Dad," says Tig, her head bobbing behind me.

Callie gives a thumbs-up sign.

Because I have no history with children, other than my own, it's difficult for me to evaluate their lives objectively. When they argue with each other—teasing and taunting and turning physical—it's hard to peel back all the layers. What part of their behavior should I ascribe to their parents' ugly divorce? What part is genetic? (Both Liz and I have woefully short fuses.) And what part is simply the typical conduct of young girls, sisters, who're so close in age?Often, I find myself deserving of blame: If I'd done something differently, been a better father, they wouldn't be facing such prickly odds. Against the advice of virtually every parenting manual, my resolution usually involves the purchase of small gifts or tokens—bejeweled sandals, charm bracelets, DVDs, colorful activity books. The journey seems too goddamn long, and a quick smile, regardless of any patterns I may be establishing, seems to help me sleep.

"This is a good one," says Tig, a few notes into a new song.

"It's from that movie we saw at Mimi's—about the girl who didn't know she was a princess."

Their hands move together, down and up, mimicking a dance they learned at last summer's camp. I take a different way home. Twice I drive around a neighboring block, letting the music play and play.

There are times when I try to force myself to remember something good from my marriage. Today I'm recalling the joy and wonder of watching Callie enter this world—an experience that was so pure and majestic it felt as though I was sailing on a heavenly slipstream. After Liz's water broke, we drove to the hospital with her feet planted against the dashboard. At a stoplight on

Fairview, she began practicing the breathing exercises we'd learned during Lamaze class—quick, whistly swallows of oxygen. "Eight weeks listening to that goddamn instructor," she said suddenly, "and this doesn't work at all." On the corner of Normandy, the pain briefly subsided and Liz spied one of her favorite diners. She asked what I thought about stopping for a grilled cheese and tomato sandwich.

"Probably not a great idea," I said.

"Jesus, I'm not crazy," she said, playfully socking me on the thigh. "I'd get it to *go*."

In the delivery room, she gripped my arm so tightly I feared she was cutting off my circulation. Her knees were high and loose strands of hair were plastered to her forehead with perspiration. According to Liz's physician, she was too far along for an epidural—"You're just gonna have to tough it out." She looked at me and rolled her eyes, as if to imply, *Is he serious?* I fed her ice chips and dabbed her neck with a cool compress.

"Think of someplace soothing," I said. "Imagine that you're on a warm, sandy beach and—"

She started laughing and grabbed the front of my shirt, pulling me close to her bedside.

"Really?" she said, her fingers turning white with pressure. "Is that the best you can do?"

Her smile turned flat, teeth against lower lip, and soon they were laying Callie, still attached by her umbilical cord, across Liz's chest. We squeezed each other's hands and watched Callie's skinny arms and legs flailing against the new air. Liz and I had our sweaty faces pressed together and I could taste the salt on my tongue. This was months before we began our incessant cycle of fighting, the animosity passed back and forth between us like a game of egg toss. We had a daughter, our first, and there was plenty of love to carry us forward.

My memories of Callie's birth were triggered by watching a pregnant woman and her husband shop for a gift at Gilberto's. I'm sitting on a couch, smoking a dark-leafed double corona, as the young couple examines a rosewood humidor.

"It's got a cedar lining," says Big Dave, who runs his fingernail along the humidor's interior wall. "It holds the right amount of moisture and gives the cigars a nice woodsy flavor."

Across from an oversize coffee table, Joe Baker, a retired plumber, flips through a glossy boating magazine. He takes a draw from his cigar and sets it against a brass ashtray shaped like a horse's head.

"This is the one," he says, removing a red marker from his shirt pocket and drawing a circle around a photograph. "Seventeen-footer."

I nod, staring numbly at the same sports highlights that have been playing on TV for the past hour.

"You fish?" he asks.

"Not in a while," I say.

Many years ago—when I was younger than Tig—my father took me fishing in Canada with some of his friends. My memories of our week in the northern wilderness are queer and disjointed. I remember stopping for hot glazed donuts during our long drive past the border. In the kitchen of our cabin, cases of Molson were stacked as high as the refrigerator, bottles turned to reveal a procession of slanted maple leafs. At night, I would lie on the couch and read comic books while the men played card games—poker, gin rummy, spades. One of the guys, called Doc, would nibble steadily from a bowl filled with cocktail peanuts and knuckles of raw garlic. Each day, a Manitoba Indian guided our three chartered Boston Whalers to various locations on the lake. And for lunch he'd carve our fish, frying walleye, bass, and perch in a blackened cast-iron skillet with butter and coarse sea salt. Over the same campfire he'd simmer cans of baked beans with fatty slabs of cured bacon.

During one rainy afternoon, I remember taking a piss in the woods. I could see the others, moving up and down like clustered oil derricks, in the smoky gaps between the trees. I heard the gentle rainwater beating against the forest's leafy canopy. Then came my father's laugh, thin and recognizable, from a place near the shore. I made my way back to the group. I was able to see what my father found so amusing: He'd baited a live frog to the end of his test line. But the tiny frog, in peril, was trying to pry its mouth from the barbed hook. Every time the frog attempted to push itself loose, it would flop sideways against my father's tackle box, hitting the plastic lid with a sickening thud. I felt a hard pit in my stomach—I wanted to race past these men I hardly knew and yank the frog from the fishing line, throw it back to freedom. But I was a small and frightened boy, still worried about what others might think of me.

More significantly, it's maybe the first time I recall being embarrassed by my father's behavior. As I stood near our boat, my sneakers growing damp with tidewater and spitting rain, I could feel my eyes purse with anger. There was a heavy stick lying in the sand, too wet for kindling, and I squeezed it in my fist. Twice I swatted the side of my leg, rapid blows—I wanted to know how it felt when wood struck bone. For a few seconds, I considered marching forward and hitting my father—on his wrist or forearm or shoulder. *This* would make him stop, I reasoned. I tried drawing my father's attention away from the frog by delivering larger and more powerful blows to my fibula, until, finally, the stick splintered at nearly the same time as I buckled in pain against the soggy ground.

"Jesus, boy," said my father, shaking his head. "What the hell are you doing?"

"Maybe he's been drinking our beer," joked one of the others.

"Don't do it, kid," said Doc. "It's killing your brain cells."

My father sat me on a rutted boulder, brushing away a slippery film of water before my jeans touched stone. I told him I thought the stick would break sooner and, when it didn't, I somehow felt obliged to finish the job.

"Look," he said, grabbing another large stick and snapping it easily with the force of his knee. "Next time, use your leverage."

I nodded.

He walked back to his friends. There was more laughter, but I couldn't hear what they said. By the time I boarded the boat again, after our dishes had been washed clean in the cloudy lake and stored in a canvas satchel that belonged to the Indian guide, the frog was hanging motionless from the fishing line. I ran my fingertips across its rubbery brown skin.

For the rest of the afternoon, huddled beneath my wet poncho, I thought about my father's cruelty. After the frog had been cut loose, its leathery corpse sloshing along the floor of our boat, I began to wish my father harm: a cinderblock anchor landing on his foot; the blade of his knife splitting his palm; or, I imagined, the long oar we used to paddle through shallow waters clocking him in the jaw. Days later, on our drive home, my father slammed his finger in the car door at a gas station—he staggered around in crooked circles, tracing the petals of an asphalt lily, stomping and cursing and shaking his wounded hand—and I wondered if perhaps I'd somehow caused his injury.

With a loud sigh, Joe Baker crosses his legs. He wears sneakers with Velcro fasteners—the kind favored by the very young and the very old. He asks me something about my daughters and, before I can answer, starts talking about his son.

"We're gonna share it," he says, removing a thread of tobacco from his tongue. "The boat—we're gonna buy it together."

I'm seated with my back to the shop's front door. A hand grasps my shoulder, squeezing twice. Then comes a soft slap closer to my chest. By the time I turn to make eye contact, Mr. Eugene is standing beside me, a tan and gold briefcase dangling from three fingers.

"Anything yet?" he asks.

I shake my head, fairly certain he's referring to Keesey.

"Okay." He heads toward his office in back. "Let me know."

I nod.

For some reason, I feel a twinge of guilt—as if maybe Mr. Eugene thinks I shouldn't be sitting here, puffing away on a six-dollar cigar, when there's work to be done. I rise to my feet and purposefully knock a large book about horse racing to the floor—I'm hoping the sound it makes will cause Mr. Eugene to look back; I want him to see my departure. Maybe it's all in my head, a bristly fabrication, but I can't afford the risk—I don't want to find myself on his bad side.

The juice is tart, peppery, causing my throat to burn and constrict. A few weeks ago, I started accidentally chewing nicotine-laced gum—square pellets that come packaged in a transparent plastic sleeve—when I lifted a few pieces from a table in Mr. Eugene's office. Later, half-jokingly, I told his assistant, Dove, I might become the first person to wean myself from the gum by turning to cigarettes. As I pull into the parking lot at Greenbriar Mall, my cell phone rattles against my passenger seat—its ringer still set to vibrate—and I can see Dennis Gaines's name on the small blue screen. I chew quickly, tucking the fresh gum near the back of my mouth.

"Fanning," he says.

Sometimes my car has difficulty making sharp turns—it grinds and squeals. I try steering into a space near the mall's side entrance, using both hands, with the phone pressed between my ear and shoulder.

"Yes? Dennis?"

There's a short, hollow pause, and I can tell he's put me on speakerphone.

"Listen, I spoke to Terry Leinas this morning—"

In a strange punctuation to Gaines's last sentence, the phone drops from my shoulder, bouncing twice against the door before landing on my floor mat. I can still hear his voice—"Fanning? Fanning?"—while I navigate the car's right front tire down from the curb.

"I'm here," I say, shifting into park.

"Did you catch that? I spoke to Terry Leinas this morning."

"Yes."

"He only wants the Appleseed line," he says. "Did you tell him that was okay?"

"No."

Between responses, I cover the mouthpiece of my phone and chew vigorously until my gum finally turns soft. "It's a whole program," says Gaines. I think I hear another voice in the background, clipped and staticky from the speaker mechanism. "To get Appleseed, he also needs to purchase Harvest and Homecoming."

Months ago, I sat in a conference room with other sales associates as Gaines explained, in excruciating detail, a new program in which various card lines would be sold together, inextricably linked. The takeaway was *packaged.*

"I understand."

"Okay," he says, followed by a short snapping noise. "Just wanted to make sure." He takes a deep breath. "I don't know where he got that crazy idea."

"Crazy."

"I know—right?"

"Right."

It begins to drizzle, tiny, caraway seed–sized drops that slowly fill my windshield. A few paces from the mall, a woman stops and reaches into her purse for a stubby umbrella. But when it refuses to lock into its upright, half-moon position, she holds the hem of the fabric across her head like a whiskery trash bag. A thunderclap in the distance makes her sprint the final two steps.

I finish my call with Gaines, turning to organize the samples in my briefcase. I mistakenly brought several mock-ups from our tony Silvercraft line—high-concept contemporary drawings on heavy cardstock. Despite its name, the Greenbriar's a middle-class mall with discount-type anchor stores, like Sears and J.C. Penney. Across from the food court is a little shop called Murphy's that sells mostly stationery, wrapping paper, and greeting cards with lower-end price points.

The air inside the mall is cool and dry. The smell of fresh popcorn comes from a red-and-white kiosk, where a teenage girl in a paper hat sits reading a textbook. She's surrounded by bins stuffed with a variety of popcorn products—caramel corn, cheddar corn, chocolate-drizzled popcorn, grapefruit-sized popcorn balls. At a neighboring kiosk, a dark-haired boy in an ill-fitting suit pitches accessories for cellular phones. There are battery chargers, ear buds, holsters for belts and handbags. He says something to the popcorn girl, who responds without looking up.

The display racks in Murphy's are neat and orderly—nearly as pristine as the retail models on the second floor at Silver Springs. Crowding the surface of a small table is an assortment of white stuffed animals, each holding a different greeting card between its fuzzy paws.

"We're dead," says Dub Murphy, who's arranging large binders filled with sample invitations along a back wall. "It's a bad time for the greeting card business."

"It's a bad time for *any* business," I say.

Dub Murphy nods. He's wearing a striped dress shirt with the cuffs rolled past his elbows. Warily, he combs back his thinning gray hair with his fingers. As I approach, I can see a small serpent of stubble beneath his lip where he missed with his razor. Shiny pennies gleam from twin eyelets on his Cordovan loafers.

"Worst I can remember," he says.

Then comes his variation of a story I've heard too many times over the past year. His grandfather started selling greeting cards and office supplies from a wooden cart. Before long, he was operating from a tiny storefront in Foster, about twenty miles south of a windswept bean field that would become Greenbriar Mall. Soon, Murphy's father had joined the business; he opened a second shop in Carbon Mills. The most exclusive section of town is called Lancaster, with its private golf club and Tudor houses and foreign auto dealerships. For nearly two decades, Murphy's was the primary supplier of custom stationery, notecards, and invitations to the high-society women of Lancaster—the Lancaster Ladies, as they were affectionately known. But a combination of factors mostly ended the relationship between Murphy's and the Lancaster Ladies. There were deaths, a sour economy. The Internet also played a role, as many of the younger women were ordering directly from Crane & Co., Lilly Pulitzer, and Smythson. Now, grandson Dub Murphy is struggling simply to pay his rent in the mall—twice in the past three years he's traded down for smaller spaces.

"What time is it?" he asks.

"One thirty."

"One thirty," he repeats. "We've been open for three and a half hours."

I nod.

"And I've made *two* sales." He shrugs. "An older woman buying a birthday card for her grandson—four dollars and twenty-six cents, with tax. Also, a young girl wanted wrapping paper—three eighteen, on sale."

"I'm sorry," I say, my fingers loosening their reluctant grip on my briefcase. "Maybe it'll pick up this afternoon. And you've got the holidays coming."

"The holidays?" He chuckles, airy and artificial. "That's almost two months away. I'm not sure we'll make it."

We talk for a little longer. Feebly, I show him a few of the cards from our upcoming lines, though I'm hardly surprised when he doesn't order anything new.

I stumble away, in desperate need of a large tumbler of scotch. Because it's only the middle of the day, and not even the appended *T.G.I. Friday's* sells hard spirits, I'll settle for a beverage with caffeine. I don't recognize any of the restaurants in Greenbriar's food court—they're imitations of imitations. I wander past a burger joint with a similar (though paler) version of a McDonald's color scheme. There's Chinese and Mexican. Also a fried chicken stand whose conspicuous mascot is a white-bearded octogenarian called The General. ("Y'all come try the General's chicken!") A self-serve soda fountain, half-obscured by an enormous wheel of replica pizza, rests at the end of an Italian sandwich shop. Casually, I remove a wax cup and fill it with diet cola. I take a loud drink. Again, I press the cup against the machine's trigger and watch more syrupy liquid spray down. I walk slowly away, half-expecting to hear a pubescent voice calling me back to pay. "I'm sorry," I imagine saying. "I'm just in another world today." But the request never comes.

Standing in a glass portico, I watch the rain tumble across several rows of parked cars. Though I need more underwear—briefs for day, boxers for sleeping—I can't bring myself to trudge back through the mall. I drink the last of my soda and stuff the cup into a cylindrical garbage pail. Two women push through the doors, shaking the water from their hair.

"Whew," says the shorter one. "I didn't expect *that*."

"No," says her friend.

They stomp their feet, letting the rain collect against a perforated rubber mat. The shorter woman takes a breath. Then she looks at me and smiles.

"Wait it out," she says.

My eyes follow them as they walk past the popcorn stand and the limitless items for cellular phones.

Nina was raised on a plot of rolling acreage near Nashville. She told me that her grandfather distilled small-batch bourbon in an old barn behind his house. Years ago, long before Nina was born, he would bottle the spirits in glass Mason jars and sell it from the back of his flatbed truck at local fairgrounds. The first time she tasted her grandfather's whiskey, when she was about ten, she ran screaming from her house, convinced she'd been poisoned.

As a schoolgirl, she relished her alone time—she would slip into a pair of knee-high rubber boots and explore the surrounding wooded hillside. "I had a small hatchet," she said, "and I'd hack my way through the underbrush, pretending to be the first person to discover that piece of land."

Nina's older brother spent his teenage years restoring muscle cars—Pontiac GTOs and Dodge Chargers and Mercury Cyclones. For a while, Nina could identify the various parts of a V-8 engine, "with floor-shifted transmission and Hurst linkage," she said.

Her parents are now retired and living in Arizona. But before they moved west, Nina's father was a reconstructive surgeon and her mother a second-grade schoolteacher. Nina has power-ful memories of leafing through the black and red bound medi-cal books in her family's den, each page more gruesome than the one before it. On occasion, she would have vivid nightmares of detached limbs and crushed craniums and faces distorted by raging infernos, skin droopy and red like melted candle wax.

There was a small pond on the northern line of Nina's prop-erty where she and her friends would swim on hot summer days. One year, after she'd watched the movie Jaws, she avoided the water altogether after her brother announced that he'd seen a "fresh-water shark" circling beneath the family's dock. She said her brother was still a devoted prankster: a couple winters ago, while they were visiting her parents, she left her rental car in a no-parking zone overnight, and the next morning her brother woke up early and moved the car. Then he secretly programmed the words *Tucson Police Department* into Nina's cell phone, linked to his number, so they would appear when he called. "It was awful," she said. "He made me believe the car had interfered with some type of late-night police action, and it had been towed. He dis-guised his voice. He also told me I owed some ridiculous fine."

By the time Nina reached high school, she had a pretty good idea that she wanted to be an artist. At sixteen, she would scour the landscape for flat slabs of shale and limestone and feldspar. She painted geometric designs and still lifes and intricate portraits on the rocks and sold them, for commission, at a local souve-nir shop. Before she left for college in Ohio, her grandfather asked her to design a label for his bourbon—now being mar-keted in traditional screw-top bottles at liquor stores. It featured Old English lettering, burnt-orange trim and, in each corner, a blooming iris, Tennessee's state flower. She still has the proto-type, hanging in her bedroom in a thin black frame. She says it reminds her of home.

One afternoon while Nina and I shared a peanut butter sun-dae, she tapped me on the wrist, gazing sharply across the table, and said, "You know, I was never one of those freaky art-school chicks." She refused to wear all black or fringe her ears with repeated piercings or smoke hand-rolled clove cigarettes. In fact, she was so intent on differentiating herself from the other "fun-koids" (her word) that she nearly joined a sorority. "Can you imagine?" she said, dragging her spoon through a puddle of peanut butter sauce. "Me at a sorority formal? Holy Christ."

Nina's closest friends from childhood are all married. And Dana Driessen, who lived across the street, has four children. This revelation makes Nina shake her head, slow and steady, as though she'd been asked to interpret a line of Sanskrit. "That life seems so far away," she says. "Like we were raised on opposite sides of the planet."

There is damage—broken toys, a mangled picture frame, wadded and torn scraps of paper. Tig has barricaded herself in the bathroom; Callie is snapping a set of colored pencils on her sister's desk. "I hate my life," she says, kicking a stool into a nearby wall. I press my palms against the air, motioning downward, in an attempt to calm her. A disconnected cable of clothing snakes across the floor. There's a new mark on the closet door, curved and black, made by the heel of a thrown shoe. The plastic and felt pieces from a chessboard are scattered around the bed. A chalky blue residue from a child's makeup kit flakes from the surface of a hanging mirror.

"Remember how you told her not to take my things without asking?" says Callie. She removes a yellow shirt from the top of her shared dresser and casts it across her arm, like a lifeguard offering a fresh towel. "Now it's ruined."

Below the shirt's banded collar is a pair of half-dollar-sized splotches of green paint.

"It's okay," I say, leaning forward to examine the stains. "I can get that out in the wash."

"She's not supposed to use my things."

I nod.

She pauses, then flings the offending shirt against Tig's pillow.

"You have to punish her."

"I'll handle it."

"No, you *won't*," she says, stomping into the hallway. "You always say that, but then you don't do anything."

"Listen, Cal—"

"You have to control her. Take something away—ground her!"

She disappears around the corner, and I can hear her slapping the bathroom door, screaming at her sister. I shuffle forward and fold myself into Tig's bed. Her linens smell from a crude blend of fabric softener and strawberry body lotion I bought her at the mall. I listen to the girls' muffled argument through the wall. I'm tired and I haven't the strength to disarm them.

Staring at the faded flower print on Callie's mattress above me, I worry about the indelible imprint Liz and I have left on our daughters. I close my eyes and imagine a thirty-something Callie, standing outside a white clapboard house on some generic suburban street. There's a lean, faceless man nearby wearing a Boston College t-shirt. Callie's voice is raised—to emphasize her point, she punches the hood of a parked car the way she's seen her parents do a hundred times. The man is gazing hopelessly at a tail of white clouds as it drags across the sky. Callie and the man are thinking the same thing: How did we get to this place?

For Callie, my sweet, rosy-cheeked child, I worry that she's simply following a pattern of learned behavior—a destiny that was kick-started the moment she was branded with her parents' damaged genetic coding. The load will weigh heavier on Callie than on her sister. It seems Tig has the ability to compartmentalize many of the hardships in her life. She possesses a lightness of being—a gift that often allows her to shed distasteful memories like a dried skin. But Callie is a thinker: she turns the unpleasantness over and over in her head to examine it from every angle. Sometimes I dream of a day when I'll sit down with Callie— with both girls—and plead with her to let go of all the dysfunction from her childhood. Though her mother and I were trying our best, we simply couldn't set a decent example. "Leave here,"

I imagine myself saying. Travel somewhere far away and find a man who's kind, gentle, and treats you well. Then build your own blueprint for happiness—maybe do everything differently than your parents.

My vision of an adult Callie fades into one from her early childhood, a legitimate memory from when she was nearly two years old. She was waking from a nap and I could hear her squealing in her bedroom. As I opened the door, I saw her gripping the side of her crib. She had removed her clothes and diaper, and she was leaping on the springy mattress. She was moving with such force that the casters on the legs of the crib wobbled against the hardwood floor.

"Look at my Mexican jumping bean," I said.

"Jum' jum' jum'," she responded, short of breath.

I pressed my mouth against her bloated belly and blew out, creating a watery farting noise. She giggled and reached forward to grab my neck. I spun her around the room, laying her softly on the terrycloth cover of her changing table. I used a pre-moistened towelette to wipe her pink bottom.

"You've got a perfect little life," I remember saying as I taped a crinkly new diaper to her waist. Then we wandered into the living room and I watched her push a miniature shopping cart, filled with plastic eggplants and wooden eggs and a rubber doll that peed water when you squeezed it.

Intimidation can take many forms. It's not always about being bigger, stronger, or, in some cases, more aggressive. Standing beside my car on Percy Street, it occurs to me that cunning is wildly underrated.

I scale the brick staircase outside the police station. A female officer sits behind a large desk, a telephone headset producing a perpetual indentation across her dark hair. Misshapen stacks of folders, manila and red and blue, cover a neighboring table. Pressed to the wall is a heavy wooden bench with silver handcuffs dangling from its armrests. A cork bulletin board is nearly lost beneath dozens of overlapping papers—announcements, reminders, newspaper stories, "wanted" photographs with accompanying biographies. Two uniformed officers drink coffee beside the kitchenette, where a crumbling wedge of Bundt cake rests on the counter. As I step forward, my movement causes a nearby water cooler to jostle and dislodge a series of gurgling bubbles.

I lean against a bookshelf, scanning the room. Keesey's facing the opposite direction, head down, his desk pointed toward the wall. I'm dressed in the same clothes I was wearing the last time I spoke to him—navy sport coat, blue shirt, and dark jeans—because it's important that he recognizes me, remembers my association with his old friend, Mr. Eugene. I take a long, circuitous walk around the outside of the room. As I pass Keesey, I deliver a choppy kick to his desk—the toe of my boot ringing against its metal leg. I pause, making certain our eyes meet, however briefly, as he glances up.

The chief's office is encased in glass, with dusty aluminum blinds that resemble the ghostly blue lines on a sheet of notebook paper. I linger for a moment in his doorway, peering back at Keesey to see if he's still paying attention. This is a tenuous plan that relies on ego and fear and an employee's white-knuckled grip to his civil-service pension. For obvious reasons, physical tactics won't work with Keesey—bullying him into a parked car with my lowered shoulder, or cracking a beer mug against his nose.

My voice is light and frail with desperation. After the chief greets me, I begin a loosely constructed story about a neighborhood dog that's been barking through the night. I give him a false name and address. As I talk, I wave my arms animatedly in hopes of rousing Keesey's curiosity. The chief thanks me and promises to look into the matter.

I follow my exaggerated route back through the police station, my eyes again locking with Keesey's. I simply want to cross an invisible barrier, make contact with *his* world. Maybe my presence will give him something to think about. There are things I can say.

Rain prattles against the tin hood of an air-conditioning unit bolted through the living room window, reminding me of the sound of gravel being dumped from a truck. A slippery wind races past the dogwoods and poplars in the neighboring yards, causing leaves and branches to scrub together in a whirl of friction. My front door, dark and heavy wood, whines with every new gust. The floor around my stocking feet is littered with torn and gutted envelopes—a congress of recognizable logos, names, color schemes. I stare at the gray and white index columns of my checkbook—dates and transaction descriptions and corresponding payments. I usually start with the least terrifying bills: gas, electric, phones (landline, cellular), and cable television. I have obscenely precise penmanship that often causes a cramp in my hand. I shake my fingers, slapping them briskly against my thigh. I inhale a long breath and steady myself for the final checks—car, rent, and credit cards. (My child support is deducted directly from my bank account.)

Every few months there are random invoices for things like car insurance, music lessons, soccer team dues, tax arrearages. Resting on the corner of my desk is a sloppy pile of paid bills, dating back to the beginning of summer. I intend to file them when I have the strength. After I finish writing today's checks and double seal each envelope with a piece of transparent tape, I stack them—longest to shortest—near my car keys for mailing.

A dull pain, shallow and throbby, radiates across the roof of my skull. I wander through the darkened house, my vision catching on a digital clock in my bedroom, a red light on the coffee machine in the kitchen, a glowing green peg on the handle of my electric razor. My lungs have trouble holding down air—great gulpy swallows wheeze across my tongue. I press my forehead against a pane of cool glass, the walls of the room shifting around me. Paired headlights on the street outside produce a curtain of smudged neon. As I lean forward, I can hear my body's weight making the aged paint on the window frame crackle. It seems like my eyes have been closed for a long time. I'm desperate for an exit strategy, a way to turn this life into something else. I lay my hands flat on the wall. Next comes the shrill howl of velocity—a horrible carnival ride with banks and graded curves and stomach-lurching dips. I can't shake all the bad memories leashed to my crippled finances.

Even in my worst nightmares, I never imagined this life. One morning I sat in the Silver Springs parking lot, hiding my head behind the dashboard. I watched my colleagues scan their identification badges against a magnetized square and shuffle through the front doors. *It should be a little easier*, I recall thinking. Enough to make a difference—lessen poverty's sudden choke-hold on our lives. If my car needs a new alternator, I don't want to lose sleep determining how I'm going to pay for it. Or if I take my daughters shopping, I'd like to be able to buy them things— frilly dresses, CDs, flavored lip gloss—without worrying about what bill will now go unpaid.

Since I started moonlighting for Mr. Eugene, my life *has* been easier. Just a little. But the hole is greasy and deep. There are still plenty of nights when I grow anxious thinking about what's down the road. I swear to God, I'll eat a bullet if I'm still peddling greeting cards at fifty. In those rare moments when I'm feeling optimistic, I think about stringing together a dozen solid years—investing most of my earnings from Mr. Eugene, rebuilding my 401(k) from Silver Springs. By the time Tig leaves for college, I see myself escaping to a small cabin in the country. I want to start drawing again; I'll build a studio from an old woodshed, with expansive views of prairieland that's crowded with soybeans and winter wheat. Maybe I'll hustle up some freelance design work—a few assignments every month. When I have trouble sleeping I often conjure warm images from this version of my future. I picture myself in a rocking chair on the porch of my cabin, drinking coffee from a white mug. The air is cool and light. A dirt roadway is half hidden beneath a cover of coppery leaves. I'm wearing a wool sweater and chinos with zebra-stripe smears of charcoal pencil. The floorboards moan as a blue-eyed Husky lies down at my side. There's always a woman, nameless and faceless, who reaches for my hand, kisses the back of my wrist. But she lives elsewhere and, soon, she departs in her creaky red pickup. A solitary hawk carves brisk, loopy spirals against the sky. In the distance I follow a trail of dust, clumpy like cotton, as it approaches. The sun's reflection skips across the hood of a rental car like the bright, slippery yolk from an egg. When the doors spring open, I watch my two daughters, in their early twenties, walk forward. They're tall and lean and impossibly beautiful. I wrap my arms around both of them, squeezing their bodies against either side of my torso. *We made it*, I think, rocking back and forth, my face arched forward so the skin of our cheeks can touch...

Staring into the darkness of my living room, I'm lost in my daydream when I hear a soft knocking coming from the rear of the house. I open the door and look down, spying a familiar orange cat with its front paws propped against the frame of the screen. I lift the hook from its eyelet, expecting the cat to retreat. Instead, he races forward and scampers into the next room, his claws abrading the shiny floorboards. He's an amber thunderbolt flashing beneath the coffee table, between chair legs, behind the couch. Tentatively, he begins lapping at a saucer of milk I've placed on a rug in the kitchen. His ears lie flat in anticipation of my fingers: I scratch the cat above his neck, in approximately the spot where a collar would fasten.

"Shoe," I say, crouching low. "That's what we're gonna call you."

In college I played football with a guy from Grand Rapids, Michigan, who had a tangle of orange, unkempt hair that flopped across his eyes. I don't remember his name, but everyone called him Shoe because it looked as though he combed his hair with a loafer or lace-up.

When the cat finishes his milk, I watch him sneak into the girls' bedroom. I collect the half-shredded envelopes from near the couch, stuffing them into a large garbage bag in the hallway. The sound of crinkling plastic sends the cat into hysterics—he darts across my feet, sprinting again to the back of the house. I kick open the screen door and watch him disappear into the black hedges. He moves so quickly the motion-sensor lights fail to ignite.

A gleaming knob of sunshine rises against the horizon. I hear the rusted-out muffler on the enormous Lincoln that delivers my newspaper. I sprinkle several spoonfuls of French Roast into a gold filter and start the coffee machine. A thin blast of steam exhales across the top of the pot, followed by a steady trickle of heated water. Through a neighboring window, I see Ted Epps standing shirtless over his bathroom sink. He drags a safety razor down his frosted jaw. Groggily, I turn back to the counter and insert two slices of rye bread into the toaster. From my living room, I hear a reporter with a British accent describing a bomb that was detonated in a crowded outdoor market near Tikrit. I shuffle into the doorway to watch the video footage, but they've already moved on to the next story—a trio of young brothers, the Tremaines, whose band performed yesterday in Times Square. I stare silently at close-up images of wailing pre-teenagers who're being crushed against powder-blue barricades. A girl who vaguely resembles Callie is shaking her head and frantically windmilling her arms as though she's trying to make herself visible to distant aircraft.

I sit on the arm of the couch and blink the sleep from my eyes. In near choreographed tandem, I hear the buzzer on the coffeemaker, followed by the popping of the toaster. My limbs are slow and heavy. "Food poisoning," I imagine saying in an early morning phone message to Dennis Gaines. "I've been throwing up for hours. I don't think I can make it today…"

Sometimes I feel like a strange alien being who loses his strength when too many days pass without seeing his daughters. I'm miraculously recharged simply by being around Callie and Tig, existing within their orbit. I suddenly have enough energy to help with soccer practice, homework, dinner, baths, and bedtime.

On the mantel of my fireplace is a photograph of the girls, illuminated by flickering television light. They're dressed in colorful flannel pajamas, and the window behind them is white with snow. As I focus on the picture, I'm struggling to remember when it was taken. I walk across the room for a closer inspection. A pointy shadow in the corner resembles a Christmas tree. Slung across Tig's shoulder is a red purse with rhinestones forming the letter T. (Was it a Christmas gift?) I stare into my daughters' faces, unnaturally bleached by a camera's flash, and try to interpret the slopes of their mouths, the camber of their eyebrows. A thin line near the gutter of a couch cushion looks like a ribbon Callie saved from a gift box. Later, she used the ribbon as a belt for her stuffed panda.

It *was* Christmas—maybe three years ago. It took a few weeks to find the bracelet she'd wanted; a manager from a tchotchkes store had to place an order with his distributor. About an hour after the girls posed for this picture, I loaded them onto a wood toboggan and dragged them to a nearby golf course where the seventh hole, a short par three, had an elevated tee box with a steep incline. They took turns riding in the front seat. On one trip, Tig tumbled off the back after we hit a bump. She complained about snow that had slithered down her boots, whining and crying because her toes had gone numb. Eventually, I ferried them home and made hot chocolate with towering silos of whipped cream. I also spread a dry towel across my lap and rubbed the coldness from Tig's feet, blowing quick puffs of air like a sprinter.

Nodding, because it's all come back to me, I return to the kitchen and pour myself some coffee. For a second time I depress the lever on the toaster—no matter how high I set the darkness dial it always requires an additional turn. As I roll my electric razor across my face, I think I hear the braying of my phone. The faint, high-pitched tinging sound of the gears in my razor is nearly the same timbre and pitch as my cell. Some mornings it tricks me: I'll stand rigid for a moment and listen to silence. Today I continue shaving, stretching to a spot in the hallway from where I can see my night table. A plastic bottle of water turns alternatingly blue and clear, matching the strobing flash of my cell. I move so quickly to answer it—third ring? fourth?—that I leave the razor running while I speak.

"It's me, Da'," says Callie, mimicking the accent of an Irish character we saw in a movie last week.

"'Ello, lassie," I say, playing along.

She tells me there's a notebook on the desk in her room that she needs for school. I've been trying to teach the girls about planning ahead; I want them to create mental checklists of the things they're liable to need in the coming days *before* they leave my house or their mother's or their classrooms. (Several times in the past couple months I've had to take one of the girls, usually Callie, back to school in the evening to retrieve a book or homework assignment. This has often meant finding a custodian willing to unlock a side door.)

"Honey…" I say, followed by a long, dejected sigh.

"I know, I know. But I didn't think—"

In the background I can hear Liz's voice, strained and tense, insisting that Callie "just have him bring it over." I can feel a tightness along the back of my neck, the same sensation I get when I'm about to put my hands on someone who's a few weeks behind on their payments.

"Be ready," I say. "I'm just gonna blow the horn."

By seven forty, I'm eating a breakfast bar in Liz's driveway. The last bite tastes dimly of the residual aftershave balm on my fingers. Callie races out the rear door, wearing white socks but no shoes.

"Oh, Cal," I say, pointing to her feet. "Those are *new* socks."

I surrender the notebook and she kisses me on the cheek. With her head leaning through my open window, she spies a pack of gum on my passenger seat.

"Can I have a piece?" she asks.

As she folds a stick of bubblegum against her tongue, I see Liz wander past a side window. It's not easy being a single mother—especially one with such a small sample size from which to draw experience. She was orphaned before she became a teenager; often, she'd observe her friends' parents with a mixture of fascination and longing. There were times, she told me, that she'd grow jealous after learning one of her classmates had been grounded. She wanted someone in her life who cared enough to punish her—provide a tangible awareness of the line that's crossed to unacceptable behavior.

In those moments when I find myself feeling a sense of compassion for Liz, I recall the stories from her often sorrowful childhood. How, soon after her parents' death, she would sit on the front porch and watch the occasional car drive past her aunt's house, as though half-expecting her parents to pull into the driveway in their Oldsmobile and tell her that it had all been a mistake—a horrible misunderstanding. To me, nothing seemed sadder than picturing a pig-tailed Liz waiting for a miracle that would never come. Or the time she was elected to her school's homecoming court, and she was the only member to march onto the football field without a parental escort. Or one Thanksgiving when she couldn't afford to travel home from college; she sat alone in her dorm room, eating delivery pizza and watching old movies on TV.

Early in our separation, I became emotional thinking about her choppy future. "She doesn't have anyone else," I told my mother. "She's all by herself in this world." I understood the trouble Liz had letting go of the girls on those first days they spent with me—I gave her time for long embraces and through-the-car-window handholding.

Liz rarely spoke about her parents. But shortly before the birth of our second child, she told me, surprisingly, that if we had another girl she wanted to name her after her mother, Tegan. This proved a difficult word for little Callie to pronounce—"Tigger" or "Teeg-nan." Soon she was calling her baby sister Tig, and it stuck. But during a mock graduation from kindergarten, Liz asked the school to use Tig's full name. And when the principal called out "Tegan Fanning," I noticed a sadness behind Liz's eyes. I placed my hand on her shoulder and together we watched Tig skip forward and receive her rolled-up diploma.

Even now, there are plenty of days when I wish things had gone differently for Liz and me. Sometimes a show of good faith will trick me into thinking that maybe we weren't that far off. A few months ago, we had a logistical discussion about the girls, tweaking weekday drop-off times to accommodate Liz's work schedule. The two of us started walking and, soon, we had rounded her block three, five times. Defenses lowered, we found ourselves sharing amusing anecdotes about our daughters—the types of things only the two of us would appreciate. Callie reading a book upside-down on Liz's couch; Tig standing in my kitchen, head swiveling round and round as she followed the blades of a ceiling fan. Liz erupted with a hearty laugh, the same one I'd heard often during our first year together, when I told her about the girls both bumping their noses as they chased a dragonfly into a wall.

Callie blows a final bubble, pink and tottery, and disappears back into the house. Maybe Liz and I didn't try hard enough, I tell myself, knowing it's a lie. Sometimes two people just aren't meant for each other. They can have wonderful children, raise them with love and patience and understanding. But as a team, two as one, they can't seem to make it work.

Tammy Margolis is jackknifed over my desk, scribbling something onto a yellow Post-it note, when I arrive at my cubicle.

"Oh, you surprised me." She stands and waves the note between two fingers. "I was just leaving you a message."

Apparently, I'm ten minutes late for a meeting. At Silver Springs, all the conference rooms are named after famous bodies of water—Atlantic, Superior, Nile. I tuck a legal pad and several folders beneath my arm and walk briskly down the hall. When I push open the doors of Pacific, a dozen faces turn to greet me. I fill a Styrofoam cup with coffee and retreat to a chair against the wall. I'm pretending to look engaged: I write down the word *diversification*, underlined twice, and nod my head. A seated Dennis Gaines is trying to catch my attention, boring almond-shaped holes into my chest. Because I know he's bothered that I haven't acknowledged him, I let my eyes sweep the room, pausing on everyone in his row except for him.

Standing at a white board, Connor Brisco is dressed in a pair of camouflage cargo pants tucked into high-gloss, over-the-calf jackboots. Around his neck is a set of silver dog tags whose diamond insets twinkle in the fluorescent light. The sleeves of his clingy brown thermal are pushed past his elbows, revealing a tattoo on his left forearm: a yin yang symbol encircled by a red dragon. He's allowed his hair to grow a little long and spiky, with dark roots showing against his scalp. There's a new corporate directive regarding in-store presentation: A month from now we'll ship expensive-looking display racks that resemble handcrafted antique furniture. Brisco's voice is high and squeaky, catching on certain words to create a short stutter.

I'm exhausted. To stay awake, I lean forward with the pointy cap of my pen digging into the soft skin under my chin. I let the weight of my head plunge the pen toward the bottom of my tongue. Across the room, I watch Maureen Sypher taking notes in a flowered journal. She's writing like a maniac, her hand moving in rapid bursts. During a company picnic last spring, Maureen drank too much sangria and got all frisky with Hayden Collings, who works in accounting. I was spooning condiments onto my hot dog—chopped onions, sweet relish—when I spotted the two of them making out near the executive parking lot. She was stroking Collings's groin, her arm nodding in a similar fashion as today. Now, it's impossible for me to see Maureen—in meetings, in the cafeteria, in line at the automated teller machine—without recalling that image of her giving Collings a dry handjob.

As the meeting draws to a close, with Brisco circling the room and making elaborate hand gestures to emphasize his final remarks, I consider my most expeditious route to the door. It's already been a long morning and I'm not sure I can tolerate another lecture from Gaines on the importance of punctuality. We all rise, in near unison, and I take three steps sideways, using beefy salesman Marc Mull as a human shield. By the time Gaines reaches the exit, I've already started to round the corner—I'm moving choppily down an adjacent hallway, slumping to make myself a smaller target. I duck into a windowless soundstage, where many of the audio cards—music, sloppy burps, barking dogs—are recorded. The walls are soundproofed, covered in bumpy foam that resembles overturned egg cartons. Gaines will wait for me in my cubicle. He probably has another meeting at the top of the hour, in about seven minutes.

I sit on a firm stool. Perched near my shoulder is a gray condenser microphone with a spongy pop screen, used to muffle certain sounds spoken by vocalists—*pees, bees* and *kays*. I plant my elbows between my thighs and fiddle with my shoelaces. This is one of my favorite places to hide. The walls are thick with concrete, which makes it impossible to get a cellular signal. And because I don't have any legitimate business with the audio engineers—on a lark, I once watched them record a singing monkeys birthday card—no one would consider looking for me in here. I'm *unreachable*, I tell myself, watching a black carpenter ant crawl across the floor.

For lunch I eat a bag of roasted pecans from a pushcart outside the courthouse. I'm sitting in the magistrate's office, between my attorney and a legal representative from another credit card company. I shift uncomfortably, rubbing my sticky palms against the sides of my trousers. My entire life—every piece of relevant financial information from the past eight years—rests in a small packet of papers, copied in triplicate, now being reviewed by the other men in this room. I take a deep breath and try to find someplace for my eyes to settle—an empty fishbowl, a framed diploma from Michigan State, a carved wooden owl.

The meeting is only a formality, I've been assured. I owe the credit card company nearly eight thousand dollars in overdue charges and accrued interest. But because I'm already paying twenty-one percent of my "reported" income to child support, the maximum the credit card folks can take is another four percent—the law only allows twenty-five percent of an individual's wages to be garnished—or about eighty bucks a month. Still, it seems unfair that I'm solely responsible for this debt, given that most of the charges were made to purchase things for the girls and, in some cases, the house I once shared with Liz.

The offer comes again: this is the third time I've heard it in as many days. If I can produce a certified bank check for $4,825.63 by the close of business on Friday, or roughly sixty percent of what I owe the credit card company, I will be absolved of my debt. As I start to speak, my attorney presses his arm across my chest, as though we're stopping short in a car.

"Mr. Kirn," says my attorney, loosening the knot on his necktie. "I sent you Mr. Fanning's financial information about six weeks ago."

Kirn nods.

"And you've had an opportunity to read through the material?"

Another nod.

"Please—did you see *anything* in there that would suggest Mr. Fanning is capable of providing you with a check for approximately five thousand dollars?"

Kirn shrugs, then shakes his head meekly.

The three men continue talking about me as though I'm no longer present. It feels like I'm in one of those films where a dead character returns in the form of a lovable apparition—*Hey! What's the deal, fellas? You're screwing up my life! There's a whole pile of money in my freezer. Just give me a little longer!* In truth, I'm hoping another year with Mr. Eugene will get me back to ground zero—a chance to pay off my credit cards, an old income tax debt, a car loan. It's like when you're playing golf and you hit a crappy shot: I just want my mulligan. A do-over.

There are papers to sign. And then another $82.11 removed from my paycheck every month. Standing on the vast staircase outside the courthouse, I watch my lawyer depart in his BMW coupe. Beside me is a marble statue of Lady Justice, Justitia, with her blindfold and sword and scales. I glance around to see if anyone's watching, then give her the finger.

A pair of Japanese markers stare down from the visor of my car like numbered (03) eyeballs. I leaf through the pages in my little black notepad. Suddenly, I remember a story Mr. Eugene told me about when his grandfather was making book. It was a more civilized time: the guys who collected for Mr. Eugene's grandfather wore suits and fedoras. Rarely was physical action required. Instead, they discreetly walked up to the men—always men—who owed them money and tapped them on the shoulders. This was usually enough. It's how they earned the nickname "tappers."

Nine days ago, I met Steve Farney in a Starbucks on Beard Street. He was down nearly two thousand dollars. As he spoke, he used his fingers to comb his young son's hair back from his forehead.

"I need a week," he said, pulling the boy close to his hip. "It's not a problem—really, it's not. I just need a week."

I nodded, watching Farney's kid break loose and press his face against a display case filled with sweets.

The orange and white sign outside of the realty office where Farney works is creaking in the breeze. The sky's gone dark and I can see him sitting behind his desk in the illuminated picture window facing the side entrance. Eventually, he grabs his briefcase and removes a tan slicker from a coat rack near the door. He drives a silver Lexus that's parked beside my car. As he crosses the lot, he extends his arm and points his key fob toward his windshield. The car gives a series of short bleeps. It's not until he pulls the handle on his door that he realizes I'm seated in the car next to him.

"*Geez*—" he says, turning superfluously in three directions. "You startled me."

I stand and tuck my notepad into the breast pocket of my shirt.

"What an afternoon!" He leans back, accidentally closing his raincoat into his door. "But I've got your money—I've got it."

I nod.

"I mean, I don't have it *on* me. I wouldn't bring that kind of money to work. But I've got it."

"Should we go somewhere?" I ask.

"I can't get it now," he says, keys rattling. "The bank is closed. But in the morning—first thing."

It's been a long day, the last ninety minutes spent waiting for Farney. I thought he'd be finished by six thirty. Planting my feet, I snap my left elbow forward and catch him across the bridge of his nose. A drizzle of blood spots his raincoat, still hanging from the seam of his car door. There's a muted cracking sound of bone striking cartilage. He's fallen to his knees, hands spread against the black asphalt. He raises his arm, quickly, protecting the side of his head because he thinks I'm going to hit him again. But I'm only reaching for my cell phone as it vibrates in the pocket of my jacket.

"Dad?" says Tig, her voice full of cheer.

"Hey, honey."

Farney uses a handkerchief to slow the bleeding.

"We have a field trip on Friday. We're going to the zoo."

"Oh, that sounds great."

After a few deep swallows, Farney tips his head back and braces himself against the rubber molding of his car.

"But I need my sneakers—for walking."

"Okay."

"I think they're at your house." There's a clunking sound, as though Tig drops the receiver. "Mom can't find them."

In the dim light, Farney's nose already looks swollen and purple. A diamond-shaped welt appears in the spot where a pair of eyeglasses would rest.

"Remind me tomorrow."

"Thanks, Dad."

As I finish my call, I listen to Farney moan, the noise echoing off the wheel well of his Lexus. I kneel beside him and lift the handkerchief, examining the damage.

"You're fine," I say, patting him on the shoulder.

It slowly occurs to me, like finger-smudged initials appearing in a foggy mirror, that Farney still has to return home. I imagine his towheaded son approaching him at the front door, the boy's sparkly blue eyes transfixed on his father's crippled nose. What would Farney say? How would he explain the wound to a four-year-old? Maybe he walked into a door, or caught himself on the frame of his car. I grab his bicep and help him to his feet. The nearest I can get to an apology is offering him a reprieve.

"Can you meet me outside that Starbucks?"

He nods.

"What time?"

His eyes twitch as he does the math in his head, charting distances and potential delays.

"Nine thirty?"

"Nine thirty," I repeat, lowering him into his car and tossing his raincoat onto the passenger seat.

He thanks me, incongruously, and I watch him drive away. He pauses before pulling out of the lot, checking his face in the rearview mirror. As I peer through my windshield, I can see a spotted trail of blood, like fallen bread crumbs, still glossy in the cones of my headlights.

A few months ago, I sat in Mr. Eugene's office with a "tapper" named Reed Desh. He'd been collecting for longer than I had, nearly five years. We traded stories about particularly challenging clients—chasing people down at work, their homes, and, in one instance, on the steps of a church after Sunday worship. I remember being surprised by something Desh said: In all the time he'd been working for Mr. Eugene, only once had he found it necessary to strike someone—an arrogant dentist from McCloud who owed eight grand on football. I watched Desh twirl a cigar cutter around his index finger and wondered if my physicality—customers who didn't pay on my second visit were often provided a little encouragement—was a reflection of my own anger seeking a corporal release, or simply a more difficult clientele.

"This guy was a real asshole," said Desh, speaking of the dentist. "But I still felt kinda shitty—I nailed him good in the stomach."

I nodded.

"He probably thought it was worth it." Desh finally returned the cigar cutter to the table at his side. "I felt so guilty I didn't go back for, like, two weeks."

A sudden gust of wind pushes a cluster of dried leaves and branches across a paved walkway, creating a hollow scraping sound. In a second-story window, I watch a cleaning woman waving a blue feather duster—jousting with the phone, a lampshade, and a black computer screen.

My legs extend before me like twin dowels. Pinched between my fingers is a caramel-colored Churchill, releasing wisps of corkscrewing smoke. I close my eyes and lean back into a leather couch. I'm half-listening to a conversation between two men sitting across from me.

"I was reading the newspaper," says Santino Sparre, who works for his father's landscaping company. "I've got this beat-up recliner—it's my favorite chair."

"Sure." The guy near Sparre is wearing a shiny sport coat with a VFW emblem pinned through its lapel. "I've got a favorite chair."

"So, she's watching some cruddy program—one of those talent shows where they take real people from across the country and have them perform."

"I know it."

"Everything's fine. She's doing her thing, I'm doing mine."

My eyes are still closed, but I can hear Sparre relighting his cigar.

"Suddenly, she turns to me and says, 'Don't you even want to sit next to me?' Like it's a *problem* that I'm, what, three feet away?"

"Jesus."

"She's gotta make trouble outta nothing."

"She wants some attention."

"Oh, *please*." Sparre slaps the arm of his couch and I open my eyes. "I give her plenty of goddamn attention. You know— last Saturday I spent forty-five minutes sitting on one of those hard little stools while she tried on shoes. Didn't say a fuckin' word."

The other guy nods.

"She wants to know you're thinking about her," says Big Dave, who's been eavesdropping on their conversation from be-hind the counter. "Even when you're not."

"Well, I'm *not*," says Sparre. He places his palms across both ears and pretends to squeeze his head. "Sometimes I'm just think-ing about reading the fuckin' newspaper."

I chuckle.

Behind Big Dave, the door of Mr. Eugene's office hisses open. I hear my last name called twice, quiet then loud.

"I'm not finished with this," I say, leaving my half-smoked cigar in an ashtray.

Mr. Eugene's on the phone, his elbows resting against his desk. I stand awkwardly, like a boy waiting to see his principal, shifting my weight from one foot to the other.

"Can I get you something to drink?" asks a disembodied voice across my left shoulder. It belongs to Dove, Mr. Eugene's assistant, who's sitting behind a glowing computer screen in the corner. He looks slightly Asian, with narrow eyes. His dark hair is cropped short, except for his sideburns, which extend angularly beyond the slope of his cheekbones. He's wearing a pink dress shirt, unbuttoned enough to reveal a thin gold chain. "We've got cold beer, soda, liquor."

"Oh, thanks," I say, locking my hands behind my back. "I'm fine."

"Have a drink," says Mr. Eugene. He hangs up the phone and scribbles something into a burgundy ledger. "Give him some of that scotch—the fancy single-malt stuff from Ricky."

"Rocks or neat?"

"Put ice in the glass," says Mr. Eugene, waving his hand at an imaginary cloud of insects. "Otherwise it's too warm. No one likes it that way."

We watch Dove dart across the room, filling a heavy tumbler with chopped ice and russet-colored liquid. I take a quick sip and, instantly, my throat squeezes closed.

"Good?"

I nod, though truthfully I haven't the palate to distinguish between fine spirits and the cheaper stuff.

Mr. Eugene rifles through some papers on his desk. He lifts a ball cap and removes a beige envelope.

"This is yours," he says, tapping the envelope against his temple like Johnny Carson doing his old Carnac the Magnificent routine. "I don't know what you said…"

I must look confused, my eyebrows pursed together in a fleshy wing.

"This afternoon I got a visit from Keesey." As Mr. Eugene rocks back, smiling, his chair squeaks in two places. "Paid the *vig*—all of it."

"Really," I say, gripping my glass with both hands. "That's a surprise."

Mr. Eugene bends low, now obscured by a stocky file cabinet. I can hear the shuffling of papers, the hissy sound of a cardboard box being slid across the ground.

"Take this." He pushes a shower radio in my direction. "For the girls." I thank him, struggling to hold the box without spilling my drink.

When I was a kid, my parents' bathroom shared a contiguous wall with my bedroom. Many mornings my father would listen to big band music from a radio resting on the tank of the toilet. He'd often sing along with the music during his shower, turning the radio's volume to headache-inducing levels. During a fight between my parents, several weeks before my father left us, I remember my mother smashed his radio with a hairbrush. "Nobody wants to hear this shit," she'd said, bludgeoning Tommy Dorsey. "It's *grandparent* music." Days later I was still finding broken shards of plastic and copper stubble on the tile floor.

"I might have something else for you," says Mr. Eugene.

I take a few steps forward, looking for a place to set my glass.

"No," he says, grinning. "A job—I might have something in a few days."

I nod.

"I'll let you know."

Standing in the cool air outside Gilberto's, I press the radio box against my ribcage. The scotch has made me a little dizzy. It takes a few moments to remember that I parked my car in the back lot.

The other day, while I was searching my drawers for a receipt, I stumbled on a mashed penny from one of my earliest dates with Liz. We were taking a long and aimless walk after dinner. In the distance came a screechy rumble, soft then louder, until it eventually caused the earth to shake. Liz grabbed my hand and started running toward a row of tightly packed evergreens. We pushed through their whisk-broom branches and shimmied

down a steep incline, coming to rest beside a pair of aged locomotive tracks.

"You have any money?" she asked. "Pennies, nickels?"

I dug through my pockets and surrendered a handful of
change. She dropped to her knees and lined the coins on the
weathered steel rails. We stood together, our elbows and feet
nearly touching, as a freight train rushed past. We could feel its
heat and velocity against our faces, a tail of coal dust and gravel
whipping across twin hills of dry soil. Liz covered her eyes with
her forearm, waving away the smoky air before retrieving her
collection of disfigured currency. She pressed the hot coins, now
lean and elongated slugs of metal, into my palm. We continued
walking and Liz told me a story about her uncle—how he was
once visited by a pair of FBI agents who opened a dark briefcase on his dining room table and asked him to identify several
photographs.

"That's me," said her uncle.

"And the men standing beside you?" said one of the agents.

"Don't know them."

This continued for a few minutes until, at last, one of the
agents asked Liz's uncle if he often played in illegal card games
with complete strangers.

"Listen," he said. "I was invited to a friendly game of poker.
But I had no idea who else was in the room."

The agents nodded and returned the pictures to their briefcase. They didn't say anything else until they reached the front
door, when one of the men leaned forward and whispered,
"Don't make us come back here."

The first time Liz heard this story, she asked her uncle about
the photographs. He admitted he knew every man in every picture—by name. "But he never gave them up," she said, stroking
a flattened nickel with her index finger. "*That's* loyalty."

We made our way to a granite staircase outside of the art
museum and sat beside each other. I found a rusted tin of canned
pears in the bushes and we took turns trying to score baskets with
our smashed coins. For a while there was only the clinking

sound of metal, hard against soft. Finally, Liz decided to raise the stakes—she said when one of us landed a coin in the can, that person got to ask the other a truth-or-dare question. We played the game for a long time, until it was too dark to see the tin's thorny mouth. My aim was better than Liz's—I made her skip barefoot through a fountain (dare), somersault down a delivery ramp (dare), and tell me the name of her first crush (truth). On what would be my last throw, in the strained gloaming, I struck the bottom of the can on the fly. With my arm still in motion, Liz called out "dare." The penny's ringing remained in our ears when I posed that she kiss me for ninety seconds. I remember both of us turned red and, before I had time to retract my suggestion, Liz scooted across the step and pressed her lips against mine. It was our first extended kiss, slick and full of meaning. We held hands the entire way home, and neither of us could keep from smiling.

For many years, I imagined giving the saved penny to one of my daughters on her wedding day. But now I'm not so sure. It remains buried in my desk drawer, forgotten beneath a stack of loose stationery and boxed pencils and my leather-bound passport.

The banner is enormous, stretching the length of the hallway, interrupted only by doors to various classrooms. Every second-grader has outlined his or her body, in pink or purple or blue, against the unfurled roll of paper. The students have created self-portraits using markers and glitter and yarn for hair. On Tig's picture of herself she pasted a loop of seashells from our trip to the beach around her neck. There's also a plaid skirt, green crépe-paper blouse, and floppy pigtails tied with pink bows. A pair of large gold hoops, formed of twisted pipe cleaners, dangles from her earlobes—a hardly subtle message for Liz and me because, in rare agreement, we've insisted Tig wait until her tenth birthday before she's permitted to have pierced ears. Her oversize fingernails are alternately painted orange and blue. Swatches of paisley fabric have been cut and shaped into knee-high boots. Below the portrait's nose—a narrow, elongated letter U—Tig spent a great deal of time detailing every Lego-sized tooth in her mouth. Finally, beside her left elbow, Tig's name is written in wandering red cursive.

Near the middle of Mrs. Archer's room is a collapsible table with punch and cookies and coffee for parents. Islands of desks, grouped in fours, are neatly spaced on the carpeted floor. Each student's name is spelled across a placard that's tacked above the pencil tray on his or her workstation. Against the far wall is a large map of the world filled with tiny pink and blue pins representing the various places the students in Mrs. Archer's class have visited. (Predictably, there's a bouquet of congested pinheads planted in Ohio, near Carbon Mills.) A wide and expansive windowsill is cluttered with various class projects—papier-mâché animals, clay statues modeled after the students' favorite historical figures (George Washington, Martin Luther King Jr., Michael Jordan), eight-by-ten reproductions of flags from other nations. Hanging beside a file cabinet is a large sheet of posterboard crowded with colorful squares. Inside each box is a Velcro-backed index card bearing a student's name and photograph. This "job list," which changes weekly, includes washing the blackboard, feeding the turtles, and emptying the pencil sharpener. I find Tig's card beneath a headline that reads "Lunch Monitor."

As I circle the desks, exchanging meek smiles with other parents, I scan a collection of poems and essays, scribbled on wide-ruled notebook paper, posted in different locations across the room. Tig has written a cute little story about a mermaid who befriends a handsome lifeguard. She's gone into splendid detail about the types of things the mermaid has chosen to carry with her from the sea—coral hairclips, starfish bracelets and, of course, "really awesome" pearl earrings. I wander past a bookshelf and notice a selection of pictures the kids have created of their respective families. Tig has drawn stiff-limbed versions of the four of us, thumbs and pinkies overlapping like paper dolls. On the left side of the page is a giant image of me, larger than the rest of the family combined. In an effort to reproduce all five fingers, she's sketched my hands, flat and extended like matted brooms. It makes me feel good when I see a chubby arrow, green and curved, beside the words *My Dad*.

In the corner of the room, Mrs. Archer rings a little glass bell. The parents and students shuffle into place, forming a meandering half-circle around her. As she begins speaking, hands clasped above her waist, my eyes dart nervously between the clock and the doorway. She talks about her goals for the class, the students, and, later, the upcoming curriculum. I grow anxious wondering why Liz can't arrive on time. With every minute that passes, I feel my agitation becoming more physical—the space between my shoulder blades starts to tingle; the leather lasts of my boots squeak as I rock from side to side; my incisors gnaw on the nail of my right thumb. Suddenly, I'm interrupted by laughter: As Mrs. Archer introduces the turtles, Bobo and Lynnette, one of the boys lifts them from their terrarium and guides them in mock genuflection. "Inside voices," says Mrs. Archer, quieting the children.

Near the end of Mrs. Archer's speech, Liz finally enters the room with the girls. Tig tries to wave but her mother catches her arm. "He sees you," she says, loud enough for others to hear.

Since the beginning of our separation, Liz has demonstrated an alarming level of insecurity. She can't bear it when the girls show me the slightest affection in her presence. A divorced friend once said Liz seemed to believe the girls had a limited amount of love to give, and some for me meant less for her. About a year ago, I met the three of them in a parking lot after they'd returned from vacation. I hadn't seen the girls in ten days and we embraced; I kissed them both on the tops of their heads. But Liz reached forward, literally pulling the girls from my arms. "They're not babies," she said, sounding perturbed. "You don't have to slobber all over them." That was probably the closest I've ever come to striking her.

It's not only the girls' love that Liz wants. She's always been a desperately needy person, since the week after her eleventh birthday when her parents were killed in a car crash. Liz and her brother went to live with their aunt and uncle near Philadelphia.

For obvious reasons, she was terrified of abandonment: Years later if she awakened at night and I wasn't beside her—maybe I'd gone to the bathroom or kitchen—she'd have difficulty catching her breath. "Hayes!" she'd scream into the darkness, until I returned to comfort her. In high school she willed herself into a fine student because it made her seem more attractive to adults, teachers, and relatives. ("You have a very special mind," her aunt would say, gushing with encouragement.) During the early months of our marriage, I discovered the importance of that period in Liz's life when we had a fight and, ridiculously, she wanted to compare our SAT scores—as if the truest measurement of a person's worth was standardized testing.

One evening when Callie was still an infant, I recall holding her against my chest and rocking her to sleep. I was singing an old Sam Cooke song and gently stroking her hair with my fingers. After a few minutes, I noticed Liz standing in the doorway. She crossed her arms and sighed, seemingly irritated. The floorboards creaked beneath her stocking feet. She wanted to know why I could sit with the baby for hours, cuddling and caressing, but was rarely able to show her the same attention. I shrugged, pressing my finger to my lips because I didn't want to disturb Callie. This became a common theme in our marriage—Liz not being the center of my universe—and together we created a noxious cycle. After an argument I'd build a wall, disgusted by the thought of intimacy. And because there was no intimacy, we'd again start to fight.

Beside the computer terminal in Mrs. Archer's room, I watch Liz usher the girls forward. She's wearing a clingy green sweater and a brown skirt that falls to her calves. For a long time I pitied her—a divorced mother struggling to make her way in this world. Some days as I waited in my car for the girls, I'd follow Liz's movements through the porch window as she folded laundry or unpacked groceries or searched behind the couch for a missing lunchbox. I could feel the emotion quavering in my throat; I had wanted something different for her, for all of us. In a gesture of goodwill, I'd occasionally surrender the contents of my wallet to Tig or Callie. "Go take this to your mother," I'd say. But that seems like another lifetime—a small kindness between two people who were once in love. Since then, we've behaved shamefully toward one another—both eager to cross distant and dreadful boundaries for the sake of being heard.

I take a few steps backward, crouching behind Tig. "I love your mermaid story," I whisper. She smiles and nods. Then we stand in silence, the four of us, listening to Mrs. Archer's last remarks. To my left, another father sighs and rolls his eyes when the "room mother" asks to say a few words. She's looking for volunteers to escort the kids on field trips. One of Tig's classmates, a brown-haired boy wearing a bright yellow soccer jersey, is playing with the zipper on his pants—up and down, up and down. When his mother finally notices, she flicks him on the ear.

"Hello, ladies," I say, once the speeches have ended. In a familiar greeting, I bump fists with Callie and Tig. "Bop it and... *bop* it."

"I need braces," says Callie.

She opens her mouth and taps her front tooth with a fingernail.

"We'll see—"

"Don't confuse her," says Liz. "This afternoon we went to the dentist. She *does* need braces."

"Okay—"

"You always do this, Hayes," she says, waving her hand dismissively. "Instead of dealing with the problem, you push it off, hoping it'll go away."

Liz lacks the mechanism that exists in most people's brains— call it a filter—that governs the appropriateness of certain conversations. Over time, I have learned to temper my responses. I lead Tig to a series of mathematical problems posted near her desk.

"Did you get a toothbrush at the dentist?" I ask.

"A pink one," she says. "And some stickers."

"Stickers are good."

"I don't like the cleaning stuff." She straightens her name-card. "It's supposed to be bubblegum flavor. But it tastes terrible, like when I'm chewing on a pen."

I pretend to gag.

Afterward, there are cookies with blue sprinkles and fruit punch. In the hallway, I point out the earrings on Tig's portrait. Liz chuckles and shakes her head and we share a moment of levity. The girls follow her through the parking lot, surrounded by scattering bands of children and parents.

"Well," I say, once we've reached Liz's car, "I'll see you tomorrow."

Both girls give me quick hugs, their ears pressed to my belly as though they're listening through a wall. As I walk away, I hear Tig complaining that Callie's backpack has been pushed to her side of the seat. "I don't have any room," says Tig. "It's not fair."

Life's not fair comes my familiar refrain—the same thing fathers have been telling daughters since the beginning of time. For a few moments, I watch them through my windshield; I see the swaying of a raised arm, fingers closed. I'm sure there's screaming—and Liz's voice, loud and forceful, insisting the girls retreat to their respective corners. Maybe this is only a pair of sisters, close in age, asserting their independence. The same as any siblings from any family. Maybe this has nothing at all to do with us.

The streets are dark and empty. Almost involuntarily, I turn right on Concord, as though I'm following a set of rails. A light at the intersection of Bayles flickers wildly, like a camera's strobe. I hear a loose branch hooked to the undercarriage of my car. I'm lost in thought and, for an instant, I half-expect to see the girls sitting behind me when I glance into my rearview mirror. The feeling is so real I nearly ask them, aloud, if they want to go for ice cream.

I watch a man in a tan robe drag a garbage pail down his driveway. When he reaches the tree lawn he spits, dribbling saliva across his chin. A large gazebo sits in the emerald center of Delmon's Circle, surrounded by park benches and wooden picnic tables. The adjoining streets are closed during Independence Day for an old-timey band concert and fireworks display.

I slow to a halt in front of Nina's house, the rims of my tires chafing against the concrete curb. We haven't spoken in nearly a week. It's late and the only light comes from her rear window. I knock on the banister and call her name, listening closely for the sound of movement. Cautiously, I make my way up her staircase.

"Hello?" she says, through a blackened screen.

After our eyes meet, she opens the door. She's wearing a gray t-shirt with the faded name of a Louisiana dance hall and men's boxer shorts folded down at the waist. An elastic headband keeps her hair from her face. She leans forward and inhales loudly through her nostrils.

"Are you drunk?"

"Um, no." I steady myself against a bookshelf, adjusting to the darkness. "Should I be?"

She laughs and retrieves a warm mug of tea from the kitchen counter.

"In my experience, booze and booty calls go hand in hand."

"Booty call?" I say, turning flush. "No, that's not…I just—"

"I'm jerking your chain."

It's been a long week, I tell her. I describe the girls' open house and my continuing struggles with their mother and the sadness I feel whenever I'm forced to leave them behind.

"Some nights," I say, looking down, "I could use a little company."

As I stammer through an apology for disturbing her at ten thirty, she places her fingers across my mouth. She brushes her nose down the side of my neck, slow and suggestive. I feel her body squeezing between my knees—her naked thighs pressed together against my groin. Then her tongue licking the bristly curve of my jaw. I lay my hands on her back, following its slope past the waistband of her blousy boxers. My palms cup around the cool, muscle-less flesh of her buttocks. We kiss, long and hard, our lips pinching wildly at slick furrows of skin. Her mouth tastes bitter and grassy from green tea. She arches backward and her erect nipples push through the filmy cotton of her shirt, like exposed bolts on machinery. I crane my head across her shoulder, a burping baby, swallowing mammoth gulps of air…

My hands race madly up and down her limbs. A jangling sound, like dropped keys, rings from below my navel as she unfastens my belt. It's nice to again feel a woman's touch on my stomach. I fear the simple connection of her hand near my penis, even accidentally, will cause me to ejaculate. In the slippery throes of passion, I steer my thoughts toward neutral ground—a distraction to make this last. *There was a ball spiraling above the horizon my junior year of college. As I turned back, reaching and stretching, I was blinded by the glare of the setting sun. Thundering through the middle of the field came the other team's strong safety. His forearm caught me below the chin, knocking me sideways. The collision was so fierce it launched my helmet into the sky, making it tumble and skid past the yardage marker. Later, one of my teammates would tell the trainer he thought I'd lost my head.* The tips of her fingernails pull the twisted, wiry hair at the crown of my pubis. Because I'm seated on a stool, she's having trouble digging her arm through the taut denim across my lap. She kisses me deeper, gently slapping the roll of flesh below my left hip. I gradually stand and, in a singular motion, she lowers my jeans past my knees.

She peels down my briefs. I feel my erection spring into the hem of my shirt, bunched and flappy across my thighs. She grabs my penis and gives it a swift tug, like she's cocking a pool cue. Soft and playful, I bite her lower lip. My wrist grazes the prickly skin of her crotch. A sticky wetness finds my middle finger and, after inverting my palm, I plunge through the slippery warmth between her legs. I stumble sideways, my knees nearly buckling. She lets out a lazy moan. My head's swimming in a jumble of thoughts, image after image, as though peering through a child's toy ViewMaster at rapid speed. I'm lost in an old familiar pleasure. I hear myself panting, my mouth and nose twined by the ropy hair across her neck…

Nina's fingers slide over the head of my penis, knuckles tightening. My hips sway forward; they bump lightly into her flexing elbow. She's naked, her magnificent body illuminated by thorns of fractured moonlight. I brace myself against the counter, my fingers clawing the slick linoleum for support. I'd forgotten how wonderful this feels, her hot breath joining with mine. I clutch her beneath her ribcage, rocking and lifting, my calves still trussed together by crumpled jeans. Then comes the blur and wizzle of rushing endorphins—a trembling that starts near the base of my spine. It's overwhelming: this sudden proof that I'm capable of experiencing these feelings again. She dribbles her green tea saliva onto my penis, moving her hand in steady arcs, like a flaring engine. I call upon another distraction: *A group of us were watching a program on the History Channel, clouding the screen with cigar smoke. There was talk of improvised explosive devices—IEDs—that detonated military vehicles with such force they literally blew one soldier into another. Months later, a recovering sergeant complained of painful lumps that speckled his bicep. The surgeons discovered something they called organic shrapnel: the blast had embedded the slivered bone and tissue remains of another soldier beneath the sergeant's skin. "Oh, Christ," said Navigator Bob. "He literally had his buddy growing in his arm."*

It's a splendid friction, this steady churning of her hand, and I grow wobbly. My forehead collides with her shoulder. At the last possible moment, I lean forward, and the angle of my penis shifts. I climax in a terrific burst; a tacky thread that scatters like buckshot—striking her thumb, wrist, and the pearly underside of her left breast. We drop to the floor, knocking over a tall wicker stool. I hold her to my chest, stroking unintelligible symbols against her temple. My semen smells sharp and acidic, like an ammonia-based cleaning solution. There's a dishtowel hanging from the handle of her refrigerator and we pass it between us.

Together we drift to sleep on the hard floor, my arm numb and tingly beneath her weight. In the distance, I can hear the wind blowing a bird feeder against an overhang of slate roof—*tickety-tick-tick*. As I fade out of consciousness, the sound becomes the clucking of my father's Buick Regal sitting in our old driveway and I'm standing across from him tossing a baseball on a damp November afternoon.

I was young; a child. My glove was clammy with moisture. We'd been playing catch for a while when he decided to increase the velocity of his throws, and they popped against the oily cowhide, stinging my palm. "Couple more," he said, raising his arm. It was becoming more difficult to see in the fading twilight and, on what would be his final throw, the ball nicked the chubby fingers of my mitt—it skidded off the laces, ricocheting into my forehead.

I remember the light blue tiles of our bathroom spinning along the ceiling of my vision. He and my mother were lowering me into a cold tub. "Keep him awake," he said, patting me gently on both cheeks. There was a two-inch incision above my left eyebrow, from the ball's seams, that needed seven stitches. In the weeks that followed the blood draining from the knotty bulb on my forehead created perpetual bruises, purple and olive smudges beneath my eyes.

A few months later, in early spring, my father took me to a field behind our local high school. He was carrying a canvas satchel filled with scuffed baseballs and a bat. "You've gotta get back in the box," he said, positioning my feet beside home plate. "Otherwise, you'll be afraid for the rest of your life." I swung at everything he threw, stepping wildly into the "bucket" with my left sneaker. I was terrified and I told him I didn't want to play baseball anymore. But the pitches kept coming and coming. Eventually, I made contact, spraying a little dribbler down the first base line. Near the end, he purposefully aimed a pitch at my lower back. "You're gonna get hit again," he said. "May as well get used to it."

I'm short of breath when my eyes open, scanning the room for a familiar sight. Nina's naked leg is hooked across my waist. We hear a dog barking from some remote yard.

"Sheesh," says Nina, her chin still pressed to my abdomen.

"What?"

"That dog." She twirls her fingers through the nest of hair on my chest. "It's outside every night."

I remember another bruise—on my left ass cheek—from that time my father made me practice batting. But he was right: My fear of being struck by a baseball quickly subsided, like a fleeting illness, and I played Little League through high school. The memory stays with me, I suppose, because it's one of the few times my father ever gave me advice.

"Ruff, ruff," says Nina.

This is nice—the two of us lying together, nearly naked, on the cool floorboards. We embrace, my arm threaded across her shoulder. It's a different perspective—Nina and me looking up at her barstools, table, and shiny red juicer.

Carved from a grassy hillside behind the local community college is a large athletic field apportioned into equal quadrants. A chalky white lattice of pulverized limestone, lines and loops, form goalie boxes, center circles, and right-angled borders. Clusters of parents crowd the sidelines with collapsible chairs and plastic beverage coolers and fuzzy fleece blankets. I'm standing along the northwest boundary, between pitches one and four, watching teams of young girls in bright soccer uniforms. In a rare alignment of constellations, Callie and Tig are playing in games at the same location. (Most Sundays, Liz drives one girl and I take the other.) A ball freckled with red and white pentagons rolls in my direction; I toss it back.

On my left, Tig is playing defense. Her team is threatening to score and she watches the action downfield, somewhat indifferent, tightening the strands of her ponytail. "Be ready, Tig," I shout, giving her a thumbs-up sign.

My head feels like it's mounted on a lazy Susan, spinning back and forth between games. Callie races past a fullback on my right, dribbling the ball through the splayed legs of another defender. She rests the bottom of her cleat on the ball and flips it sideways with her heel, getting enough space to make a clean pass to a teammate streaking toward the goal.

A firm hand stings me between my shoulder blades. As I pivot, I'm engulfed in an awkward "guy" hug—arms extended, hips held at a safe distance.

"This is a surprise," says Sully. "Melanie's team is playing against Callie's."

He hooks his thumbs down the waist of his trousers and rocks back on his feet. For a moment his eyes scan the neighboring horizon, his pupils large and black. He follows the movements of a figure on a parallel sideline.

"Oh, look at that." He pretends to fan himself. "Do you know the Chases? Greg and Paula? They've got a new nanny. She's, like, twenty-three. From Denmark or Sweden—some Scandinavian country."

Together we watch a young blonde, dressed in bulky sweater and jeans, walking with a toddler gripping her index fingers.

"She's pretty."

"*Please*," says Sully, slapping my arm. "I could not live under the same roof with that girl."

I chuckle.

"I'm not kidding. I don't know how he does it. He must be queer."

Hand in pocket, I snap a piece of nicotine gum from its foil-backed sleeve. I tuck it against my palm with my thumb. After a series of dry coughs, I raise the slick pellet toward my mouth and, sneakily, deposit it under my tongue.

Suddenly, there's a distant memory in my head: a serpent coiled around Christ's right arm. This was twenty years ago—we were seniors in high school. Sully was hugging Christ's neck, trying to fasten a second snake, made of rubber, against the statue's head with silver duct tape. I was aiming my father's old flashlight, long and heavy as a thighbone. Several feet from the statue's base, Cale Boyd was spraying words into the grass with Day-Glo paint: *Go Cougars!* and *Ground the Eagles*. The whole thing only lasted a few minutes; soon the three of us were crammed together in the cab of my pickup.

We rounded a corner, fast and deliberate, and a pile of garbage slid across the dashboard—cassette tapes, disposable pens, two empty cans of soda. Sully stacked four crackers on top of each other and jammed them past his teeth. Cale sat in the middle with a weathered football pressed between his knees. Using his fingernail, he scraped dried mud from the ball's pebbly skin.

As the pickup reached Fairfax, we passed a sheriff's cruiser heading in the opposite direction. Though it was nighttime, I lowered the sun visor to hide my face. But I'd forgotten about a photograph pasted to the visor's underside—a wavy-haired girl crouched beside a roiling stream. I quickly returned the visor to its original position.

"That's tragic," said Sully.

"Years from now we're gonna see this fucking truck on a scrap heap," said Cale, shaking his head. "And I bet that picture will *still* be up there."

Her name was Audrey Killian, and she was my first real girl-friend. On the cool October night that the three of us "decorated" St. Edward's High in anticipation of our football game against the Eagles the following afternoon, Audrey had already started her freshman year at Bowdoin College in Maine. We'd been apart for nearly four months.

No one said anything for the rest of the ride. We pulled into the front lot at Dairy Barn—an old-style drive-in with intercoms mounted on orange poles. The speakers hadn't worked since our parents were kids. But if you waited long enough, someone would come take your order. Mostly, we got our food from the counter inside.

The truck was still running when Sully and Cale reached the cashier. I stayed and watched the waitresses from across my steering wheel. They all wore pink-and-white dresses with matching aprons that tied against the smalls of their backs. Outside Dairy Barn was a rectangular trash bin made of hard industrial plastic. Its roof sagged beneath the weight of a pudgy boy from my chemistry class. He was wearing pointy, Western-style boots that he banged together to make a pesky clapping noise.

"The fryer's broken," said Sully.

He was holding an orange tray with two burgers wrapped in wax paper and two Royal Crown colas. Cale set his meatball sandwich on the hood of my truck. He sprinkled parmesan cheese from a green container—seven, eight, nine shakes—onto the saucy bun.

I was looking down, removing the pickle slices from my burger. Then everything went dark as something blocked the streetlight from my window. It was Sid Lapanelli, a freakin' human eclipse. He was a defensive tackle on our football team.

"You do that thing?" he asked.

I nodded, dropping the pickles onto the black asphalt.

"I wanna go look."

"Shit, Lapanelli," said Sully. "You stupid fuckin' yeti. That's the *last* place you should go."

It seemed Sully had more to say, but he was interrupted by Deborah Zearey wrapping two slender arms around his waist. She was wearing tight corduroy jeans, tan clogs, and a snap-front denim shirt. She told us there was going to be a party at Dempsey's—a decaying cabin on the southern side of town, hidden from the road by a rogue trail of dogwoods and conifers.

"It'll be fun," she said, walking toward her sister's Chevy Impala. "You guys should come."

"I might," said Sully.

I took a bite of my burger and smiled.

"He's scared of her," I said.

"*Scared?*"

"A girl like Deb," I started, taking a long pull of soda, "she was dating seniors in eighth grade."

Now, I navigate my way between twin soccer fields, a blister of nicotine gum squished against my back teeth. Sully's yelling for his daughter to use her elbow, "like I showed you," so she won't get knocked off the ball. I extend my arms and applaud, exaggeratedly loud, in Callie's direction.

There was nothing especially significant about that autumn night. Sully, Cale, and I received weeklong suspensions for "defacing and vandalizing the property and surrounding grounds" at St. Edward's. Also, the following Saturday we were required to clean our mess under custodial supervision. I remember we spent a lot of time trying to convince Sully to call Deborah Zearey. Six days later, he finally asked her out. The two dated for the better part of the next eight years before, on a cloudless spring morning, exchanging marital vows. Cale and I were groomsmen. As a joke, we tied a rubber snake around the doorknob of their bridal suite.

Predictably, there's a long list of instructions from Liz as I load the girls into my car, all delivered in a stern, uncompromising voice. She wants Callie to get started on a timeline for her social studies class; Tig has to finish an assignment—two worksheets, front and back—for mathematics. Both girls need to do at least thirty minutes of reading—their books are in their backpacks. Also, she reminds me to prepare only *healthy* foods for their lunches the following day. "That means no fruit rolls or gummy snacks or chips," she says, emphasizing each word by tapping my windshield with her index finger. "Are we on the same page?"

I nod because, really, there's no other response. But on the drive home, I tell Callie and Tig to *please* dispose of their lunch-box detritus at school—even if there are leftovers—to prevent any "problematic" conversations with their mother. The girls are old enough to understand the myriad of differences between their parents. According to experts, as long as Liz and I are consistent with our conduct and expectations for the girls when they're in our respective company, Callie and Tig should be fine.

The girls are still wearing their soccer uniforms when we stop at the mall. The rubber nubs of their shoes clack against the slippery floor. Both girls need new dresses for a monthly manners and etiquette tutorial that starts at a local country club next Friday.

"We have to wear white gloves," says Callie, waving the brochure.

"I have gloves," says Tig. "I also have mittens."

"This is a different kind. They mean fancy, dinner-party gloves."

In a small and pricy children's clothing boutique, I watch the girls try on a series of dresses. Callie's favorite is a taupe, lace-trimmed model with delicate spaghetti straps. As she takes a few generous twirls in front of a three-way mirror, the dress's hem gets caught on her shin guards. She adjusts the side seams against her hips and, for a moment, looks ten years older—a college student preparing for a sorority mixer. Then Tig skips into the room, seemingly enchanted by the flowing train of her evening gown, a sheer and sparkly taffeta that inflates after every step.

"Oh, geez," says Callie, framing her face with outstretched fingers.

"Don't you love it?" asks Tig. "It's like a Cinderella dress."

She's staring forward, eyes riveted to her own reflection. Fortunately, the gown is so expensive that we can eliminate it based on price, and we don't have to discuss its grotesque lack of subtlety.

"Go look through your size," I tell Tig, whose head drops between her sagging shoulders. "There are lots of other nice ones."

Eventually, Tig settles on a sleeveless yellow sheath with a watercolor rose pattern. She asks me several times if she can wear the dress out of the store. But I remind her that she's still "sticky" from soccer. "Besides," I say, rubbing her hand, "it's for special occasions."

As we wander past the food court—Callie orders a cinnamon-dusted pretzel, Tig a watermelon slushy—I plead with them to keep their plastic-wrapped dresses from dragging against the ground. They slow to examine a pyramid of exotic shoes in a window display.

"Oh, Dad," says Tig, her voice quivering with excitement. "Those would be *perfect* with my new dress."

She's pointing to a red, spiky-heeled model with a faux-ruby broach fastened to its closure strap.

"No way," says Callie. "They're too high."

"It doesn't matter," I say, ushering them forward. "You already have shoes—the patent leather ones."

The girls race ahead, crossing a smooth tile bridge that bisects an illuminated fountain. A few feet beyond the other side is the entrance to Carmella's Paper & Things. I linger near the doorway, looking for a familiar face above the geometrically arranged racks of stationery and greeting cards. An elderly woman with coarse, chemically treated hair is balancing four small boxes in her arms. She lifts a set of notecards toward her chin, changing its angle to cut the light's glare against the transparent plastic casing. The woman nods, suddenly, and responds to a voice coming from the rear of the store. Nina appears from behind a cardboard display stand. A tremor of anticipation rushes through me like a hard vibration. I rap gently on the outside window. The elderly woman lowers and raises her head, seeking an unobstructed line of vision, as though she's trying to place me. Nina waves, then breaks into a playful jog.

"Hey," she says, tripping the shop's motion-sensor chime. "Look at you on a Sunday."

Behind me, the girls are clinging to their hangered dresses. They scuffle to my side, like metal ingots near a newly activated magnet—Callie licking her fingers, Tig using a straw to scrape the last droplets of her slushy from the bottom of its cup. After a moment, Callie rubs her chin, eyebrows raised in an expression of curiosity. She's trying to process this sudden dispatch of information. It's the first time she's seen her father show interest in a woman. Tig is also weighing the exchange, her eyes darting back and forth between Nina and me.

"Guys," I say, guiding the girls forward. "This is a friend of mine."

Nina introduces herself, shaking their hands with bouncy fist pumps.

"Oh, I *love* those." She gestures toward Tig's icy drink. "Sometimes I have them mix two flavors—cherry and blueberry, or lemon and tangerine."

Tig beams, glancing into her empty cup.

"Just finishing a little shopping," I say.

"We got party dresses," says Tig.

"But they're not for a party," says Callie. "We're starting Breeson's next week."

"Their mother signed them up for etiquette classes," I say. "In *theory*, they'll learn how to behave at social functions—the proper way to eat soup, which is the salad fork."

"Good things to know."

"And there's dancing," says Tig.

"Not, like, funky dancing." In a brief demonstration, Callie wiggles her hips and claws at the air with her fingers. "It's the kind of dancing where you have to *touch* the boy."

"*Eeeeew,*" says Nina.

"I know," says Tig.

From inside the store, the elderly woman calls to Nina, sounding testy and impatient. I apologize for the intrusion. "Oh, please," says Nina, making a slashing motion with her arm. Instinctively, I lean forward and kiss her quickly on the lips. The girls' eyes grow wide and, sweetly, Tig breaks into a gentle smile.

"Okay, say goodbye."

The three of us walk toward the parking lot. Tig stomps with her right foot, discharging a clump of dried mud from beneath her cleated sole.

"How do you know her?" asks Callie.

"Well, I guess from work."

"She's at your office?"

"No." I pull Callie close, hugging her against my waist. "She sells our cards at that store."

"You met her there?"

I nod.

"Is she your girlfriend?" asks Tig.

"She's a girl. And she's my friend."

"*Daaaddd,*" says Callie. "That's not what she means."

Near the mall's entrance, Tig deposits her cup into a garbage pail.

"We just like hanging out together," I say, shrugging.

"Have you been to her house?"

I nod.

"Has she been to *our* house?"

"Yes."

"Did she see my room?" asks Tig.

"I think so."

"What about dinner—have you taken her out to any restaurants?"

"I have."

"It sounds like she's your girlfriend."

"Sounds like she's your girlfriend," repeats Tig.

"Okay," I say, unlocking the car.

As the girls lay their dresses in the trunk, they notice the worn leather satchel that belongs to the college professor who owes money to Mr. Eugene. Tig snickers when Callie raises the nude sculpture. I usher them away and, before I've had a chance to start the ignition, Callie shouts from the back seat for me to turn on the radio—a pop station that's heavy on bass and high-pitched teen warblers. Tig removes an activity book from a pocket in the door and asks me for a pencil. During the drive home, we're mostly quiet except for Callie, who's singing along to the music.

At a lengthy stoplight Tig adjusts herself, bracing her feet against the front seatback. "Sheesh," she says suddenly. "I think she's your girlfriend."

The chair is lean and armless. I rest my hands against my knees, then fold them across my lap. To stop my legs from trembling, I squeeze my ankles together and concentrate on touching my heels to the floor, as though I'm depressing a two-pedaled clutch. I can feel my stomach contracting into a knobby fist. The room is swaying, up then down, like a ketch in choppy waters.

Behind me the door is closed. Against the far wall, I watch a white-faced clock sweep away each excruciating second. A hefty manila folder rests on the table in front of Dennis Gaines. There is also a bottle of mineral water in case his throat goes dry. Sitting quietly in the corner, Rose Potiker crosses her legs. She's holding a yellow legal pad and a gleaming gold pen. When I entered the room, she was introduced—by rote—as a representative from the human resources department. This is not the first time I have been down this road.

As Gaines talks, his words are slow and measured. He has spent hours rehearsing this speech, reviewing it with Potiker —searching for the precise balance of candor and compassion. There can be no ambiguity, no mossy grays. However, it's important that Gaines and Potiker, dual ambassadors of Silver Springs, come across as earnest and sincere. There is legal precedent: They don't want disgruntled former employees tripping them up over some careless remark and turning litigious. My head grows heavy and hot. Perspiration beads along the back of my neck, soaking into the cool collar of my shirt. Gaines keeps talking, his voice now borrowing the tone and timbre of droning machinery. I'm trying to listen because there are significant details about the breadth of the company's layoffs and my severance package and termination dates for my family's health care benefits—Gaines slaps a sheaf of papers labeled "extended Cobra coverage"—but I can't shake the image I have of myself exiting this room, dizzy and sluggish, newly unemployed.

After a long silence, Gaines describes the difficulty they had in making this "hard, hard" decision. "It wasn't performance based," he says, looking down at the table. He tells me it was rooted in the company's continued declining stock. There's a trace of melancholia in his voice—as though, incredibly, he's expecting a sympathetic response from me. But I can only muster a blank stare into the lopsided dimple of his navy and yellow necktie. My arms have turned numb, lying like dead fish across my thighs.

"Would you like something to drink?" asks Potiker, inching forward. She too knows the drill. As soon as they can get me hydrated and upright—by now I have surely exceeded my allocation of time—they can trundle me out the door and start their next scheduled beheading. But I can't move.

A flurry of dark thoughts races through my mind. I worry about my rent and my child support payments. I feel a sharp pain in my lower back as I consider breaking the news to Liz. There are soccer team fees and music lessons and braces for Callie's teeth. I imagine trying to register for extended health care benefits—a series of recorded voices ushering me from one computerized sentinel to another until, finally, I am placed on interminable hold. *Please have your company ID number ready...* The last time I lost my job it took me three days to speak with an actual person, only to discover the monthly surcharge for continued medical coverage resembled a mortgage payment. Twenty-two is the figure that skates across my subconscious— the interest rate on my Visa card if I'm late with a check. The girls will need school supplies and packed lunches and white gloves for their etiquette classes. On the corner of my nightstand is a small booklet of green vouchers that I mail to the bank every month for my car loan...

Gaines extends his right hand.

"If anything changes," he says. "We'd bring you back."

"In a minute," says Potiker.

I'm standing near the door, holding a bright packet of papers, though I don't remember leaving my chair. I desperately milk down my final moments of service at Silver Springs. It occurs to me that as long as I stay in this room, nothing can change—nobody will know I've been fired. To the rest of them, it's simply a meeting about a new line of greeting cards or my expense account or an altered company policy for billing clients. I lean my forehead against the doorframe, Gaines and Potiker watching from beyond my left shoulder. I remember an old comic book where Superman, flying at hyper speed, reverses the earth's orbit to push back time. If there was only a way to return to the ignorance and safety of yesterday. Or even this morning. I consider falling to my knees and pleading for mercy. I can tell them about my painful divorce and my doe-eyed daughters. I'll promise to work longer hours; I'll take a pay cut...

But it's all too late. Gaines's fingers brush against the copper strike plate around the doorknob. Time has slowed to a muddy slither. I can hear the pop of the metal latch and spindle. Then we're standing between twin rows of cubicles, my former colleagues hunched over their desks—answering e-mails and talking on phones and filling out crowded spreadsheets. I brace myself against a nearby copy machine. Potiker places her hand on my shoulder and leans forward. "Do you need any boxes?" she whispers.

Once I'm alone, I gaze silently at my dark computer screen. I will be given a chance to copy my personal files onto a disk, with company supervision, at a later date. Apparently, there's a history of destructive behavior: In the past, discharged employees, in fits of rage, have infected corporate systems with damaging viruses, or stolen software and company secrets. Slowly, I begin removing items from my corkboard walls—photographs of Callie in her soccer uniform and Tig in a swimming pool; newspaper clippings; cartoon panels; crib-sheet calendars from the girls' school. I wrap the painted rock paperweight in a roadmap from one of my first sales calls. There are files and pens and corporate policy manuals.

It doesn't take long for word of the layoffs to spread. Soon, Bill Sweeney's hunched over the crown of my cubicle, his eyes dimly following my movements. I surrender a butter knife I filched weeks ago from the cafeteria.

"Shove this in my ear," I say.

His mouth curves into an injured smile.

"Man," he says, nervously tapping his shoe against the carpeted floor. "I'm really sorry."

I tilt back in my chair. After a few moments of silence, I sweep three large stacks of worksheets into a metal trash can. They strike the bottom with a mighty *whoof*, loud enough to turn the heads of several people sitting nearby. Most of my former colleagues have retreated into protective cocoons, feigning ignorance. They're spineless ninnies who fear by acknowledging my termination they're somehow putting themselves at risk, as though my firing is contagious. Twice I catch Tom Naifeth staring across the aisle at me, curiously looking for signs of a breakdown—tears, cursing, balled fists. But whenever I look back he drops his head.

"Do you have any—" starts Sweeney.

"No," I say, ripping a pile of papers in half. "I've been unemployed for less than a half-hour. I have absolutely no idea what comes next."

Sweeney's a decent guy. Last fall, during a sales conference in Madison, Wisconsin, we got drunk together at the university's student union. After our third round of drafts, we invented a game called Pathetic Middle-Aged White Men. We set his digital wristwatch on our table and took turns engaging college girls in conversation. The objective was to talk for as many minutes as possible without having our marks excuse themselves—"In disgust," said Sweeney, spanking a wooden bench. There were bonus points for physical contact initiated by co-eds—touching a wrist, rubbing a forearm, etc. Though my memory's hazy—we drank a lot of beer—I recall winning the contest after chatting with a thin-lipped blonde for eleven minutes. Mostly, she and I talked about an aging quarterback for the Green Bay Packers.

On the ledge beside Sweeney's elbow, I unload some of the clutter from my desk: stapler, tape dispenser, plastic ruler, two pairs of scissors. It feels as though I'm hosting a miniature yard sale. "Help yourself," I say.

He promises to contact a friend who works for a publishing company.

"Maybe they're looking for sales reps," he says. "Or graphic artists. You did some of that, right?"

I nod, depressing the spring-loaded roller mechanism that releases my top drawer. It's filled with saltine crackers, condiment packets (ketchup, mustard, sugar), loose paperclips, wood and plastic coffee stirrers, Post-it notes, blunt pencils, rubber bands, soiled business cards. I dump the contents into a garbage pail. I use a can of compressed air to blow out the dust and crumbs clotted along the drawer's welded seams.

"Hey," says Josh Dyer, who appears behind Sweeney.

I toss him a cellophane package of sour balls.

"Oh, God," he says, stomping his leg. "I was gonna clean *my* office today."

When Sweeney realizes I haven't the strength (nor interest) to describe my circumstances to Dyer, he pulls him aside and quietly announces the layoffs. I watch Dyer's eyes lock against something immediate and tangible—my nameplate, my abandoned stapler. His reaction is natural: He's eager to know how this sudden and alarming information will affect his own mortality. As he stares at the now-closed conference room door; he must surely wonder who's next. He bends forward, clutching Sweeney's arm.

"Is there a list?" he says, his voice rising into a troubled register.

Before Sweeney can answer, Dyer lurches down the hallway. He aimlessly dips his head into several neighboring cubicles. In typically dramatic fashion, he appears to lose his balance near a soda machine, clawing to support himself against the silvery side of a drinking fountain. Sweeney blots his neck with a folded handkerchief and crosses his arms.

Many of the things I'd long intended to save—files, records, receipts, and binders filled with next big ideas—are now being rapidly discarded. The byproducts of countless hours of work, pages crowded with note-taking and brainstorms and minutes from staff meetings, are being stuffed into flimsy convenience-store bags that I'll tote to a giant dumpster in the loading dock. Sweeney refuses to leave, motivated by a queer combination of friendship and fear. We both jump when we hear the piercing wail of a female voice.

"Oh, no," says Kelly Krasnoff, smudged whiskers of mascara framing her eyes. "Hayes…"

She reaches forward and squeezes my hand. Her skin feels cold and slippery.

"It's okay—"

"You're in my prayers." She pauses, examining a picture of Callie and Tig sitting at a picnic table. "*All* of you."

She bends at the waist and gives me a hug, patting my shoulder with her bony fingers.

It only takes ninety minutes to purge the cubicle of any signs of my existence. Beside the keyboard, I leave a single Post-it note with a smiley face drawn in black marker. I use a dolly, the kind favored by hotel porters, to cart my belongings through the main lobby. Because the dolly's not permitted outside the building, I need to carry my boxes—all three of them—to the trunk of my car. On my second trip, I notice a few other employees who didn't survive the ax. A woman crying on a bench between twin flowerbeds is being consoled by a friend. I recognize an editor from "humorous paper cards" as he drags a large box across the asphalt by its floppy lid. Two women are embracing beneath an enormous red-and-blue Silver Springs sign. In the shadow of a Dutch maple, I see a doughy guy in a navy jumpsuit with a walkie-talkie pressed to his ear. Stitched to his left breast is a colorful shield-like emblem. When he turns, I can read the word *Security*, in white Century Gothic lettering, emblazoned across his back. It doesn't take long before I spot several other security guards—walking, riding on mountain bikes, driving in mid-size sport utility vehicles. As I recall, during the last batch of layoffs there were reprisals—acts of petty vandalism—by dismissed employees: broken windows, smashed picture frames, graffiti (the word *urine* written in Sharpie marker between Silver and Springs in the company logo).

Still, it seems like the ultimate indignity to be trailed by these minimum-wage rent-a-cops after losing a job. I can feel the day's shock and anxiety changing into anger. I stand beside the rear bumper of my car, staring across the parking lot at a stocky security guard with thinning brown hair. He's looping around several rows of striped spaces, slow and choppy, creating the circumference of a large circle with me near its center. A few times he speaks into the mouthpiece of his walkie-talkie, then lowers it into the black harness on his belt.

My right fist clenches, bouncing against the outside of my thigh. He's not carrying a weapon. Feral and clammy, I consider the possibilities—a series of metaphorical lines drawn in the sand. I'm ready to release my demons. If he passes the Toyota, parked a dozen yards away, I'll throw something from one of my boxes—a coffee thermos or a heavy glass candy dish. And if he speaks to me, asks why I'm still here, I'll slam my painted-rock paperweight into the side of his head.

A couple minutes later, I watch the security guard climb into an SUV and drive toward a neighboring warehouse. I sit behind the wheel of my car and gaze through the windshield. An art director I met during one of last year's RFIs is walking along a hurricane fence, smoking a cigarette and talking on his cell phone. His head snaps back and he explodes in laughter. This is my final image of Silver Springs, I think, as I follow the roadway that snakes between the company's hilly front courtyard.

The disturbingly bronzed faces of the Tremaine Brothers are painted on the side of a freebie fast-food glass filled with scotch and ice. The house is dark except for the pink nightlight glowing in my bathroom. Three boxes overflowing with the former contents of my office now rest on the living room floor. I've turned my chair sideways, using the arm of the couch as a footrest. I watch the occasional car drive down my street, tires gasping against the wet pavement. A cold, steady rain sounds on the roof like uncooked rice poured into a skillet. I'm chewing a cigar, spitting bourbon-colored saliva into a ceramic ashtray.

Last year, after an orthopedic surgeon diagnosed twin herniated discs in my lower back, he gave me a prescription for pain medication. I have taken my last couple of Vicodin tablets and, predictably, they've made me feel loose and dreamy. On the sidewalk outside, Mrs. Gaynor is retrieving her terrier's tootsie-roll turds with a transparent plastic glove. I raise my arm and, in a child's game of perspective, squash her between my thumb and forefinger. A rapid double-bleep comes from the girls' bedroom, heralding a new hour. It's a rubber wristwatch of Callie's that I've tried to disarm a half-dozen times.

I'm like an emotional drunkard, staggering down a set of seedy alleyways. I'm terrified by what's ahead—filing for unemployment benefits, scraping up my child support payments, hunting for a new career. I'll have to update my résumé, write a cover letter. (I make a mental note to purchase quality paper stock in light gray or celery.) There will be interviews for lower-paying jobs and decisions to make about whether we can still afford the girls' extracurricular activities. I remember my first few days at Silver Springs, sitting through orientation meetings behind packets of neatly segregated papers from HR. One of the representatives even discussed the company's unremitting goodwill should we ever lose our jobs—a premise that seemed distant and unnecessary, at the time, given that the room was crowded with people in their initial hours of employment.

But strangely, I also feel a tremendous sense of relief. A liberation. Tomorrow morning—and a foreseeable future of tomorrow mornings—I can sleep late. There are no more sales calls or invoices or testy conversations with retailers about back-ordered product. I see my "career" in social expressions sinking to the bottom of a very dark lake. Before I started working at Silver Springs, I'd never purchased a single greeting card. Instead, I used permanent markers to scrawl short messages—*Happy Birthday, Callie! Love, Dad*—across the shiny surfaces of wrapped gifts. Reaching down, I remove a sample holiday card from the nearest storage box. I display the card, half-opened, in the soggy ashtray and use a torch lighter to ignite its painted Christmas tree. The air fills with whirling black smoke and the stink of chemicals.

During the early months of our separation, Liz took the girls to visit her extended family in Vermont. By the second week, I was physically heartsick—the girls and I had never been apart for more than a couple days—and I spent my nights pacing circles in the darkness of this room. The distance between us was unfamiliar and suffocating. In my loneliness, I'd break down, weeping, my face buried deep in the seat cushions of the couch. This was my new life, and I worried that I'd always feel wounded and incomplete. I had trouble focusing: At my desk or behind the wheel of my car, I'd conjure favorite memories of Callie singing into a hairbrush microphone or Tig cooing in her crib.

I'm now visited by a similar emptiness, and I try to control my breathing beneath the invisible icebox lying across my chest. I ignore the blinking message light on my phone. I recognize the numbers—calls from Nina and Sweeney and another guy at work. I fish out a small deck of business cards from my wallet and build a squat-shaped hut on the back of a glossy magazine. Three times I try to set it ablaze, but my lighter's out of fuel. In a fit of frustration, I heave the lighter against the wall and it splinters into a trail of fractured pieces, coiled springs, tiny gold screws.

After I finish my drink, I wander to the garage. The cement floor is cold against my stocking feet. I slip my hands into a pair of black padded gloves and begin slugging the heavy bag that dangles from the ceiling. With every blow I can feel a transference of energy, prickly shockwaves running down my forearms. I deliver right crosses, left jabs, and uppercuts; I swing sloppy roundhouses that connect with a horizontal stripe of tape at eyebrow level. Then a series of combinations—jab, hook, straight— that makes the support chain squeak with friction. I don't picture my bosses' faces superimposed on the canvas skin; I'm only out for exercise—a way to burn off some of the day's disappointment. I lean forward, pulling the bag into an imaginary clench, and pepper its sides with short rabbit punches. My shirt is soon dark with perspiration, sticking to my armpits, belly, and back. I wrap my arms around the heavy bag and, suddenly, I'm squeezing it for support—spinning in a slow and clumsy two-step. In the distance, I hear a muffled clacking noise. Maybe it's a rodent rummaging through the trash or a passing truck's broken tailpipe. But it reminds me of the *bracka-brack* sound my football cleats would make against the loose gravel road as I jogged to the practice field with my high school teammates. I remember we had an old stone well with a hand pump that we'd use to draw water on hot summer afternoons. Sometimes we'd lie in the stubbly ryegrass and talk about everything that was still possible.

Tears are spilling down my cheeks, mixing with a sheen of warm sweat. I fall to my knees and then my back. Staring into the whiteness of the ceiling, I smell gasoline—a leak from my car or an unused lawn mower. What if I stay here? How long would it take for someone to notice I was missing?

After a sleepless night, I let the shower run until the water turns cold. I don't shave or eat breakfast. With a news channel playing absently behind me, I drink a soda and read the small story in the morning newspaper about the layoffs at Silver Springs. The sky is pale as zinc. I watch three kids loading onto a school bus, their backpacks slung across their shoulders. As the bus squeals away, I can see a guy following in a red Chrysler. He slaps his steering wheel, presumably frustrated by the bus's slow pace.

I make my bed and clean the bathroom, scrubbing the mildewy tiles around the tub with an old toothbrush. I start a load of laundry. In the basement there's a toy carriage Tig once used for her dolls, surrounded by hills of undersized clothes stored in plastic garbage bags. Beneath a glass-brick window is a battered steamer chest filled with the girls' artwork and school projects.

Though it's only my first day of unemployment, I'm already struggling to feel useful. In the kitchen hallway, illuminated by a pair of high-watt bulbs, I set up my ironing board and painstakingly press a basket of wrinkled clothes—chinos and button-down shirts and dresses that belong mostly to Tig. Cautiously, I slide the iron's hot prow between the pleats of a denim skirt. I pump long, foggy blasts of spray-starch from an aerosol can. When the iron's heated footprint touches a damp collar or cuff, transparent clouds of exhaust rise with a cheery sizzle. Soon the doorframes are heavy with rows of hangered clothing. If you look at them through squinted eyes, they resemble colorfully fringed curtains.

Next comes a strong memory—a runny collection of memories joined together—of watching my mother in our old laundry room. She wore a pastel housedress, standing over a whiny ironing board. The empty sleeve of a pink blouse jiggled beside a dark industrial sink. Resting on a nearby counter was a portable radio playing staticky country-western music. I was crouched beneath a Ping-Pong table in a neighboring room, arranging plastic soldiers around a tin castle that closed into a convenient carrying case. There was also a papier-mâché model, Mount Olympus, that I'd built for a second-grade assignment on Greek gods. I set up a pair of snipers behind its snowcapped peak.

The phone was pressed between my mother's ear and shoulder. She weaved her iron through a column of imitation pearl buttons on her pink blouse. As I pretended to detonate the door of my castle, I watched my mother hang the shirt on a rubberized clothesline above our hot water tank. She spread a new item of clothing on her board—a pair of cotton trousers—and pulled a squiggly knot from the phone's cord.

"That's stupid," she said, swinging the iron like a gavel. It struck the lid of the washing machine with a metallic clang. "We're already a month past due."

She was speaking to my father. It wouldn't be long before he was living somewhere else. I could see my mother's head drop, chin into chest. A deep sigh, followed by the phone being returned to its wall cradle three times in rapid succession—*pow, pow, pow!* Then I heard a piece of plastic, splintered by the force, bounce against the cement floor. One of my soldiers had a bayonet fastened to the end of his rifle and I drove him forward, goring an imaginary enemy.

Maybe this was the first time I knew my life was about to change. In the basement's cold silence, I heard my mother sniffling. She removed a freshly folded undershirt from a pile and wiped her eyes. I may have asked her if she was okay; I know I was worried. She leaned forward and took a loud drink from the spigot. Then she smoothed down the waist of her dress and returned to her laundry.

A few hours later, I remember sitting with my father at the kitchen table. He'd fixed himself a plate of food: salted crackers, raw onion, and a tin of sardines. Balanced on three cookbooks behind me was a small black-and-white TV. Between bites, my father watched a football game—Oklahoma versus Texas. He poured beer into a tall glass, waiting for its foamy head to retreat before taking his first swallow. It wasn't until he'd nearly finished with his meal that he spoke his first words to me.

"This is no good," he said, skewering a tiny fish with his fork and shoving it into his mouth. At the time I didn't know if he was talking about his food or something of greater consequence. Something a seven-year-old boy couldn't possibly understand.

I look down and see one of my undershirts curling across the lip of the wicker laundry basket. It's the same brand of white V-necks my father wore—the type my mother probably used to dry her eyes. "This is no good," I say aloud, the iron's hard-fiber handle still gripped in my hand.

The grass is shaggy and half-covered by blond leaves. Because the eastern side of the house is exposed to direct sunlight, it's subject to star-shaped blisters of cracking paint—above the door, near the gable of the tarpaper roof. One of the shutters on Callie's bedroom window is loose, listing sideways like a droopy eyelid. There are several missing bricks on the front landing—a residential-code violation that's punishable by fine. A capsized skateboard rests against the exposed root of a purple ash that cranes across the driveway. The grounds are pocked with the typical clutter associated with children: deflated soccer ball, bicycle helmet, red jump rope tied to a wobbly handrest beside the door. The girls' names appear in faded white chalk on twin stones cresting from an L-shaped flowerbed.

My heart feels as though it's humping through my chest. I steady myself against Liz's car, pressing my arm into the passenger-side window. The back seat is crowded with books, broken pencils, hairclips, and shredded foil wrappers from honey-roasted peanuts. I peer into the house and see the back of Liz's head, her hair fastened into a low ponytail with a white rubber band. She's seated at the dining room table, bathed in muted light from her laptop screen. My hand rises slowly. I tap the wood, soft then harder. She walks across the kitchen, not realizing it's me until she's nearly at the door.

"The girls aren't home yet," she says.

This afternoon I'm taking Callie and Tig shopping for Halloween costumes. I nod, explaining that I arrived early to speak with her. A squirrel races frantically down the driveway, disappearing beneath the rear porch. Liz looks defensive; she crosses her arms and straightens her spine. I take a deep breath, my heels settling against a nubby shoe mat.

"I lost my job."

I'm hoping if the words come quickly, they'll disarm her—carve through any petty disagreement she's prepared to revisit. I simply want to share this information. But I fear if we get side-tracked by another argument—homework assignments, dietary concerns, impending bills—my sudden layoff will make me an easy target: *Oh, Christ*, I imagine her shouting. *You can't even hold a goddamn job.*

"They released a bunch of us," I say. "It was in today's paper."

There's a long silence. Liz's eyes grow wide and she clutches the doorframe with both hands. For a moment, she rocks forward on the balls of her feet and I think she's going to be sick.

"Oh, my God," she says finally.

I give her an abbreviated summary of my meeting with human resources—extended medical coverage, severance package, unemployment benefits. I tell her the child support agency will continue withdrawing her payments directly from my bank account. Lastly, because the color still won't return to her face, I proffer a lie—a series of lies—about promising leads in the job market.

As her hands linger above her hollow cheeks, I watch her eyes turn red and watery. She steps back and bumps her head against the pantry door. I follow her into the living room. The gray couch we bought at a warehouse sale years ago is striped with clothing—jackets and scarves, thermal shirts and sweaters. She sits on a battered Mission-style chair—*my* chair—and buries her head in her palms. At first it's difficult to hear her, the sounds leashed together in a furious moan. She's pitched forward, chest to knees, and her shoulder blades rise against her sweatshirt with every heaving breath.

Like a swimmer, she lifts her mouth for air. I see wet tracks running down her face, glassy in the afternoon light. She begins to ramble, her speech sprinting ahead of her thoughts. I nod in blind agreement. She's worried about our finances—already depleted from a long divorce. She wants to know about the girls' music lessons and soccer, the mortgage, *food*. "Next weekend Tig has three birthday parties," she says, wiping her nose. "That's three gifts—about seventy-five dollars. Do *you* have seventy-five dollars? I don't."

A great wave of momentum carries her toward new ground. After a couple short breaths, she takes a dimly introspective view of things, wondering aloud how her life turned out so wrong. She treads through her personal history, recalling the years before we met. There was a cute little apartment in a five-story walk-up, with linen curtains, twin flowerboxes, and stained pine rafters. She was the business manager for an independent record company, a Bohemian outfit where employees wore t-shirts with clever phrases emblazoned across their chests and, twice weekly, were permitted to take home as many CDs as they could carry. She had a "woody"—her word—for the head of A&R, a grungy-looking guy with bleached hair and a perpetually stubbly chin. On Friday evenings, most of her colleagues would gather in a bar downstairs called the Barking Spider for margaritas served in Frisbee-sized stem glasses. The back room had billiard tables, dartboards, and a garishly lighted trivia game that people would play for shots of liquor.

One night while watching a friend of mine work an Addams Family pinball machine near the hallway to the restrooms, I met Liz for the first time. We were both tipsy and I interrupted her conversation with a woman named Dee Dee by squeezing into their wood-paneled booth. They were talking about some guy Dee Dee had recently started dating—he was attending a wedding in California and wanted her permission to call his old girlfriend, who lived nearby. "That's crazy," I said, boldly draping my arm across the seat behind Liz. "He's asking for your approval to screw around." They silently nodded above the salted rims of their glasses. By the end of the evening, Liz had scrawled her phone number on the back of a business card. We came together in the parking lot for a quick, tequila-tart kiss with our friends watching from their cars. This was ground zero of our relationship: the exact moment in Liz's story when her life began to unravel.

Of course, there were signs—dozens of them during our courtship—that we were a poor match. After a weeklong business trip to Indiana and Kentucky, I pushed back a longstanding date with Liz to watch a football game with my buddies. This would become a touchstone during future arguments, pulled from the ether whenever Liz wanted to cite my lack of readiness for a romantic relationship. "I was *really* looking forward to being with you," she'd say, hot with rage. "Talk about a red flag. You should've been *excited* to see me—more than a stupid game."

Her rants were always filled with little phrases of corroboration—"people say" or "my friends notice"—as though there was a clandestine community supporting her many erroneous claims about me. Too often I'd seen the way she gathered encouragement: rambling aimlessly to a friend, her voice gaining strength like a steam engine, until the person across from her, anxious and confused, simply nodded their head. In Liz's mind, this slight gesture was proof of devotion—an indication that her friend was going "all in" behind Liz's hand. "You're so wrong," she'd tell me, jabbing her finger against the air. "Ask Rachel Lutz—we were just talking about you."

By our last year together, I'd finally convinced her to see a counselor with me. But the visits were frustrating—Liz rarely dropped her guard low enough for us to accomplish any real work. Once, when our therapist suggested medication, Liz smashed a box of Kleenex. She was convinced that I had proposed the diagnosis—that I'd secretively badgered the counselor into recommending pharmaceuticals. After every session we'd leave the therapist's office with a punch list—"Don't make it a punch-*out* list," the counselor would joke—of behavioral tips to focus on during the subsequent weeks. *Be empathetic. Encourage your partner. Respond with sweetness.* Typically, we'd consult our respective lists for the first day or two following appointments. But by week's end, we'd revert to our old habits.

Before our final visit to the counselor, during an especially ugly fight about the girls' hectic schedules, Liz tore her punch list into confetti and dumped it on my head from the second-floor landing. My memory of that day remains vivid, perhaps because there was a singular moment, as I was standing alone in the bathroom, Callie's and Tig's young voices reverberating through the tile and painted drywall, that I could literally see my marriage screech to a merciful end. I was staring into the mirror above the sink, my hair and shoulders littered with scraps of paper. I pressed my palm against the reflective glass—a solitary figure stranded inside a suffocating, real-life snow globe.

For a long time, during the most difficult part of our divorce, we transferred the girls in public places—schoolyards, restaurants, library lobbies—for our own protection. According to experts, we'd be less likely to engage in damaging conduct if we were surrounded by other people. Objective witnesses. Still, there were days when we couldn't contain our rage, and one of us would ignite this monstrous bonfire of resentment by taking a cheap shot after the girls had been sealed in the car. Invariably, the exchange was followed by a blizzard of breathtakingly malicious voice and text messages—soon-to-be former spouses shedding any pretense of civility, probing for weak spots in the person they once loved most. Cruel remarks about fleshy hips, disturbed relatives, issues with intimacy.

On a brilliant summer morning, shortly after Liz learned how much she would be receiving in monthly support payments, I waited for the girls in my idling car. A gentle breeze pushed an empty bag of potato chips across the parking lot at Dinks. In the few seconds it took me to retrieve the shiny green trash, Liz had worked her way to my door. She was clutching a bristly stack of bills against her chest, frayed envelopes and awkwardly twisted papers. Her voice was loud enough to draw the attention of a family waiting near the drive-thru window. In the distance, I could hear a woman telling her son to turn away.

Liz's words were quick and compressed. I saw her gas bill and, below it, in familiar blue and orange, a statement from the phone company. Her nostrils tightened into boneless arches. We were close enough that I felt her warm spittle against my neck and chin. I didn't have the language or capacity to slow her down.

I raised my eyes and surveyed the space behind her, looking for the girls. As I stepped forward, I could see her free arm moving away from her body, a narrow flash of butterscotch winking from her closed hand. By the time our bodies were even, toes to heels, the thumb side of her fist was crashing into my abdomen—a clumsy punch that threatened to dislocate her fingers. But then came a sudden sting above the crown of my pelvis. It wasn't until I saw her arm withdraw, slow and straight, that I realized what had happened. Gripped in her clubby hand was a spike—a yellow pencil that belonged to one of our daughters. I paused for a moment, trying to process her actions. The blood was hot, sucking my shirt against my skin. I felt the wetness leaking into the waistband of my trousers. I don't remember reaching down, but when I looked at my palm it was murky red.

"Oh, God," she said, the pencil still clasped in her fist like a broken handle.

All the hardness erased from Liz's face, in the blink of an eye, as though it had been carried away with her last breath. Then she started to cry—violent, gulpy sobs that shook her shoulders and made her arms tremble. I watched her struggle to speak, her dried and crinkled lips fighting to produce a recognizable sound.

Without warning, two small shadows appeared against the black pavement behind my car. The girls were squeezed together, Callie partially shielding her sister. Both girls were pale—I could see their eyelashes twitching like the mouths of spiny fish. Their mother was weeping, her face buried in the hinge of her elbow. I braced myself against a lightpost. The girls were gazing at the rusty-red pinwheel on my shirt. In a moment of clarity, I understood that the scene must've been confusing and, worse, terrifying for them. The lie came quickly—a torrent of make-believe designed to restore sanity in their troubled world. "The car door," I said, blurting the disjointed words as I dropped to my knee. In a calm and reassuring voice, I described how I was reaching for something in my glove compartment—"something for Mom"—and I caught myself on the sharp corner of the car door. "You know how Mom hates blood." I tapped Liz on the leg and she nodded, dabbing her moist eyes with her shirtsleeve. "I think it just freaked her out."

This seemed wholly logical to the girls, too young and innocent to know better.

"Dad cut himself on the car door," said Callie, as if it was the only possible explanation—the only thing that could've happened

Outside Liz's house, I hear the sound of my daughters' shoes scuffling up the driveway. I crouch beside Liz and place my hand on her back, preparing for the girls to enter the room. By now, they'd hardly find it surprising to see their mother fighting back tears. But I worry about the example I'm setting. Despite years of tension between Liz and me, I don't want the girls to think I dislike their mother. It's a small gesture, my hand moving down Liz's curved spine, but it shows my daughters I'm capable of compassion.

"Dad's in the house," says Tig.

She's standing in the doorway, her backpack resting on the ground. After a brief silence, we hear the screen door slap closed.

"Where?" says Callie.

"I'm in here, honey," I say.

Both girls are staring at us. It's been a long time since they've seen us together, in this house. Tig's eyebrows flare down against the bridge of her nose, as though she's suddenly been called upon to solve a math equation. She sees the wet streaks on her mother's face.

"Everything's fine," I say, pre-emptively. "I just got some bad news. At work. And I was sharing it with your mom."

"Did someone die?" asks Callie.

"No," I say. "It's nothing like that."

"Dad," says Tig, unzipping her coat, "did you get in trouble?"

On a different day, I might suspect a niggling remark from Liz had put this idea in Tig's head.

"Yes," I say, patting Liz on the back and rising. "I got in trouble at work—for taking too many ketchup packets from the cafeteria."

"*Dad*," says Callie.

"Really." Tig crosses her arms and tries to look serious. "What happened?"

"It's nothing you guys need to worry about," I say, kissing them both on their scalps. "Okay—who wants to get Halloween costumes?"

In tandem, they leap against the wooden floorboards, rattling a crystal antelope on the bookshelf that Liz and I bought in Portland. From Tig comes a rapid surge of ideas, one after the next, starting with the vampire queen her friend Kimmy suggested.

"I was also thinking about being a diva or a cheerleader or, maybe, a fairy with sparkly wings and a glow-in-the-dark wand."

"That's retarded," says Callie.

"Hey—what did I tell you about that language."

"Retarded's not a curse word."

"But it's not nice," I say, stealing a glance at Liz, who's still collecting herself. "I don't want any more insults."

"I still like fairies," says Tig.

"Me, too," I say.

"I wasn't talking about *fairies*." Callie shoves her backpack beneath the dining room table. "You don't know if they're gonna even have glow-in-the-dark wands."

"They might," says Tig, skipping toward the door.

"Cal," I say, pulling her close and speaking softly into her ear. "Let her be excited about something. Okay? It doesn't hurt anything."

"Well, it hurts *me*."

"Oh, no it doesn't." I kick her gently on her bottom. "Give her a break."

Turning back, my eyes catch on a photograph on a ledge near the window. It's the four of us shortly after Tig was born— Callie's peeking over the side of a blue pram, with Liz and me behind her. I hear one of the girls tinkling in the bathroom behind me.

"You can keep them for dinner," says Liz, suddenly.

I nod.

"You know," she says, words caught in her chest, "before I met you, I never had any money problems."

I want to remind her that before she met me, she didn't have children. But I'm silent, waiting the obligatory three-count—so she'll know I heard her—before starting my retreat.

The girls are already sitting in the back seat of my car when I leave the house. As I walk past the kitchen window, I feel movement coming from the other side of the glass—Liz rising from the chair and, perhaps, fixing herself a cup of hot tea.

A massive, single-story building sits near the end of a strip mall on Sandusky. Until recently, it housed a popular super store—a chain specializing in dry goods sold in laughably large quantities: towers of toilet paper, back-breaking crates of canned soups, mattress-size sacks of ground coffee. As the owners of the space search for a new "permanent" tenant, they've signed a series of month-long leases. There's a costume shop through Halloween and, starting in mid-November, a holiday repository called Christmas Towne that will feature several racks of discontinued Silver Springs products.

After the electric doors glide soundlessly apart, the girls and I are greeted by a seven-foot-tall mannequin with a machete buried in its head. A battery pack activates the mannequin's right arm, lunging aimlessly forward, and a sinister, horror-movie howl. The sudden movement surprises Tig, who jumps sideways.

"He got you," says Callie, filled with glee.

"No."

"You were totally scared."

Tig shakes her head, then presses against my leg.

We pass an information kiosk where a teenage boy, dressed in shimmery black cape and Gothic face paint, gazes mournfully into space.

"I think he's a vampire," whispers Tig.

"No," says Callie. "He didn't have fangs."

The girls wander the aisles, examining the plastic-wrapped costumes hanging from corkboard dividing walls—popular movie villains, cartoon characters, overly gruesome accident victims, princesses, superheroes. Cautiously, Tig approaches a rubber-mask version of a harrowing alien, with distended eyeballs and serpentine tongue. She touches its crooked nose with the tip of her index finger.

"*Eeeewww*," she says.

"That's a gross one."

She nods, disappearing around a corner to inspect the next row. From the corner of my eye I notice Callie working her way toward an "adults only" section: spiked brassieres, studded leather G-strings, French chambermaid outfits, and thigh-high vinyl boots. I shuffle into the entrance, covertly blocking her path. A dozen yards away stands a gargoyle statue with its gray arm extended. Every few moments, I watch Tig reach for something in the shadows. It's not until I move closer, across a generous aisle, that I see what the gargoyle's holding in its clawed fingers: a silver chalice teeming with wrapped candy.

"Tig," I shout into a bullhorn with phony police department emblems. "No more sugar!"

I hear giggling, followed by the patter of sneakered feet.

The girls continue shopping and I stroll around the perimeter of the store. I stumble upon a section crowded with highly detailed costumes designed for people who take the holiday too seriously—astronaut helmets with working lights, robot masks featuring voicebox converters, fleece-coated camel suits for two. This little trip with the girls is a welcome distraction from my firing. But my eyes seem drawn only to the assorted price tags, as though they've been illuminated by a spear of white light. I'm reminded of the way it feels to live without money, eternally weighing cost against need. Dinners of boxed macaroni or canned soup. Calls to my sister for another round of hand-me-down clothes for Callie and Tig. Using a shoe tree and a mallet to stretch the girls' soccer cleats for one more season.

During a disastrous period several years ago, before I started moonlighting for Mr. Eugene, I would occasionally resort to petty theft. After loading shopping baskets at local convenience stores, I'd tuck a final item or two beneath my arm—disposable razor blades, batteries, school supplies, shampoo. Usually I wore a quilted winter parka to shield the stolen goods. Though I was often ready with an excuse—"Oh, geez," I imagined saying if the alarm sounded, "where's my head today?"—it was never needed. I could talk my way out of trouble, I reasoned. *This is all just a silly mistake, a misunderstanding. I'm terribly sorry.* Surely no criminal—for that's what I was, a criminal—would pay for his paper towels and dish soap and ibuprofen tablets, only to filch a bottle of conditioner. (Who steals *conditioner?*) Once, repulsively, I included the girls in a last-minute scheme when I didn't have enough cash in my wallet, allowing Tig to leave the store with a pricy bottle of children's vitamins in her hand.

It was shameful behavior. And worse, as a father of two young daughters fighting for shared custody, it was profoundly dangerous. Even a single store manager dismissing my story—a mistake, a misunderstanding—would have cost me the thing I value most in this world. Risking it all for a spool of dental floss or a tube of moisturizing cream. But strangely, the guilt rarely stayed with me beyond the car ride home. Somehow I was able to justify my conduct: This wasn't really me. Rather, it was an aberration, a form of survival during an especially trying time.

With each genuine purchase, I grew more aware of its corresponding financial consequence. I became a whiz at simple mathematics, adding (and subtracting) the rounded-up price of every item that found its way into (and out of) my shopping cart. On Sunday mornings I'd dismantle the newspaper, leaving the sports and editorial sections for later in favor of countless pages of colorful coupons. There were savings on breakfast cereal, iced cookies, laundry detergent, seedless grapes. Using a pair of sharp scissors with a molded plastic handle, I meticulously cut each coupon along its dotted border. Then I collected them all in a neat little stack, smallest to largest, held together by one of the girls' elastic ponytail bands.

For months I was the jackass who clogged the checkout line as clerks deducted thirty-seven cents from halved peaches or potted meats. Invariably, I was ahead of a frustrated housewife who struggled to entertain her kids—squeeze toys, chocolate-covered raisins, extraneous photographs in tabloid magazines. A couple times my coupons had expired and the cashier was forced to page her manager for an imposing-sounding code to reboot her register. During our interminable wait, I could feel the eyes of the customers behind me burning spiteful holes into the back of my head.

Tonight the girls and I are on the clock. Liz expects them home by seven-thirty. As I walk toward the middle of the store, Tig races between a pair of arching displays.

"Okay, Dad," she says, pausing to catch her breath. "I know what I want to be."

Resting against her outstretched forearms is a gauzy helix of yellow and white fabric. There's also an oversize hat with a bouquet of artificial flowers stapled above its brim. I push back several folds of scratchy polyester to reveal a label that reads, *Southern Belle.* Hooked across Tig's elbow is a flimsy parasol.

"Interesting choice," I say.

"She doesn't even know what that *means,*" says Callie, appearing from behind a replica mummy.

"That's fine." I playfully cup my palm across Callie's mouth. "She likes the costume—that's all that matters."

"I like the costume," says Tig, smiling broadly. "It's got a hat and an umbrella and a really puffy dress."

"Geeth," says Callie, slobbering against the seams of my fingers.

I lead them toward the checkout line.

"What about *you?*" I inspect the items cradled in Callie's arms. "Did you find something?"

"I'm gonna invent a costume." She reveals a hinge-top kit filled with stage makeup (black, white, and red), lacy spider-web gloves, tarnished silver chain with fearsome skull pendant, and a skin-tight t-shirt featuring a bedazzled Stratocaster guitar. "Maybe a zombie rocker."

"Love it," I say, rewarding her ingenuity with a slap on the shoulders.

"Can I use some of your makeup?" asks Tig.

"No—you've got your *own* costume."

"I just want a little—"

"Of course," I say, stepping between the girls. "There's enough for both of you."

"Dad—this is *mine*."

"That's silly." I look down, making sure our eyes meet. "In this family we share."

After a moment of contemplation, Callie reaches forward and rips the parasol from Tig's arm.

"Fine—then I'm using this umbrella."

"Dad!"

As I grab for the parasol, Callie tries screening it with her body. I tickle her along the ribs, hoping to lighten the mood. But she cocks her arm and threatens to throw the fragile umbrella into the nearby gargoyle statue.

"Cal…"

She plants her hind leg, like a pitcher beginning his windup, and as the parasol rushes past her ear I pluck it from the sky.

"I *hate* having a younger sister!"

She kicks an empty box in Tig's direction.

"Stop it."

The three of us walk silently toward the register. A pack of teenagers stands a few feet away, jointly paring down a heap of merchandise in their shopping cart.

"You might not believe this," I say, lowering my lips near Callie's cheek, "but one day you're gonna share everything— shoes, shirts, sweaters."

"Doubt it."

"*Not my stuff,*" says Tig.

The teenagers have finished with the cashier—a middle-aged woman wearing a rhinestone tiara and a button that reads *Happy Freakin' Halloween*—and they haul their purchases to the parking lot.

"One day," I repeat, shaking my index finger. "One day."

The three of us sit in the parking lot at the Shrimp Boat restaurant, sharing a family-size order of fried clam strips. Balanced on the lowered armrest of my car's front seat is a pair of plastic cups, one filled with tartar sauce and the other with ketchup. Tig sucks a drink of orange soda through a straw.

"Okay," she says, tucking her feet beneath her buttocks. "Would you rather take a bath in throw-up—like, from a bunch of different people—or eat a worm sandwich?"

"Eeeeew, nasty," I say.

"Worm sandwich," says Callie. "But I'd put a *lot* of mustard on the bread."

"The worms are still alive," says Tig.

"And they're wiggling in your stomach," I say.

Callie sticks out her tongue, revealing a tan clump of chewed clam and breadcrumb batter.

"It's still better than sitting in a bathtub of other people's puke," says Callie.

Tig nods.

"It would get all in your hair and nose and—"

"C'mon," I say, snapping my fingers. "I thought we were supposed to make good choices. You know, like, would you rather have a snowmobile or a surfboard?"

"Snowmobile," says Callie.

"Snowmobile," repeats Tig.

"Anyway," says Callie, shoving a clam strip between her upper gum and incisor like a giant fang. "There's nowhere to surf in Ohio."

For some reason Tig finds this amusing and giggles, splashing her lap with orange spittle. As she's blotting dry her tights with a paper napkin, I watch a familiar figure emerge from a liquor store. He's holding a bottle of booze by its neck, sheathed in a brown bag. He walks past several neighboring storefronts and pauses near an optician, his left shoulder braced against a steel awning post. The headlights from a small, fuel-efficient car set him aglow, turning his shadow into an elongated Rorschach test.

He's wearing a camel-hair overcoat and a dark plaid scarf that's knotted around his neck. A group of teenage boys passes, disappearing into a chain store that sells video games. His name is Chris Effinger, and he works as a computer programmer for a large insurance company. He flexes forward in his wingtips, allowing the toes of his shoes to scoot across the edge of the curb, as though he's a swimmer positioned on a starting block.

For obvious reasons, I never make collections when I'm with the girls. But Effinger and I have had a hard time connecting— last week he was called away on business, and the week before he was suffering from a stomach virus. I only agreed to meet him this evening, with the girls, because our exchange promises to be brief—a simple surrendering of cash.

I let him wait, preparing the girls for distraction by turning the radio to their favorite station.

"He's an old friend," I say. "This will only take a minute." I rise from the car and brush off my clothing. "No fighting—leave each other alone."

I approach Effinger and he nods, adjusting his bottle of liquor against the inside of his forearm, as though he's toting a football. He turns up the collar of his coat and blows a couple quick puffs of breath onto his free hand. Nubs of lint from his scarf cling to the day's-end stubble beneath his chin. There is a moment of silence and his eyebrows kiss together, draining toward the bridge of his nose.

He speaks in an animated cadence, his shoulders arching against the smooth fabric of his coat. In a familiar refrain, he recounts several of his failed selections—college and pro games that took unsatisfying turns in the waning minutes. Then he focuses his contempt on the half-dozen messages I left on his answering machine.

"I'm good for it." He reaches into his pocket and removes a stack of folded money, slowly counting out eighteen bills into my exposed palm. "I'm not goin' anywhere."

I take a couple steps to my right to shield our encounter from the girls, whom I know are watching. He continues talking and I find myself staring at a frothy star of saliva in the corner of his mouth. When he's finished he mentions a game from this coming weekend—seemingly in the hopes of reading my reaction. We shake hands awkwardly: I'm slow to respond and his fist is gripped around my fingers.

As I walk back to the car, I can see the girls' faces floating hazily in the windshield. A streak of ketchup rises crookedly from Tig's lips. Crumbled remnants of fried clam strips speckle my seat. The music is loud and the girls are punching the air in time to the beat. I lower the volume—"Awww, Dad!"—and take a sip of diet cola. My windows are fogged with moisture from the girls' breath.

"That man looked angry," says Callie.

"He's a baddy," says Tig.

"No, he was just a little upset." I wipe a greasy fingerprint from the console at my side. "He was running late for—late for something."

"What was he giving you?" asks Callie.

"Just some files for work."

"It didn't look like files."

"He was mad," says Tig.

"Did you make him mad?" asks Callie.

"I hope not."

I reach across my shoulder and pass around a handful of individually wrapped towelettes, the kind that smell like disinfectant cleaning solution.

"What were you talking about?" asks Callie.

"Stuff."

"*Dad.*"

"Just stuff." I turn forward in time to see the group of teen-age boys leaving the video game store. "Nothing important."

"Why was he angry?"

"I'm not sure he was angry—"

"He *looked* like it."

"Yeah," says Tig. "He looked angry."

I shrug.

"Who wants dessert?"

"You're just changing the subject," says Callie.

"Hey, Dad," says Tig. "Are *you* a goody or a baddy?"

"I hope I'm a goody."

"Geez," says Callie, rubbing the damp cloth across her mouth and nose. "He's our dad."

"And dads are goodies," says Tig.

"Pheeeew," I say, pretending to wipe the flop sweat from my brow.

"Not always," says Callie. "Hitler was a baddy."

"He was," I say. "But I don't think he had any children."

Together they pack their flimsy boxes and napkins into a white paper sack. Tig is staring ahead, chewing on the plastic lid of her cup, when Callie leans forward, conspiratorially, and says, "Some dads are bad people."

I nod.

"But *not* our dad," says Tig.

"Except," I announce, raising my index finger and pointing at them in the rearview mirror, "when you guys don't clean your room."

As I gather the garbage, I can see Callie rolling her eyes. I jog to a dumpster pressed against the side of the restaurant and glance back at the car, watching the girls swaying again to their music. It's hard to know what they truly think of me. They rely on me, they love me—I'm sure of it. But I wonder about their image of me during the rest of the time. They've surely fostered opinions about my work and behavior and the days I spend without them. It makes me curious. I'd like to know if their vision of me is similar to the one I have of myself. I worry that the best parts of me are often obscured by all the ugliness with Liz, or by some brief and mysterious action, like meeting a stranger in a darkened parking lot. Sometimes when I bark orders at the girls—clear the table, get ready for bed—one of them will shake her head and say, "You're always angry, Dad." I'm not sure if this is how they really feel, a legitimate impression, or if they're simply snapping back at me in frustration.

The thing I want most in the world is their happiness. And it would break my heart to discover they didn't know this about their father. Instead, years from now, maybe they'll associate me with the hardships and pain of their adolescence—similar to memories of a churlish teacher or schoolyard bully. This pattern of thinking makes me want to embrace the girls and draw them hard against my ribcage, then take them on a shopping spree through the mall. I need the good memories—skating rinks, camp-outs on the living room floor, fried clam dinners in the back seat of my car—to outweigh the bad.

In the distance, I see Tig's hands clapping behind the passenger window. She bends forward and her hair brushes the back of the front seat. As I walk toward the car, my fingers sink into the pockets of my jacket. I feel Effinger's cash rolled and banded into a fat tube. "Are you a goody or a baddy," I hear Tig's voice asking in my head. It's not so easily definable, I tell myself, releasing the tight lump of bills. The only thing the girls know is that I can buy them snow boots and school supplies and weekly Chinese dinners.

These men, like Effinger, aren't much different from me, except at breakfast each morning the first thing they do is turn to the betting line in the newspaper. Mr. Eugene provides a service—a distraction from their otherwise somniferous lives. And I'm nothing more than an errand boy, a UPS man in reverse, taking instead of delivering.

A few months ago, I came home with a splotch of blood on my shirtsleeve that I got from slugging a guy in the mouth for missing three payments. I was helping Callie with her math when she noticed the stain. I told her it was salsa from lunch.

"It doesn't look like salsa," she said, raising her eyebrows.

That was probably the closest I've come to telling the girls a little something about my work for Mr. Eugene—and only because I'd had a couple of whiskeys. To get the shirt clean, I had to scrub it with a special type of prewash detergent.

The door swings open as I approach the car. Tig raises her arms and squeezes me around the waist.

"Callie turned up the music again," she says.

"That's okay."

She seems disappointed that I'm not more upset with her sister.

After we buckle ourselves into our seats, I suggest a quick stop for donuts. Both girls squeal with excitement.

"You know why?" I ask, peering into the empty darkness. "Because I'm a *goody*."

Tight fists of dirt leap across the sidewalk, forming shallow parabolas that leak stones and twigs onto the grassy curb. From my car, I watch two men digging a chest-deep hole in the cold earth. Nearly five yards of space is demarcated by gas company warning flags—orange nylon sheathed around flexible wire rods. One of the men, wearing light blue coveralls and a yellow helmet, retrieves a pick-ax from his truck. He pauses to clean the lenses on his safety glasses with the thumb of his glove. Before he casts a swing into the dark pit, he says something to his partner. The other man nods and then retreats to a neighboring lawn, where he uses a shovel to knock the mud from his boots. His breath is a curling white mist.

This morning I waited almost ninety minutes for Mr. Eugene to arrive at Gilberto's. I sat in the lounge and tried to read a newspaper, my eyes jumping absently from one story to the next. Four times I lighted a short double Maduro until, finally, I simply chewed its soggy end. My heart would skip whenever the alarm on the back door sounded. There were three deliveries—cigars, beverages, mail—before Mr. Eugene entered and I was waved into his office.

"That's a bad break," he said as I stood silently against the wall. He knew I had lost my job. "Fucking economy."

I placed my collection on his desk, nearly six thousand dollars in a salmon-colored Silver Springs envelope. He took a sip of coffee from a Styrofoam cup, then examined his toasted bagel, lightly buttered, on a creased sheet of wax paper.

"Did you tell your girls?" he asked.

I shook my head.

"Probably for the best." After taking a bite of bagel, he scanned the space around him until Dove appeared with a fresh stack of paper napkins. "No need to worry them."

I nodded.

Then he said something I couldn't hear. Dove moved about the furniture as if on wheels, darting between a card table and a pair of file cabinets. He presented a few pages of legal-type documents to Mr. Eugene.

"Tough times," said Mr. Eugene, breadcrumbs sparking from his mouth. "I'll throw you what I can."

I thanked him, avoiding eye contact. He knew my reasons for coming to see him today instead of my usual Tuesday. His thumb and forefinger rubbed against his napkin in a circular, frictiony motion, as though he was sprinkling salt onto uncooked beef. The phone rang twice, then stopped. He counted out my money and pushed it toward the corner of his desk. Next, he peeled off two additional hundred-dollar bills and folded them in half. His lips formed the words, "For you." He placed the new currency on my existing pile and tapped it, twice, with his middle finger—a judge lowering his gavel to signal a finality to our transaction.

After a long sigh, he started discussing some new business with Dove. Warm beads of perspiration formed in the bristly snarl of my hairline. I shifted my weight from side to side. Sometimes, if the laces on my boots are too tight, it slows the circulation near my ankles and my feet grow numb. My vision began to absorb a dozen meaningless objects from around the room. I felt like an accident victim in that sluggish moment before impact, when the world slows to a sticky crawl and everything, a riot of detail, swells to an outsize proportion. There was a bundle of *Daily Racing* forms behind Mr. Eugene's chair, the top copy defaced with a crosshatching of red lines and ovals. Pinned to a bulletin board near his desk were three rows of betting lines, clipped from newspapers, arranged by days of the week. A bookshelf against the rear wall supported team media guides, sports compendiums and almanacs, binders, old magazines, and four baseballs—the highest one, in a protective globe of transparent plastic, autographed by Joe DiMaggio. Resting on the billiard table was a large sombrero, its rhinestone accents, blue and red and green, gleaming beneath a suspended lamp.

My breathing grew quicker, almost breaking into a pant. I steadied myself by holding a bentwood chair. Then my mouth tasted like old pennies. I was desperate; I wanted some small assurance from Mr. Eugene—anything that would help me sleep at night. I tried to speak but the sound wouldn't leave my throat.

"Dove, Dove," said Mr. Eugene, gesturing in my direction. "Get him a glass of water."

"I'm sorry."

My hand was shaking as I raised the water to my lips. Mr. Eugene waved me closer.

"You need more?" he whispered.

"I—" My voice cracked. "I can do other things."

"I know you can," he said, patting me on the hand.

"It's just—some weeks there aren't many collections."

He leaned back, nodding.

"It'll pick up," he said. "Best time of year. Football, basketball, hockey—the seasons overlap."

He sat quietly for a few minutes. I could hear Dove paging through some papers behind me.

"You travel?" asked Mr. Eugene.

I nodded.

"Okay." He squeezed my wrist. "I may have something—a little errand. Gimme a few days."

Again, I thanked him. As I moved for the door, he slapped the side of his desk and said, "Hang in there"—the same words as on a ridiculous greeting card, one of Silver Springs' best sellers, in which a cat dangles by its claws from a tree limb.

The two gas company workers crouch now beside the lip of their hole, exhaling fringy clouds of cigarette smoke. I recognize the car as it turns into the mouth of the driveway. I shut off my engine and walk briskly across the street. The ground is littered with fallen acorns that snap and crunch beneath my feet.

As she emerges from the driver's seat, she's holding a plastic bag pressed to her chest. She peers down to find her house key in the waning afternoon light. Silently, I follow her—waiting and waiting. At the base of her staircase, something makes her glance back—an unfamiliar sound, a premonition. She jumps, nearly losing hold of her bag.

"Jesus," she says, stomping her heel in the gravel. "What's *wrong* with you?"

"I just wanted to surprise you."

"Oh, you did." Nina leans forward and plants a kiss on my cheek. "I think my heart's gonna explode."

Inside her doorway, she removes her jacket and tosses it across the back of a chair. She's wearing a tight black shirt and black jeans.

"Very sexy," I say.

"You like?" She takes several steps toward the sink, imitating a model on a catwalk, then completes a slow spin and reveals her backside. "I call it my Dirty Sandy."

"How's that?"

"From *Grease*," she says, snapping her fingers. "Remember Olivia Newton-John in the last scene? Dirty Sandy? When she tramps it up for John Travolta?"

I nod.

"But I'm not gonna sing."

We're silent as she unpacks a few items from her shopping bag—avocados, low-fat milk, a carton of zucchini muffins. I sit on her couch in darkness, trying to find a comfortable position.

"So—" She lights a tray of half-melted candles on her coffee table. "I left you a couple messages."

Staring down at my boots, I lick my thumb and erase a smudge across the right toe box. She pours two glasses of red wine from a bottle near the refrigerator.

"I know," I say, pressing the heels of my palms against my eyelids. "I'm sorry."

The seat cushion tilts as she sits down beside me.

"Is everything okay?" she asks. "Did I do something?"

"No, no." I give her knee an affectionate squeeze. "I lost my job."

She slides her hand across my shoulder and pulls me toward her neck. I can smell the fresh alcohol on her breath. She kisses my ear, my forehead. We sit together, embracing, our bodies softly knotted near the calves and elbows. The walls dance with a warm, yellowish glow. On the windowsill is a small cactus poking from a clear jar that's filled with layers of colored sand—purple, green, red. There's also a pair of antique apothecary bottles holding a plum liquid. It reminds me of a strange cocktail I once heard Big Dave mention, called the Lean: codeine-based cough syrup mixed with Sprite and a Jolly Rancher candy.

Nina takes another sip of wine and lies back, making the couch gasp. In the warmth and safety of Nina's apartment, with her steady heart thrumming against my arm, I suddenly recall moments from my recent past that make me cringe with embarrassment—a call from the supermarket ("This is Helen Sidel in accounting…") about three bounced checks; a young convenience store clerk announcing that my credit card had been declined; dozens of ambiguously named companies appearing in my phone's ID window as they call to collect on long overdue accounts. During my divorce, I listened to a woman in Silver Springs' payroll department as she explained the terms of the legal garnishment that was being imposed on my paychecks by the state's Department of Child Services.

A wisp of Nina's hair spills against the collar of my shirt, coming to rest on my chest.

"Do you have any leads?" she asks.

"Not one."

I picture several stacks of tightly banded money, all hundreds, sitting on Mr. Eugene's desk. Enough to cover *months* of future expenses—child support, car payments, rent.

"What about getting back into design?"

"Sure." Reflexively, my right hand curls around an invisible brick of cash, too much even for both pockets of my jacket. "You know where they're hiring?"

"Um, no," she says. "It was just an idea."

"I'll look."

I know what's coming—the next tense stage of my relationship with Nina. In the months after I lost my design job, I learned a large part of my self-esteem was tethered to my work. I was unemployed and I had a failing marriage. It was difficult to feel good about myself. I'd go days without showering or shaving. My only contact with the outside world was through my daughters and, sometimes, a brief conversation with Liz. Calls from friends and family went unreturned. Twice a month—if I was lucky—I'd pull myself together for job interviews. Typically, the person (or persons) leading the interview would leaf through my portfolio, nodding in places, and erupt with a series of well-rehearsed exclamations—"Marvelous!" and "Outstanding!" and "Love this one!" A few weeks later, I'd invariably receive a postcard thanking me for my interest in Name-of-Company's vacancy and—regretfully!—informing me that the position had been filled.

Some days I was short with the girls, snapping at Callie for leaving food on the counter or kicking a ball in the living room or turning the TV up too loud. One afternoon she refused to put away her clothes—she stood defiantly in the hallway and screamed back at me. In that moment—an accumulation of moments—I was overcome by rage; it felt like someone had ignited a road flare in my cerebral cortex. I reached forward, pinning her jaw closed with the web of skin between my thumb and forefinger. "You will *not* talk to me that way!" I shouted, drunk with emotion. I burned with the unforgiving fuel of failure—lost job, ruined marriage, mounting debt, and, as if I needed more proof than this, the failure of my impending single parenthood. Eventually, I noticed Tig in her bassinet, her tiny face red and wet.

My body went limp.

As Callie retreated into the shadows, damp eyes blinking, I made excuses for my behavior. "I wasn't *choking* you," I said. But they were young, my daughters, and they saw what they saw. A thin red crescent, like a clown's lopsided smile, still marked Callie's neck. I stammered for something that would make sense to her, finally settling on an apology. But it wasn't clean and, soon, I too was crying, my knees pressed against the hardwood floor.

I could hear the boards creak as Callie moved closer, tentatively placing her little hands on my shoulders. I reached into the darkness, pawing for a flannel nightgown or a pebbly pajama bottom, and drew her into a warm embrace. We stayed that way for a long time, until Callie tapped me on the head and said, "Dad, I can't breathe." Then, because life isn't always linear for a child, she asked for ice cream with colored sprinkles.

Months later, after I started my new job in sales, I slowly began to feel better about myself. It's not that I took pride in my work—I detested nearly every visit I made to a vendor. This time, though, my self-esteem was inextricably linked to my income. I once again had a little money in my pocket; I could take my daughters out for dinner, buy them both a new pair of bedroom slippers. There was a curious satisfaction in paying my bills on time—a systematic pleasure that came each month when I dumped a bundle of sealed envelopes into the drive-thru mailbox at the post office. It seemed to provide some small order to a corner of my chaos.

But now I feel as though I've taken a dozen steps backward, like I've landed on the wrong space in one of the girls' board games and, distressingly, I must move my token back to the beginning. My thoughts shift to peewee football during my youth: I recall this one Saturday when my team scored a touchdown less than three minutes into the second quarter, extending our lead to thirty-five points, and as we prepared to kickoff, the referees huddled the opposing coaches together. After a few moments of conversation the refs started waving their arms and we were awarded the victory. It seemed the league had a mercy rule—"to avoid further humiliation"—in which the game would come to an "immediate and premature end when one team is leading by at least thirty-five points."

I close my eyes and uncross my ankles. Nina runs the ball of her foot down my shin, toes splayed. That's what I need—a mercy rule for my life. A quick surrender, a tiny white flag. The chance to start again, march onto a new field the following Saturday and shed everything bad like a soiled uniform.

"You okay?" asks Nina. I nod.

My fingers are cold and she rubs them between her palms, blowing concentrated breaths as though cleaning a pair of spectacles. She never says *It'll get better*, and I'm relieved. The last time I lost my job, when my marriage was also foundering, I heard that phrase at least twice a day. *It'll get better.* But it doesn't always get better, and so the words sound empty—a shallow sentiment embossed on the cover of a greeting card.

Maybe I fall asleep.

Later, in the flickering candlelight, I straighten against the couch. I hear the soft exhale of air through Nina's nose, a gentle half-snore, like wind through the teeth of a comb.

Her face is coated in white pancake makeup. Smudgy black ovals encircle her dim eyes. She leans forward and parts her lips, which glow a fiery shade of red. Callie gazes longingly into space, as though summoning an old dream. I worry about the thoughts skating through her head; beneath her shiny mask she appears sullen and lost. I sit across from her at the kitchen table, kneading my fingers through a bowl of packaged candies.

"You excited?" I ask.

She shrugs her shoulders and her painted mouth twists into a shriveled flower bud. We talk for a while, about school and sack lunches and her friend Abbey's new puppy. She briskly scratches her eyelid, seemingly forgetting about the still-damp makeup.

Eventually she starts in on the words she's been waiting to speak, disguised beneath generic observations about holidays and classmates and families other than her own. A perpetual knot of tension floats in her belly, drifting aimlessly, waiting to be tugged in competing directions—one end gripped by her mother, the other by me. I learn that Callie fills with anxiety, to the point of distraction, whenever Liz and I are scheduled to attend the same event. Her eyes are glassy and dark when she tells me that she's always aware of her parents' proximity to one another in confined spaces. She fears the smallest misunderstanding—a drop-off time, an unpaid bill—will mushroom into something catastrophic and public, causing deep embarrassment for her. She has furtively developed survival techniques for such situations—the most reliable, she claims, is simply distracting Liz or me with a suddenly intense thread of conversation. Maybe a question about homework or technology or a current news story. Also, she occasionally feigns illness—stomach, head—to interrupt pending conflicts.

I lay my head against the table, ear to Formica. My heart feels as though it's been cast of lead. There's nothing worse than seeing your child suffer—especially when the damage has been done by your own hand.

Tonight the girls' school is hosting its annual Halloween parade, where the costumed kids from each classroom march through a lighted courtyard in front of the assembled parents. In the past, Liz and I have stood on opposite sides of the quadrant, smiling politely if our paths crossed. But one year, I remember, we had an animated discussion about automobile insurance. In the moment, pulled along by the argument's heavy undertow, it's difficult to break loose—even as I'm staring down at my daughters' troubled faces.

"I'm sorry," I say, gathering Callie's hands in mine.

She is peering into the distance when we hear a *shushy* sound from the hall. Tig appears in the doorway, the papery fabric of her costume rubbing against her legs. She looks at her sister and me, pauses for a moment, and then shuffles away as though she just remembered something important.

"I'm going to try my best not to make you uncomfortable," I say.

Callie nods in the same dismissive manner as a parent listening to his child promise to make her bed every morning. I'm searching desperately for something to say that will make this right, return the smile to Callie's face. But there are no words, only actions.

I slowly unwrap a peanut butter cup and slide it toward Callie. She takes a small, timid bite and chews silently, her thumb turning the chocolate-covered candy against the table.

A couple weeks ago I collected nearly five grand from a roofer named Sam LoPiccolo. We met in his driveway, and as he handed me the money, folded in a section of newspaper, I could see his young daughter glaring out the window of his house. I felt a pang of guilt at taking a considerable portion of his income—money he should've been using to buy food and clothing for his family, or repair the listing door on his garage. It was the nearest I've ever come to telling someone he should quit gambling. As I walked back to my car, I spotted a pink and white princess-themed scooter resting in the grass—the same kind of scooter that my girls owned when they were little. I could picture Callie racing down the sidewalk of my old neighborhood as I followed in her tracks, pushing Tig in a chrome stroller on one of those cloudless summer days that seemed like it was never going to end.

Through my windshield, I watched LoPiccolo use a piece of wire to steady the handle on one of the storage bins near the back of his truck. His daughter was still framed in the window, standing beside a white curtain that was tethered with an ornate band of rope. I wondered what came next for LoPiccolo—how many late nights away from his family would it take him to earn back his losses? Would this episode spark loud fights with his wife, force his daughter to shutter herself in her room to escape?

For a few minutes, I thought about apologizing. I wanted to cast a light on our similarities, explain that my motivation was no different than his for hanging shingles or wagering five hundred bucks on Oklahoma State. We both had families to support—and we were only looking for a way to make life a little better. He had chosen one road, I had chosen another.

I'm not sure why it suddenly seemed so important that LoPiccolo, a guy I'd only met once before, didn't resent me. But I sat for a while in my parked car, long after he'd stubbed out a cigarette and retreated into his house. I imagined the two of us sharing a couch at the cigar shop, exchanging stories about our children. Maybe we'd be drinking beer and when we were finished, one of us would pat the other on his knee and say something encouraging, like "Fight the good fight." Later that night, we'd brush our teeth and wash the cigar smoke from our skin. Then we'd kiss our daughters lying peacefully in their beds.

I'm still thinking about LoPiccolo's money, and how it was bundled in newsprint on the car seat beside me, when Callie tucks the rest of the peanut butter cup into her mouth. She still looks apprehensive as we rise from the table and meet Tig beside the bathroom mirror. Soon, both girls are jockeying for position—swinging elbows and inflating their chests. Tig wants to wear a pair of plastic high-heel shoes, but I tell her they're not practical.

"Oh, sheesh," she says, flipping her hair across her shoulder. Then she follows her sister to the car.

The scream is terrifying. I sit up in bed and try to decide if I dreamed it. But after a few moments of silence, I hear another long shriek and the pounding of footsteps across the living room floor. I race down the hall, nearly colliding with the girls' old dollhouse.

Tig's standing on the couch, swaddled in a colorful fleece blanket, her eyes as wide as lightbulbs. I see Callie hunched forward, as though preparing for a water landing, threads of saliva jiggling from her lips. She spits furiously into the rug.

"My mouth," she says, fanning her tongue with her fingers. "It's on *fire*."

"What happened?" I ask.

Callie's body contorts with a series of dry heaves. She lurches forward, arms flapping madly against her sides. A milky arc of vomit lands between my bare feet.

"*Here*," says Tig, pointing to our end table.

Beside the telephone is a small foil sleeve, its underside mottled with smooth, transparent squares.

"Oh, Cal," I say, lifting the packet of nicotine gum. "Did you chew this?"

She nods, wiping her mouth with the cuff of her pajamas.

"How many times have I told you?" I give her a drink from a bottle of water. "Don't take my things without asking."

I wrap my hand in several layers of paper towel and begin cleaning her mess.

"This gum isn't for you," I say, covering my mouth and nose with the stretched collar of my t-shirt. "It's—it's *medicine* gum."

"Who ever heard of medicine gum?" says Tig.

"It's disgusting," says Callie.

My palm is filled with regurgitated pellets of Cap'n Crunch cereal. I fold them in a clamshell of paper towel, leaving a soggy white heap beside the rug. The room smells of ammonia and warmed dairy.

"We were lookin' for something else," says Tig. "You hided—"

"*Hid.*"

"You *hid* our Halloween candy."

This year they spent the holiday with Liz. But now their candy, in matching plastic jack o' lanterns with black handles, sits on top of my refrigerator.

"Of course," I say. "Otherwise I'd be finding Kit Kat and Skittle wrappers stuffed between the seat cushions of the couch."

"That wasn't me," says Tig.

"It sure was," says Callie.

"Get dressed," I say, turning off the TV and pointing them in the direction of their room. "And put your jammies down the hamper."

In the kitchen, I make coffee and drop a couple slices of cinnamon bread into the toaster.

"Do you guys want scrambled eggs?" I shout.

"I want bacon," says Callie.

"Me too," says Tig.

"We don't have bacon." I press my hand against the dull side of a knife, for leverage, and chop a wedge of cheddar cheese into tiny cubes. "How about eggs?"

"Sure."

"Callie won't let me share the mirror."

"Callie," I say, brushing the cheese into a bowl of blended eggs. "Let your sister share the mirror."

A hard rubber ball caroms down the hallway, striking the base of the stove and hurdling into the sink.

"Careful," I say. "You just missed my coffee."

The ball came inside a goody bag that Tig received yesterday at Ellen Linwood's birthday party. She took inventory of her prizes, aloud, as I stood in the foyer of the Linwoods' house and waited for Tig to put on her coat. Soon there were other parents, pressed casually together. One mother leaned down, whispering into her daughter's ear. The girl then thanked her hosts, timidly, refusing to take her eyes from a shiny green ring on her index finger.

The first thing I saw was the back of his head, partially shielded by the upturned collar on his corduroy jacket. He was wearing khaki trousers and rubber-soled hunting boots. As he turned into the light, where I had a three-quarter view of his face, I began to recognize his features: skinny gray lips, steeply angled cheekbones, Roman-style nose with a faint vertical crease along its bulbous end. He looked at me and smiled. I remembered reading his name on the contact list from Tig's school. Last spring he owed Mr. Eugene nearly six thousand dollars, as I recall, from wagers made mostly on professional sports—basketball, hockey. He drives a silver Audi with a ski rack strapped to its roof.

I dropped to my knees, pretending to help Tig with the zipper of her coat. ("Dad, I've *got* it," she said.) My chin was pressed against my chest, eyes down, as though I was preparing to launch into a somersault.

He runs a small manufacturing company with his father—they make rubber O-rings for certain types of heavy machinery. I had been waiting for him outside, near a parking space beneath a sign with his name. There wasn't any trouble. He asked me if we could stall for a few minutes, until his father was gone. The money was in a safe and it would be an awkward conversation, explaining things to his ol' man, with me standing nearby.

"Look at this," he'd said, removing a large box from his back seat. He set it against the hood of his car. It was a new single-serving coffee machine, with cylindrical cartridges and a plunger-style handle. "It's amazing. Makes coffee, tea, hot cocoa." We watched his father walk to a black Cadillac, big as a hearse, on the other side of the parking lot.

The guy knew the security guard by name. It didn't take long for him to retrieve the money, in fifties and hundreds, from a safe behind his father's desk. He put it in a cotton sack with his company's logo silk-screened across its sides.

In the Linwoods' foyer I turned sideways, exchanging good-byes with my face aimed in the opposite direction; I focused on a reddish tree in their front yard. "Geez," said Tig, pushing my hand from her shoulder. She nearly tripped as I nudged her down the brick steps.

He didn't seem to remember me—there was no nervous chatter or noticeable blush. Maybe he was only being polite. On the drive home, I worried he might tell his wife or one of the other parents from Tig's class. My mind played out a paranoid game of telephone. I followed a sequence of imagined connections between his wife and Liz and Tig's teacher and the school board president. Anxious, I pulled onto the side of the road for long enough that it drew the girls' attention.

What could he say? I ran through a range of possible excuses, make-believe answers to a call that would likely never come. *It was a favor—I was doing a friend a favor by picking up a package. Believe me, I didn't know it was going to be a pile of money.*

There's a loud knock against the doorframe of the kitchen. Tig's swinging her hairbrush into the wall, high to low, like she's hammering a nail.

"Stop!"

I pour the eggs into a skillet that's spitting hot butter.

"Dad," she says, crossing her arms. "She's totally hogging the mirror."

"Stand here." I deposit three marshmallows into her outstretched hand. "Eat these—*slowly*. When you're finished I'll tell Callie it's your turn in the bathroom."

As she chews, she makes a pleasant humming noise from deep in her chest. She's staring at a collection of drawings and photographs tacked to the refrigerator.

"I remember this," she says, nodding toward a picture of the three of us in a canoe.

"I hope so."

Using a white-handled spatula, I sweep the eggs in a clockwise motion. It doesn't take long for them to turn bright and rubbery.

"Did it rain?"

"Not until we got back to the cabin," I say. "But I had to paddle the whole way—*by myself*."

"Right," she says, leaning closer, as though she's searching for a hidden clue. "We had hot dogs."

"And baked beans that we cooked in a can."

"I didn't like those."

There is orange juice and milk. The cinnamon toast has been buttered and cut on a diagonal. I set a pair of triangular stacks around a jar of strawberry preserves.

"This is gonna get cold," I say, scraping the eggs onto a serving plate. "You can have the mirror *after* we eat."

She sighs, tossing her hairbrush into the air and catching it against her stomach. Callie and Tig sit across from each other at the table. Tig makes a face at Callie, who responds by raising her middle finger.

"*Oh*," says Tig. "Callie gave me a bird."

"It's not *a* bird, stupid. It's *the* bird."

"Guys!" I say, clapping my hands. "That's the last time, Callie." I turn toward her sister. "And I saw you teasing, making faces. No more."

They begin eating, slow and intense. It's so quiet I can hear a squeaking joint in Callie's chair.

"After we're done," says Tig, "Dad said *I* get to use the bathroom."

"Tig—did you just hear me?"

For emphasis, I strike my fork against the side of my plate. The ringing sound is followed by a spongy piece of egg leaping across my wrist and into my cup, creating a delicate backsplash of coffee. The girls gaze into one another's eyes, holding this pose for a beat, and then break into laughter.

"Omigod!" shouts Callie.

Tig leans across the table and peeks into my cup. She wrinkles her nose in disgust.

"Drink it!" says Tig.

"Yeah, drink it!"

Together, they pound the table with their fists and chant, "Drink it, drink it."

Because they're my daughters and nothing brings me more joy than making them happy; because only moments ago they were having an argument over the stupid mirror in my tiny bathroom; because, really, in this unkind world it's the least a father can do—I lift my cup and take a long sip. Both girls have stopped laughing and they're now transfixed to my mouth. Pressing my fingers against my chest, I grab my heart and slide my chair from the table. I stagger in sloppy circles, dragging my right foot and peering up at the ceiling. Then comes a loud moan. I lower my fist into the arch of my ribcage and perform a ridiculously dramatic version of the Heimlich maneuver on myself. After three rapid pulls, I step forward and discharge a coffee-soaked loogie of scrambled egg onto the floor. Callie and Tig scream with delight (or terror). They race from the table and surround the wet spot.

"*Eeeeew*," says Tig. "It looks like a smashed snail."

"We just studied the human body in science class," says Callie. "It looks like a miniature pancreas."

"Oh, geez." I reach down and clean the egg with my napkin. "I probably shouldn't have done that."

Callie places her hands on her hips. She turns sideways and tries to raise only one eyebrow. "You know, Dad," she says, tapping her foot. "You gotta live a little."

I chuckle, wondering where Callie learned such an expression—and how it would apply to my spitting eggs across the kitchen.

"Okay, let's eat," I say.

The girls scurry back into their seats. Tig holds a piece of crust between her teeth, aiming it at her sister. I shake my head and they both start laughing again. A trickle of juice runs down Callie's chin. In a theatrical flourish, Tig hides her eyes in the crook of her elbow, as though she can't bear another moment of this madness.

Spread across my desk are the classified sections from two newspapers. With a purple marker that belongs to the girls, I've encircled a handful of prospective jobs. I'm generous in the scope of my experience—there's a medical supply company in need of a technical illustrator, and an exporter requiring someone with knowledge of international sales. I also search a number of employment-based websites. A boutique greeting card company in Lubbock, Texas, has a posting for an entry-level sales associate, though the suggested salary, less than half of what I was earning at Silver Springs, makes relocation seem absurd.

I have printed the most promising opportunity and tacked the page to my bulletin board: a local sign business is looking for a part-time graphic artist. In the margin, I scribble a brief checklist—they require a cover letter, résumé, and samples of my work.

Not long ago, I spoke to a friend of mine who's a bank manager in Milwaukee. He hates his boss and decided to test the job market. He told me that in the ensuing six months, he applied for more than a *hundred* vacancies. In response, he received a single interview request—from the business office of a small university. The furniture behind me glows a cathode-ray blue from a football game on TV—Oregon versus Washington State. The announcers prattle endlessly about a "lightning bug–quick" quarterback for the Ducks who's a former gang member from South Central Los Angeles. I click on a link for a website illustrator because, beside "job location," is the hopeful description *Anywhere, U.S.A.* I scroll through the document and review the position's various "responsibilities." Though I have the ability to "work under tight deadlines," I wonder if "maintaining and growing social media" is a deal-breaker.

During a timeout in the football game, one of the marching bands plays an old song—the Moody Blues' *Nights in White Satin*—that reminds me of my sister. As children, we spent many Saturdays listening to a portable radio in my bedroom while we created a pretend world with small army men and plastic figurines. For a long time, when we heard this song, we thought the lyrics were referring to knights with a K. "They wore these satin bibs across their armor," Cameron would say, convincingly. "For identification, like a uniform."

I haven't seen my sister in months, since a long weekend last summer when the girls and I drove to Illinois for a visit. She lives in Winnetka, near Chicago. As we pulled into her sprawling driveway, past twin rows of mirror-image topiary, the girls pressed their faces against the car windows. "Aunt Cammy lives at a college?" asked Tig. There was a swimming pool, a tennis court. And though my niece and nephew aren't yet of driving age, my sister and her husband own four cars—each worth more than I earned in my best year. Later that night the kids played under a nanny's supervision while I ate dinner with my sister and her husband in their Spanish stucco wine cellar.

After discussing our respective children—schools, friends, hobbies—it became increasingly difficult for us to find common ground. Even then, long before I'd lost my job,

I was living paycheck to paycheck. To keep the conversation alive, I told them about a sales call I'd made near Cincinnati a few months earlier. During the drive home, my car suddenly died on Interstate 71—the steering grew stiff and I had to navigate my way to safety on the highway's greasy shoulder. I described a series of tows, from one repair shop to another, until I could find a qualified mechanic. "I spent eighty bucks before the problem was even diagnosed," I'd said, gazing lamely at my brother-in-law for some sign of shared recognition. My engine had thrown a rod: It would cost seventy-five hundred dollars to repair—more than the car's Blue Book value. But the kicker, the part of my story that brings a smile to the faces of most listeners, is when I explain how I went ballistic in the dealer's showroom—I'd met all of the manufacturer's service requirements and, despite "catastrophic engine failure," a dashboard warning light never illuminated. "Listen, I can understand if I kept driving with an obvious engine problem," I'd said. "But there was nothing—not a single blip." Now, my sister *was* smiling, though I believe it was more from embarrassment.

The great thumbs-up, pat-on-the-back payoff is when I reveal that my persistence and stubbornness proved successful: The dealership replaced my engine at no cost. But after a moment of silence, my brother-in-law turned to my sister and asked if there was rosemary in his grilled trout.

A short while later, before bedtime, Tig took my hand and led me into the doorway of my niece's closet. Tig's eyes were wide and glassy. The space was larger than my bathroom, and against its opposing walls were dual levels of hangered clothing—dozens of skirts, dresses, slacks, and tunics. Many of the outfits had not yet been worn, with colorful store tags still blooming from their sleeves. Directly in front of us, like a gleaming Mayan altar, was a display rack for my niece's shoes—bejeweled sneakers and Mary Janes and white leather sandals, all conjoined in perfect little pairs.

Tig took a mighty breath. I half-expected her to fall to her knees, genuflecting before this great monument to consumerism. "Someday," she said, in a voice filled with wonder and longing, "I want a closet like this one."

On the drive home, near the Indiana border, the girls began fighting over the angle of a portable DVD player. As I tried to quiet them down, the conversation turned to their cousins and how they each had their own handheld gaming device. Then came the inevitable queries about the vast disparity in our lifestyles, questions I'd been expecting since the moment the girls and I stepped into the arena-sized foyer of my sister's house.

"If Aunt Cammy's your sister," said Tig, "how come she has a giant mansion with a swimming pool and we don't have anything?"

"We have lots of things."

"Nothing good," said Callie. "Not like them."

Briefly, I considered correcting the girls. I thought about listing all the amazing things in their lives—the things that truly mattered. But I couldn't muster the strength; it felt hollow and insincere. Earlier that morning, drinking coffee and watching the kids race around the yard, I had indulged in a starry-eyed fantasy, pretending for a moment that my sister's house belonged to us. *This afternoon maybe Callie will take a tennis lesson, maybe Tig will go horseback riding with friends.* I pictured myself behind the wheel of a slate-gray Porsche, like the one parked in my brother-in-law's garage, heading to Lake Michigan for a sail…

I was brought back to earth when Cameron joined me on the terrace, her terrace. It took a few minutes before I realized what she wanted to discuss, her eyes riveted to a flawlessly manicured bed of tulips below us. She sat on a lounge chair and removed her cork-soled flat, rubbing the redness from the ball of her foot. There was an allusion to my failed engine story of two nights earlier, then a stuttery reference to her husband's investment firm. Next, she provided an outsider's perspective of my divorce, liberally using words like "traumatic" and "heartbreaking." Eventually—awkwardly—she made her point: If I needed financial assistance, I "shouldn't hesitate to, well, you know—reach out to us."

I thanked her, wrapping my arms around her slender shoulders. It wasn't simply that my sister was offering a handout—I was her brother; she was supposed to lean on *me*. Rather, I was terrified of what existed for my future. In a roiling swell of images, like a deck of playing cards blown from a table, I saw myself catapulted from a German sports car and into my poorly lighted kitchen; I stood beside the sink, phone to ear, mustering the nerve to ask my sister for money.

This is what I'm thinking about as I trawl through endlessly dismal job listings on my computer, wondering if any single salary would cover my sister's landscaping bill. It's almost a relief when I hear the sudden pecking noise from my back door; I'm grateful for a new distraction. I rise from my desk and walk to the rear of the house. In a now familiar routine, the cat sits in the open doorway and stares tentatively down my hall. He takes a few steps forward, then retreats to the patio. I stand motionless, my right arm propping back the screen. As he creeps toward the pantry, where I've set a dish of food and water beside the stove, I cautiously ease the door back into its frame, not wanting to startle him with any abrupt sounds.

"Good evening, Shoe," I say.

His face is buried in kibble, his hind legs resting between his front paws. A dander of dried mud coats part of his tail, as though he's been dipped in chocolate batter. I retrieve a wire-bristle hairbrush from inside a toy crib near Tig's desk. Then I follow a slow, circuitous route to reach the cat, trying to avoid his line of vision. Gentle as dust, I lower the brush against his fur— the cat pauses, briefly holding his position, before returning to his food. My strokes are long and light, showering flakes of crusty dirt onto the floor. A steady purr echoes across the water dish.

"Listen, pal—it doesn't get any better than this."

Crouched beside the cat, I see a pair of bow-tie hairclips swept against a heating vent. I want to write myself a note to purchase a broom—we used the old one for a school project, cutting the handle into a frame for Tig's Apache "deerskin"—but I fear any unexpected movements will chase the cat away. Instead, I repeat the words "new broom, new broom" with each pull of the brush.

The bartender is wearing a white blazer with gold buttons. Against his hip he braces an enormous tin of cocktail peanuts; he uses a soup ladle to refill a column of silver bowls that lines the bar around him. Afterward, he unfolds a pair of paper napkins and presses them gently into the bases of matching baskets. Beside three beer taps is a large, glass-sided popcorn machine, similar to the ones at movie-theater concession stands. He grabs a plastic trowel and guides a small avalanche of popcorn into each basket.

Across the room, two elderly men share a table. Resting between them is a single scoop of tuna salad on a wrinkled lettuce leaf. The men spread the tuna onto saltine crackers and wash them down with tumblers of cider. Whenever one of the men speaks, his counterpart leans forward and cups a hand to his ear.

I'm sitting on a dark wood chair with burgundy leather cushions, held in place by copper rivets. A giant-screen TV flickers with a business program—across the bottom are twin crawls displaying real-time results from the New York Stock Exchange and NASDAQ. I stretch my legs and stare through a wall-sized picture window, watching four golfers take turns putting across the eighteenth green. It's cold outside, nearly ski weather; three of the golfers are wearing stocking hats. A tall, skinny kid in a turtleneck raises his putter like a rifle and pretends to shoot one of the other guys. There's horseplay, laughter. A bearded man dressed in a fleece pullover lifts the skinny kid's golf bag and threatens to drop it into a kidney-shaped water hazard. Then he returns the yellow flagstick to its hole and the group disappears around the side of the clubhouse. I can hear the scratching of their spikes against the asphalt cart path.

Sometimes I grow resentful of other people's happiness. I study their lives from a distance and wonder why things can't be easier for me and the girls. As the bearded guy in the fleece pullover flashes past the window, I tell myself that his children got what they wanted for their birthdays—maybe laptop computers or touchscreen cell phones. This year he'll take his family on vacations to warm and exotic places. His wife's renovating the kitchen; his kids have straight teeth and college funds. In a near whisper, I repeat Callie's customary mantra: *It's not fair.* It hasn't been fair for a long time.

There are days when my misery is paralyzing; it feels like the darkness is permanent. I fantasize about loading the girls into my car and driving to a different town in a different state, starting over again. I imagine this new life from an idyllic perspective—it wouldn't take long for me to find a rewarding job, save a little money; and the girls would make immediate and lasting friendships. Because it's only pretend, a daydream that I control, Liz has been conveniently cropped from the picture. And there's a magical new woman (Nina?) to help raise my daughters.

Behind me, the four golfers noisily enter the room. The skinny kid orders a Coke and grabs two handfuls of popcorn, trailing slippery kernels on the floor. A black man wearing the same white blazer as the bartender appears from the kitchen, balancing a serving tray near his shoulder, and sets a BLT sandwich and chips on an empty table. A few minutes later, there's a knocking at one of the exterior glass doors. The bartender releases the latch and an athletic-looking guy in a Titleist cap walks toward a water cooler, pausing briefly to talk with the two elderly men. He sits down and takes a loud swallow of water. When he removes his cap, his bark-colored hair is curled around an invisible crown. He chews a bite of his BLT and nods when our eyes meet.

His name is Chase Loomis, and he's the golf pro at Carbon Mills Country Club. I have his photograph in my coat pocket, clipped from a club newsletter. As he eats his lunch, he changes the TV channel—first asking if anyone minds—to sports highlights. During a replay of last night's Bulls' game, he groans when a guard for the Knicks buries a difficult three-pointer with time expiring.

"See that?" he asks rhetorically. "Two goddamn guys in his face."

After he finishes his sandwich, he asks the bartender to toss him a frozen Milky Way. He's still holding the candy bar when he rises and heads into the locker room. I follow him. On my left is a steam room and individual shower stalls that share a contiguous wall with a half-dozen sinks. A stainless steel shelf beneath a wide mirror holds disposable razors, shaving creams, spray deodorants, three kinds of mouthwash, blow dryers, talcum powder, hand cleanser, two popular brands of cologne, and glass jars filled with blue-tinted antiseptic liquid and plastic combs. Nearby is a C-shaped desk with folded towels, golf tees, scorecards, stubby eraser-less pencils, breath mints, and various sizes of adhesive bandages.

"Can I help you?" asks a bald man behind the counter.

I shake my head.

Before the lockers is a large bulletin board with club announcements, tournament brackets, rankings (juniors, men's open, and seniors), handicap index, and a selection of stroke tutorials culled from magazines. I wander down the center aisle, turning from side to side. It's not until I retrace my steps that I see Loomis, cap on head, standing over a urinal. He zips his fly and raises his knee, removing a speared leaf from his golf spikes. After he washes his hands, he smiles hastily at my reflection in the mirror. He starts to leave and I grab his sleeve, tugging him back against the sink. I touch my finger to my lips and crouch down, checking beneath the toilet doors for visible shoes. His face contorts, eyes squinting into an imaginary sun; he frees his arm from my grip. As the words are rising in my throat—the sound is audible yet indistinct—a braying comes from my coat pocket. I fumble with my cell phone, nearly dropping it onto the tile floor. In the process, I accidentally depress the *answer* button—I'd meant to hit *ignore*—and, absurdly, place the phone to my ear.

"One second," I whisper, patting him on the shoulder.

A long pause followed by a woman's voice. When she explains that she works for St. Vincent's Hospital, I see a thousand nightmarish images rushing through my head—Tig injuring herself on the school playground, Callie getting hit by a car as she crosses the street. I feel my skin turn cold as the blood drains from my face. Now, instead of patting Loomis's shoulder, I'm clutching it for support.

"You okay?" he asks, I think.

It takes me a moment to understand what the woman's saying, for my brain to decipher this new information, because I'm praying—"Please, please, *please* let them be okay"—that my daughters haven't been harmed. She tells me that last spring I had a series of tests, as part of a standard physical examination, and my insurance only covered sixty percent of their cost. I still have an outstanding balance—and would I like to satisfy that balance right now, over the phone, because the hospital accepts all major credit cards.

"Fucking *balls*," I say.

"Pardon," she responds.

I hang up the phone and return it to my pocket.

"Jesus," I say, turning to Loomis. "I thought something happened to one of my daughters."

He looks confused.

"They're fine." I splash cold water onto my face and blot the wetness with a paper towel. "It was something else."

Together we walk past the scorecards and golf tees and cluttered bulletin board. Near a corridor that leads to the pro shop, he slows to tuck his shirttail into his khakis.

"Well, this is me," he says, gesturing with his thumb. "Did you need something?"

I'm silent, my thoughts still preoccupied with the silly phone call.

"Maybe you wanted to schedule a lesson?"

Almost as though someone has waved smelling salts beneath my nose, I snap out of my fog—shaking my head like a cartoon character orbited by a halo of blinking stars and whistling birds. I escort Loomis into a corner, beside a glass-encased fire extinguisher and ax. I'm not sure he hears anything after I speak Mr. Eugene's name; he's fiddling with his belt buckle and staring somberly at his tan golf shoes. Predictably, he tries to defend his compilation of losing wagers—"Desmond twisted his ankle" and "the Blazers' plane was delayed by weather" and "the officiating was for the pits." He doesn't have the money, he confesses, cringing as though he just hit a lousy bunker shot.

Normally, this wouldn't be a problem: We'd arrange a payment schedule over the coming weeks, with a seven percent interest rate commencing after the first month. But before his recent run of bad luck, Loomis had been winning—he'd had a remarkable string of nearly four months when he was in the black.

"The son-of-a-bitch is late," said Mr. Eugene, a few days ago. "He came here every Wednesday—like clockwork—to get paid. Now he's gonna *stiff* me?"

Leaning against the nameplate of a nearby locker is an old nine iron, its grip threatening to unravel. I sit on a wooden bench and pass the golf club between my fingers, watching the light skate across its silver shaft. I'm thinking about Tig climbing the painted monkey bars at her school playground, hand over hand, until she reaches a small steel pedestal at its summit. On the ground below is a rubberized carpet that interlocks like the pieces of a giant jigsaw puzzle. I sometimes worry that its padded surface doesn't offer enough protection, especially if a child should fall from a considerable height.

"I need something by Monday," I say. "At least half."

He nods.

I write my phone number on a page torn from my notepad and slide it across the bench. Before he reaches the door to the pro shop he calls back to me, blindly—we're no longer in one another's line of sight—and says he's glad my daughters are okay.

I sit motionless, my forearms resting on my knees. Across the aisle sit a young boy and his grandfather. They're wearing damp swim trunks and bathrobes. In the time it takes me to return the nine iron to its locker and pull up the elastic of my socks, the boy has dressed in street clothes—wool sweater, corduroy pants, high-top sneakers. His blond hair is still tousled and spiky from the chlorinated water. I smile thinking about how much longer it would've taken my girls to ready themselves for the outside world. Last week, I waited nearly forty minutes for Callie to finish her preparations for dinner at a dark, unpopular Mexican restaurant. ("She might see a boy," said Tig, after we'd called her sister a third time. "At least that's what she *thinks*.") As I stood in Callie's doorway, she screamed about her jeans feeling tight in the thighs—she completed a series of squats and deep knee bends, surrounded by the twisted remains of a half-dozen other ill-fitting trousers. When Tig shuffled to my side for a closer look, Callie threw a pillow—"Mind your own business!"—and dislodged Tig's headband.

Over the next few minutes, our life resembled a scene from a slapstick comedy about parenthood: I reminded Callie that we don't invade other people's space (with pillows, glass figurines, closed fists); Callie, now teary-eyed, repeatedly slapped her thighs and hollered about her body; and Tig returned to the bathroom, cursing her sister for ruining a "perfect" hairdo that took her "about a hundred hours" to get right. Later, during the car ride to the restaurant, I told both girls that they were spectacular beauties, which was met by loud groans, and that it didn't matter what they wore because I wasn't letting them go out with boys until their twenty-fifth birthdays.

"You can't stop me," said Callie, kicking the back of my seat.

"Me either," said Tig.

"I think so," I said. "I'm bigger and meaner than any boy-friend."

"Sheesh," said Tig.

"You're *definitely* meaner," said Callie.

I lie sideways on the bench. Spilled against the baseboard are coins, ball markers, and a pair of broken breath mints.

Some days it felt like I was too close to the dissolution of my marriage—foundering in a sea of subpoenas and hostile e-mails and heavily blurred memories. Other times, though, it seemed like I couldn't draw myself near enough to the elements that truly mattered. I would focus on some niggling detail—a breached agreement, an angry exchange—instead of a more significant target. And, as always, it was Callie and Tig who caught most of the shrapnel.

One Saturday long after Liz and I separated, I was reading a newspaper when Callie wandered into the living room followed by her sister. I remember asking them what they wanted for lunch. We discussed a few options—frozen pizza, leftover chicken, fast-food hamburgers. I was still leafing through the entertainment section, looking for kid-friendly movies, when the girls climbed up beside me on the couch. Suddenly, as though it was the most natural thing in the world, Callie said it was time for her mother to bring her stuff over. When I told Callie that she and Tig had everything they needed in my house—books and beds, toys and toothbrushes—Callie shook her head.

"No," she said. "Now we're ready for *Mom* to move here."

I could feel the pebbly goose flesh rise along my arms. Liz and I had spoken to the girls about our long-pending divorce, but they were still young and didn't understand what lay ahead. I squeezed them together on a single seat cushion and looked them in the eyes. Then I explained the ways in which our lives would be different now—they would spend roughly half of each week with their mother and half with me; they had two bedrooms and two backyards; they even had a pair of closets in my house that we'd stock with new clothes.

"Well," said Callie, exhaling. "We liked it better the other way."

"Yeah," said Tig. "Th' other way."

The air seemed heavy and hard to breathe. The room felt as though it was slowly rotating, like the floor of one of those restaurants perched atop a tall building. I held the arm of the couch for support. The girls were having trouble processing—they had heard Liz and me say we were going to "try" this new way of living and were under the impression it could be repealed. Perhaps that's why neither of the girls melted down at my initial departure—they believed it was only temporary.

Callie was clutching my finger and Tig was gazing up at her sister, as though waiting to read her next reaction.

"We're going to see how this works for a while," I said.

Callie's forehead raised and her lips turned white with worry. One of her front teeth was missing, and I could see the pink tip of her tongue mashed through the vacant space.

"But…but…what if Mom needs us?" asked Callie.

"She can come over whenever she wants," I said. "And you can always call her."

"Mom makes my lunches," said Tig.

"Well, I'll make your lunches—on the days you're with me."

"Dad," said Tig, crossing her little arms. "You don't know how."

"Sure, I do."

Tig crinkled her nose and spit out an imaginary wad of gum.

"So, when *is* Mom coming to stay here?" asked Callie.

I told them I wasn't sure that was ever going to happen. Their mother and I were having trouble living together—we argued too much and nobody seemed happy.

"I was happy," said Callie.

"I was happy," repeated Tig.

Then Callie's face warmed with new light. She slapped her thigh and raised her fingers to my mouth. It was a child's simple idea, something that made absolute sense to a pair of young girls. She suggested a set of rules for her mother and me, similar to the ones she and Tig had to follow. If Liz and I fought, we'd each retreat to separate rooms until we cooled down. Then, if the trouble continued, we'd both be given timeouts.

"That's a good idea," said Callie, beaming with pride.

Though I'm not sure Tig understood, she nodded her head in support of her sister.

Because their faces were bright and full of optimism during this difficult moment, I tried to sound hopeful. But as I spoke my voice cracked and I had to wipe my eyes with my shirtsleeve. They had weathered a powerful storm by holding tight to something that no longer existed, and I couldn't bring myself to knock it from their hands. This was more important to them than gifts on Christmas morning or crisp dollar bills left by a tooth fairy. They only wanted what they once had—and they'd been struggling, in silence, to get it back.

Together the three of us sat in my living room, our eyes darting from face to face. Callie was anxious and she rubbed her palms against her knees. Tig was chewing on a strand of hair, head cocked like a curious dog.

"Let's see what happens," I said, which was the most I could offer.

Callie's shoulders slumped. A few years later, she would not have allowed me to get away with such a vague answer. But for now, it provided a glimmer of hope, which was enough for two hungry girls who wanted cheeseburgers and vanilla milkshakes.

Not long ago I was convinced I'd never have a meaningful romantic relationship again. I was simply too damaged—incapable of trusting another woman and, in turn, certain that I no longer possessed the tools to reciprocate. But now, with distance and a wink of good fortune, it feels as though Nina is pecking away at that wall. I'm suddenly finding charm in her idiosyncrasies, cautiously embracing what once would've driven me in a different direction.

I think it's cute that Nina scribbles daily reminders on the back of her left hand—*do laundry* and *wine store* and *air in tires.* It didn't bother me when she removed all the pepperoni from her half of a pizza we ordered. "I like the flavor they leave on the cheese," she said. "But they give me wicked heartburn." I even smiled—cracked a joke—when she excused herself twice during a movie to relieve her dime-sized bladder.

She tells wonderfully absurd stories, long and rambling, jackknifing back against themselves until the listener's lost and uncertain of her intent. The other night she was describing a sculpture she welded together for an art class in college when the tale fractured into a half-dozen snaggy tributaries. Soon she was talking about the first time she visited her local drugstore to pick up a prescription for birth control. Only seventeen, she filled her shopping basket with hair products and chewy candies and a cap pistol for her young nephew. She was trembling as she approached the pharmacy counter and, ultimately, it took two more trips—and lots of unneeded purchases—for her to muster enough nerve. "Geez," she said, sighing loudly. "What was I talking about?"

Sometimes while we're kissing she'll abruptly pull away, as though she's heard a distant voice calling her name. She'll stare curiously into space for two beats, three, before returning to my lips. When I asked her about this habit, she patted me softly on the knee. "Just wanna make it last," she said. "Like a yummy dessert."

Of course, we're still in the discovery phase. But I know she's good for me—at this time, in this place. I have a tendency to overthink my problems, examine them from every angle until they cloud my mind, and Nina can often sense when I'm carrying too much weight. On one occasion, sitting across from me at a diner, she blew a pellet of torn napkin through her straw and it landed in my soup. "Take it easy, sport," she said. "In a thousand years you'll be a pile of dust and carbon. No one will care about any of this."

I smiled because, indeed, she was right. And for at least the next few hours, Nina made all the bad stuff disappear.

A small window, like a porthole on a steamer ship, is set into a panel of white drywall. Several colorful duffel bags are stacked between a set of matching end tables. Near the bathroom, a toy dump truck rattles to the huffy beat of a multi-speakered stereo system. I'm sitting with a magazine butterflied across my lap, turning the pages without looking down. Instead, my eyes follow the slender figure of a twenty-something dance teacher, dressed in a skimpy navy leotard, as she prepares a neighboring studio for class. She cranes forward to retrieve a plastic cone and her heart-shaped ass, framed by the slanty-eyed leg holes of her singlet, rises in the doorway. She's so limber that her chin nearly taps the toes of her slippers, shimmery black hair trailing against the floor like spilled motor oil.

Her image summons one of my strongest memories from adolescence—an evening about six weeks before my junior year of high school, when I sat beside Jessica Novak on a picnic table during a gentle rain. We were attending a keg party behind the house of some kid I barely knew. In the hazy streetlight I could see the water beading against Jessica's lower lip, snapping tiny lariats of mist whenever she spoke. I reached for a cup of beer we'd been sharing and my fingers landed on her wrist. Then came a loud report from the woods nearby—an air gun or a bottle rocket left over from Independence Day. As she turned to face me, in the shallow darkness, it suddenly seemed as though everything in my life had been leading to that single moment. I leaned forward and placed my mouth against hers, my heart erupting like a piece of timber driven through a log splitter. In a swift gasp, all the noise and raging tumult around us dissolved into a sluicy silence.

We held our lips together for a long time. She curled her fingers around the back of my neck and I could hear her silver bracelets clinking. My head was filled with a jumble of ideas, seeds in a breeze, and it was difficult to parse truth from fiction. "Jessica Novak is my girlfriend," I repeated to myself. This couldn't mean anything else—hands sliding across damp skin, my knee pressed between her thighs. I allowed my imagination to sprint recklessly forward: I pictured the two of us on dates and doing homework at my kitchen table and necking in the back seat of my mother's car. But Jessica Novak saw things differently. It took nine days for her to return my phone calls. She wasn't my girlfriend—not then, not ever. While we were kissing, this boy she liked, Dylan Cano, had been sitting with some friends on the hood of a nearby car; she simply wanted to make him jealous.

Now, still gazing at the dance instructor, I'm interrupted by Callie and Tig. Both girls are wearing pink and white ballet outfits.

"Good class?" I ask.

Tig reaches forward and places her hands on my cheeks, mouthing the words, "I love you."

"I love you too, honey."

The two girls explode with laughter, slapping palms and shaking their heads.

"She didn't say 'I love you'—"

"No!" says Tig, leaping in front of her sister. "*I* wanna tell him."

Rising from my seat, I pull the straps of their gym bags across my shoulder.

"It looked like I was saying, 'I love you'—right, Dad?"

I nod. As we move toward the exit, I peer back at the dance instructor. Her door is now closed.

"I didn't say that." Tig squeezes the sleeve of my jacket so I'll stare her full in the face. "I was saying 'Elephant shoes.'"

"Look, Dad," says Callie, mouthing an overly enunciated version of the strangely paired words. "Try it."

I move my lips silently, repeating the phrase several times. "Elephant shoes, elephant shoes," I say, softly at first. "Elephant shoes, I love you, I love you…"

The girls are still giggling as we reach the sidewalk. With an abrupt sigh, Tig stops and rests her fists on her hips. Earlier in the week, when I was pleading with Tig to clean her desk and finish her schoolwork, I'd promised her a flavored sports drink from a vending machine at ballet class. "Next time," I say, reminding her that we're headed a few doors down to purchase new winter jackets. But she's not making any more deals, and I fish through my pockets for loose change. As Callie and I wait beneath a saggy metal awning, she practices a series of dance moves—setting her feet in first position, raising her leg past her waist, twirling in tight, overlapping circles.

Tig returns with a bright red mustache and a smile. The three of us walk past a takeout chicken restaurant, a video store, a delicatessen. Callie says the dance studio often smells like fried chicken, which makes it hard to concentrate. In the doorway of a discount clothing store, Tig raises her drink too quickly and splashes the front of her leotard. "Oh, Tig," I say, spitting into a handkerchief and blotting the saturn-shaped stain beneath her neckline.

The girls race down the bright, wide aisles to their favorite section of the store. By the time I reach them, Callie's flipping through a spindle of "skinny" jeans and Tig has several gauzy blouses folded across her arm. I remind them of our purpose: we're here for winter jackets. But neither girl seems interested.

I drift between a half-dozen racks crowded with gloves, scarves, and stocking hats. There are dress coats with faux-fur collars, pea coats, ski parkas, short jackets, and long dusters. I examine a snowboarding shell, designed for layering, with yellow and white piping. A double-breasted model made of wool and cashmere (only ten percent) has oversized buttons that are loose to the touch. Nearly obscured by a misplaced bathrobe is a tan car coat with matching belt. I consider putting it aside for Callie, but it's out of our price range.

From behind a great wall of signage and snow pants, I hear a familiar voice—she's loud and animated, her dimpled arms flashing across a fissure in the display stand. I hold my position, waiting and watching, intent on moving in the opposite direction from this woman, satisfied to glimpse her from afar. But she's not traveling alone and as I measure her footsteps, I back into her friend's shopping cart, causing a long enough delay that I see Shirley Curtin round the corner and, more significantly, she sees me. Next comes an awkward embrace, quick and shaky.

"How *are* you?" she asks, eyebrows arched in a manner that suggests pity.

From my old desk at Silver Springs, I could lob a box of condolence cards and strike Shirley Curtin, who survived the layoffs and remains Dennis Gaines's administrative assistant. She's stroking my hand with her plump fingers. As I start to speak, Callie and Tig appear beside me—each girl carrying a few prospective items for purchase. They're both talking at the same time, raising sweaters and indicating various details—zippered collar, "smooth" fabric. Before I can respond, Shirley Curtin slaps the handle of her shopping cart and exclaims, "These are your daughters! I haven't seen them since they were little."

"We're supposed to be looking for winter coats," I say, guiding the girls toward a neighboring aisle.

"I used to work with your father," says Shirley Curtin, suddenly, alarmingly. "At Silver Springs."

The girls are more concerned with their clothing, Callie practicing the closure on a pair of corduroy trousers, Tig pulling a coiled thread from a shirt.

"We miss him very much."

I place my hands on the girls' shoulders and give them a gentle shove. Soon we're surrounded by junior outerwear, protected from Shirley Curtin by an assortment of circular racks and jumbo placards. Because I promise each girl a *single* outfit—pants and shirt or dress and tights—they're surprisingly accommodating in our search for coats. After twenty minutes, Callie has agreed on a blue, waist-length ski jacket, and Tig a slightly longer style with a detachable liner.

On the drive home, the girls eat chicken fingers and curly fries from the restaurant beside the dance studio. I lower the volume on the radio and listen to their conversation. Tig talks about a boy in her class who got a bucket stuck on his head during a science experiment. He looked so ridiculous walking into things— chair, wall, desk—that even the teacher was laughing. For some reason, this story inspires Callie to describe a horrible smell coming from the hallway outside her classroom. "You know what?" she asks, sharing a cup of honey barbecue sauce with her sister. "This kid—Evan Hintz—had kept a fried-egg sandwich in his locker for, like, *two* weeks." It fills me with warmth to hear them talking this way. No animus or rancor—only two sisters who, though it'll take them years to acknowledge it, are often best friends.

A giant moon hangs suspended in the night sky, like a locomotive light in a black tunnel. Tig takes a sip of her drink and sighs.

"The next time someone gets sent to the moon," she says, "they should go when it's full."

"Why is that?" I ask.

"Look," she says, gesturing toward the horizon with a curly fry. "There's a lot more space than when it's all skinny."

Callie bursts into laughter, kicking the back of the passenger seat. I hide my smile against my shoulder.

"Oh, geez—that's crazy," says Callie.

"Honey —"

"The moon is *always* the same size, dodo."

"Don't call her that."

"It's going around the earth and reflecting the sun's light," says Callie. "We're just seeing it from a different angle."

"Hey, that's pretty good, Cal."

"We learned it in school—she should know that."

I wave my finger in the rearview mirror and Callie shrugs.

"Man," she says, returning to her food.

The girls are mostly quiet for the rest of the trip, except for a small burp from Tig that makes them both giggle. Then, several intersections from their mother's house, Callie leans forward, chin on fist, and asks a question I was hoping wouldn't come.

"Does that woman work someplace else?"

"Huh?"

"The woman from inside the store. She said she *used* to work with you."

It would be easy to bend the truth—a little half-nod and a change of subjects. Maybe deal with it another time.

"No," I say, easing the car to a halt beside a school crossing sign. I turn sideways, addressing the girls with my torso wedged between the two front seats. In a simple, abbreviated account: I explain the troubled economy and foundering retailers and their combined impact on greeting card manufacturers. I speak in generalities and, after a few minutes, the girls have lost interest. I take a deep breath, pat them on the knees. Again I start from a broad perspective, defining the term "layoff" and the typical numbers involved—"sometimes *thousands* of people," I say, eyes wide. As I continue rambling, hoping this shower of imposing-sounding words will somehow temper the blow (for both of us), Callie crosses her arms.

"Dad," she says, staring forward. "Did you get fired?"

Now both girls are looking up from their meals. Tig's mouth is parted, her chicken finger hovering eternally above her lap. I return to the obscurity and safety of adult language, discussing severance packages and extended benefits.

"You got fired," says Callie.

"Laid off," I say.

"That's the same thing as being fired, right?"

They are young girls and this is what they want: a way to understand my anxiety and chaos. A definition distilled to its purest form. I nod. And though I'm still not certain Tig has a handle on things, she has heard the word *fired* before—and it frightens her. I see her eyes fill with water, her lower lip arching across her upper teeth.

"Oh, sweetie," I say, kissing her wrist. "It's gonna be fine—I promise you."

There is only silence. We hear a car whoosh past, then Callie munching on ice from her soda.

"How's it gonna be fine?" asks Callie. "You *need* a job."

"We're okay." I break into an exaggerated smile. "I've got a few possibilities. And a friend of mine has been giving me work as a—" I pause, choosing my words carefully, "freelance contractor."

"What's that?" asks Tig.

"Well, it means I don't have to go into an office every day."

"Will you still have a desk?"

"Probably not."

She nods.

The three of us sit quietly for a few more moments. Then, because children have a tremendous capacity to forge ahead, they ask me for handfuls of the chocolate-covered raisins in my glove box, as if it's the most important thing in the world.

Liz is wearing dark sweatpants and a frayed cardigan sweater that once belonged to me. She's illuminated by a cone of orange light from a lamp above the front door. As I kiss the girls goodbye and hand them their stuff—school backpacks, dance bags, new coats—Liz pounds the doorframe to catch my attention. At first, I pretend not to notice and peer down at my cell phone as though I'm reviewing messages. But Tig leans back into the car and says, "Mom wants you." I roll down the passenger window.

"Thanks for taking them," she says.

I nod, lifting my shoulders into a sort of half shrug. I want to respond with a similar display of goodwill, a few kind words of my own, but the door closes with quick finality.

This is a true story. Two summers ago, the girls and I spent a long weekend at a friend's lake house in upstate New York. There was a closet stacked with old board games, and one evening we decided to play Life. We spun the numbered wheel and drove our little automobile game pieces along the snaking road, acquiring property and stocks and piles of colorful cash. But when I landed on a red space that ordered me to "Get Married," I physically couldn't do it. We continued with our game—I obligingly inserted a pink peg into my car and the girls agreed to call "her" my girlfriend instead of my spouse. "Geez, Dad," said Callie. "You've got issues."

I work hard to conjure one of my fondest memories of Liz, one that's remained in focus through years of rancid smoke. Once when Callie was still an infant, I awakened in the middle of the night to a half-empty bed. I made my way through our house, shuffling from room to room. Eventually, I noticed that our back door was open—I pressed my face against the screen and let my eyes adjust to the darkness. It took a few moments before I heard Liz's slippers scraping along the driveway. She had Callie strapped into a harness-type contraption that fastened across her frontside, like a reverse backpack, providing Callie with forward views and unfettered range of motion for her limbs. In the gentle night air, I listened to Liz as she whispered to our daughter. "And this one time," she said, "your father took me ice skating." Liz was walking with an exaggerated bounce to her step in hopes that the up-and-down motion would ease Callie back to sleep. "At first, he kept pretending to fall. Oh, he's a Silly Billy. He was flopping and sliding so Mommy would hold onto him as we skated around the rink. Isn't that funny?" I stood in the doorway for a while longer, though once Liz turned the opposite direction it became difficult to hear. She finally returned to bed, with Callie resting between us, and I wrapped my arm around the both of them.

True to his word, Mr. Eugene has provided me with more work —at least four or five additional collections a week. After scribbling a few things in my little black notebook, I tuck it beneath the rubber bands on my car's sun visor. I'm sitting outside a bowling alley called Claymore Lanes, counting thirty-five hundred dollars against my lap. The money came from Mike Claymore, who agreed to pay off his son's debt, handing me a paper sack through my window before his evening rush. Then he stood in an empty parking space and had a smoke, cupping a cigarette between his thumb and index finger. I watched him silently as he exhaled lungsmoke and scratched his ham-sized forearms. On his way back inside, he stomped out his cigarette and nodded at me.

I'm driving home and eating a turkey sandwich, the kind with shredded lettuce that spills across my front seat. Also, criminally, I have an open bottle of beer squeezed between my thighs. At stoplights, I dip my head below the window and take quick gulps. An enormous, cellophane-wrapped pickle spear makes my car stink of garlic.

As I pull into my driveway, I hear my cell phone—it's hidden between deli sandwich paper and Mike Claymore's bag of money. I shift my car into park and examine the phone's luminous display window.

There's a familiar heaviness to her voice, as though she's been afflicted by some untreatable bronchial condition. She's the kind of woman who never says, "I'm fine," and exchanged greetings become referendums on her list of illnesses and ailments, real and imagined. Tonight her knees are sore. And she fears the pneumonia that settled in her chest last winter has returned.

"And you?" asks my mother, after a long silence.

I don't have the strength to describe everything in detail, then respond to her inevitable roster of motives and consequences. Instead, I provide a brief and dispassionate account of my life over the past weeks.

"Ma," I say, after she asks me what comes next. "I have no idea."

She launches into a story about a great-uncle who during her childhood had a particularly difficult five or six-year period— foreclosure, bankruptcy, prostate cancer. She remembers visiting him in the hospital and hearing him tell her aunt that he *hoped* the disease would take him. As my mother continues talking, I take the white paper from my sandwich and press it flat against my knee. Removing one of my Japanese marking pens from the car's visor, I absently start to sketch the garbage cans near my yard—corrugated side panels, indentations, tiny rivets sprouting from each tunneled handle. I use a stippling technique to create shadows against the bumpy driveway.

It's been a long time since I sat down to draw, and I nearly forgot how it clears my head. The sound of paper crinkling beneath my hand causes my mother to raise her voice. She's moved on to her predictable ending: an inflated example of a man who fought the good fight and, ultimately, magnificently, was rewarded with a successful second career.

"You know," she says, pausing for dramatic effect, "he was a *millionaire* when he died."

That's perfect, I tell my mother. Because my goal is to die with more than a million dollars.

"Don't be a smart mouth."

As the conversation resumes, my mother suggesting a variety of temporary employment opportunities—retail sales, teaching, hawking plumbing supplies for a "national chain" like her friend Janice Dykstra's son—I add more to my picture. There's a knotty wooden fence and a pair of low-hanging telephone wires. Even after my mother and I finish talking, and I've promised to have the girls call her over the weekend, I spend another twenty minutes rendering the garage door.

The next morning I'm third in line at a convenience store. There are five items in my basket, including wintermint toothpaste for the girls and another box of nicotine chewing gum. Eventually, the cashier waves me forward. She rings up my purchases and drags my bank card through a slot in her register.

During my financial struggles, I've developed a highly acute sense of checkout-counter protocol. There's an appropriate delay, an acceptable period of time—no more than twenty seconds—from when a cashier swipes a bank card to when the customer's receipt is ejected. I smile weakly and drum my fingers against the handle of my basket. It's been nearly a minute and the teller's staring into a glowing screen on her register—a screen that's congested with numbers and codes and other important information concealed from the customer by angle and intent.

"It's not going through," she says finally.

"What do you mean? It's a money card—from my checking account. I have enough—"

"Dunno." She shrugs. "But it's not going through."

The woman behind me pretends to read a label on her box of hair dye. Typically, I pay for things in cash, removing enough money from my freezer on Sunday nights to last me through the week. But a few days ago I bought new coats and clothing for the girls, nearly emptying my wallet.

"Can you put my things aside?" I ask, without making eye contact. "I'll come back."

Standing in the parking lot, I dial the customer service number on the back of my card. Twice I'm instructed to enter my account information by depressing the tiny cell phone keys. I'm routed from one representative to another—"Oh, that's a different department, but it will be my *pleasure* to connect you." After a lengthy wait, I speak with a supervisor who informs me that a "legal hold" has been placed on my account.

"I'm sorry," I say, softly knocking my head against the roof of my car. "What does that *mean*?"

I'm told the legal hold was initiated by the state's Department of Children's Services—the agency that garnishes my monthly support payments. There's nothing else, she insists, and then offers to connect me with someone in the bank's legal division. I leave a long, panic-stricken message for my attorney.

Although I have a collection in Boardman, about forty minutes away, I'm too distracted to make the drive. I stop at the Roasted Bean, on Cadiz and Lake, for a cup of coffee. I'm trying to figure out why Children's Services would freeze my bank account. (Can they *do* that?) I haven't missed any payments, and since losing my job the agency has started withdrawing the money directly from my unemployment benefits. I'm seated at a table by the window, my eyes skipping back and forth between my cell phone and coffee cup.

Across the room, a college-aged boy wearing a hooded sweatshirt and laceless sneakers is typing into a laptop computer. Without looking up, he says something to a woman behind the counter, a *barista*, and chuckles at her response. A young mother enters with two small children. She bends down to examine the selection of pastries in a glass display case. An animated little girl, unmistakably her daughter, waves a rubber pretzel at her toddler brother. "Don't tease him, honey," says the mother.

The girl is dressed in a brown overcoat and polka-dot stockings. She wanders toward the college kid with the computer and rests her chin on the soft arm of his chair.

"We have a *pewter*," she says.

It takes a moment for the college kid to determine the voice's location.

"It's bigger than that."

"I bet," he says. "Do you know how to use it?"

She shakes her head and her pigtails flop across the bridge of her nose.

"My dad says I'll break it."

"Well, they *are* fragile."

She digs her fingernails into the fabric of the chair.

"We have a dog."

"Really."

"Her name is Missy," says the girl, leaning forward and kicking up her feet. "But we might have to get rid of her, 'count of my brother."

"I'm sorry to hear that."

"He's got allergies." She hooks her thumb across her shoulder, as though she's preparing to cast a fishing line. "That's him over there."

The college kid glances in the direction of the register and nods.

"Lydia, honey," says the mother. "Please leave that young man alone."

The little girl squats down and inspects the buckle of her shoe.

"That's a very pretty name," says the college kid, peering over the arm of his chair. "Lydia."

"There's a girl in my class named Dorothy."

The college kid smiles, as though he's waiting for something else.

"*Lydia!*" says the girl's mother, stomping her foot. "Come over here."

The sudden noise makes the toddler start crying. The mother turns her stroller toward the exit and places a white bag filled with baked goods into her purse.

"Well, I gotta go."

"Nice to meet you, Lydia," says the college kid.

Although her mother's waiting beside the door, the girl appears in no hurry to reach her. She carefully navigates each step so her feet only land inside the outlines of the black tiles. Finally, the girl's mother grabs her by the elbow and practically hurtles her in front of the stroller. "Hold the door," says the mother, in a firm voice. The college kid watches them leave and then returns to his work.

It's not until late afternoon that I hear back from my attorney. I'm lying on my couch, eyes covered by a lukewarm compress. I reach blindly for my phone and knock over a clay dish Callie made at summer camp. (It doesn't break.) After an imposing silence, my attorney explains that there's been a clerical error, a mistake in the transcription of certain dates, and according to the flawed records at Children's Services I'm nearly five thousand dollars in arrears. When I suggest that the agency simply make the correction—and unfreeze my goddamn bank account—my attorney bursts into laughter. He reminds me that we're dealing with the worst possible bureaucracy and, although they're clearly at fault, we must now "request" a hearing. In short, we must ask for permission to notify them of *their* mistake. He promises to file the necessary paperwork in the morning.

It's dark when I stumble into the kitchen. My appetite has vanished; unless I'm with the girls I rarely eat more than one meal a day. I look sluggish and gaunt, like a character in an El Greco painting. The house is cold but I refuse to change the thermostat. For a couple weeks last winter I let the girls keep their room a few degrees warmer. The following month my gas bill was almost double its usual rate.

I pour a glass of bourbon and drink it in three swallows. To soothe the afterburn, I use a grape juicebox as chaser, steadying its spaghetti-thin straw against the hinge of my lips. There's a blinking message from Nina and one from my sister. I wrap myself in a fleece blanket and collapse in my chair. Sometimes before bed, Tig will ask me for a "human burrito"—I'll roll her tightly in a comforter, arms pinned to her sides. She'll laugh and wriggle as I lay her on the mattress.

I kick my feet onto the coffee table and pull the ends of the blanket together beneath my chin. Then I stare numbly into space, watching an occasional pair of headlights climb across the living room wall.

The house still smells of broccoli and broiled meat. I'm rinsing the last of the dishes, scraping dinner's greasy remains into the trash because the whirling blades of my garbage disposal were disabled by a coin. About a week ago Callie winged a quarter at Tig and missed. (Later, I'd learn she never tracked the coin's path or made any attempt to retrieve it.) The next morning when I tried to grind our leftover breakfast, French toast and link sausage, I heard the disposal catch on something hard and tinny. I needed a flashlight to make out the scratched quarter lodged beneath the U-shaped rotors. I bloodied my knuckles against the drain while navigating a screwdriver, hammer, and rubber-grip pliers. "Jesus, it's really in there," I said, as Tig aimed the light.

The girls are doing homework at their desks. I shout for them to turn off the music, but I have trouble hearing their responses above the sink's running water. A salad plate slips from my hand and cracks into three neat pieces. I gaze at the floor from a few different angles, fighting the light's glare, making certain there isn't any slivery glass to threaten the girls' bare feet. As I discover a small nest of dropped (and dusty) foods beneath the cupboard doors—M&Ms, Spanish peanuts, pretzel sticks—I hear a muffled thump from down the hall. It's followed, in quick succession, by a scream and the slap of wood against wood.

On my way to the girls' bedroom, their door swings open and a hardcover book hurtles into a framed photograph of a mountainous landscape. There's a short delay—one beat, two—before the picture slides from the wall and topples over. Callie's sinking her fingernails into Tig's biceps, using leverage to plow her sister into the ladder of their bunk bed. Tig has Callie's hair gripped in her fists like reins. They're yelling and pushing and trying to kick each other. I step between them.

"What's going on?"

"She's an *ass*," says Callie, feeling her scalp for proof that her hair's still attached.

"Hey—"

"Well, she *is*."

I flick Callie on the shoulder.

"I *hate* her," says Tig, examining the red crescent marks on her arm.

Apparently, Tig was listening to a song on their boom box and Callie changed it—because, according to Callie, a few minutes earlier Tig had changed one of *her* songs before it ended.

"Doesn't matter," I say. "What's the rule about putting our hands on someone?"

"Not to do it," says Tig.

"Unless it's your *stupid* sister," says Callie.

"Enough!"

I lead them both to their desks on opposite sides of the room and return the compact disc to its case. Tig brings her palms together. "Please can we listen to it?" she asks. "If we *promise* to be good?"

I shake my head.

"See what you did," says Callie.

"No." I press my fingers above Callie's ears and turn her head toward an open mathematics textbook. "You're not supposed to be listening to music until *after* you've finished your homework."

"Mom lets us," says Tig.

"Don't lie," says Callie.

"Sometimes she does."

"Like when—"

"Hey," I say, clapping my hands together. "In *this* house, there's no music until you're done with school stuff."

I stand in the middle of the room and cross my arms, waiting for them to start working again. After a few moments of silence, I shuffle into the hallway and listen with my back to the wall. Tig begins speaking in quick, dynamic bursts. But she halts in midsentence when I clear my throat in that blustery way of someone who wants to be noticed.

In the living room, I've spread bills and notices and folders across the coffee table. I'm trying to determine the number of outstanding checks that will be affected by the sudden hold on my bank account. According to my attorney, the child support agency intends to withdraw a portion of my artificial arrearage—maybe a third, maybe more—by week's end. "The bad news is, you'll never see that money again," he said. "The good news, though, is after your hearing they'll credit the account, and you won't have to make any additional support payments for a while."

There are utility bills, dance lessons, dental payments. I'm also putting together an estimated budget for the next few months: I leaf through my little black notebook, recording recent and future transactions on a ruled spreadsheet I created from an old sketchbook. A brambly heat starts behind both of my ears, in tandem, expanding across my nape and scapula. I can feel my breathing accelerate as a helix of black spots crowds the periphery of my vision. Over the past couple days, I've crunched the numbers in my head; I know we're going to have to make more sacrifices. But staring at all the columns and figures together for the first time, I realize the disparity between my income and expenses is even greater than I imagined.

Leaning back, I massage compact ovals against my eyelids. It's been a long time since I've had a good sleep—most nights I lie in bed for hours, maybe reading or listening to the radio. Once the lights are finally turned off, my mind is occupied by a never-ending cycle of problems, as though they're slots on a roulette wheel. Each spin delivers a different concern.

To find sleep I often have to distract myself, literally forcing pleasant thoughts into my head—images from the girls' ballet recitals, the flutter in my stomach the first time I kissed Nina, a fingertip catch I made during a game in college. But it's a battle to maintain my focus. A few nights ago, I called upon a memory from my early twenties: standing outside a restaurant converted from an old mill, and listening to its giant waterwheel chugging in the Chagrin River. A group of us who were home for the holidays had decided to meet, and I'd had a few cocktails. I was joined in the parking lot by Julie Emmett, a petite blond that I knew from lifeguarding the summer I turned sixteen. It was cold enough that we could see our breath. She was wearing a fleece-lined denim jacket, Navajo-print skirt, and black motorcycle boots. For some reason, Julie Emmett had peeled down the waistband of her skirt—was she showing me a new tattoo? A scar?—and I was gaping at the taut skin of her abdomen. In the restaurant's strained light, I could see a strip of downy yellow fuzz below her navel. A hundred times since that night I've dreamed of laying my hand on her bare waist, and it's this memory of Julie Emmett—or, more precisely, her exposed, twenty-two-year-old pelvis—that I summoned earlier in the week to help relieve my anxiety and lead me toward sleep.

But the picture grew cloudy. I was interrupted by a series of inconvenient details, each sparking a new set of loosely connected worries. I remembered Julie Emmett drove a blue Honda, and that only made me think about my impending car payments and insurance premiums. Recalling the way snowflakes settled in her hair started me fretting over winter heating prices. There was even a memory of Roger Lennon ordering a drink in the bar—and because he's now an orthodontist, I began to calculate the cost of braces for my daughters.

In my living room, I sort through the bills, attempting to rank them in order of importance. There's a small laceration on my right hand, across the bridge of my middle knuckle. Yesterday I caught my skin on the zipper of a guy's jacket during a trip to Boardman; he needed another week to finish his payment. He seemed like a nice man—owns a sporting goods store, sponsors a youth-league hockey team. (Resting above his desk were three trophies and corresponding photographs.) After he learned I had daughters, he even gave me a pair of replica football jerseys. But I've had a lot on my mind and, some days, the weight seems too great. The drive to Boardman took longer than I expected, and I had heartburn from a lousy sandwich I'd bought along the way. We made a plan to meet again next week, near me. Still, there was this pressure, an immovable freight on my shoulders and neck and knees. I was cold then hot, feeling a dampness beneath my collar. He was talking and waving an invoice for camping supplies, his voice receding into a steady hum. I couldn't get comfortable—my heart would quicken and slow; I had this tingly itch along the backs of my thighs. Then he was looking up at me, as though he expected some answer to a question I hadn't heard. He kept nudging my wrist with the back of his hand—*Huh, huh? Know what I mean?* I don't remember my arm cocking back, elbow crossing the plane of my shoulder. But I can still see his face as I came forward, all thrust and fury, like the finished motion of a tennis serve. My fist struck him in the chest and, a second time, across his clavicle where the zippered closure of his warm-up jacket drew blood.

On the ride home, I kept glancing at the girls' new football jerseys on the passenger seat—blue and red and white—until, finally, I tossed them into the back of the car. Near the entrance of his store he'd offered me a small towel and some iodine for my hand, but I avoided looking him in the face. More than fear or anger or sadness, he seemed disappointed, as if I'd been a stray dog he'd cared for and fed only to get bitten. I surprised us both by hugging him, awkwardly, his chin pressed into my shoulder. I wanted him to know that I had a capacity for kindness and understanding. *This isn't who I am*, I felt like telling him. On a different day in a different month I might not have raised my fist.

The shriek is loud and unexpected, causing a reactionary twitch from my right arm. The movement leaves a diagonal pen mark across a check I'm writing for electricity. As I return to the girls' room, I'm greeted by a rubber-tipped cheerleader's baton being launched like a javelin, narrowly missing Callie's head. I grab Tig by the waistband of her jeans and lift her from the ground.

"That's very dangerous," I say, aiming her toward the bathroom. "Get ready for bed."

I retrieve the baton and stand watchfully between the two girls.

"I want that," says Tig.

She kicks her foot and a spume of toothpaste squirts from the corner of her mouth.

"I'm sorry, but you've—"

She takes her free hand and slaps me on the thigh. In response, I lay the baton against my knee and fold its soft, tubular metal in half.

"Oh—" says Tig, her toothbrush dropping to the floor. "You ruined it."

She's crying, deliriously swinging her arms in our confined space.

"See," shouts Callie. "That's what you get for throwing things."

"Mind your own beeswax," I say.

"It *is* my beeswax—she almost hit me."

Tig watches me drop her V-shaped baton into the garbage.

"I *hate* you!" she screams, running from room to room. She resembles an insect hurling itself against a hot floodlight.

After about ten minutes, I agree to buy her a new baton— "I'd rather have rollerblades," she says—if she can improve her behavior.

"Great," says Callie, climbing into her top bunk. "You're rewarding her for almost spearing me?"

"No one's being rewarded."

"Well—"

"Cal," I say, placing a bottle of water on the highest step of her ladder in case she gets thirsty during the night. "I'm just trying to make it till tomorrow."

She snickers.

"What?"

"My teacher would call you a drama queen."

I smile.

"Maybe she's right."

I turn off the light and Tig waves me back to her bedside.

"Dad," she whispers, "cuddle my feet."

"Honey, it's late."

"Real quick—just for a minute."

I crouch down, sitting on a corner of her blanket. She squeezes her bare feet together, right over left, like a diver's. I gather them in my palms and tug, hand after hand, upward toward her ankles, as though I'm pulling a fire hose. "Cuddle, cuddle, cuddle," I say, because that's how she likes it.

A replica of China's flag is pasted on the center panel of a foam trifold board. My living room is littered with glossy photographs torn from magazines, rough sketches on white paper, colored pencils and markers, spools of ribbon, adhesive-backed gold stars. Earlier today I received a call from Liz. Because she had to work late at the construction company, she needed me to take the girls. I'm seated at my computer, proofreading several paragraphs Callie wrote about China's history for a school assignment while she and Nina lay out materials for the rest of the presentation.

"Hey, Dad," says Callie. "If a Chinese kid loses an upper tooth, her parents will plant it in the ground so the new tooth grows straight."

"That's interesting," I say without turning around.

"They'll get a tooth tree," says Tig, who's coloring on the couch.

"Same for bottom teeth?" asks Nina.

"Oh, no." Callie slaps the wood floor. "They throw the bottom tooth onto a roof—so the next tooth will grow upwards."

"That's crazy," says Tig.

Nina rises and walks into the kitchen for a glass of juice. I follow in close proximity, laying my head across her shoulder.

"Having fun?" I ask, rolling my eyes.

"They're sweet girls," she says.

Before I can press my body against hers, Tig appears in the doorway.

"Are we making cookies?"

Nina explains that she promised Tig they'd bake cookies—at some future, indeterminate date.

"Another time," I say.

"We've gotta go shopping," says Nina. "We need the proper ingredients."

Tig cocks her head, casting a suspicious eye at the two of us.

"Okay," she says reluctantly. "But I don't like any nuts in mine."

"No nuts," Nina confirms.

As Tig turns to leave, the toe of her oversized flat strikes the refrigerator door.

"Tig," I say. "Whose shoes are those?"

She gestures toward Nina with her thumb.

"Did you ask—"

"It's fine," says Nina, softly patting my wrist. "They're old and stinky."

Tig looks down, as though expecting a suddenly offensive smell to rise and meet her.

"Well, I like 'em," she says.

"Me too," says Nina.

I watch Tig shuffle slowly back into the living room. At first, I was tentative about connecting Nina to my world with the girls. I didn't know how they'd respond. Here was someone new to share their father's affection—a woman who wasn't their mother. But Callie's school project came upon us without warning, and most of my art supplies are still boxed in Liz's basement. And so, almost accidentally, we're forced to see how the pieces fit together.

The girls took to Nina immediately—especially Tig, who peppered her with questions about hairstyles and favorite foods and the plastic tackle box she uses for a purse. Though Callie's more reserved, she's grateful for Nina's assistance and she thanks her several times. They glue a pair of black lacquer chopsticks on the board beside a short paragraph about Asian cuisine. Tig's desperate to be included; she asks if anyone needs a shaker of glitter that's squeezed against her knees.

For a moment, the image of the three of them working together rekindles all my best fantasies about family life—the fine and easy exchanges that rarely existed when I lived with Liz. I close my eyes and listen to their conversation, sweet-throated sparrows on a common branch. Maybe this will be enough—a chance for the girls to see a healthy relationship between two caring adults.

The girls are tired and slow to rise from bed. On my third visit to their room, I strip the covers from their languid bodies. Callie screams, complaining of the cold. Tig hooks my leg with her outstretched feet. "Carry me like a baby," she says. I lift her across my forearms, rocking her back and forth on our way to the bathroom. She lets her flannel pajamas gather around her ankles as she drops to the toilet.

I've started preparing their lunches when Callie yells for me—though she wants to remain on her bunk while dressing, she needs her clothes. "Really?" I ask, rummaging through her messy drawers and tossing her the first of every item I see—jeans, undies, socks. But she doesn't like the shirt I've selected and it sails across the room.

"Then *you* come pick," I say.

She's still calling me—"The gray one!"—when I return to the kitchen. A light snow has begun to fall from a bone-colored sky. The girls are excited when I tell them they can wear their new winter coats. It's not until we arrive at school that I notice the tags attached to Callie's sleeve.

"Don't rip it," she says, pulling away. "Use a scissors."

"You think I have a scissors in my car?"

From a pocket below my seat, I remove a folding knife and carefully sever the store tags, leaving a pair of stubbly plastic threads near Callie's wrist. She leans forward so I can kiss her on the head; Tig offers me her face. As they join a procession of fellow students, I call to them through my open window, if only to maintain our connection for a few additional seconds, reminding them to eat their carrots and grapes before the rest of their lunches. This is what I'm thinking about—Callie and Tig gleefully discovering a ladybug-shaped chocolate at the bottoms of their bags—when they disappear from sight.

The satchel smells of cigar smoke. It's lying on the passenger seat of my car, and every few miles I glance down, eyes locking on its tarnished brass closure. A couple hours ago, I was eating a tuna sandwich in a diner when my cell phone began to rattle against my water glass.

This Sunday there's a football game between the Steelers and Colts. Although the line is close—Pittsburgh getting two and a half points—Mr. Eugene's taking a large number of bets on Indianapolis. I've been asked to drive to Atlantic City and lay off some of his action: I'll wager big on the Colts to cover any potential losses. With a game like this one, he'll only pocket the vig.

The drive should take me a little more than seven hours, though I've already stopped once, shortly after crossing into Pennsylvania, for gas and coffee. I kept the satchel gripped in my left hand, even while I was taking a piss. I'll follow 80 East almost the entire way and, if I'm lucky, arrive soon after sundown.

My windshield's messy with roadspray and flecks of snow like stars glimpsed from a fast-moving spacecraft. A pair of enormous semis, seemingly hinged at the bumpers, passes on my left, nearly blowing my car into a guardrail. In the hilly belly of the state, furred branches on conifers and Jack pines are newly shaded white. A trail of grease smoke rises above the treetops, like a crack in the sky.

A sadness creeps through me as I replay the previous few hours. Before leaving, I'd stopped at home to pack some things for the trip—change of clothes, Dopp kit. I was rushing because I still needed to pick up the money from Mr. Eugene's office. If the ground hadn't been covered with fresh snow I might have missed it. But across the rear lawn, beside the driveway, I noticed the first small marking in the reflection of my car door. It was a narrow red streak, interrupted in places like a scored line. I followed its path to the back of my house and, near the corner of my deck, I saw the orange cat curled into a spiny ball.

As I approached, the cat retreated a few steps, allowing more redness to spill from his underside. He rested on his side, panting, his eyes sad and black. Between his hind legs I could see the damage: his stomach had been torn open and pink entrails, like ribbons of soft cheese, lay against the cold earth. I tried to rub him behind his ears but he only dragged himself farther away. Twice he let his tail flop sideways into the snowy grass. I spoke to him in the same gentle voice I use to comfort the girls through illness. If I wasn't in a hurry I could've rolled him into a basket and carted him to a vet, though it probably wouldn't have made a difference.

His breathing grew slower and his head seemed too heavy for his slender neck. I covered him with an old towel from the garage. I figured this might be enough, a sign of human interest, to frighten away predatory animals. Then I sat in my car and watched him from my side mirror, hoping he would rise again and sprint into the barbed woods beneath the telephone wires. But there was only the quavering of my old towel, up then down, with the intervals growing longer between the two until, finally, I couldn't determine if there was any movement at all.

Ahead the horizon is dark and I lose myself in a succession of lies about felines and their powers of restoration. Shoe only needs to rest; his lacerated belly will heal on its own. A week from now he'll appear at my back door as though nothing's happened, a jagged scar the only reminder of his injury.

On a hillside to my left I see a small clapboard house partially hidden by a roving column of bur oaks, some of their branches still protected by fiery leaves. The scene stirs a memory from high school, shortly after we'd won the league championship my junior season. Sully and I were driving to a party in a wealthy suburb called Devon Hills. We arrived early and waited on a sloping side street. There was a white house not unlike the one I'd just passed, only larger, and a hunched willow blocked three of its windows. The air was damp and red leaves stuck to the hood of my truck. For a fleeting moment I was filled with hope and promise—we had our entire lives ahead of us and, no matter how wonderful things seemed, they would only get better. But that wasn't true. And, years later, I learned nothing would ever feel that way again.

Now, a bullwhip of black highway ahead, I'm traveling to Atlantic City with a case of money. This is not the life I imagined for myself. I expected my share of struggles but, eventually, I believed all the pieces would come together, like a number sequence falling into place. Instead, there came a moment when the hard times simply swallowed everything else.

I can often see the effect it's having on the girls. "No one's happy," said Callie, less than a month ago. "Not you, not Mom." I sat in our lightless kitchen, fingers knitted across my lap, and tried to figure an exit strategy for this part of our lives—at least a way to release the tension. But I couldn't form a single lucid thought.

On the road in front of me, an old Cadillac briefly drifts onto the shoulder and launches a rooster-tail of gravel that pings beneath my car. I watch a pair of large crows land on a droopy wire fence in the distance. There's a packet of nicotine gum clattering across the dashboard. Once, when Nina and I were kissing, she remarked that my cinnamon gum reminded her of being a teenager—of warm diet colas and corduroy jeans and making out with boys in her parents' driveway.

In astrophysics there's something called a Lagrange Point, where a small object positioned within the gravitational pull of two larger objects can be "held" stationary in space. I can't help but apply this theory to my own universe: No matter how I try to shake free, it seems I'm always caught between my ex-wife and financial despair. For me, the laws of motion have suddenly become irrelevant.

She's not pulling away, I tell myself. In fact, it's the opposite—a cry for greater intimacy, an increased closeness. Soon after Nina helped Callie with her school project on China, a slippery attempt to weave Nina into the fabric of our family, we spoke at length about the arc of our relationship. She made it clear that she's not interested in killing time. We have enough in common, a powerful enough connection, for this thing between us to own a certain significance. There weren't any ultimatums. But she wanted me to know that she's worth the effort, and sacrifices would need to be made.

"I understand that you have a lot on your plate," she said. "Raising your daughters, finding a job. But I can't always be your second choice—someone to be shoehorned into your schedule when you're feeling lonely late at night."

She is right, of course. And if we both want the same thing it will require plenty of work on my part. Standing up to Liz when she makes last-minute changes to our parenting schedule. Finding a babysitter on evenings when I have the girls. And, perhaps most importantly, a way to fully commit myself to Nina when we're together. Making sure that she is a priority. Too often, I have asked her to serve as my sounding board or therapist: she's endured long discourses on the girls' behavior or my damaged exchanges with Liz or my anxiety about finding work.

"I'm trying," I told her, though I'm not certain it's the truth. Moving forward, I'll need to step outside of my comfort zone— if that's even the proper terminology—and push myself toward a more vulnerable place. This is what she wants: a stake in whatever exists behind my protective shell.

During our conversation the other night, she raised her voice. It was the first time I remember seeing in Nina a glint of anger about the two of us.

"You have to decide how much I mean to you," she said, slapping the counter with her exposed palm. "Are you in or out?"

There were more words between us, and I did my best to provide an explanation. I'm *in*, I'm definitely *in*. But there is so much water running past the stone. I asked for patience and a little understanding. It's not easy to make corrections in a life that's deeply settled. I want it all to work, watch it come together in a neat tributary. Still, it feels as though sometimes the cascade is too great. And there are days when I simply need to turn things off. Call it resting or recharging my batteries. That doesn't mean I don't care about Nina or wish to spend time with her. Rather, it's an inherent selfishness---a part of me that doesn't long for anything other than a resounding quiet and a chain of undisturbed moments alone.

On long car trips the girls like to track the number of fast-food restaurants they can see from the highway. (I'm certain they think it provokes a subliminal message and I'll be more receptive to their frequent pitches for burgers and pizza.) Though I'm only in Bloomsburg, I've already counted a hundred and eighteen. In fairness, I haven't devoted my full attention to the game—I've only been following the colorful signs from the corners of my eyes. In the circular lobby of a rest stop, drinking peppery coffee and stretching out the soreness in my back, I pause to lean against a Plexiglas arcade game filled with stuffed animals and boxed toys. By inserting a dollar, the player gets to operate a chain-linked crane for thirty seconds in hopes of retrieving one of the prizes. A rubber-nosed koala appears to be straddling a light gray elephant. I notice my reflection in the smudged glass and follow the movements of my lips. "Elephant shoes, elephant shoes," I whisper.

Waiting in line at a hot dog stand are two girls in their late teens. Despite the cold weather, one of them wears a form-fitting t-shirt and sandals. She's talking on a cell phone, loud enough for others to hear, and holding a bag of red licorice in her free hand. The second girl sways from side to side, gazing down at an open textbook. I close my eyes and try to imagine my daughters in five years, in ten. Callie will be finishing college, Tig will be starting. There's so much distance between now and then— plenty of time to repair some of the damage their mother and I have caused, or create new wounds. I picture Callie in the crimson jersey of some unidentified university, racing down a soccer field on a cloudless fall afternoon. Maybe Tig's watching from the sidelines, visiting her sister during a long weekend. Neither of them has a single worry except for homework and boyfriends and what they're going to wear later that evening.

I turn sideways and my forehead leaves an oily streak on the hard awning of the arcade game. Because I'm not ready to squeeze myself back in the car, I feed a dollar into a lighted slot and grip the crane's joystick. My initial play is for a smiling puppy with green eyes and matching collar. However, I soon discover that the grommets on the crane's silvery jaw are intentionally slack, and the puppy falls twice before my time has expired. I kick the machine against its base, nearly causing my coffee to topple over.

"It's a rip-off," says a young boy who's watching from behind me.

I return to the road, my car whistling as it gathers momentum on the interstate's slick entrance ramp. I twirl the radio dial from one staticky station to another. About forty minutes outside of Atlantic City, traffic slows to a crawl. It's not until I crest above a second hill that I realize this isn't typical of the evening commute. Dotting the soggy median are four state troopers, lights flashing, and two ambulances. A black SUV rests on its side between a badly damaged Ford sedan and a now lopsided minivan. As I creep past I watch a woman being lifted onto a stretcher. There's an icy drizzle, and one of the patrolmen shields the injured woman's face with a notebook. A broken taillight rises abruptly from the grass like a large and shiny strawberry. A white-haired man with a rectangle of fresh gauze taped to his head is talking with a state trooper. He brings his hands together with a clap.

In another lifetime, when I was still a child, I remember being awakened one night by the sound of steel scraping against cement. My bedroom window overlooked our driveway, and I pressed my face to the glass. Even in the splintered light of our front porch I could see that my father's car wasn't sitting properly. Later, I heard my parents talking through a heating vent that ran past our kitchen table; my father had been drinking, and on his ride home, tipsy and tired, he rolled into an intersection. The driver of the delivery truck didn't see my father until he clipped the front of his car, removing his bumper and grillwork like a bottle cap. Although the impact wasn't direct, it spun my father's car sideways into a high curb.

The only other person I knew who had been struck by a car was Ricky Chambers' grandmother, and she'd been killed instantly. I lay in darkness thinking my father must be invincible: he'd survived an accident, with a truck. At the time I'd been reading lots of comic books, and I fell back asleep wondering if my father was, indeed, some type of superhero. I spent the following day searching our house for clues—a mask or costume or utility belt.

The rain grows heavier as I approach Atlantic City. Red and blue and yellow lights shimmer in the smoky darkness. I park beneath the Tropicana, a towering hotel complex with a lemon-shaped crown on its roof.

A standard "suite" has been reserved under my name and paid for, less incidentals, by Mr. Eugene. I let my wet clothes fall on the carpeted floor of my room. After storing the leather satchel in my closet, beneath a jacket and folded blanket, I take a long shower, aiming the hot water against the small of my back. I'm tired, and I lie on the bed, allowing an old movie to play softly in the background. It seems as though I only close my eyes for a few minutes, but when I wake it's nearly midnight. I dress quickly and eat dinner in a steakhouse—New York Strip, string beans, two beers. Then I make my way through the casino, walking intently, satchel thumping against the hinge of my knee. At the sports book I slap down thirteen decks of cash before an attractive teller and wager the entire amount on the Indianapolis Colts, still giving two-and-a-half. I pocket my betting ticket and head toward the street for some fresh air.

The boardwalk glows beneath a canopy of iridescent light. A cold breeze swirls across the ocean's shore. The rain has stopped, and feathery footprints of steam rise from glassy puddles. A group of men in their late twenties stumble past, talking loudly and slurring their speech. In the middle is a thin guy wearing a white beauty-pageant sash that reads *The Groom*. There's a clanking sound whenever he lurches forward. I look to the ground and see a ball and chain fastened to his left ankle. One of his "friends" squeezes the chain's slack and tosses the heavy ball down the boardwalk. As the chain tightens, the groom is pulled awkwardly behind it. The others shout insults and spray him with beer. An older couple in slickers and rubber-soled shoes takes a circuitous path to their hotel, avoiding the loud revelers.

Despite the late hour, the boardwalk is crowded with pedestrian traffic. I watch a man tilt his head sideways and take a large bite from a foil-wrapped gyro sandwich, squeezing a clot of yogurt sauce onto the front of his shirt. He nearly collides with a woman in a fur coat and spiked heels as she teeters past. Beneath a green awning stands a bearded, long-haired man playing an acoustic guitar. His case is sprung open and its red felt interior littered with coins and dollar bills. A pair of college-aged guys wrestles playfully nearby. The larger of the two grips the back of his buddy's neck with one hand.

I wander past a souvenir shop and notice a selection of maritime-themed jewelry boxes in the window. There's also an earring tree shaped like a lighthouse and a collectible plate featuring a painted version of the boardwalk. I make a mental note to buy a present for the girls before I leave—something that can be boxed and giftwrapped, because Tig likes to guess what's inside. Tomorrow she has a playdate at Henley Krupin's house and, if it's not too cold outside, the girls will chase each other up and down Henley's sidewalk with three friends from their class. Then, probably around dinnertime, Liz will pull into the Krupins' driveway and Tig will spend the first ten minutes of the ride home asking why she can't live on Henley's street.

In a half-fantasy, I imagine the Colts defeating the Steelers— maybe by a touchdown—and collecting Mr. Eugene's money. I wouldn't need a mortgage broker or credit check—instead, I'd simply dump the contents of the leather satchel onto the real estate agent's desk and ask for the house across from the Krupins', the one that's been on the market for eighteen months. I picture Tig's rapturous dance across our new lawn, all toothless smile and flapping pigtails. "This is the best thing *ever*," she might say, her slender arms locked around my waist. And, of course, she would be right.

There are two layers of curtains shielding my window, leaving the room in perpetual darkness save for a finger of daylight poking through the center seam. Pushed against a wall is a room service cart cloaked in white linen. It holds a tepid pot of coffee, an empty juice glass, an arched crust of wheat toast, and a plate streaked with dried egg yolk. I'm sitting on the end of my bed, staring sleepily at the images on my muted television. Lying across my left thigh is my hotel bill, neatly bound in a small cardstock folder embossed with the Tropicana logo. An hour ago the Pittsburgh Steelers defeated the Indianapolis Colts. I have placed the now-worthless betting slip into an envelope for my return trip home.

The call came while I was packing my overnight bag. There's another "little errand" that Mr. Eugene wants me to run, in Morgantown, West Virginia. "We'll talk once you're on the road," he said.

In the parking lot, scraps of blown paper collect against the tires of my car. A wrapper from a packet of gummy candies, my daughters' favorite, dances into a mulch-covered flowerbed. I unfurl a creased road map and approximate the distance of my drive, using my thumbnail as a measuring device. I have a narrow margin of error: As long as I can leave Morgantown by, say, ten tomorrow morning, I'll be able to pick up the girls from school. Any later and I'll have to contact Liz about adjusting our schedule.

Not far from the highway's entrance ramp is a large cemetery encircled by a scabby iron fence. Instinctively, I hold my breath. It's a game the girls play: stop breathing out of respect for those who can't breathe. I reach the neighboring block and exhale. *Whew*, I imagine Tig saying, *that was a long one.*

When Cameron and I were children, my mother took us to a fair in Percy County—it had rides and games of chance and animal husbandry contests. At one point my mother made us peer into her mirrored compact to see our faces, which were powdered white with confectionary sugar from enormous slabs of fried dough called Elephant Ears. During the drive home, the sky parted with heavy rains and crinkled threads of lightning. The storm was so fierce that my mother pulled to the side of the road beneath a shelter of trees that resembled a miscolored cloud formation. Cameron and I passed the time taking turns drawing in a spare notebook—Ferris wheels, carnival barkers, smiling bovines.

Later, once the rain lessened, we slopped through the muddy entrance of a graveyard. We chased each other between the rows of stone markers—tall spires and polished-marble chests and smooth white crosses. It wasn't until I plucked a small American flag from a veteran's plot that my mother stopped us. In the trickling moisture, my sister and I stood against the door to our car as my mother explained the reverence associated with cemeteries. I remember staring past her shoulder, horrified and breathless, learning for the first time that the bodies of dead people were buried under the ground. I have no recollection of what I thought cemeteries were for prior to that moment. But as we continued our ride home, my sister and I had lots of wide-eyed questions for my mother. Are the dead people wearing clothes? (Yes.) What if they wake up? (They're dead.) Can they see who comes to visit? (They're *dead*.)

It's late afternoon and my headlights reflect in the glittery license plate of the car ahead—*Indiana, The Crossroads of America.*

I leave a message for Nina, then my thoughts turn to Callie and Tig. I wonder what they'll be eating for dinner and if they have any homework and if their mother will make them take baths. A few days ago, I received a halting e-mail from Liz threatening legal action if I didn't start returning the girls on time. It seems that over the past several weeks, the girls have been a combined forty-seven minutes late—she'd counted—in clear violation of our shared parenting agreement.

Shortly after I cross from Delaware into Maryland I see a sign for an indoor water park, with corkscrewing slides and wave machines and a "white sandy beach" facsimile. It sparks a memory from when the girls were very young: Liz and I sitting on a wooden glider, rocking forward and back, in the shadows of a friend's lake house. We watched a group of teenagers diving from an aluminum platform strapped to six floating drums. The teenagers giggled and screamed and slapped water at each other. Beside me, Liz was nursing Tig while Callie filled a yellow plastic pail with sand and stones and tiny clumps of weeds. Two sparrows swooped low to the ground, in tandem, and Callie followed their trail, a beat behind. Later, we all sat at a picnic table that had been converted from a section of barn door. Liz and I ate a salad of wild greens, tomatoes, and red onion. We grilled a marinated flank steak and cut Callie's into nibble-sized pieces. It's one of the few times we truly felt like a family.

Maybe it's different for the girls because this is the only life they've known. Although many of their friends have idyllic-seeming families, I think Callie and Tig are cautious when processing this information, not unlike when an adult strolls past an expensive automobile. We know it exists, but only for some other person in some alternate universe. *Stop staring. That'll never be you.* I'm thinking hard, trying to determine what parts of the girls' childhoods can objectively be labeled as *happy*. Years ago, during the worst of my divorce, I watched my attorney draw a long line on a sheet of legal paper. Then he made a small dot in the middle. "The line represents your life," he said. "And this *little* spot is where you are now. It may seem overwhelming, because you're stuck in this space. But ultimately, it's just a blink of time."

As the soupy Maryland countryside chugs past my window, I'm hoping all the sadness of the previous six years can also be condensed into a tiny pen mark on a scrap of paper, and when Callie and Tig are old enough they can reclaim the narrative of their lives.

For three straight summers, the girls attended a day camp about thirty minutes from town. There was swimming and canoe races and crafts and a small "canteen" where kids could purchase penny candy and lanyard cord. During one of my roughest economic periods, I met with Liz several weeks before the end of school. I was clear and concise, relying only on the sober truth: without her help, our daughters would have to miss camp.

After the words had all come out, floating between us like the windblown seeds of a dandelion, Liz crossed her arms and her face turned red. She began thinking aloud, offering what initially sounded like a disjointed list of purchases and tasks—new brassieres, leaky sink in the second-floor bathroom, rain slicker, repairing the ragged and crumbling front landing. Ultimately, she admitted these were sacrifices she was willing to make to cover her half of the camp's expense. Soon we were working together, two adults surrendering their needs like high-valued playing cards, to ensure the least amount of disruption in their daughters' lives. Liz broke into a smile when, near the end, I offered to forgo a (make-believe) vacation in Tahiti. This was the way divorced parents were supposed to behave—a solitary unit chugging along in their children's best interest. It showed me—*both* of us—that we could operate in a nobler manner, reach up to a higher plain of existence. We abandoned our anger, however briefly, to take a meaningful step forward.

Moments after I enter West Virginia, I'm driving across a long suspension bridge that connects two sides of a shingly reservoir. Nearly hidden in the hillsides are small houses, dim and dreary, that look as though they've been sketched by charcoal pencil. A tangle of roadway disappears into curves and canyons. Every few dozen miles there are packed-dirt tributaries that lead to unforgivingly steep knolls designed to "catch" runaway trucks. In the humped valleys beneath I can see acres and acres of barren farmland. There's also a small town, stippled with lights, of red brick and limestone and white-bordered windows. From this height the town resembles the centerpiece of a model locomotive set. If I did nothing more than hold my steering wheel straight, perhaps squeezed on both sides with my knees, it would only take a handful of seconds for my car to bust through a steel guardrail, somersault down the side of this mountain, and explode in dancing flames near the town's vacant ballfields.

For the last couple hours, my cellular service has been spotty. I emerge from a tunnel and notice that my message light is blinking. There's a random call from the girls' ballet studio reminding me our payment is nearly a month past due and—stammer, unnatural pause—we also owe for holiday show costumes. I stop for fuel and a caffeinated soda. When I raise the drink to my mouth, I can still smell gasoline on my fingers.

It takes another hour to reach my hotel, on the banks of the Monongahela River. My car has the stale feel that comes after long trips—spilled nubs of licorice, improperly folded maps, sticky pop stains, and wilted shreds of sandwich lettuce. There's also the tangy reek of perspiration. As I walk across the parking lot, I'm greeted by spirals of light snow like swarms of mayflies. I'm presented with my room key and, not wanting to be alone, I retreat to a soft gray chair in the lobby beside a polished grand piano that looks unplayed. I stare through the decorative panes of a floor-to-ceiling window, watching a bellman load a collection of hard-skinned suitcases into the back of a taxi. He's wearing a cap, the same type favored by policemen and ship captains. Its flat top has turned slushy white. A heavyset woman presses money into the bellman's gloved hand and cautiously lowers herself onto the back seat. She turns toward the hotel's exterior lights, and for the first time I can see that she's holding a small, persimmon-haired dog against her chest. I hear a muffled squeak as the door closes, and I'm not sure if it's the dog or a hinge in need of lubrication.

It takes several minutes for all the words to unravel and settle in their proper order. I'm seated on a tightly stretched bedspread in my hotel room, staring at the silent phone resting against my lap. Beneath the thermostat is a small desk holding a pad of cream-colored paper, a leather-bound room service menu, a curved lamp, a ballpoint pen with the hotel's name stamped across it. A hesitant clicking noise comes from a hidden radiator. I have eaten both squares of complimentary chocolate and their gold wrappers lie flat on my night table, ironed smooth with a Gideon's bible while I spoke to Mr. Eugene.

Since I began working for him years ago, he's never asked me to put my hands on anyone. Maybe there was an implication, a suggestion for a little physicality with those who'd refused to make their payments over an extended period. But tonight is the first time that he's asked for it explicitly.

The boy's name—and he *is* a boy, no older than twenty-one —is Luke Fowler. According to Mr. Eugene, Fowler, who's a guard on a nearby college basketball team, had agreed to shave points during a recent game against Seton Hall. But in the final six minutes Fowler stuck a pair of three-pointers and made five free throws, surpassing the betting line by four. "We lost a lot of money," said Mr. Eugene testily. My reaction was swift and logical: Shouldn't Mr. Eugene have "people" who handle this sort of thing? Slowly it occurred to me that *I'm* his "people."

During my junior year of college, one of my teammates, star running back Nate Purify, got his cleat caught in a gap of artificial turf. He was returning a punt and he planted his right foot, preparing to make a hard cut to his left. But his leg suddenly buckled—there wasn't a defender within ten yards. The following day, a group of us visited him in the hospital. He'd blown out his knee, rupturing both his anterior cruciate and medial collateral ligaments. We could see the flaky dander of dried saltwater branching from the corners of his eyes. After eleven months he was permitted to run again, but he'd lost his primary asset on the field—his quickness. He was benched by the middle of the next season in favor of a fleet-footed sophomore. Then, years later, I heard from our offensive coordinator that Purify had been arrested for passing bad checks near his hometown in Nebraska. It made me wonder about the randomness of life—a chance seam on a swatch of fake grass; the length of an interchangeable cleat; the violent torque that accompanies a sudden momentum shift by a large and rapidly moving object. Would it have made a difference if Purify's foot had landed, say, an inch or so to the left? Could that tiny correction have had an impact on the rest of his life?

In the morning, I'm still thinking about the fragility of human joints—knees and ankles, wrists and hips—as I walk down the main thoroughfare on campus. There's a corner eatery that smells of warm biscuits and coffee. Its walls are covered with athletic paraphernalia—team uniforms, pennants, autographed balls, and framed newspaper stories. Suspended above the service counter is a wooden menu shaped like a scoreboard. All of the sandwiches are named after famous local athletes. As I wait for a toasted bagel, I take several playful twirls on a stool. My eye catches on a glossy photograph the size of notebook paper. I lean forward for a glimpse of the university's current basketball team. Seated in the front row, third from left, with his hands flared across his bony knees, is Luke Fowler. His shaggy brown hair is carelessly parted on the right, spiky tufts springing in odd directions. Twin cowlicks droop low across his forehead. The picture was likely taken in early fall; his skin still holds a faint blush of suntan. His lips are parted in a lean smile, revealing a chipped incisor.

Outside, I eat my bagel and follow a steady stream of students as they make their way to class. Rising from a distinctive brick building with white trim is a four-sided clock tower. I recognize the architectural style as Second Empire or Beaux-Arts. I hear a strange *clackety* noise coming from one side; it's a long-haired kid in a ski parka riding a skateboard. He's whistling and his arms are outstretched, as though he's mimicking an airplane. I watch him disappear down a winding path. He seems unfettered by the daily stresses of life; as I watch the final wave of his fingertips, I try to recall the last time I felt so carefree. For some reason, I have a powerful image of standing beside a window in my childhood bedroom, wearing my Little League baseball uniform and pounding the pocket of my glove with my right fist. There's music playing from a shoebox-shaped radio on my desk. I'm watching my sister and her friend in our backyard as they lie on lounge chairs and read magazines. Later, I will have three hits in a game against the Expos and eat bubblegum ice cream with my teammates, picking out the pale nuggets of gum and saving them in a paper napkin. I remember the sweet summer air rushing through the car's open window on the drive home and a sensation as though it was going to lift me from my seat, weightless and windswept.

But this life has stolen away all my lightness. I'm plodding through an unfamiliar town in search of, ultimately, a paycheck. I've committed to do unspeakable things. I've surrendered to a pattern of behavior that even five years ago I would've found appalling. There's a short thread that connects Luke Fowler to Nate Purify to me. We all shared the same dreams, wanted similar things. And now I'm being asked to extinguish that spark in Fowler, give him a glimpse of all that remains—the opposite of hope.

Beside the entrance to one of the university's libraries, I call Liz and explain that my business is taking longer than I expected. She agrees to pick up the girls from school and, surprisingly, offers me a trade for tomorrow afternoon. I continue my tour of the campus, kicking a small peak of frozen mud near the base of a large statue—a frontiersman on horseback. I dial my home number and cup my cell phone against my ear. Three times I listen to my outgoing message, in which Callie and Tig take turns providing instructions until they both break into laughter.

Not long ago, during a drive to the grocery store, Tig announced that "for Christmas or my birthday" she wanted a set of matching gloves, hat, and scarf. In response, Callie told me about a style of earrings that resemble the pull tab on a zipper. These will be the first things I buy after receiving my next payment from Mr. Eugene.

Perched behind the highest row of seats in the university's field-house, I watch the final moments of basketball practice. The sounds of squeaking sneakers and bouncing balls echo through the rafters. A line of players forms at each basket and they take turns shooting free throws. The coach wears a navy sweatsuit trimmed in gold and a white-tipped whistle around his neck. His slicked-back hair shines under the fluorescent lights. A muscular black kid in a reversible tank top is dribbling down the sideline as one of his teammates half-heartedly plays defense. Eventually, they join the rest of the group near center court in a lopsided huddle, hands together, and shout a word I can't understand—team? win?—before heading toward a darkened tunnel.

I make my way down a series of ramps and through a concrete hallway. There's an enormous loading bay designed to accommodate eighteen-wheelers stocked with circus equipment and monster cars and stage sets for ice-skating shows. As I continue around the horseshoe-shaped corridor, I hear the playful banter of ballplayers—laughter followed by the heavy spank of large feet chasing large feet.

In a shaded alley, I climb onto a parked Zamboni and rest my arms across a tacky steering wheel. The locker room door is clogged with a knot of sweating, churning bodies. I wait and listen to their muffled voices and the steady *hoosh* of running water. As the first pair of players exits the concourse, wet hair steaming in the cold air, I retreat to an icy bench beside the shuttered ticket windows. Both athletes carry jugs of orange sports drinks in their long fingers.

A few minutes later, Luke Fowler shuffles out with two teammates. Fowler's wearing untied high-top sneakers that wobble each time they're lifted from the ground. When he and his friends reach a neighboring tree lawn, I rise from my seat and follow them. There's plenty of distance between us—they cross a series of streets and courtyards and footbridges. Finally, the largest of the three leans forward, as though he's dropped something slippery, and vanishes into a revolving door.

I walk through a hump of plowed snow, creating a noise like a finger being dragged across a balloon. Fowler and his buddy are talking beneath a floodlight. When Fowler raises his hand to demonstrate a jump shot, an L-shaped shadow forms along the sidewalk. They are waiting for someone—another member of the team who's jogging down an adjacent path, his red duffel flopping against his hip. Soon they're trailing each other into the same building as the first guy.

The lobby is warm and it smells of fried onions. I watch Fowler's back as he waits in line, a bright tray spinning on his index finger like a basketball. A glass sneeze-guard covers steel vats of food resting in a trough of hot water. I'm standing near a long conveyor belt on which students place their trays after they've finished eating. I move through the dining area and, when no one's looking, steal an apple and a packet of goldfish crackers.

It takes about forty minutes for Fowler to finish his dinner and pass me seated on a ledge in the hallway. He says something to one of his friends, but I can't hear him above the ambient noise of the cafeteria. As he weaves his way through campus, deep in conversation, his arms thrash against his sides like he's trying to stay afloat. And I can't help but think he resembles Callie during one of her little tantrums—limbs swimming furiously against the air, face red and creased.

Near a bookstore, Fowler breaks from his group and leaps over a crippled fence. He's alone now, moving purposefully between buildings and down side streets. I keep pace—I consider approaching him outdoors. For the first time, I start thinking about my intentions once I reach him. Maybe I could simply dislocate his shoulder or fracture his shooting wrist.

A silver Honda slows beside Fowler. The passenger door creaks open and an attractive blonde steps onto the curb. Fowler kisses her, then reaches into the car and grabs her canvas bookbag. Together they walk a few blocks and, as they turn down a wooded path, Fowler appears to look in my direction. I pause and pretend to read one of the student flyers tacked to a wooden kiosk. By the time I glance back, they're gone. In a sort of half-scramble, I try to retrace their footsteps.

I remove my black notepad and pen from my pocket. It's remarkable what people will tell you if you ask them the right way. Posing as a sportswriter—"I'm late for an interview"—it only takes a few minutes to get directions to Fowler's dormitory. The common room beside the foyer is crowded with students lounging on couches and stuffed chairs, their eyes directed at a large console television. Two girls in bathrobes and fuzzy slippers scuffle toward a pair of vending machines. A few tiles in the linoleum hallway have been uprooted, revealing a scribbly residue of dried glue.

I scale the two stories to Fowler's floor up a stairwell that stinks like rotted produce. On the wall to my right is a masking-tape square, roughly the height and width of a pitcher's strike zone. The painted cinderblocks beneath are pocked with dozens of white crescents where a ball, or balls, have found their mark. I sidestep a teepee made from old pizza boxes and a rug that looks like it's been burned. A stereo is cranked ridiculously loud, the same type of hard-throbbing, hip-hoppy music that's played on Callie's favorite station.

A student in a denim jacket blows cigarette smoke out of a parted window. Nearby, a wooden chair hangs randomly from a hook on a wall. The baseboards are cluttered with swells of debris—plastic cups, fast-food bags, pencils, single shoes, loose batteries. Many of the doors are decorated with sports posters and message pads and photographs of swimsuit models. On Fowler's door, 306, is a decal of the school mascot and a basketball schedule with the scores of past games written beside each opposing team in black marker. There's also a green shamrock made from construction paper. I knock twice, soft then hard. When no one answers I turn the knob and slip into the room.

The noise and clamor behind me fades like the ending of a song. Overlapping pyramids of light from the street below shine through a frosted window. Pressed into a far corner is an unmade bed, blanket and sheets tangled together beneath a pile of scattered clothes—hoodies and sweatsocks and dark indigo jeans. I stumble on a collection of books fanned across a crinkled rug. There's a small university-issue desk of blond wood and a matching dresser whose drawers are pulled to arbitrary depths. A portable CD player sits on a small stool below the window. Felt pennants of various college and professional sports teams form a wheel against one wall.

On Fowler's desk is a laptop computer, two souvenir mugs (Aloha Classic, Battle of Big Star) filled with pens and pencils, Xeroxed syllabi, dog-eared sports magazines with his name circled in scouting reports, a team binder, a fancy stack of returned homework assignments and an examination blue book displaying his letter grade—B+—on its cover. The doors to the closet have been slid apart, revealing silky warm-up suits and hanging shirts and a tower of pristine-looking athletic shoes.

Beside a frameless mirror are three shelves supported by thin silver brackets. Each shelf holds a combination of photographs and prize ribbons, plaques and trophies. I examine a few of the pictures, turning them toward the streetlight for a better view. In one, a baby-faced Fowler is wearing his high school uniform, his arms draped across the shoulders of two teammates. Another shows him and a date dressed as dark-eyed spooks, not unlike the zombie-rocker costume Callie wore for Halloween. Finally, there's a teenage Fowler standing presumably with his parents at his sister's graduation. The four of them seem incredibly happy—Fowler's smiling and holding his mother's hand; his father is kissing Fowler's sister on the cheek, knocking her mortarboard cap askew. I'm still clutching the photograph when I sit down on a padded chair near the bed.

At my high school graduation, I remember having my picture taken with Cameron and my mother. As the three of us posed together on the school lawn, I saw a kid from my class, Paul Cabot, standing on a bench and spraying himself with a shaken bottle of ginger ale. All I could think about was the disparity in our futures: By the middle of August I'd be gone from Carbon Mills, and Paul Cabot would be attending a local community college and working a construction job with his father. I watched a tail of blue exhaust from my mother's station wagon after she dropped me at college and, as she disappeared into the wooded horizon, I thought about all that lay ahead for me—classes, football, girlfriends, a high-paying job in some big city. The last thing I expected was to return home. Now, peering down at Fowler's family, I wonder about their expectations for him.

In the seamiest gullies of a parent's imagination there are horrifying visions that we try to suppress. Awful, fearful things like car accidents and drug overdoses and lurking sex offenders. A couple times I became so overwhelmed by these types of intrusive thoughts that I rose from bed and parked outside of Liz's house, keeping watch all night to make certain the girls were safe. In Fowler's parents' darkest dreams, I'm sure they never imagined a scenario like this, someone waiting in their son's room to cause him pain...

The rapid stutter of moving feet in the hallway is followed by silence. I lean back and cross my legs at the ankles. On the nightstand rests a postcard from someplace warm, a glossy depiction of palm trees and a clear blue inlet. I'm reminded of a circular wading pool from when the girls were little. We'd use a garden hose to fill it with water and Tig, either naked or in a swim diaper, would sit with her shoulders propped against one side. I have a wonderful memory of Callie lying in that pool, her toes poking above the water line and her arms spread across its curled lip. I was reading a newspaper in the morning sunshine and when our eyes met, Callie nodded, as if to suggest, "Ain't this the life, Dad!" It seems like a hundred years ago, and it seems like yesterday.

All this travel and stress has left me exhausted. I keep nodding off, my head snapping back each time my chin touches my chest. Then comes sleep's dizzy embrace. The snow falls in steady waves, like an advancing infantry. Callie and Tig are seated on a sled behind me, mouths parted, as they try to catch snowflakes against their tongues. I'm pulling them toward a hill on a familiar golf course. Tig complains about the cold and, later, about Callie's boot digging into her side. Suddenly I'm running—my lungs turning numb with icy breaths. I feel the rope of the sled cutting into my hand. "Hurry!" screams one of the girls, although the howling wind makes the voice difficult to identify. A pair of arms is squeezing my waist, tugging me sideways into the shared warmth of another body. It's Nina—her lips dry and cool against mine. "I *knew* she was your girlfriend," says Callie, clapping her mittens together. And then it's the four of us trudging into a swirl of white. We finally reach the top of the hill and take turns steering the sled down its powdery slope. I stand on the wooden slats and bend my knees, gaining speed as the runners hiss beneath me. The snow and swift-moving air cause my eyes to water. I leap a small mogul, then another. I'm traveling too fast—bare trees and crooked skyline slurred above my outstretched arms. I land with a hard impact that produces an ominous crackling noise. Then the ground gives way and I tumble into a steep chasm. I try grabbing a pointy ledge, but it crumbles loose under my touch. The compressed layers of earth rush past like a flickering movie. I'm falling and falling, the velocity pushing my arms against my ears. A strange voice is speaking from somewhere on the surface, loud and hollow-sounding. I squeeze my hand, attempting to make a fist, but there are twin pieces of smooth, varnished maple pressing against the skin of my palms…

I jerk sideways and my fingers curl around the arms of a chair. It takes a moment for me to place my surroundings. An intercom system in the hallway announces the dormitory curfew—"all visitors must leave the building at once." Still resting across my lap is the photograph of Fowler's family. I use the cuff of my jacket to remove a smudge mark on the glass, between his parents. In the gap under the door to the room, I follow the light as it changes shape with each passing footstep. I settle the soles of my boots firmly on the floor, shoulder-width apart. My mind is filled with images of Callie and Tig in their ballet costumes, sailing through the air. They're taking turns demonstrating their newest moves before class begins—arabesque, brisé, grand plié.

The first sound comes as I'm picturing the silk flower stitched to Tig's neckline—it's the metallic jiggle of a turning doorknob, the spring-clip and tumbler engaging the deadlatch. I watch three stripes of light skitter across the copper bulb. Then he's only a large shadow pasted against a fluorescent background. The door closes behind him and he drops his duffel beside the closet. Next comes the baritone rumble of urine meeting water from a significant height. I'm still concealed in the darkness when he reaches his desk, turning on his lamp and removing his sweater. Maybe he hears me breathing or sees my reflection in a framed poster of the Pittsburgh Art Museum; he pivots around on the heels of his sneakers. His eyes are wide and his right elbow is raised level with his ribcage, as though he's positioning himself for a rebound. He grabs a rubber dumbbell, presumably for protection, and takes several steps backward, his chest shuddering to a wildly syncopated beat. His mouth opens but he can manage only a panicky moan. He turns from side to side—he appears to be looking for some misplaced object that will help this all make sense…

I stand and use my fingers, flat and rigid as a spade, to strike the medial nerve that runs near his bicep. His arm goes momentarily limp, and the dumbbell drops to the floor with a loud thump. He lifts his opposite shoulder, as though he intends to throw a punch. But I catch him with a forearm-cross beneath his chin, making his lower teeth rattle against his upper ones. I consider driving my fist into cheekbone, followed by a rapid succession of choppy jabs, but something stops me. He scrunches his face, forming a bowtie of wrinkles across the bridge of his nose; he resembles Tig when she's been given a piece of unwelcome news. His hands fall to his sides and he tumbles onto his mattress, lifting a feathery gasp from the box spring. He reaches forward and pauses, as though waiting for permission, and retrieves a bottle of water from his nightstand. I return to my chair.

After a quick drink he starts to speak, his sentences clipped and stammery. His voice is higher than I expected. He doesn't need an explanation for my presence: He talks about the game against Seton Hall, describing how large the basket seemed during the final few minutes—he hadn't felt that good in a long time, maybe since high school. Then come the excuses about gambling debts and lost income and a father who's been out of work since they discovered a tumor on his bladder last June. I gaze down at the photograph balanced across my thigh.

"That's not him," he says.

He tells me the people in the picture are his old girlfriend and her family. Somehow I feel deceived, robbed of the parallel world I invented for Fowler based on my interpretation of the image. I toss the portrait to the ground. He sighs and nervously adjusts the elastic on his left sock. To occupy my hands, I remove a three iron from a golf bag leaning against the wall and twirl it between my fingers.

His words are coming slower now as, seemingly, he searches his memory for more material from which to make a connection—a way to reel me toward a place of communication and understanding. He starts to look me squarely in the eyes. There are spontaneous descriptions of his old CYO gymnasium and endurance training and a four-team parlay he bet last month...

We're interrupted by some movement outside the door. In the quiet that follows, I hunch forward and bounce the rubber-gripped golf club between my boots. Fowler is anxiously kneading a corner his pillowcase. Behind me the window groans against a gust of wind.

I don't know what's next. We're both waiting for me to take action, physically or otherwise. But I keep visualizing Fowler lying on his dormitory floor, injured, alone. And I can't shake the notion that he's somebody's son. That he has two loving parents waiting in western Pennsylvania to hear from him, and there's nothing that would terrify me more than learning that one of my daughters was in danger...

He crosses his legs and rests his chin against his fist. On his dresser is a white bottle of laundry detergent and a glass Mason jar filled with coins. There are also three painted figurines of professional basketball players in various states of activity—shooting a jumper, driving the lane, blocking a layup. Taped to the side of his mirror is the same team picture I saw in the restaurant and, below that, a child's drawing of a backboard with Fowler's number (24) in crayon...

I've hurt lots of people—twisting arms and bruising ribs and drawing blood. But this feels different. It's the first time violence has been compulsory. A mandate for thuggish behavior. Fowler's also much younger than the others, closer in age to Callie than to me. Suddenly I'm thinking about how long it would take to move past any serious injury I might cause him. Is it something I'd mostly forget by the end of my long drive home? Or would it replay whenever I watched a basketball game on TV?

His pupils dart back and forth. He's silent now, desperate for his next topic of conversation—a way to extend this civility between us. The slope of his eyebrows makes him seem eager and vulnerable. For the first time, I notice a small dimple in his left cheek that softens his jawline. Squashed beneath his thigh is a stuffed panda, only its ears and forepaws visible. It could be a gift from his old girlfriend or a keepsake from childhood. Fowler scratches his head but fails to comb down the loose hairs that blossom beneath his fingers.

Maybe there's just some coldness, some blackness in each of us—an undefinable element—that drives us beyond the borders of reason. A grim and sparky interference that wreaks chaos with the needle of our moral compass. A place where logic and absurdity are blended into a viscous film, like the bonding of twin chemical agents, until we can no longer determine the difference between these competing solutions. In my case, I see the bright faces of my daughters working both ends of the continuum—I'm fighting between a desire to do what's right and a compulsion to do what's necessary, in this moment, for my family. It feels as though the dormitory walls are inching closer, like the teeth of a vise. I adjust the thin string bracelet on my left wrist that Tig wove for me in a school art class. I inhale three large gulps of air and everything starts moving at a leadened pace. As Fowler lowers his arm, it seems to linger for fractions of a second in each position along the way down, like single cell animation. The knuckle on Fowler's left index finger is swollen and discolored. His head totters sideways in an isolated twitch. Then he looks toward the door—two, three glances—as though he's willing a visitor to disrupt us. On the nightstand his cell phone vibrates and stops…

We've been together for long enough that my heartbeat has slowed. The querulous impulse that's led me here seems to have downshifted into a lesser gear. Fowler starts to talk, gesturing into the empty space above my head with his puffy finger. The words are swift and unpunctuated, audible only as a ripply braid of sound. I watch his mouth waggle, down then up, and I know that if I don't make a decision soon I'll lose my nerve. My left foot moves forward, almost mechanically, planted against a fold in the rug, as though I'm preparing to leave. I rise from my chair with the golf club still resting gently in my hand. My arm curls around the back of my body, elevating the blade of the three iron to a slot behind my opposing ear.

This next part isn't premeditated; it simply happens. I see the club's shaft swing down in a silvery blur, my arm snapping ahead as though I'm tossing a horseshoe. I hear the fluttery *whish* of smooth metal carving through air. But there's no impact, no meaty clap as if the blade had struck his shin or bended knee.

Because I never strike him, he never screams out, in terror and pain, as though the metal-faced club had turned the bony flesh around his patella into a crumbling clot of dirt.

Instead, the kid simply follows my practice stroke, parting his lips into a narrow oval. Again the golf club rises and, instinctively, Fowler tightens his eyes and flinches—preparing for the worst. But this time I let the three iron fall blindly down my back, like a hidden ball trick, until it comes to rest against the tendons below my calf. I'm filled with a muddle of emotions: anger and disappointment and a crippling desire to provide a better life for my daughters. It occurs to me, with the finality of a braying horn, that there's nothing else for me here, only a stretch of lighted highway to lead me home again.

In the moist radiator heat, I remove my jacket and drape it across my shoulder. I move closer to the door and nearly trip on the handle of Fowler's duffel bag. As he whimpers into his chest, laying uninjured against the sagging mattress, I think about how Callie and Tig enjoy standing across the hard toes of my boots while I walk them like stiff-jointed robots into their room. "Make scary noises," they'll sometimes say, knotting their faces into funny grimaces. I'll drop them onto their beds and raise my hand, rapidly waving my outstretched fingers from side to side. "Here comes the propeller," I'll announce. Then I'll burrow a fingernail into their belly buttons and swivel the rest of my hand until they're laughing hysterically. To make me stop, they'll turn onto their sides and fold themselves into a defensive ball, like Fowler is now…

A spotlight from the courtyard beside the dormitory gives the glazed windows an incandescent glow. There's a slight squeaking noise as Fowler's shaking causes the bed to jiggle. A phrase I often repeat to the girls after some lesser misbehavior abruptly blooms in my head. "You know better," I say, aloud, although I'm uncertain if the words are meant for him or me.

Now comes only the hard truth of two men aimed in different directions, neither knowing what exists ahead. I take a deep swallow and, powered by an unexpected motion, push my way into the hall. As my boots scrape against the floor, I notice a spidery darkness on the dull gray cinderblocks. My shadow appears asymmetrical. There's a ghostly bulge rising from my right shoulder, where my jacket lies softly, like a child's backside or a droopy sack of grain.

ACKNOWLEDGMENTS

My deepest appreciation goes to my family, Richard Messer-man, Sue Barberic, Katalina Speck, Guy Intoci Jr., Peter and Ben Henkel, Eric Hamilton, John Forgetta, Veronica Richter, Don DeLillo, Peter Scott, Kathy Kitterman, Alex Greenberg, Tony and Brent Gilberto, Jo-Anne Pavell, David Ross, Steve and Ellen Ross, Bill Barone, Duncan Kennedy, Dan Gehn, Danny and Tiffany Ferry, Bertis Downs, Adam Grossman, the Hertzers, the Shlonskys, the Hubbards, Ron Antonucci and Sarah Willis, Greg Kelly, Jack McCallum, Hank Hersch, Tony Constantino, the Markeys, Michael Minotti, the Mitchells, the Morfords, Mitch and Sawyer Opalich, Don Rhymer, Richard Gilden-meister, John Ruby, Jared Levin, Kiki Roberts, the Bugenskes, Mark and Katrina Cassell, Amy Hanauer, Scott Lynch, Alex Seli-outski, the Sicklings, Laurie Friedler, and Peter Kaplan.